# LANCE DU

By

# Duncan Peberdy

Coronavirus continues to be a dreadful blight on the UK and across the world, and this novel does not attempt to trivialise the profound devastation families have been caused by the tragic, and sometimes unnecessary, deaths of their loved ones.

There is more comment on this after the end of the novel.

**First Edition** published in the UK on Monday 21ˢᵗ June 2021 by DroitwichNet Limited - 10 Mosel Drive - Droitwich Spa – Worcs - WR9 8DB

This story, and the characters at the heart of it, are entirely a work of fiction, created by the author's imagination. However, real places, real people and events around Covid-19 have been embroidered into the fictional tapestry to provide a sense of realism. For the main characters, any resemblance to actual persons, living or dead, is entirely coincidental.

Copyright © Duncan Peberdy 2021

The right of Duncan Peberdy to be identified as the author of this work has been asserted in accordance with the Copyright, Designs and Patents Act 1988.

All rights reserved. No part of this publication may be reproduced, stored in a retrieval system, or transmitted in any form by any means electronic, mechanical, photocopying, recording or otherwise, without the prior written permission of the copyright owner.

A CIP record for this book is available from the British Library.

This book is sold subject to the condition that it shall not, by way of trade or otherwise, be lent, re-sold, hired out, or otherwise circulated without the publisher's prior consent in any form of binding or cover other than that in which it is published and without a similar condition including this condition being imposed on the subsequent purchaser.

ISBN: 978-0-9927903-4-9

Copyright © Duncan Peberdy, 2021


Cover Illustration © Neil Duffy




Printed and bound in the UK by Penrose Group
Ashford, TW15 1YQ
**www.penrosegroup.co.uk**

# St. Richard's Hospice

CARING FOR LIFE

Reg. Charity No. 515668

**50%** of the net profit from the sale of all formats of **Lance Dune House** are being donated to St. Richard's Hospice in Worcester.

For more information on the great work that St Richard's Hospice provides for the people of Worcestershire, please visit:

www.strichards.org.uk

Updates on income raised from book sales will be posted on:

www.thecovid19Murders.com

# First Edition
June 2021

# LANCE DUNE HOUSE

For Elaine
Sophie & Steve
Tom & Verity
Lola & Charlie

This could be the one!

# Part One

ONE
## Just Around The Corner

Edward Claines came upon Lance Dune House by pure chance.

It was a cold wet day, in January 1977, where the incessant drizzle, slowly descending through already damp air, made it more difficult to drive, especially if you were looking for somewhere unfamiliar, and the cold made you wish your own home had better windows. Edward was looking for Ogbourne House, where he had an appointment to meet the owners, Paul and Nicola Eastleigh, and to quote them for his secondary glazing that would help them to keep the cold outside their farmhouse. Along Bow Brook Lane, all the properties were big and separated with quite random distances between each other, and each driveway entrance offered a name rather than a street number for identification. As Edward peered through the drizzle looking for Ogbourne House, it was the *'For Sale'* sign next to a small single-story lodge just inside yet another private drive that caught his attention. The next property, a few hundred yards further along the rural lane, was the one the Eastleighs were expecting him at.

Once Edward had sat with the Eastleighs and demonstrated the benefits of his secondary glazing compared to other local companies, and then explained why he could offer substantial price-savings over the well-known national firms, the 'property for sale next door' came up in conversation as Edward went from room to room with Paul measuring windows. He'd assumed, as he'd driven slowly past, that it was the lodge adjacent to the *'For Sale'* sign that was being sold, but now learnt from Paul that the lodge was part of the main property, and that the house, Lance Dune House, was 'going for a song' because it needed a lot of work; new roof, new windows, heating, at the very minimum they thought. A project for someone. "I was almost tempted to buy it myself," said Paul, "but the Mrs thought there was too much for us to do at our time of life."

There was no sight of the house for sale from either the road or from the windows in Ogbourne House as Edward measured them in preparation for their insulating glazing that he instinctively knew the Eastleighs would buy from him. Intrigued by what a 'project' might look like, on the spur-of-the-moment after leaving his appointment, Edward turned his Jaguar in by the lodge and headed up towards the house along the longer-than-anticipated drive with fields fenced off to the right-hand side. It already felt like he was heading to a destination.

As the property was reached, the tarmac drive delivered the Jaguar to a gravelled forecourt in front of an imposing front door. The drizzle stopped falling onto the windscreen and mid-afternoon winter sun appearing for the first time today, that would soon be replaced by dusk, brightened up the saturated sky.

From the neighbour's comments, Edward had been expecting the house to be almost derelict. Yes, it didn't look lived in and the wooden window frames were mostly near rotten and mossed over in places, but still intact, and there were no holes visible in the roof. Neither was there an answer to Edward's knock at the large black front door, so he walked around to the rear where there was an enormous overgrown lawn, flower beds full of weeds and fields as far as he could see beyond. Peering into the house, the natural light from one bay window highlighted a still-furnished sitting room containing a large fireplace with its metal guard, a beautifully crafted Chaise Longue upholstered in plain green velvet, mounted on four stubby dark mahogany legs, and two dark brown leather armchairs. In front of the fire, the dark red-oak herringbone parquet floor was partly covered by a large intricately patterned Persian rug. Swirls of dark brown and vermillion florals clinging to black branches on a faded ivory background. The kitchen, similarly belonging to a bygone age, had dark kitchen cabinets and a farmhouse table with six chairs on a black and white tiled floor, like an infinity chess board disappearing into the hallway. Within a few minutes every ground floor window had been peered through and Edward's shoes, totally impractical for the wet outdoors, were starting to leak. Externally, the rendered walls had once been white, and dark stains descended the walls from where the guttering leaked. If prospective buyers were looking for somewhere they could immediately move into, or were judging the book by the cover, then this wasn't the place for them. Edward wasn't to know until he drove straight from the property to the estate agent to collect a brochure before going back to his office, that the property had two reception rooms, five bedrooms and three bathrooms, and the grounds totalled 1.8 acres – not that such a measurement meant anything to Edward apart from that it was big. The acreage excluded the drive to the road, where that one-bedroom lodge was included in the sale.

'Room for a tennis court' was stated in the brochure, as was the distance to private schools in Worcester and, in the other direction, Stratford-upon-Avon. The charming location, affording superb walking and riding, on the edge of a much sought-after village, and the wonderful unspoilt views onto open countryside, all pitched the sale at those with sufficient money to enjoy its location and hold a position in society that it assumed buyers would be attracted from. Edward, already a self-made successful businessman, aspired to hold such a respected position in society for himself.

Lance Dune House, following the death of the previous owner, had been on the market for over twelve months. The family selling had initially turned down some offers that were considerably below the original optimistic valuation, but the agent, now probed by Edward who discovered there were no outstanding offers, and probably anxious to realise his commission on the sale, suggested that an offer below the asking price would now be considered differently to when it had first been listed and declined. There had been plenty of interest in and viewings of the property, but the 'needs some improvement' really meant rewiring, replumbing and the addition of a heating system, then there were the windows and maybe the roof. It was indeed a project for someone. Given that it was now over twelve months, the children of the deceased owner had most probably envisaged ways that they would spend their inheritance and were almost certainly now getting impatient to do so. Edward judged that any shortfall in their expectation when split between the three of them, would not be perceived as so much of a loss individually. Edward could sense that there was a deal to be done.

Turning over the final page of the brochure, now open before him on his desk, revealed a full-page image on the rear cover of a wonderful unspoilt view across the picturesque countryside from the beautifully mown rear garden. Edward called his bank manager to see if he could finance the purchase of Lance Dune House, together with a short-term facility as a bridging loan. That would give him a few months to make the necessary improvements before completing the sale of their existing home and moving in. If it was affordable, then he would arrange a viewing with his surveyor, and then tell Helen, his wife, all about their new home.

There had been no thoughts or plans or even any 'what-if' conversations about moving from his present home just yet. Edward and Helen had only been in their current home, a modern 4-bedroom detached, for a little over two years, and they had both considered that property, already far better than either of them had experienced in their own childhoods, to be their *forever home*.

Whilst he waited for a call back with the 'in-principle' answer he was expecting that would allow him to proceed, Edward cracked-on with the secondary glazing quotation for Paul and Nicola Eastleigh at Ogbourne House, his soon-to-be new neighbours.

But acquiring his project was not quite the plain sailing that Edward hoped for. Barclays agreed his mortgage in principle, and John, his surveyor, strongly advised the full replacement of the roof. Secondary glazing would keep the need for replacement windows at bay for a few years, but a full central heating system as well as the wiring and plumbing that was known about, was also needed.

A realistic offer, that Edward believed reflected the investment needed to bring the property back to full habitation, was made, and quickly rejected. He didn't know how far below the asking price had previously been offered, but he did know that being on the market for over twelve months was unusual. Would he like to increase his offer? He was asked. Not yet. Perhaps not at all, even though the facility from Barclays would allow him to. He wanted to play hardball and win on his terms.

Edward rang one of his former colleagues at the Jaguar garage. Christopher owed him a favour and payback time had come.

"Chris, I need a favour." And Edward told Chris that he needed him to visit Grant Welsh, the Estate Agent, look at some country properties, and then to arrange a viewing of Lance Dune House just outside Feckenham with this wife, and to make sure he was suited and booted. "It needs a lot of work, so when you've been, just tell them that it's probably too big a project for you, but you'll have a think about it, and then give me a call."

And when Chris and his wife Susan had been to the property and then phoned Edward, he was asked to wait 48 hours and then go back to the Agent with an offer that also reflected the cost of essential work, but which was crucially £6,000 below what Edward had himself already unsuccessfully offered.

1977 was a vastly different time to today in most respects, including house buying. Offers were accepted on face-value, there was no requirement to provide any evidence of your financial wherewithal until later in the process. Turning up in a Jaguar with his wife and being smartly dressed certainly gave the appearance that Chris's offer was to be taken seriously. But needless to say, with a higher offer having only recently been rejected, the Agent was instructed by the family to decline the new lower offer. They also said that if Edward's offer was still on the table, they would now accept it. £6,000, the reduction of the new offer, was after all, only £2,000 less for each of the family, and the new reduced offer that Chris had submitted, put a fresh perspective on Edward's own offer.

Following his client's instructions, the Agent phoned Edward, who expressed his surprise at the call, and advised him that if his original offer was still there, that the family would now accept it.

Christopher had repaid the favour, and a month later than expected, Edward and Helen Claines were the new custodians of Lance Dune House and Edward now arranged for Helen, who after a couple of years of trying was now three months pregnant, to visit it for the first time. With his ownership of Lance Dune House, Edward was moving into a new social class, and he was taking Helen with him into that world.

# TWO
## Edward Claudius Claines

At the time that Edward Claudius Claines raped Shirley Phillips, in the grounds of Lance Dune House, he was forty-one years old. Shirley was just eighteen.

It was 1977, Tuesday the 7$^{th}$ of June to be precise, and the occasion for the party at Lance Dune House being uniquely held on that Tuesday, was the additional public holiday tagged onto Spring Bank Holiday Monday to give the whole country an extra-long weekend to celebrate Queen Elizabeth's 25$^{th}$ year of rule. Her Silver Jubilee. The year that Virginia Wade won Wimbledon. The year that Fleetwood Mac released Rumours. The year Elvis Presley died. The year that the last public execution with a Guillotine took place in France. The year Pele retired. The year Tina Phillips was forcibly conceived against the will of her mother, by Edward Claudius Claines.

Edward Claines, before he added the Claudius middle moniker that was not allocated to him at birth, had become a successful self-made business owner. His abundance of good looks, unfailing confidence and depth of charisma made him instantly likeable, and he intuitively knew how to lead customers, like Paul and Nicola Eastleigh, down cul-de-sacs without them even knowing that they were being effortlessly cajoled into a buying position where saying 'yes' was the only logical outcome. Unless they now wanted to look, and be expertly made to feel, stupid.

Long before 1977, Edward had cut his sales teeth in the men's clothing department at the Russell and Dorrell department store on Worcester's High Street, and then in 1966 as he hit 30, Edward took a job with a significant pay rise and life-changing commission to sell Jaguar cars, mainly to the rich and famous. Even though the introduction of a drink drive limit first became law in 1967, some Jaguar showrooms continued their unique practice of popping open a bottle of champers shortly before midday, every day, to toast customers collecting their new Mark X or E-Type Jag. Once celebrities such as Steve McQueen, Brigitte Bardot, and Tony Curtis were photographed with their E-Type, there was no shortage of customers willing to part with their £5,500 – more than the cost of a modest 3-bed semi in most parts of the UK! – and earn Edward more commission than he could shake a stick at.

Two years later Edward joined the golf club. The owners of the Jaguar garage were members, many of their customers belonged to golf clubs, and it was undeniably an investment that would raise far more income from the resulting commission on new car sales than the combined cost of membership, professional lessons and the essential attire of pastel patterned Lyle and Scott knitwear.

Life for Edward was on an upward trajectory. In the blink of an eye five years had passed, he and Helen, a receptionist from the Jaguar garage, were now married, and a four bedroomed detached house purchased, albeit on a mortgage, in anticipation of children, and because it offered suitable off-road parking for his company Jaguar. Never one for team sporting endeavours during his childhood, golf became more than just an opportunity for business networking, it spoke to Edward's values about being the very best you can be at everything, and each year his handicap lowered. It was in the 19$^{th}$ hole with a glass of single malt Irish whiskey in his hand, ice, no water, when his epiphany – that moment of sudden revelation with the potential to take his life to the next level occurred. Edward felt perfectly at home in the golf club; he had the money to always 'pay his way' in the bar and he could hold a conversation with anyone on cars, politics, business and most things, perhaps with the exception of team sports. Except he now realised, according to his epiphanous moment, that at the golf club he belonged to a very small minority. Not quite the exception to the rule, but it was generally true that most of the golf club members owned their own businesses, some because of family connections and inheritances, and others who had identified a brilliant opportunity, taken the plunge and invested their time and money into their venture.

Edward knew instantly that if he really wanted to succeed in life, really succeed and improve his already good life even further, then he had to be the boss of his own company. Wasn't it so rightly a truism that Edward had heard many times, that very few people get rich working for someone else? Edward determined that this was exactly what he wanted for himself and his family. His new home full of children and holidays in Switzerland. He'd never actually had a foreign holiday, but some of his customers took their Jaguar Mark 2's [conjure up an image of Colin Dexter's Inspector Morse behind the wheel of his red Mark 2 Jaguar] across Europe each summer and that sounded fun. Improving his golf and going on golfing and fishing holidays that he'd heard so much about also appealed. Yes, running his own business became a fixation, a must-do ambition, his very purpose. Only what could he do? What did he know apart from inside leg measurements from his time at Russell and Dorrell, and that wasn't something that in the least interested him, or Jaguar cars? There was no way that he could set up in competition with his current employer, nor did he think it possible to raise the capital to do so in another town.

We are now in 1973. Almost two years have passed since Edward determined that he must own his own business, and frustratingly he still hasn't identified what that business might be. He doesn't want to just run his own business; he wants to run his own highly successful business. Failure, or even just mediocre success is not an option. And then one Sunday morning, Edward is at the golf club playing in a charity event with a 'Shotgun start.' To those unfamiliar with a 'shotgun start,' instead of everyone starting from the first hole and playing to the eighteenth green, eighteen groups of four players all simultaneously start from a different hole and play their eighteen holes in sequence. For example, if you start at hole five, then you'll finish at hole four. Seems a bit strange, and folklore suggests that when this format was originally devised and with everyone waiting in place at their respective starting hole, a shotgun, that could be clearly heard at every starting tee across the course, was supposedly fired to signal the start of play. When used for a charity day or another competition, the great thing is that instead of there being several hours between the first and last groups of players finishing their own rounds of golf, everyone pretty much finishes at the same time, making it far more sociable, especially if there's a meal and prizes to be given out.

On this particular day for the charity event, seventy-two members are randomly paired with a partner and compete in a 'Foursome' against another pair. In a 'foursome,' each pair play with one ball and take it in turns to hit the ball from the tee into the 4.25-inch diameter hole on the green.

The fact that the competition was in aid of charity was not important, what was ultimately life-changing for Edward was his serendipitous pairing with Bob Munday, and the conversation the two of them had as they set off from hole seven. The 'shotgun' format meant that everyone was in their starting place long before necessary, and the 'Foursome' format of playing the same single ball against their opponents, meant that they were in conversation together for the next four hours and into the clubhouse. It was during this one round of golf that Edward found the business opportunity that would change his life.

Bob Munday owned a small house building company. He might have taken it over when his father retired, but the apprenticeship his father gave him meant that he knew every trade himself; footings, brickwork, plumbing, wiring, tiling, plastering. Bob Munday could competently turn his hand to all of these trades when required. No one would ever take Bob Munday for a mug on a building site.

During the course of their conversation as Edward listened intently to Bob, like he did to all of his Jaguar customers, a throw-away comment from Bob almost stopped Edward in his tracks. "If I were starting again, I'd probably have a go at that secondary glazing. Have you seen how much *Everest* charge for some aluminium extrusions and a pane or two of glass? Daylight robbery if you ask me."

As Edward focused the conversation on secondary glazing, something he knew nothing about, he discovered that in the early 1970s the demand for better window insulation that eliminated ice on the inside of bedroom windows in homes that still did not have central heating, was outstripping supply. *Everest*, with their national TV adverts, had created a demand that they couldn't satisfy, and there were customers a plenty who couldn't or wouldn't *'fit the best'* and their associated prices, creating opportunities for smaller local companies to capitalise, that were already being taken.

Was this the opportunity for his own business that Edward had been looking for? He wanted to know much more about it.

Workings Saturdays at the Jaguar dealership meant a day-off in the week, and usually Edward took Mondays off to give him the equivalent of a proper weekend and time to play golf. The next morning, following his conversation with Bob Munday, he was in the library as soon as it opened to consult the *'Yellow Pages'* for details of window replacement companies in Birmingham. Close enough to visit, but not too close to be doing business themselves around Worcestershire. The first company he telephoned wasn't interested in talking to him, but the second, based in Acocks Green, to the south east of Birmingham, was happy for Edward to visit right away when he explained that it was his day off. He would set off now and be there within the hour. There was no time to lose, and Edward was buzzing with impatience to discover if this really was the opportunity he pictured in his mind as a result of his conversation with Bob Munday.

By the end of the day, Edward had learnt enough to know that this was his opportunity to start a business. It was an unbelievably simple process; the products were in demand and commanded bigger profit margins than Jaguar cars – or at least the profit margins that he was aware of – and around Worcestershire the local competition to the national companies wasn't yet in place. All it required were aluminium frames, which could be purchased in straight cut lengths, single or double-glazed units, which were purchased already manufactured from a glazier, a workshop to assemble the frames, and then to fit them at the customer's house. Aluminium Patio doors, which he learnt were a large part of the business in Acocks Green, were trickier, mainly because of their size and weight which needed two people to fit them into an opening in the side of a building rather than added as secondary glazing, but the aluminium frame manufacturer provided training and it really wasn't that complicated. So keen was Edward to move Bob's idea forwards, that as soon as he left the Acocks Green premises he found a payphone and called the contact he'd been given at the aluminium frames manufacturer and made an appointment to visit their Wolverhampton factory the following Monday, his next day off.

Terry, the Acocks Green owner had started his business using a garage lock-up as his first workshop, but very quickly had to find a bigger workshop as the volumes of orders and materials required grew, and within two years he was already employing four full-time staff to make the frames and install them. There was plenty more work if he wanted to increase the distances he was prepared to travel. Edward was more than pleased with his visit to the frame manufacturer, and now had confirmation of the high profit margins available.

Two weeks later Edward was enjoying a Sunday morning round of golf with Bob. Edward had set the game up specifically to give him the opportunity to talk more to Bob, and his mind wasn't on the golf, which strangely made him play much better. During their fairway walks, Edward updated Bob on his meetings and research into the secondary glazing business. Edward didn't want to play at it, he didn't want to start his business as a part-time venture whilst selling Jaguars.  Edward wanted to create the most professional and successful secondary glazing business possible, and his only slight reservation was around committing to business premises and then not achieving the levels of work that he thought were realistically possible. But he was in luck.  Logistics in every business sector were changing, and increasingly Bob's building materials were being delivered on a just-in-time basis directly to site and they didn't need to use all the storage space in his builder's yard. There was plenty of room to get Edward going, and always someone there in his office to sign for deliveries etc. Before the eighteenth hole was reached, a deal was struck.  Bob would get a 50% discount on the windows that he needed for his houses – which still left a small profit for Edward, such were the huge margins being generated by this new business segment, and in addition Edward would also pay Bob 10% of his profits in cash.  Edward could now start his business with almost no overheads, and he only needed to buy stock to supply what was already sold.  The informal window contract for Bob's houses would instantly give Edward the purchasing volumes that attracted better trade prices, so it was a great arrangement.  In return, rent free premises staffed during office hours would be at Edward's disposal.  His only capital outlay to get going would be some benches, specialist storage racks for glass encasements, tools, and a modest van to the outside of which those glass encasements could be secured for delivery to site.

Edward and Bob shook hands, on Tuesday morning Edward took a handwritten letter of resignation to his employer, and later that week *Heat at Home Limited* was established with the tagline *'Keep Your Heat at Home.'* Corny perhaps, but in 1973 it heralded the start of a cash-rich business empire that is still going strong almost fifty years later, having been acquired in 2018 by a German window frame manufacturer at the third time of trying.

# THREE
## The Queen's Silver Jubilee Year – 1977

To mark the Queen's 25$^{th}$ year since her succession to the throne, and the first year that *Heat at Home Limited* had turned over more than £1 million, Edward decided to embellish his name by adding *Claudius* to fill the hitherto absence of a middle name. It had a certain ring of grandeur about it, he determined. Almost mystical. It would help set him apart. It instantly seemed appropriate and not at all out of place for his own almost imposing looks. At six foot three, Edward cut a dashing figure without trying. He was neither slim, nor overweight, and maintained his figure without the need for an exercise regime by being careful about what he ate and drank. But in truth he was always on the go, he was not someone to waste his evenings in front of TV screen when there were quotes to do, stock to buy, or a new product to research. On his wedding day, dressed in a Morning Suit comprising of a dark charcoal long-tailed jacket, dark grey trousers with a subtle matching charcoal stripe, and a grey waistcoat, his red tie provided a perfect contrast to the similarly dressed best man and ushers with their grey ties. He didn't out-shine his wife, but he was an equally commanding figure to her radiant beauty. They presented a veneer of being the perfect couple, although Edward never treated Helen as his equal, but considered her to be more of his beautiful possession.

Just thirty minutes with a Solicitor and it was done; to add 'Claudius' really was that simple. New business cards were printed even though plenty of the current ones were still in the stationery cupboard.

*I Claudius* had been last year's *must watch* TV programme; it would have been a proverbial water cooler moment only the water cooler hadn't yet made it into the workplace, and Edward much admired the tenacity and power of the Roman Emperor to get roads, aqueducts and even canals built, and to brutally overcome any opponents plotting to dispose him from his emperorship. Somewhat ironically he would not have chosen the name if he'd known that the actor portraying Claudius, Derek Jacobi, was not a womanising red-blooded male like himself. "What! He *bats for the other side*" is probably much too understated for how Edward would most likely have misogynistically vocalised that discovery when it was eventually made.

After just two years of business, the previously spare space in Bob's building yard was hopelessly insufficient to meet the demands of storing stock and assembling orders that Edward and his commission-only sales team were generating for a growing workforce to manufacture and install.

Bob was genuinely sorry to see Edward leave; they had become good friends despite their difference in age and losing the 10% of profits that came his way as cash-in-hand every month, was going to be missed too. It had been a win/win arrangement that generated under-the-counter cash for Bob that financed new golf clubs, short golfing holidays, and more things that his wife didn't need to know about, without detracting from the housekeeping that she expected.

By 1977, the unit on the small industrial estate that initially had far too much capacity when they moved from Bob's, was now itself bursting at the seams. A bigger or additional facility was actively being looked for to satisfy council contracts, new building developments as well as the secondary glazing business that continued to grow. Front doors of homes built from the 1920s to the 1960s with small inlays of stained glass were being replaced on every street by aluminium-framed doors with full length panes of frosted glass. By the time uPVC came along to dominate the replacement window market, and grow Edward's business and profits even further, yet more capacity would be needed.

Edward's only business fault was that he couldn't delegate effectively; he wanted to be in charge of every aspect of his business. At the Jaguar garage he sold the cars and wasn't allowed to get involved in any service work or after-market accessories. Those parts of the business were run by others. That was the structure not to be deviated from. By contrast, at *Heat at Home Limited,* he rightly considered that at all times the buck stopped with him, and that it was his business to know that neither too little nor too much stock was being purchased, that production created the minimum waste offcuts possible, and that the installation teams were kept busy. All very laudable to have an overview of, except for the fact that he now had a full-time purchaser, a fulltime head of production, and effectively a gang-master to make sure that installation engineers and vehicles were fully utilised, and they should have been left to get on with their expertise without Edward's daily micromanagement. Edward paid well, and for now his employees put up with it.

Getting the sales in was Edward's own expertise, and one that he was keen to upskill his commission-only sales ladies in their suitably short skirts with. For residential customers, a 50% deposit was always taken with the order, and that already covered ALL of the business costs for that job. Not only would he take along samples of his own products, but also some lesser quality aluminium frames that he would infer his competitors were using to keep their costs down.

"You know what Everest say," Edward would tell potential customers, "you only fit double glazing once, so fit the best. But it doesn't have to be Everest," he would add. Only *Heat at Home* were massively cheaper than Everest, and Edward played hard on being as good as Everest but at a much-reduced cost. If anyone tried to negotiate the cost a little lower, then a 75% deposit or even full payment up front would be his requirement to seal the deal. Despite VAT being introduced at a rate of 10% when Britain joined the European Union in 1973, there was plenty of profit margin to give the appearance of taking 'cash without a receipt' and save the customer their 10% VAT charge in order to shake hands and close a deal, even though the VAT, in most cases, was being charged and paid to HMRC. The result, even happier customers who told all their friends, was a win/win. Great for business. No victims. Just the psychology for successful selling.

## Tuesday 7$^{th}$ June 1977 – Queen's Silver Jubilee Bank Holiday

Since February, workmen had been busy making Lance Dune House habitable. Replacement roof trusses supported the new red tiled roof, central heating had been installed for the very first time, and the rewiring and new plumbing completed. When the bridging loan ended in April and Edward and Helen moved in, there was still much to do, and by the time of the Queen's Silver Jubilee the new kitchen was still not complete. When Edward purchased the house, he initially anticipated the modernisation of Lance Dune House taking several years, but his wife's pregnancy, after several years of trying, had accelerated his plans, and by June the new family bathroom and nursery were now already completed.

Arriving home from anywhere was a great pleasure for Edward. He loved turning off Bow Brook Lane into the drive by the lodge and accelerating his newly acquired Jaguar XJ-S, with its 3.6 litre V12 engine purring away beneath the bonnet, alongside the fields as he approached the gravel forecourt. He'd told Helen about his idea to show the house off with a garden party on the Queen's Jubilee bank holiday, and as much as she didn't really want the time and trouble it would take to organise given her maternal state, she knew that there was no point trying to argue against it. Everyone would love driving up to the house and everyone would see how well Edward was doing for himself. It was too good an opportunity to miss, even if the house wasn't quite finished.

The rear lawn, immaculately striped with a surface that would have put Wimbledon's Centre Court to shame, had a smattering of different coloured Croquet Hoops arranged to the left side with balls and mallets lying ready to be swung into action. Beyond the lawn, the views across the rolling countryside of woodlands, streams, and orchards to the gently climbing Berrow Hill, provided a truly idyllic setting. On this beautiful summer's day, the sales brochure image had sprung into life right in front of their eyes. Immediately past the lawn was an open field, with a meandering line of Birch trees at the far end hugging and overhanging a small stream. The field was separated from the lawn with a *ha-ha*, a small dry moat that would keep wildlife out of the garden without the need for fences that would spoil the view, that was not obvious when looking from the rear crazy-paved patio.

Unless you were lucky enough to inherit this extensive family home, or even luckier and win the Littlewoods Football Pools, it was a property that only someone who generated wealth for themselves and others could buy. In 1977, even a Premium Bonds jackpot win selected by ERNIE would have been insufficient to acquire such a magnificent home. In just a few short years, Edward Claudius Claines had fully vindicated his move from selling Jaguar cars for other people to supplying his own secondary glazing and replacement doors and windows. Lance Dune House, hidden away in rural Worcestershire just outside the quaint village of Feckenham, was his proof.

His world, with an impending child and heir, had gone from good to great.

## FOUR
### Edward's Jubilee Garden Party

There was a marquee, just in case the unpredictable British summer weather proved to be exactly that, and Shirley Phillips, just eighteen years old, was one of the waitresses employed by the company hired to provide the catering. A cold buffet, sausage rolls, mini sausages on a stick, cheese and pineapple on a stick, and a selection of sliced white bread sandwiches including egg and cress, ham salad, cheese and tomato, together with some bowls of coronation chicken. Guests would collect their own food from the buffet, and the young girls would clean away used plates, top up champagne flutes and supply fresh bitter or mild from the Watney's Party Seven cans when required.

Open house from 2-7pm the invites had said. Bob Munday and his wife came, as did new neighbours Paul and Nicola Eastleigh, along with Chris and Susan who had viewed the property and helped Edward by putting in a lower offer. Previous employers and colleagues from Russell and Dorrell and the Jaguar dealership were all keen to see what Lance Dune House was about, and all equally impressed with the house and what Edward had achieved. In addition to the mixture of their friends and his 'friends,' with the latter being mainly business contacts who he purchased from or sold to, plus a few waifs and strays from his golf club, his own employees were also invited. The company employees had seen the house before. With all the other work taking priority, secondary glazing had been fitted for now and full window replacements would have to wait.

There must have been over fifty people at its busiest, although most of them had arrived for 2pm and staggered away by 5pm, and when it was all over at 7pm, and the last cars had rolled off the gravel, Edward returned to the garden where the cleaning up operation was in full swing. The young waitresses and the owner of the catering company were putting glasses back into cardboard boxes, waste food into bin bags, and unused food into Tupperware containers.

Edward was knackered. Throughout the five hours he made sure that he'd circulated fully and spoken to everyone, spending a little longer with Bob Munday and his wife, and given the waitresses an encouraging pat and squeeze of their buttocks at every opportunity. It was not out of keeping with the misogynistic times and, for the most part, women just put up with it. In fact, the absence of such behaviour, socially and in the workplace, would have been more surprising. That didn't make it right, it was just the then cultural norm. In 1977, when men thought they still ruled the world.

The June sunshine shone brightly all afternoon and the marquee got some use as respite from its rays. Helen Claines, seven months pregnant and exhausted well before the party finished, took herself off for a relaxing bath when the last of the guests had driven away, and would then go straight to bed. She had enjoyed being the centre of attention but would preferred to have waited until the building work was complete and her pregnancy over before having a party with so many people. She had witnessed Edward in his element; the welcoming host ensuring that everyone enjoyed his hospitality and had his personal attention at some point during the afternoon.

Jim, the catering company owner, commented how lovely the setting was with field and trees at the far end. "We might have to get a few sheep to keep it under control," quipped Edward. "But the stream is lovely, and I think we've got some small trout in it," he added. "Why don't we all grab a drink and wander down for a look?" The field didn't yet belong to Edward, but instead belonged to the farmer whose father had originally sold the land so that Lance Dune House could be built. That was a small detail that Edward didn't feel needed correcting.

Jim wanted to get the van packed up and head off home. Edward thought that was a bit short-sighted and not what he would have done himself if he was looking for more work, but Shirley and Denise, the other waitress, were keen to have a look. Then just as they had glasses filled and ready to go, Denise's father appeared to collect her from her bank holiday employment. Shirley had arrived on her moped and wasn't dependent on a lift home. Denise's father was invited to join them but declined, and so on the humid summer evening it was just Edward and Shirley who made their way across the lawn, carefully down the steps built into the middle of the *ha-ha* wall, and across the field, with Edward's arm supportively around Shirley's shoulder as they both crossed the field in unsuitable shoes, trying not to spill the bubbly contents in the flutes.

Although still two months away from being a father for the first time, technically Edward, at forty-one years of age, was more than old enough to be eighteen-year-old Shirley's father. Shirley innocently saw nothing wrong in being alone with the much older man. During the afternoon, out of sight, Shirley had helped herself to a couple of swigs of Champagne from the bottle – strictly against the on-duty rules that forbad such behaviour. She'd never drunk Champagne before; *Babycham* yes, and although the taste was very agreeable, she had no idea if the *Pol Roger* she had been serving all afternoon was any good, although she'd overheard Edward repeating a few times throughout the party to guests that *"if it's good enough for Winston Churchill, then it'll do for the friends of Edward Claudius Claines."* Pol Roger is what they had served to customers at the Jaguar garage.

Edward had ditched his jacket but was still wearing his tie. Shirley was in the short black skirt and white long-sleeved shirt required for waitressing but had removed her black tights and white lace apron once the party was over. Her legs had been overheating all afternoon and it was a great relief to feel the cooler evening air circulating around them. It was the first proper drink that Edward had taken. There was no obvious footpath across the field, but the grass and ground were dry from weeks without rainfall, and they picked their way towards the line of Birch trees at the far end. Edward complimented Shirley on her long flowing red hair, similar to his wife's, now released from the bun that held it up whilst working, made a flattering comment about the alure of her whiter-than-white legs, and occasionally lowered his arm so he could squeeze her buttock.

Edward flirted with all the ladies and had many girlfriends before Helen. Helen suspected his infidelities, and if they were fact, they were tolerated. In part because if he was wayward there hadn't yet been any indiscretions that had required 'dealing with,' and also because of the comparatively luxurious lifestyle that he now provided her with. Far more affluent than either of their own quite humble upbringings. She'd only been the receptionist at the Jaguar dealership, and now here she was, a trophy wife to look pretty on his arm and create a house full of kids. She hadn't even been told about the new house, as magnificent as it was, until after Edward had committed to buying it. It was Edward that had the work ethic, a workaholic who willingly paid for all the help that was needed around the house allowing Helen to be a lady-that-lunches, and only allowed himself the relaxation of a half-day every Sunday that was spent on a male-only golf course somewhere or other. Although Helen had been a virgin when they married, she considered Edward to be a selfish lover, only ever interested when he was interested, and always just wanting to 'get straight on with it' for his own hurried gratification. She felt that it left her unfulfilled sexually, but as she not had anything to compare it with apart from when she pleasured herself, and that was mostly a much better experience, she wasn't really sure. Such things were not then the topic of conversations when ladies lunched or enjoyed a spa day together.

The bank of the stream gently sloped down from the tree line, and they stood silently for a while in the bright evening sunshine, looking for the fish he had spoken of. The sunlight perfectly picked out the riverbed through the shallow clear water. "Can I paddle in it?" she asked as she kicked off her flat shoes and handed Edward her Champagne as she placed her bare right foot into the stream. "Oh, it's lovely. Cooling my feet down a treat." As Shirley paddled about, the sunshine perforating the tree cover extenuated the redness of her hair, Edward sat on the grass bank and longingly watched her.

# FIVE
## Unlawful Sexual Intercourse

Edward was conflicted by the contradiction he recognised between Shirley's youthfulness and the fully womanly figure she cut.

"How old are you?" he asked.

"I'm eighteen."

She should have stopped at that, but carelessly and innocently added, "but don't you get having any wrong ideas."

Only he was having wrong ideas, very wrong ideas. Lance Dune House hadn't yet been consummated; Helen had refused him sex for the last three months to 'protect the baby.' That of course didn't mean that he wasn't getting any sex. There were always housewives willing to save on the cost of their windows, especially those who'd seen the "*Confessions of a Window Cleaner*" film and thought that freely offering their sexual availability in lieu of part-payment not only saved money, but also satisfied a need that they also weren't themselves getting enough of at home. He was incredibly careful selecting who he transgressed with, mainly favouring the older woman who wouldn't come after him as if he were now a much-besotted puppy, and who were unlikely to end up 'in the family way.' Edward didn't like using a condom.

But Shirley was none of these things. And neither she nor Edward were drunk.

After paddling around for a few minutes, she came and sat on the bank next to him. Her legs were wet below the knees from kicking the water up, and as she leant across his chest where he lay on the grass to pick up her Champagne from where he'd placed both glasses, he moved up and kissed her on the lips. Completely surprised by the kiss she received but had not engaged in, she moved back, not with a recoil, just back, and Shirley made no verbal objection to what had just happened. Edward turned towards her and placed his right hand on Shirley's wet leg and in a single swift action moved his hand upwards, underneath her skirt and within her knickers. Her pubic hair was thick and plentiful. Now she attempted to recoil instantly, but before she could start to move towards safety he was on top of her, simultaneously kissing her whilst fumbling with his trousers to release his bulging penis. She couldn't move. He was both too strong and she was now frozen in terror with him astride her. She wasn't a virgin but had only had sex with one boy and it hadn't been like this. Both of them losing their virginity together hadn't just happened, it was a conscious decision that had been spoken about, planned for, condoms purchased. But now by this beautiful stream in an idyllic setting Edward pushed her short skirt up, forced her knickers to one side and entered her dry vagina with no concern for her feelings, with no excuse for his crime and with no protection from his sperm. She wanted to scream but her voice wouldn't work; it didn't matter that no one would hear her. He thrusted away, his breath getting louder and louder as he continued to kiss her whilst she wrestled her face from side to side. Almost as quickly as she had been ambushed, suddenly his gratification was over. But it was over for Edward only in so much that he had finished, that he was out of her and now kneeling to the side as he buttoned his trousers back together. There was no talk between then. If it had been consensual he could have offered his thanks and commented on his enjoyment and asked how it had been for her – not that he ever asked his wife the same question. Neither was there a 'sorry, I couldn't resist you' to convey any admission of guilt for his transgression. Hadn't she hinted to him that she 'wanted it' too with her *"now don't you get having any wrong ideas"* statement teasing him?

"I'll see you back at the house," was all he could mutter as he picked up his own glass and turned away from the stream and started to make his way back to the house without even looking back at her.

It might not have been the bad sex that gets *The Literary Review* all in a fluster, but for Shirley it was far worse than that. Her vagina now throbbed with physical pain from the unwanted intrusion. God it was so sore. Her head now throbbed with the emotional pain. The guilt. 'Had she brought it upon herself?' 'Had she drunk too much and led him on?' He hadn't deliberately singled her out, after all Denise and her father, and even Jim were all invited to wander across to the stream with them. Would she have gone if it had just been her that he asked? She didn't now know. It was too confusing. It was too late now.

Shirley sat and cried her heart out. The dusk was descending to expel the daylight when she started to walk barefooted first across the rough field and then the tightly mowed lawn back towards the house, terrified of finding him there.

Shirley replayed in her mind the trauma of what had just happened. She had been drinking, she had taken her tights off, she hadn't objected at any point when his arm was tight around her shoulder or when he grasped and squeezed her buttock. She had lent across him to get her drink, and she hadn't recoiled or moved away or verbally warned him when he kissed her. She hadn't wanted him, but maybe it was her own fault that she hadn't made that clear enough? In the immediate aftermath, Shirley now wrongly thought that she was partly to blame in some way.

But there should have been no need for the young innocent woman to feel any responsibility for the misdemeanour that was his, and his alone. She hadn't drunk enough, even with her relative inexperience of alcohol, to let it cloud her judgement or actions. Nor had Edward. She hadn't encouraged him in any way apart from being present with her good looks, and she wasn't to know that his wife was withholding his access at home to any sexual gratification until after her baby was born. His physical strength and the speed at which it all happened took away her control. There was no consent for what he did. No justification.

Intoxication had not clouded either of their judgements, and being taken advantage of only for her beauty, her youth, and her non-consensual availability by the idyllic stream that summer evening was clearly a rape. Only wrongly thinking that she had somehow unwittingly encouraged him, Shirley didn't fully know it. Let us also not forget, and history will attest, that in 1977 women were more subservient than they are today, that the police and courts were institutionally misogynistic, and crucially we were almost ten years away from the first convictions corroborated by newly developed DNA evidence.

Shirley certainly hadn't wanted it. She hadn't encouraged him or even flirted with him, but still she stupidly felt some responsibility. He was a successful businessman, a married man with a beautiful wife, a beautiful house, and a beautiful car. Would anyone believe that a man surrounded by such beauty would be capable of something so ugly? Shirley didn't know that there were plenty of women he had taken advantage of when too much alcohol had clouded their judgement. It would only be his word against hers if any accusation were made. It was almost too much to bear for such a young soul.

Shirley needn't have worried about encountering Edward again that evening; the coward was nowhere to be seen having retreated back into the sanctuary of his home and taken comfort for his misjudged actions in the contents of an Irish whiskey bottle – a single malt with ice of course.

Shirley located her belongings in the Marquee, then headed off home to Droitwich on her moped to run a bath and re-run the horrid experience through her mind time and time again. It was not overly late, but her parents were already in bed. She didn't know what to do; if anything at all.

As she sat in a hot bath full of Avon bubbles, Shirley still couldn't decide if she had been partly to blame. She had no idea that the consequences of the rape earlier in the evening would determine every aspect of her life moving forwards, as well as impacting the life of the daughter she was now unintentionally and unknowingly creating.

It was far from over.

In fact, it was only just beginning.

# Part Two

## SIX
## She Blinded Me With Science

At the end of June 1977 Shirley Phillips missed her period. There was no internet then for Google to inform you of at least ten reasons why you might miss a period and not actually be pregnant. Stress was one of them. Shirley was concerned, especially given what happened three weeks earlier, but she'd missed her period before. Before she'd ever had sex. When she was in the middle of her 'O' level examinations. She put it down to stress. She hadn't told anyone about the incident with Edward Claines, and since then Shirley had been withdrawn, had no appetite and put her gynaecological omission down to the stress caused by her own stupidity on the evening of the Queen's Silver Jubilee celebrations.

If only she'd turned down the opportunity to work that day and joined the street party celebrations with her family instead, then none of this would have happened. A real *sliding doors* moment, which was kind of ironic since sliding patio doors were a made-to-measure best-seller offered to home improvers by *Heat at Home Limited* which Edward Claines made great money from.

By the time she missed her second period, Shirley knew it was something substantially more than stress. She'd been in denial; her appetite had returned but she had regular bouts of nausea which had been hidden from her parents. The only home pregnancy test that had recently become available had to be asked for at a pharmacy, something she didn't want to do in a small community where almost everyone knew everyone, so without telling her parents, two weeks later Shirley made an appointment to see her GP. A man. A sample of urine was produced in the surgery toilet and 48 hours later a positive result was declared.

Being raped by Edward Claines was the only occasion that Shirley had physical intimacy in 1977, and she was able to pinpoint the day of conception with 100% accuracy. She was now ten weeks 'gone.'

The GP referred her to the hospital in Worcester for a twelve-week scan, gave her some leaflets about abortion, which had only been legalised a decade earlier and was slowly gaining its place as an alternative contraceptive. However, even though she was eighteen, Shirley wouldn't be able to opt for an abortion without the knowledge of her mother, such were the regulations at that time.

She was going to have to raise that conversation with her mother, and having been born into a Catholic family, Shirley assumed that the course of action that her mother would insist upon was already known to her. No abortion. Child to be given away. A forced adoption. That's how it still was in 1977 and by the time her pregnancy reached full term in 1978, it would be no different.

Shirley never shared the exact date of the conception with anyone except her GP. Her mother accompanied Shirley to her twelve-week scan, which everyone knew was just an approximation, not a precise science, and continued to get an "I can't tell you," each time she relentlessly enquired as to who the father might be.

"Is that because you were *'at it'* so often you don't know, or because it's SOMEONE WE KNOW?"

"It's neither Joan."

Shirley had always enjoyed a closer relationship with her father, Patrick, who like Joan had anglicised his name when they moved from Ireland in the 1950s in search of work. 'No Blacks, No Dogs, No Irish,' in that order, was commonplace signage to ward off the unwanted when looking to rent accommodation. As a result, Padraig became Patrick and Siobhan became Joan – no formalities of a Deed Poll, just a selection of the closest English equivalent – and, as they both could sufficiently mask their Irish accents for long enough, flats and employment soon followed, and their new names were used by work colleagues and friends without them knowing that better sounding alternatives were available. Their life hereafter, on bank accounts, rents, mortgages, and healthcare forms, lost many connections to their country of birth and childhood.

Shirley called her mother 'Joan' whenever there was tension in the conversation between them, and this was one such time.

She couldn't bring herself to tell her mother that a much older man had forced himself upon her and that she hadn't been a willing participant, which by now she had fully convinced herself to be the truth. She just wished she'd been having her period on that fateful evening, presuming that the presence of a panty liner in her knickers would have stopped him in his rapist and adulterous tracks. It would at least have stopped her getting pregnant. It was only now that Shirley thought of his poor wife and the fact that she was so heavily pregnant that day; she must have given birth by now? She didn't know exactly how far 'gone' she had been at the party in early June.

To the outside world, at just twelve weeks pregnant, Shirley's body, with a bit of help from her selection of loose clothing, was still to outwardly advertise her maternal condition. She would not be going back to college in September and her mother would insist that she was not staying in Droitwich to put shame on her Catholic parents for having a daughter who was scandalously a single mother. No, she would be sent to stay with relatives in Ireland *'for work experience'* and then shortly after the birth would be expected to give up her baby, without question, for adoption. "And you can throw those leaflets away too. There'll be no abortion in this family." Family indeed.

Three weeks' later, Joan and Patrick drove their only daughter Shirley to Holyhead in North Wales where she boarded the B&I Ferry with a single small suitcase as a foot passenger on her way to Dublin, where her Aunty Nuala, Joan's younger sister, and Uncle Fergal, her husband, would meet her off the boat on the other side of the Irish Sea and drive her to their childless farm in County Wexford, about an hour's drive south of Ireland's capital.

The evening before she left for Ireland, wearing a purposely tight jumper and loose coat, Shirley hopped on her moped and drove the nines from Droitwich to confront Edward Claines at his home. As she was leaving early tomorrow with her parents, Shirley was determined to face up to him. It wasn't the first time she'd tried to do so, but last time his car hadn't been on the gravel forecourt, so she assumed he wasn't home either. But this time his car was parked out front and she pulled up beside it.

Shirley was relieved that it was Edward himself who answered the door. His wife answering would have made it far more difficult for her than it already was.

She removed her helmet and shook out her long red hair.

"Remember me from your Jubilee party?"

"Well, yes," with an air of 'but why are you asking?' in his voice.

She now unbuttoned her coat exposing the bump extenuated by the purposely selected tight jumper.

"This is your doing," was all she said.  There was no change in his demeanour, and without checking to see if he was being overheard from within the house, and without lowering his voice, he asked,

"Do you have any evidence that it's mine?" adding,

"Is it money you want to make it go away?" both almost as matter-of-fact statements as much as questions, with the latter sounding a little sinister. Where was the 'Oh my god, I'm so sorry,' or something similarly remorseful she had expected? Or wanted. Or needed.  Why wasn't it a completely dumbfounding shock to him?

"Unfortunately, my parents are Catholic so it's not going to *go away*, but you probably ought to tell your wife before she finds out from someone else."

As Edward started to speak again, Shirley could hear a baby crying loudly in the house.

"I no longer have a wife.  Sadly, Helen died in childbirth last month," he calmly announced.

Shirley stood for a moment. That news of his wife's death during childbirth, delivered so matter of fact, knocked her sideways.  It was only a few months since Helen had been right here at the party, her pregnancy as large as life itself with the promise of new life, and radiantly looking forward to her birth. Now Shirley really didn't know what she wanted from him, except for him to be fully aware about the consequences of his actions.  She had planned to tell him that her parents were sending her away, and that she'd be back by next summer.  But with the shock of his news and hearing the cries of a baby that had already lost its mother, Shirley turned away and ran back to her moped. Putting on her helmet and setting off for home without buttoning her coat.

'Oh fuck,' thought Edward. But he of course didn't know that tomorrow she would be on her way to Ireland or that her parents still hadn't elicited his identity as the baby's father or the criminal circumstances of its conception. He had a nanny to look after baby Helen, named after her mother in order to preserve her memory, but now he knew that sometime next year Helen would have a half-brother or half-sister and he was concerned how that would look to friends and family – especially his late wife Helen's parents – as they would surely find out.

Edward only assumed that before too long Shirley would be back requesting money, especially now he'd stupidly put that idea into her head, and that he'd deal with that at the time. Not once did he consider that the child might need the love and support of its father. Not once did he admit to himself any feelings of remorse towards the young girl for his actions or consider how that might be affecting her. Not even now he discovered she was pregnant. He was only concerned with the potential for negativity towards himself from others, and the consequences for his own reputation and how that might affect his business if those actions became public knowledge.

# SEVEN
## Ireland 1977

Fergal and Nuala's farm in County Wexford had its own private single-track drive from the minor road through unfenced fields on both sides. But those fields were full of sheep and there was no similarity with Lance Dune House. There was no similarity either with any part of Shirley's life in Droitwich where there really wasn't that much for teenagers to do. Here there was nothing. Perhaps even less than nothing outside the farmhouse walls. Like many of the farms there, sheep was what they did, and there are three times as many sheep across the whole of County Wexford as there are people, even though sheep farming isn't the dominant agricultural practice. Shirley hadn't been sent to Ireland just to remove her from Droitwich so that fellow parishioners at the Sacred Heart wouldn't learn about Patrick and Joan's wayward daughter; there was a bit more to it. It was still a common practice in the 1970s, just like many preceding decades in that Catholic-dominated country, for unmarried mothers to be sent away from the prying eyes of neighbours to isolated baby farms run by Nuns, so that their resulting babies could be given away to far-more-worthy married couples. They weren't actual farms, but large houses in both urban and rural settings, often run as laundries to gainfully employ the misfit singletons. Sending them away also stopped the expectant unmarried mother from parading around their local community with her illegitimate sin on show for all to see, and thereby casting a great shadow of shame across the whole family. Why is it only now that we recognise the shame was on the families and the church for sending them away? Because when these mostly young women returned to their family homes after months of absence, everyone knew explicitly why they had been away, but as nobody had witnessed their pregnancy, so nobody spoke of it. An open, but unspoken, secret.

By 1977 such practices were only just starting to change, but it was still relatively rare for an unmarried mother not to be sent away, which is, after all, exactly what Joan, and very reluctantly Patrick, had arranged for their daughter. Nor was it totally against Shirley's will as being with her family was potentially better than the church-sponsored alternative. The family had visited Aunty Nuala during many summer holidays, and as much as

Shirley loved the countryside as a change to her small town at the edge of West Midlands' civilisation, she knew that in a few weeks the holiday would be over, and they'd be home.  But to be here now, so isolated for maybe seven months was a different proposition altogether. Farming wasn't a Monday to Friday occupation, and whilst Nuala and Fergal were occupied seven days a week on their farm, and especially as Shirley increasingly became unable to help in the latter stages of her teenage pregnant state, there really was nowhere to go and almost nothing to do.  When necessary, Nuala would take Shirley to Wexford for any medical appointments at the hospital, and most Wednesdays Shirley would accompany Fergal when he went to the Wexford Farmers Co-op sheep sales in Enniscorthy.  In truth, without her friends and almost castaway in the middle of nowhere, Shirley had too much time to worry about her future.  Nuala had no experiences of childbirth to inform and reassure her with, and she continually wondered how she would be able to care for a child, let alone face the even worse prospect of giving her baby away?  The medical staff were not reassuring, almost as if it were Nuala they were talking to, and instead treating Shirley as if she was not part of it.  Perhaps they were so institutionalised against the right of any single woman to be pregnant outside of wedlock?  Or they were doing a great job at not helping Shirley develop any sense of emotional bonding with her baby, as that would surely help her want to 'donate' the infant into a childless marriage somewhere?  Maybe even America?  That is what she would do. Right?

As her bump got bigger, so did Shirley's worries as the seemingly horrific and ever-closer prospect of a large baby coming through her vagina troubled her more and more.  She could vividly remember that the attack by Edward Claines had caused her great physical pain, so how would she be able to cope with a birth?  Even if her mind told her that millions of babies had been born exactly that same way before, and she'd now witnessed and helped Ewe's produce their lambs without the assured levels of maternity help she was anticipating.

What if she needed a Caesarean?  What if she poohed herself in the delivery room; Shirley had seen loads of sheep do that whilst lambing. Come to think of it, what if she didn't make it to the delivery room on time?  What if she didn't want to give the baby up for adoption like her mother had insisted would be the case? These were all the worries that a young woman, without the support of her mother or the system in Ireland, was having in the turmoil of her mind.

"Do you want to keep the baby?" Nuala broached the subject as she drove home from a hospital appointment where the nurses had once again suggested that giving the baby up for adoption would be the best course of action for everyone. She would need to sign the paperwork at some stage.

"I don't have any choice. That's what mum's expecting. She won't let me take it back to Droitwich, and I've not got any way to provide for us both myself." More resigned statements of facts from Shirley than a direct answer.

"But if you could stay with Fergal and me for longer after the baby is born, maybe a year, would you want to keep YOUR baby then?"

Joan had asked her younger sister and brother-in-law to hide Shirley away from the world, to remove Joan's own embarrassment from her daughter's 'doing,' and to help arrange for the baby to be adopted. It wasn't cruel or heartless to Joan, it was simply the practicality of how 'things were done' in the Ireland that Joan and Patrick had left behind twenty-five years earlier, when adoption had been made legal in Ireland. The same practicality that made them change their names in England.

By 1977 there had already been many scandals in Ireland around the forced adoptions, with stories of broken families and lost children, many of whom were now old enough to seek out their real birth parents and, in many cases, cause problems for current relationships from whom the mistakes of teenage lust and indiscretions had been previously hidden. The secrecy and confidentiality that it had been assumed started and ended on the day of any adoption, was now not legally the case. Too much trouble had already come from these adoptions, tens of thousands of them across Ireland, and the newspapers and investigative TV programmes were slowly exposing how large the scale of the 'baby trade' had become. Nuala didn't want that for her niece. Was there a way for Shirley to feel that abandoning her child was not the only course of action open to her?

Nuala raised the subject with Fergal. They had been trying themselves for a child and it just hadn't happened. There was no opportunity in the 1970s for the medical profession in rural Ireland to play God and assist with their fertility. It was just accepted that either it did or didn't happen. They were used to that with the Ewes in their care. Adoption was usually the answer for such childless married couples. She had thought – but only in her own mind – that perhaps she and Fergal could adopt Shirley's baby; that would be better than it going to total strangers. But what if in a few years Shirley's circumstances change and she now wants to reclaim her baby? Shirley would know exactly where HER child was, and she'd be on the birth certificate.

For Fergal, adopting his niece's child was too complicated and not something he wanted Nuala to pursue. In truth, he didn't want to adopt another man's child, even if he didn't know who that man was. The child would never be of him, and for Fergal any adoption would cause as many problems between them as it potentially solved for Nuala.

"But here's a thing," he asked Nuala. "What if we agree to share our home with Shirley indefinitely and that her and the baby come and live here for as long as they want? Wouldn't that work? Shirley wouldn't have to give the child up for adoption, and you'd have a baby in the home."

There were no social pay-outs for single unmarried mothers, Shirley would have to work on the farm to pay her way, and whilst they didn't strictly need the help, it would make things easier and financially they could stretch to it. When the child was older, Shirley could always get a job in Wexford or Enniscorthy.

A child's parents are the people who raise them, and after Shirley agreed to the arrangement that Nuala and Fergal surprised her with on Christmas Day 1977, plans were made for the three of them to support the baby growing up on the farm. Adoption papers would not now need signing, but who was going to share the news with Joan? Who was going to tell Patrick that his little girl wouldn't be coming home anytime soon? That communication was put off until after the baby arrived.

On the 7th March 1978, Tina Nuala Phillips was born at Wexford County Hospital, at 4.15am to be precise, following a fourteen-hour labour, and weighing in at 3.3kg, or 7lb and 4oz in today's post-Brexit world.

Nuala and Fergal adored having a surrogate daughter and granddaughter as part of their family, and whatever the original intentions Shirley's parents may have had, adoption of this red-headed and loud-lunged baby was not something that any of those on the small sheep farm in Glasscarrig could now contemplate. They now told Joan that Shirley was keeping her baby daughter, and Joan told Shirley there was still no place in her home for a single mother and child, even if they were her own and Patrick's daughter and granddaughter.

In fact, ten summers in County Wexford would pass before Shirley and Tina left the farm to return to England. During those ten years, Joan and Patrick had visited every summer, driving over via the Holyhead to Dublin ferry, and every time they drove over the Menai Strait onto the island of Anglesey, Patrick bitterly regretted going along with Joan's plan and grudgingly sending Shirley away for the sake of family pride; Joan's pride. Joan had no such self-recriminations about her actions selfishly designed only to maintain her own bigoted Catholic respectability.

Helping to nurture three hundred sheep, mainly Suffolk and Charollais, on rolling Irish pastures may seem idyllic, but repairing fences, moving stock around the farm, offloading bags of feed, is physically demanding. There's a real pleasure in lambing, helping the ewes bring their lambs into the world, but also incredibly tiring and being up in the middle of the night, albeit in lambing sheds, is emotionally draining too.

Shirley wanted more for herself and Tina than their existence on an Irish sheep farm, but without the support of her mother and father she considered herself to be trapped there. She had no social life, and it would take her years to save up in order to make a new start elsewhere. Where else would she go and if she needed to work to support them both, who would look after Tina; she wouldn't be able to afford childcare.

In January 1988, when Joan learnt that Shirley wanted to return home she was prepared to help, but still not to have her and Tina living with them. This time she was overruled by Patrick who declared that if their own daughter and granddaughter were not welcome in the family home, then he would leave too. Joan didn't know if he meant it; she thought he might. Patrick didn't know if he meant it, he thought he might, but thankfully he never had to find out how far his resolve would need to be tested. And in June 1988, after a two-month delay to get passports, Shirley and Tina bid goodbye, but not farewell, with both in floods of tears, to Nuala and Fergal, who had been more of a family to them than 'you know who.' This time Fergal drove them the 90 minutes north from the farm, just beyond Dublin to the airport and Aer Lingus delivered them safely back to Birmingham. It was the first time that either of them had been on a plane and the first time that Tina had been outside of Ireland.

Joan had felt coerced into giving Shirley six months to find her feet and get their own home. It was the motivation Shirley needed to get Edward Claines to make amends for his two-minute error that she had paid so dearly for, and he hadn't. She wouldn't be without Tina whatever the hardships ahead might be. Life on the farm had been very tough at times, but neither of them had been poor, Fergal had paid her for her hard work, and she had some savings put away.

But why was it only now that Shirley, who's life had been on hold for ten years, felt so certain that the time and opportunity had come to move on?

# EIGHT
## 22nd January 1988 – Who's DNA Is It Anyway?

In November 1983 and July 1986 respectively, two teenage girls, both aged only fifteen, went missing from neighbouring villages in Leicestershire. Tragically, both were found strangled to death in order, the Police presumed, to conceal the identity of the 'man' who in both cases had first raped them. Samples taken from both victims identified that it was almost certainly the same person responsible for both attacks; both samples confirmed that the attacker had type A blood group and carried an Enzyme present in only 10% of men.

A young man with learning difficulties had admitted his guilt to the second murder, but not the first. That young man would probably still be in prison today, some thirty-five years later – and that's a really sobering thought – if it were not for the discovery of DNA profiling that had been developed at the University of Leicester by Professor Alec Jeffreys, by which individuals could be uniquely identified from their body material; hair, semen, blood, saliva, etc. That discovery determined beyond all doubt that the young man with learning difficulties was not the 'owner' of the forensic samples recovered from either crime scene.

From the separate locations the two girls had been found, the Police believed that they were looking for a local man, and with the newfound ability to link the DNA recovered to a specific individual, five thousand men local to the two villages were requested to provide blood and saliva samples to the investigating team. The five thousand samples all tested negative for a match, but the crime was eventually solved, quite by chance, when someone was overheard in the pub bragging about the £200 a work colleague had paid him to provide a false sample in his name. That work colleague was Colin Pitchfork, and after a sample of his DNA was checked against the forensic evidence recovered from both crime scenes and proven to be an identical match, on the 19th of September 1987, Colin Pitchfork was arrested and charged with both murders.

DNA Profiling was the scientific breakthrough that has provided substantive evidence that has since helped to convict tens of thousands of criminals around the world. Pitchfork confessed to the killings; it transpired that he had an earlier conviction for indecent exposure, and his case made legal history as Pitchfork became the first person convicted on the basis of scientific DNA evidence. He was sentenced to thirty years imprisonment in January 1988.

The news of the arrest and the sentencing were both reported globally, such was the importance to corroborating forensic evidence from DNA profiling. Briefly it became the lead story in Germany, Brazil, the United States of America, Australia, and even China. But it was in a small farmhouse in Glasscarrig, not too far inland from the Irish Sea, when on the 22$^{nd}$ January 1988 Shirley Phillips was watching the ITV 10 o'clock News with her Aunt Nuala and Uncle Fergus when another breakthrough came. The news report into how Pitchfork had been detected not only explained how DNA profiling could match individuals precisely to bodily matter, but that your DNA could confirm parentage. In other words, the DNA of a child would match 50% with its mother and 50% with its father. This was now scientific fact, not science fiction.

Tina's Birth Certificate may have had *"Father Not Known"* officially recorded on it, but thanks to the scientific advances in DNA, that piece of paper was no longer the only evidence of parentage.

Shirley had wanted much more out of life for herself and Tina, but the roof over their heads, being able to stay together with the love and support and security from Nuala and Fergus was a compromise worth giving up on other dreams for. Until that news about DNA that provided her with another option. What if she had not watched the news broadcast? The effect was to immediately transport Shirley's mind back over the years to the moment when she stood on Edward's doorstep in her tight jumper that announced her pregnancy to him. He hadn't been concerned for the health and wellbeing of either herself or the baby. All he could say, she remembered it word for word so clearly, was:

"Do you have any evidence that it's mine?"

"Is it money you want to make it go away?"

In 1977 Edward had denied and rejected Shirley and her unborn child on the basis that it was only her word against his. There was no known ability then to prove parentage. But now there was, and it didn't require any 'backdated' forensic evidence from the time. A spit of saliva, a single lock of hair, or a few drops of Edward's blood was all that was needed to extract a DNA profile from and match it with Tina's.

The TV news correctly forecast that the detection of serious crimes would never be the same again.

Shirley Phillips, on a sofa in front of a small TV in the Irish Republic, had just identified a way to have Edward Claudius Claines take at least financial responsibility for the upbringing of his child, and to compensate herself in some way in order to make good for everything that occurred as a direct result of his actions, and his actions alone. She didn't have a coherent way to describe to herself what she meant, but she was adamant that her daughter would have some of the life chances Edward had removed from Shirley. She loved her daughter, positively rejoiced in the fact that she hadn't been able to 'make it go away' with Edward's money; that had honestly been her first thought whilst she was in self-denial, in advance of her first scan and before her mother told her then, without any room for doubt, what was going to happen *'to put this mess right'*. She loved Nuala and Fergal too, for without their love and acceptance, she might still have been made to give up her child. Tina.

The conviction of Colin Pitchfork for dual murder, reported globally on the 22$^{nd}$ January 1988, had been the reason why six months later Shirley and Tina flew 'home' to start their lives again.

Forensic science had a new weapon in its arsenal. Shirley Phillips had a new purpose in her life.

A better life for Tina and herself that Edward Claines would not now be able to refute any responsibility for was now her focus. Had he married again, had he now got more children. Shirley didn't care about any new wife or new children that Edward may have, she just wanted justice for what Edward had put her through. Justice for the rape. Justice for what Shirley now perceived as an enforced exile from her parents and the removal of her life choices for over ten years.

Yes. Shirley wanted revenge, and thanks to DNA she now had that opportunity.

She would miss Fergus and especially Nuala, she couldn't thank them enough for what they had sacrificed to provide a home for Tina and herself, but for ten years her life had been treading water, and now it was time to swim with the current.

## The Absent Father

For those same ten years, especially at the start of them, Edward Claines presumed, but not feared, that at some stage there would be another knock at his door and both Shirley and her child would be standing there. Apart from her first name and the facts that she had been eighteen and lived close enough to get to his home on a moped, Edward knew nothing else about her. He assumed that unless she had in fact 'got rid of it,' that somewhere not too far away he now had a second child, and that it and the mother were still living locally. He wondered if his name had been registered as the child's father. He of course didn't know that Shirley and his baby daughter were in Ireland or that the father had to be present for that responsibility to be officially recorded on the birth certificate there.

Edward saw no point in worrying about that 'knock at the door' moment happening. He would deal with it when the time came.

But he was curious as to why had she not come after him for any money yet?

She must have had that abortion.

That would be it, he wrongly assumed.

How wrong that assumption had been would shortly become clear, and present Edward with a very real situation that we would now have to deal with.

# Part Three

NINE
## Time Stands

Tina Phillips should have enjoyed one more year at St. Mary's National School in Ballygarrett before leaving Irish primary education, but in her new home in Droitwich they still operated a middle-school system, so she would have moved school twice in quick succession anyway if she'd stayed for her final year in the Catholic School. Shirley had at least waited until the end of summer term for them to leave Ireland. She didn't think that they would return to live there again.

Back in Droitwich at her parental home, Shirley was reunited with her teenage bedroom. It hadn't been touched in the intervening almost eleven years, even the same weird mix of posters were still on the wall: Bay City Rollers, David Bowie, David Soul. In 1977, both her parents had assumed that once nature had taken its course in Ireland, the baby would have been *'offered for adoption'*, which sounds a touch more human than *'forcibly taken from her,'* and Shirley would return home to Droitwich alone with the pretence that nothing had ever happened. Her mother would have preferred that convenient lie; one most likely that would never have been the subject of conversation again.

*'It's like I died, and you kept this room as my memorial'* thought Shirley. Perhaps her parents, especially her father, had experienced her not returning until now as a bereavement of sorts? She wasn't going to ask why her room had not been updated like others in the house and give her mother yet another opportunity to 'tut' and apportion blame elsewhere. *'Well, it's nobody's fault but yours for what happened,'* Joan would most likely have said.

Still possessing looks that allured, Shirley Phillips was for the most part unrecognisable to the young woman that departed to Ireland just over a decade ago. Her long hair was gone; totally impractical on a working farm, it had been cropped into a something shorter than a bob, and her complexion made ruddy by her outdoors existence. She'd picked up an Irish lilt in her voice that made her accent hard to place, neither rural

Worcestershire nor rural Ireland. Her frame had filled out too. Again, the manual work on the farm added curves and her adolescent cleavage had blossomed. Childbirth had also been partly responsible for that.

In the Droitwich library, Shirley asked if they kept back copies of local newspapers, and was taken to the upstairs reference section, located in a side room, where print copies going back around twelve months were instantly available. The microfiche, that archived older copies on film without taking up masses of space, would take a few days to arrive from the Archive Service if required. It was all free.

Shirley presumed that Edward Claines had been a member of a golf club, many of his friends were there on her fateful day and she remembered hearing golf references in many snippets of conversations as drinks were topped up and replenished. In fact, she could clearly remember the whole day, from almost losing control on the gravel at the front of the house when she arrived on her moped, to Edward nonchalantly walking away up the gentle incline of the water's bank almost as if, well as if nothing of particular note had happened to him. She had replayed the details of everything that remained trapped in her mind so many times throughout the years. It had never left her; the touches of her bottom throughout the afternoon were not just from Edward. Would she have gone across the field with him if she hadn't drunk any champagne? Why didn't Jim or Denise go with her instead of finishing the clearing up? Denise would have been there if her father had turned up a couple of minutes later to collect her. What if she hadn't let him put his arm around her. What if, what if, what if?

What if Edward Claines had not just been a gentleman, but instead a decent human being too? There wouldn't then have been the need for any 'what ifs' to continually attach themselves to Shirley's thoughts – a sort of PTSD – Post Traumatic Sexual Defilement that had already lasted eleven years.

But at no point since, has Shirley been able to recall fully the immediate aftermath. She must have walked back across the field and lawn she so clearly remembered crossing earlier with Edward. Her belongings, helmet, keys, coat, must have been somewhere. The journey home on her moped was a blur, and she'd forgotten about sitting in the bath for so long that the bubbles had all dissolved into the now cold water. She remembered acutely the vaginal pain of the moment down beside the stream, how it physically affected her walking back across the field, and the pain when climbing the stairs to have a bath. But she had now forgotten that it was still painful the following morning and for a few days thereafter. Those few minutes of being taken advantage of against her will affected Shirley's attitude towards men for the rest of her life, robbing her of the ability to let someone get close to her and vice versa. She also believed, as her mother had been all too quick to remind her on many occasions, that no decent man would want to have anything to do with an unmarried mother and someone else's child. There were no other single mums at the school gate in Ireland or at any of the school social events that she mostly stayed away from. Nobody said anything to her face or crossed the road to avoid her, but neither were the circumstances of her single motherhood ever asked about. No man in such a small rural Catholic community would dare to ask her out. Shirley accepted the situation, the alternative would be not to have her daughter, and irrespective of how she was conceived, that was the one thing that had kept her going. Until that breakthrough in DNA science put her and Tina's lives on a different track.

The golf club used every opportunity for free advertising in the local papers, and results from competitions were published along with cheesy photos of trophy-holding men in their latest jumpers with even brighter multicoloured diamond-designs. Edward wasn't in any of the photos, but his name was amongst the competition listings. He was still a member. Starting with sports section on the back cover, Shirley had been looking through the back pages to find evidence of his membership at St. Augustine's Golf Club, but now she closed another copy of a recent paper that confirmed her research, there was a photograph of Edward, larger than life itself, on the front cover. Adorned by a red cape with a thick black border, a black-only cap with a shape to it reminiscent of those worn by Scott Tracy and the other Thunderbirds Puppets, and a long heavy-looking gold chain around his neck. Edward had been successfully nominated and seconded by his pals to be the new Mayor of Droitwich Spa. It was a good news story. Now fifty-two years old, his successful company that employed many local people also sponsored one of the boy's football teams, and his ceremonial year as the town's Mayor, normally a reward for Town Councillors rather than high-profile locals, was to raise funds to support selected charities.  The Rape Charity *Crisis* wasn't one of his three nominated good causes they reported.

Early that same evening Shirley cycled to St. Augustine's Golf Club. It was a Monday evening and not at all busy.  Her mission wasn't to confront Edward; she could have gone to his house for that, but she checked the car park and didn't spot a Jaguar.  Only she wasn't to know that his last Jaguar had proved mechanically unreliable and he'd now gone German, purchasing a 7-Series BMW in Bavarian Blue – who even knew that was a colour?

The BMW was far more suitable for his golf clubs than the Jaguar too, and the salesman hadn't even recognised or promoted that advantage.

Shirley was in search of the bar manager.  She wanted to know if there were any bar jobs going.  There weren't, "but we regularly need temporary staff when there are dinners, regional competitions, and then there's the summer ball in August," he explained.

Shirley told him two white lies.  That her name was Tina, and that she'd worked in a pub in Ireland.  In truth, she'd helped out with the drinks in the village hall at a couple of farming events, but nothing there had been dispensed on draft or from optics.  "Leave me your details and I'll be in touch."

"I've only just moved back here," she replied, "and I haven't got a phone installed yet."  Clearly, she didn't want him phoning and asking for 'Tina.' "I'd be happy to do a couple of trial evenings for free to show you how capable I am."  She offered.

That hadn't been offered before, he admired her confidence, and there was frankly nothing to lose, and so it was agreed that she would work two trial shifts the coming Saturday and Sunday evenings.  There was a competition on Sunday, so it should be busy throughout the day.  It turned out that 'evenings' at the golf club meant from 4-9pm.

"You'll need to wear long black trousers and a long-sleeved white blouse. Clubhouse dress rules," he added.

Shirley's only concern was remembering that her barmaid-name was Tina. Was it a mistake to have taken her daughter's name for the purpose?  She didn't know.  But it was a help that she was given an oval gold badge with

TINA in Dymo tape capitalised across it. She was shown how to work the electronic cash register – she'd got her own four-digit pin that she had to enter before each sale – and a run through of optics, draft ales, and bottles, shown where to put empty bottles, where to find spare packets of nuts and crisps. If any of the optic spirits were getting low, she'd have to ask the bar manager to bring a replacement, and likewise, if any beer ran out, he would connect a new barrel up.  That made it all sound like she'd be on her own, but in fact she was working on both days with Pat who was perfectly nice and pleasant, but spent her time talking with the members when she wasn't needed to serve. Pat was probably in her early to mid-fifties, and 'Tina' was glad not to have someone being overly chatty with her; wanting to know all about her and her business.

Tina's Saturday shift at the golf club had been perfectly pleasant, but without any sight of Edward.

When 'Tina' arrived for work on Sunday afternoon, there still wasn't a Jaguar in the car park, but there was a 7-Series BMW in the 'Reserved for Captain' parking space that she failed to notice, despite the eye-catching Bavarian Blue metallic paint.

# TEN
## Edward's DNA

The golfers had started to return from their afternoon competition rounds and full of banter, each trying to outdo the other with their generosity and peacock-posturing at the bar. She might not have recognised Edward Claines from almost eleven years ago had she not seen his Mayoral mug shot in the paper. He had put on some weight and his hair was now receding and cut differently. He had no idea who she was when he came to the bar, and she returned the air of non-recognition.

"Good evening sir, what can I get you?"

"All the staff know my poison; I've not seen you here before. Who are you then?"

Which was frankly a stupid question as 'TINA' was front and centre on her name badge.

Shirley pointed to her name badge.

"Ah Tina. Well Tina, I'd like a double Jameson's whiskey. No water, just two lumps of ice."

No please or thank you. Just an attempt to caress her hand as she gave him the change from his £10 note.

"I quite like you Tina, and what a lovely accent you have" he oozed chauvinistically. "I'm sure you'll enjoy working here. I'm Edward. Club Captain so don't forget what I always drink."

"I'm sure I won't."

And he was gone. Away to interfere with whoever was running the competition day.

It was a warm summer day. Clubhouse rules still required men to wear ties at all times, but jackets could be removed once the most senior person present had removed theirs. The Club President was not there today, so when Edward, as Captain, removed his navy-blue blazer, emblazoned with the St. Augustine's Club Crest, and put it on the back of the chair he was sat at, most others followed suit.

Shirley saw her opportunity. "I'm just popping to the loo" she told Pat. She didn't need the loo, but once in the cubicle she took the opportunity for a pee and removed from her trouser pocket a small roll of clear Sellotape. She now widened her fingers and wrapped the tape several times around the back and front of her left hand, so that the sticky side was outwards. It was a 'trick' her Aunty Nuala had taught her in Ireland for removing stray sheep hairs from the best furniture in their seldom-used lounge. With the sticky tape arrayed around your fingers and palm, you just ran the front and back of your hand across the cushioned seating, and unwanted sheep hairs stuck to the tape. When you clasped your fingers tightly together, the tape came off easily to be thrown away.

Before coming back to the bar, she went across to where Edward was sitting and, as she said, "excuse me," and lent across to his right-hand side to collect the two empty glasses with her right hand, her left hand ran across the collar on his blazer and the tape collected the stray hairs that had earlier fallen from his head. Not many, but enough. His right hand connected with her right buttock. "Yes, I am going to like you Tina" he smirked. She didn't care. He wouldn't be smirking next time she saw him, and as she turned away from the table her left hand went into her pocket where she contracted her fingers and wriggled her hand free from the Sellotape, leaving it concealed within the pocket, with his DNA attached to it.

She was tempted to leave there and then. Nobody knew her name or had a contact number for her, but 'Tina' wanted to make sure that Edward saw her as much as possible so that he would recognise Shirley when he saw her next. Which wouldn't be long. When her shift finished she was told that they would be happy to use her for events over the summer. "I'll get you my number as soon as I have the phone installed" she promised. She wouldn't be back at St. Augustine's Golf Club even if they were paying her double the going rate.

Back home, Joan once again said, with her air of superiority that put everyone's backs up, what a stupid idea it was trying to do a part-time evening job when she should be at home looking after her daughter.

"I think you're probably right Joan, I'll look for something else. Most of them were horrible people anyway."

Back in her bedroom where she'd already removed the pop posters from the walls, Shirley took the Sellotape from her pocket to inspect her catch. Four or five good strands of hair, some smaller ones, dandruff. She put the tape on her chest of drawers and went back downstairs to 'borrow' an envelope from her dad, returning to pluck all the hairs from the tape with her eyebrow tweezers and drop them into the empty envelope. She was going to put the envelope at the back of her sock drawer when she remembered where she used to hide things that she didn't want her mother to find when she was a teenager living at home. Underneath the carpet in the built-in wardrobe there was a small fill-in piece of floorboard that could be lifted to reveal a small makeshift safe place. That would be safer. But she hadn't been capable of creating such a hideaway. The previous owners must have created it.

Downstairs, in the room directly below, her parents and daughter were in front of the TV watching a tribute show to Russell Harty who had recently died. Tina was only still up because there was no school until the end of summer and her mum had been out most of the afternoon and evening.

Taking great care, she put her eyebrow tweezers between the floorboards and eased the small length of wood up until she could squeeze her fingers beneath it and lift it out. Expecting the small void to be empty, there was a white and red plastic bag which revealed itself to be a *Woolworths* bag when opened out fully. Inside was her short black skirt and knickers from that traumatic evening after the Silver Jubilee party. She'd forgotten all about them, or, more correctly, just blocked it out. With the 'new' evidence in her hand, she now recalled that it had been her intention to burn them when no one was around and had hidden them there until that was possible. Only the events of being sent away to Ireland had overtaken her, and Shirley now thought 'What if Mum and Dad had moved and somebody else found them when replacing the carpet? Or what if they had given my room a makeover and found them?' Taking the items from the bag, she didn't have to look too hard to see that they were still soiled with his escaped semen. A few tears of remembrance rolled down her cheek, but the find, this rediscovered evidence that had no value at the time, but now, with DNA profiling that could implicate Edward in her rape, it only strengthened Tina's resolve to take her next action. He could still claim it had been consensual, but she had another trick from her time in Ireland to bring into play. One that was almost true.

Shirley was now even more committed than ever to get even with Edward. There would never be full closure, but she had this opportunity now to improve her daughter's life, and Tina was her first thought in all of this.

The Woolworths Bag was returned to the void with the envelope slotted in beside it. She put the carpet back without putting the wood back in just in case it made too much noise and aroused suspicions in the room below of something not being right in the room above. She must remember to do that in the morning.

Shirley went to sit with her daughter to learn about who Russell Harty was, why he was so beloved by the British public, and how he died.

# ELEVEN
## The Ultimatum

"TINA, it is Tina, isn't it? What brings you here?"

The following afternoon, Shirley had gone to the offices of *"Heat at Home Limited"* where a Bavarian-Blue 7-Series BMW was parked in the 'Reserved – MD' space.

When she walked in, the receptionist was away taking a customer through to the showroom.

*Heat at Home* had moved with the times. Secondary windows for residential properties were almost a thing of the past. Everyone now wanted the new uPVC replacement units – no more painting and maintenance, and consumer credit was starting to be taken up in large numbers only expanding their market potential. Building societies were part of the 80s credit explosion and keen to offer additional loans and re-mortgages to homeowners whose property prices had substantially increased and now had a low loan-to-value ratio. They'd also invested in machines that stuffed your walls full of government-funded heat-retaining insulation if it had been built with an empty cavity. *Heat at Home* would also sell you a complete conservatory. The business that had always boomed showed no signs of slowing down.

And so, by chance it was Edward himself who welcomed Shirley into his empire. She hadn't expected him to remember the name she used the previous evening. Was it because he'd had to tell her what he liked to drink without having to ask for it, or was it because she gone over the table and lent across him to collect glasses whilst running her left hand across his jacket to collect stray hairs?

"Is there somewhere private we can talk?"

"Come through to my office."

"Well Tina, I didn't expect to see you so soon," went the small talk as Edward led the way through the showroom to his office, "Even though it is of course a pleasure," he confidently proclaimed.

"Can I organise a cup of coffee or tea for you?"

"No thank you. I'm not expecting to be here long."

"How can I help you then Tina?"

"You don't recognise me, do you?" He answered with a facial expression that meant *'what do you mean, I only met you for the first time yesterday at the golf club?'*

"My name's not really Tina, and apart from yesterday the last time I saw you was over ten years ago when I stood outside your home and you asked me two questions about my early pregnancy."

Edwards face visibly sunk as he immediately recalled clearly in his mind exactly the scene she described. He got up and closed the door which he'd left open.

He had long forgotten about that moment, although in the very aftermath of it, he had expected another knock at the door to be imminent. But for many years now he'd completely forgotten all about it.

"You asked me if I had any evidence that my baby was yours, and how much it would cost to 'make it go away,' by which I assumed you meant how much money would I need to get an abortion?"

She was determined not to let him speak until she had said what had been going through her mind for months, and quickly added,

"Well of course I didn't have any evidence then – it would have just been your word against mine. But I hadn't had sex for almost a year before that evening, and you knew exactly what you did to me. There was no doubt that she was yours." She would have liked to have told him that the effect had been so traumatic that she'd been unable to let herself get close to anyone else since, let alone have sex, but Shirley didn't want to give him the satisfaction of knowing that her self-esteem, her very sense of self-worth, had meant both of those were true. "But you know that they now have this thing called DNA. That chap who raped and murdered those two girls was sent to prison for life because of it. I came to the golf club to get some of your DNA. I took some hairs off your jacket when I collected the empty glasses from your table, and those hairs, if necessary, will prove that you are the father of my daughter. And I didn't know until last night that I still have the skirt and knickers hidden away from the day when you attacked me, and they're still stained with your '*stuff.*' I was going to burn them, but my parents sent me off to Ireland to have my baby and the only reason that I was allowed to keep her was because I told the authorities that I had been raped. *Father unknown - due to rape* is stated clearly on her birth certificate."

'How is the girl, what's her name, is she as beautiful as you, have you got a photo?' These are the questions that Edward Claudius Claines didn't think to ask. Instead, after a few moments of silent contemplation about his own position, and nothing else, he asked,

"Have you come here to blackmail me for your silence then?"

"Silence? Who said anything about silence? Now it can be proved without any doubt that you're the father, I want you to take responsibility for what you did, to provide financially for our daughter. How you choose to do that, well, that's up to you Mr Mayor." She'd already lied about the '*due to rape*' being on the Birth Certificate that actually only recorded *Father Unknown*, but he wasn't to know that.

There was a knock at the door as the receptionist came in and asked if he could come through and speak to some customers in the showroom.

"Sorry Jess, I've got something I must deal with first. Hold my calls too until I'm finished here."

"You asked me before if I wanted any money to make it go away. It's too late for it to go away, but I now want you to at least make amends financially for what you did to me by providing properly for your daughter. I'm not after anything for myself. Is that unreasonable seeing how you could now potentially go to jail?"

"It doesn't sound like I have any choice. Do I?"

"CHOICE. Oh, that's rich. Unlike ME, I didn't have any choice when your raped me. But YOU now have a choice alright to do the right thing here." She wanted to go further and tell him that there was a choice that he made on that horrible evening almost eleven years ago, and on that occasion HE made the wrong one. "But I made up my mind a long time before coming here, that if you don't help us now, that I will go straight to the police and tell them that you raped me. I'll now be able to give them my old clothes and your hair, and then I'll be talking to the Benefits Office about getting ten years of child maintenance arrears from you."

The evidence was stacking up against him. She had the clothes, it was documented that the baby had been conceived because of rape, DNA was a thing that could put people in prison, and Mrs Thatcher was on a crusade to make absent fathers take responsibility and fully pay for raising children that resulted from their sexual indulgences, instead of the state picking up the tab. The personal cost to Edward's reputation of the truth coming out was going to be far higher than even ten years of maintenance arrears payments, and that reputation was far more important for Edward than any monetary payment. Uppermost, in his mind at least, was that he was the Mayor, that he was the Captain of the Golf Club, and that he was the owner of a successful local business. People in Droitwich looked up to Edward Claines, and the combined prominence these positions gave him seemed more significant than that of his moral and financial obligations to his unknown daughter. Did this new situation have the potential to make everything Edward had worked so hard for all come tumbling down around him? Did she actually have a daughter? Now he came to think of it, it sounded plausible. Any circumstances with his own daughter never crossed his mind.

"What is it you actually want then?" is what Edward said. What he thought was 'How do you want to go about blackmailing me then?'

"I just want two things, and if you don't want anything to do with OUR daughter, you'll never hear from me again.

Firstly, I want you to provide us with a small house, rent free forever.

Secondly, I want you to provide me with a monthly income, so I don't have to work all hours and can be there as a single parent to bring her up properly.

It's your choice. You shouldn't have done what you did."

She had him over a barrel, but he needed to buy some time to work things out.

"You're asking for an awful lot there," is what Edward calmly said. 'Fuck, fuck, fuck,' is what he was angrily thinking. But he wasn't angry at himself like he should have been, he was angry for not having the upper hand.

He waited for her to answer, but she just remained silent waiting for a 'yes' or a 'no.'

He leafed through the pages of the open diary on his desk.

"I need some time to work out what I can do for you. Come back this time next Monday and I'll see what can be done." He wanted to talk to his solicitor, but he didn't want to tell her that. What was the minimum he could get away with? "I'm sure we can figure out something acceptable by then."

"There's not much really to figure out. Either you help your daughter like I've asked, or you don't. I'm not going to accept anything less than I've reasonably asked for. The choice of supporting your daughter or the risk of going to jail is yours. It's not blackmail; it's a choice you can willingly make.

I'll be back next Monday then. And I WILL go to the police and the Benefits Office if you mess me about. I've already lost ten years of my life, there is literally nothing more for me to lose."

And with that she got up, and like Edward leaving the stream on that evening back in 1977, Shirley left his office without looking back. She was trembling inside; it had been so difficult to confront him with such seeming confidence. She was thinking only of providing for their daughter and was now completely driven to achieve that.

It was no longer about one word against another, no longer about twisting the facts to suit a different narrative.

Would Edward risk Shirley going to the police with her historical rape allegation? A claim that crucially now had DNA science that could seemingly put him, and him alone, at the scene of?

Was she just being reasonable in the circumstances?

# TWELVE
## The Payback

As soon as Shirley left his office, Edward picked up the phone to call his solicitor. The number was one of his stored autodials. As the ringing started he slammed down the receiver. 'I can't tell anyone about what happened,' he thought. Needing to think more about the uncomfortable situation he found himself in, he went to greet the waiting customers in the showroom with all the charm and attention as if he'd just closed a big order and not with an appearance instead of being burdened with the threat of being outed as a rapist looming over him.

Later that afternoon, when he'd returned to his office and asked Jess to hold all his calls again, after he'd given the situation and the now necessary consequences of his actions more thought, instead of calling his solicitor with the aim of minimising his exposure, Edward called his friend Bob Munday, the builder. It would be another ten years before everyone shouted 'Yes we can!' to Bob the Builder, as he then became affectionally known.

Edward determined that renting a house would cost more in the long-term and would require a monthly payment to a landlord or agent, and there would be contact with him every time something went wrong in the house and needed fixing. He would buy something and that would be the end of it.

"Bob, straight to the point. I need to buy a small house, somewhere in Droitwich. Have you got anything that's not selling?"

"You of all people should know how prices are rising like never before with all the demand," answered Bob. "Everything's selling. Can't build 'em quick enough. What are you looking for?"

"A deal as always – you know me Bob, a deal. Just a starter family home – just cash, no mortgage to arrange."

"Should I ask why or for whom?"

"Best not to, I think."

"Ok, leave it with me, I'll find out what's available and give you a call back tomorrow. Is that OK?"

"Just perfect Bob, thank you. Much appreciated, as always."

That evening, sat in the Orangery at Lance Dune House with a glass of Jamieson's and ice in his hand, Edward finally accepted that he had no choice but to do as Shirley asked.  There was no point fighting it, and although it was painful for him to admit, it was in his own best interests too. Being the salesman he was, Edward needed to feel like he had the upper hand, that he was the one in control of the negotiation.  But he needed something that he could negotiate with.  On his terms.  With the calming help of his whiskey, he determined that he would use some of his savings to buy the house and put Shirley on the payroll, but only until the child was twenty-one.  Or should it be eighteen?  He also decided that the house would be put in trust for the girl to inherit.  That way he would have evidence that there really was a child and when she was born, and confirmation that it wasn't a scam.  That really was the small doubt he was clinging to.  The house would be the girl's and couldn't be sold until she reached twenty-one or her mother died, whichever was the longer. In other words, the mother could live there as long as she wanted or whilst she breathed.  His solicitor would have to know that there was a child to provide for, which was not uncommon, but not the real reason why he was being so generous.

That was it.  Only how much should he pay her? And how would he deal with that?

As promised, Bob Munday called back the following morning.

"I've got a lovely three bed detached just off Blackfriars Avenue, it's at the end of cul-de-sac so it's quite discreet.  It's a bit small, but as a favour you can have it for fifty-four thousand.  It's almost finished and should be just over sixty on the market right now.  It's unbelievable how much land prices are going up this year."

"Haven't you got anything under fifty thousand?"

"Not a thing.  The new developments won't be ready until next year now, and the way things are going they'll be nothing under fifty thousand by then anyway."

"OK, can you put my name on it for a week? I'll know for sure late next Monday, but I'm almost certain to take it off your hands." And with that Edward said that he'd see Bob at St. Augustine's Golf Club on Sunday and rang off.

'Fifty grand for something not much bigger than the Lodge at the end of my drive' thought Edward. It's a shame that the Lodge has only got one bedroom, he mused, but he wouldn't want them living at the end of the drive anyway. But he determined in that moment to fix the Lodge, replace the windows, put in a kitchen, and make it liveable, just in case it was needed in the future for something similar.

Next Edward rang his solicitor.

"Listen John, bit delicate this, but I've just discovered that I have another child and I need to make some financial arrangements to look after her." He was about to explain when John interrupted.

"Are you sure that it's your child? Nobody trying to take advantage of you are they?"

"I'm afraid there's no doubt, and I don't want to avoid my responsibilities. I was thinking of putting the child's mother on my payroll to provide her with a monthly allowance that would pay the rent, buy clothes, shoes, food, etc.."

"I wouldn't put her on the payroll Edward. For one, it will make people in your accounts department suspicious. And, if she works anywhere else, that employer will also need to know that she's getting a Tax Allowance for her supposed employment with you, plus you'll have National Insurance and other add-ons. Besides, it's not really a business expense, so I think your Accountant would have something to say about that. In fact, you'd probably be better off talking to Andrew and see what he thinks best."

And with a "You dark horse you," John ended the call. He wasn't surprised, everyone who knew Edward well, knew of his appetite for the ladies.

So later in the day Edward phoned Andrew to half-explain the situation he found himself in and was advised to put Shirley's monthly allowance through the books as a consultancy fee so he could fully offset the payment as a business expense. The alternative was to pay her himself, but he would have to pay tax on the additional salary he took to cover the cost. "Get her to set up her own business and invoice you monthly. *Heat at Home* is more than big enough now to warrant hiring a marketing consultant or something like that. A bookkeeper to do her accounts will be no more than a couple of hundred each year."

## The Deal

"Ah, take a seat Shirley" he directed when Jess showed Shirley through to his office the following Monday afternoon. He took control.

"I've got the following offer for you. With regards to a home, there's a small housing development just off Blackfriars Road and a brand new three bedroomed detached house will be ready for you in about six weeks' time. I'll set up a trust for the child [he still didn't know her name – he hadn't asked] with the house registered to the trust. It will legally be hers at the age of twenty-one, but there will be a clause allowing you the right to live there as long as you wish.

The house will be purchased in full, but you will be responsible for everything else. By this I mean everything such as rates, the utilities, repairs, furnishings, etc.

Now, with regard to a monthly income, you will invoice the company each month for a marketing consultancy fee of one thousand pounds. Each April you can increase this by 5% or the rate of inflation, whichever is the greater. You will be responsible for your own tax and you'll have to pay a bookkeeper or accountant to help you. Given that you won't have any rent, that income should be sufficient to provide more than just the basics for you both. You can invoice the company until the child turns twenty-one, at which point you are both on your own. And you can start invoicing me this month so that you have some money towards furniture and kitchen equipment. You can check with the builders what it comes with as standard."

A three bedroomed detached house. Way better than she had hoped for. A thousand pounds every month. Again, much better than Shirley had hoped for. And all without a real fight. Edward really didn't want to risk damaging his local reputation.

"Thank you Edward. You've done the right thing by your daughter. How do we go about the arrangements?"

"Well, there's something I want from you in return. I need to know, to have your word, that I will never be named as the father. The money for the house will be paid for through my solicitor and not directly traceable to me. I don't want anyone coming after me for child maintenance payments or if they do, our arrangement will end; you will both be worse off. This is way more generous than just me paying my dues."

"I think you're conveniently forgetting how this all came about Mr Mayor." She thought he needed a reminder of the outward appearance he was almost on the verge of protecting. "But if you keep to what you've just offered, which I would be pleased to accept, then I promise you your secret will be safe with me."

Neither of them had considered what would happen if the business were sold or if it struggled financially and couldn't then afford to pay a monthly fee for a marketing consultant. Thankfully, it would never be a problem.

Shirley didn't know that Edward was spending more than £1000 per month to send his 'other daughter' to an elite boarding school in Birmingham. But irrespective of that, his lifestyle, BMW car, clothes, demeanour, all gave the impression that it was more than affordable to him.

Edward hadn't considered that the consultancy arrangement would provide him with an unwanted monthly reminder of his biggest mistake when he had to sign-off her invoice for payment. He still wasn't as adept at delegating work to those really responsible for it.

The meeting, perfectly matter of fact and devoid of any emotion from either of them, ended with Edward arranging for Shirley to come back in two weeks' time for an update. He asked her to bring their daughter's identity documents with her so that the legal side of things could be dealt with by his solicitor. For the first time, he would find out his second daughter was called Tina Nuala Phillips; from her Irish passport, and that her birth date was nine months after the first and only party he ever hosted at Lance Dune House. He wouldn't get to see her Birth Certificate.

# THIRTEEN
## How Life Transpired

Shirley told her parents that she had found an unfurnished home to rent close by, that it was a new build and that she and Tina would be moving there in around six weeks. She had some savings that would pay her rent for over six months and get her some basic furniture to start them off. She would now be looking for a part-time job that would fit around Tina's schooling. The house was in the catchment area for Witton Middle School, one of just two middle schools in Droitwich, and only a five-minute walk away. The town centre was also a five-minute walk in the opposite direction, so she wouldn't need any transport. She'd passed her driving test in Ireland so she could drive the small lorry crammed full of lambs to the market in Enniscorthy when required, and now needed to find out if her licence was transferable here or if she'd need to take another test.

Inevitably there was a hold up on the new house, not because of Bob Munday's building skills, setting up a Trust had just taken time, and the Land Registry Documents were needed with the change of plot number to house number and a postcode allocated. By then, Shirley had set-up a company and submitted two invoices that would help her buy furniture. She also had some savings from Ireland.

On the final day of August 1988, two days after the Bank Holiday and the day before Tina started at her new school, they moved into their new home off Blackfriars Avenue. For the next ten and a half years, until Tina's twenty-first birthday, every month Shirley's invoice was promptly paid in full. Shirley quickly found a great job as an assistant cashier at the Alliance and Leicester Building Society in Droitwich that perfectly suited school hours, and she enrolled on a part-time course with the Open University - a certificate in Business Management - so she could at least start to understand some of the principles she was invoicing for each month. It also helped her advance from her starting position as an Assistant Cashier, to later become their West Midlands Training Officer.

And that's how Shirley led her life. She allowed her Auburn red hair to grow long again, worked hard for the Building Society and, with the additional money each month from Edward, provided very well for herself and Tina. The experience with Edward and the subsequent ten years in Ireland as an unspoken social outcast as she raised her young daughter, both had a substantial impact on how Shirley viewed men, and she never allowed herself to be romantically or sexually interested in men throughout the rest of her days. Edward's picture was regularly in the papers, especially during his Mayoral year, but Shirley never saw Edward Claudius Claines again in person, although she sent him an unsigned 'Thank You' card when they moved into their house and enclosed another one with her final invoice in March 1999. Shirley was now fully on her own. Tina, now a mother herself, had left home two years ago, which was ironic considering the house was now unknowingly hers as she was twenty-one, but Shirley was fully in control of the things in her life that she could control, and she had a much better relationship with her mother than at any time since before her teenage years.

Fergal and Nuala visited every year. It was usually just a week or less towards the end of July when the demands of sheep farming were at their lowest and someone could be found to manage the farm in their absence. Joan was perplexed as to why they always stayed with Shirley and Tina and not her and Patrick.

## Home in Droitwich Spa

Today, Droitwich Spa is a proper little town of around 23,000 people nestled in the Worcestershire countryside just over 20 miles south of Birmingham, equally accessible from Junctions 5 and 6 of the M5 as you head down towards Cheltenham and Bristol. Worcester, the county city, is 6 miles to the south, Bromsgrove 6 miles to the North, and both are considerably bigger and attract better retail and leisure facilities. Part of the charm of Droitwich is that there isn't a McDonalds or a KFC; just a Droitwich-sized Dominos and a Subway. The Lido park has an uncovered outside swimming pool operational from May to September, good quality free tennis courts to use, a bowls club for the old 'uns, and a bandstand hosting a full programme of Sunday afternoon concerts throughout the summer. Hop on a train and you can be at Grand Central in the centre of Birmingham in 30 minutes, or Worcester in 9 minutes if you depart from the other platform.

Serving all the surrounding villages too, Droitwich Spa High School, that also incorporates a sixth form, takes pupils from the two middle schools, situated either side of the town centre. One of which, Witton Middle

School, is where Tina Phillip's education continued when she arrived from Ireland in 1988. Droitwich was very much smaller then; The Ridings and Copcut Rise estates were still to be built, as were the Clover Ridge developments. The Ring o' Bells and Spring Meadow pubs were still in business, as was the little 'open all hours' shop at the bottom of the Holloway that did fabulous bacon butties as a side-line. And the Copcut Elm Pub, today a *Hungry Horse*, situated on the A38 heading out of town towards Worcester, was yet to be painted bright pink and renamed Trotter Hall as part of Mad O'Rourke's little pub company chain.

In the 1960s and 70s the much-missed comedian Rik Mayall grew up in Droitwich, and Gareth Southgate lived there when he played for Aston Villa in the late 1990s.

It was far from a cosmopolitan second half to Tina's childhood, but she wasn't stuck literally miles from anywhere on a farm, and now there were afterschool clubs, a leisure centre, and the wide-open spaces in the park to explore. There were friends, kids to play out in the streets with after school, and there were boys. There was nothing remarkable about Tina's progress academically or socially, except that her home life lacked the influence of a male role model. Granddad Patrick was always on hand, and unlike her grandma Joan he took every opportunity to spoil her rotten.

In her first year at Witton, Tina discovered that her Irish education had already equipped her with the skills and knowledge that her classmates were now being challenged with. She was bored, easily distracted, and should really have been put up a year. But a British education is all geared around successfully reaching another birthday and not an academic or vocational ability. Instead of being an 'A' student, she muddled through achieving C grades without much effort. And by the time she reached 16, she'd had enough of school and left to work for Texas DIY, filling shelves, operating the checkout, pointing customers in the right direction across the DIY shed in Droitwich to find their home improvement purchases. With no rent to pay at home, it was good money. Good money that attracted Tina to cider, boys, and sex. She was happy, except for the fact that bringing young men back to the house was a complete no no, and so her virginity was abandoned at sixteen adjacent to the Lido park. In St. Peter's graveyard.

The dead there didn't mind, and Tina can't now remember who was on top of her, or underneath her for that matter!

For her eighteenth birthday, Tina indulged herself with a tattoo. On the inside her ankle so it could be discreetly covered by socks, or tights or trousers. By 1996, the norms of society were hugely different to those experienced by Shirley, and an eighteen-year-old woman had no qualms about getting repeat prescriptions for the contraceptive pill.

When Alfie Rogers got eighteen-year-old Tina Phillips pregnant in 1996, he was twenty-four years old. Until that point, he'd had no reason to take responsibility for anything in his life. He was a rudderless soul with no aims or directions for himself. No dreams to guide him, and no work ethic instilled in him by his parents. He was a chancer who loved a drink, more than one, and the occasional smoke of socially acceptable illegal substances.

Alfie left school at sixteen without any qualifications, but he was far from stupid. His English and Maths were far better that most of those with pieces of paper to prove their capabilities, but he failed to get to examinations and the high school staff had long given up on his and especially his parents' attitude towards schooling to care about getting him there. It would be quite different today we are led to believe.

Droitwich town centre has a quaint and renowned sunken High Street, supposedly moulded by brine streams that caused the undulating subsidence along its length, with a cobbled surface that is lined with many pretty timber-framed buildings. Alongside the bypass, known affectionately as the *'dual track,'* Berry Hill is a large industrial estate with a community of small, medium, and large companies that offer a range of temporary employment opportunities for the unqualified. Alfie had worked his way around the industrial estate, performing a range of unskilled manual tasks that habitually bored him within a short space of time. At one company he'd been there long enough to get a fork-lift truck operator licence, and that had helped him get employment elsewhere.

In his earlier days, that combination of drink and cannabis had made Alfie late or completely absent from work on too many occasions. When friends gave him work on building sites, sometimes with the full intention of helping him to learn a trade, as soon as he had enough spare money in his pocket to not care, he didn't.

Always looking for a quick buck, easy money, if the opportunity arose for a bit of ill-gotten dishonesty, pilfering from a warehouse, folding a banknote to make it look as if there was an extra note so he could purposely short-change someone, he'd take the chance. But Alfie wasn't a criminal. Never did anything that couldn't be twisted around to have the explanation of an 'honest mistake.' Nothing would stick to Alfie; he was like Teflon, especially not employment, and well known around the town's pubs, everyone considered him a loveable rogue.

# FOURTEEN
## The Twenty-Week Scan

Tina Phillips, still a few weeks short of her nineteenth birthday and, as you know, had never known her father, which was most likely why she wanted her own baby, due in around four months' time, to have Alfie, the baby's father, around to help bring him up and provide that father figure for it. They learnt today that their child was going to be a boy. Jake.

Tina, not unlike her mother, is one of those impatient people who likes to have everything arranged as soon as possible, typically before it is really required. During her first scan, not until fourteen weeks because she was in denial for so long about the reality of the situation, Tina still had some forlorn hope that it might all go away by itself; Tina asked the nurse if she could tell if it was a girl or a boy that was starting to disfigure her good looks. In reply Tina and Alfie were told that it was still too early, but today the baby was lying in a position that removed all doubt, and so when they confirmed that they really did want to know, the nurse informed them with a beaming smile that their impending 'little bundle of joy' was going to be a baby boy.

The ultrasound scan confirmed that the baby's development and heartbeat were both normal, and there was no indication of any of the abnormalities being checked for, most of which are statistically a concern when the mother is considerably older than someone as young as Tina.

By the end of the day, 'Jake' had been decided upon together, and Tina had instructed Alfie that she wanted to be married before the baby arrived, and so he'd better get on and make that happen too. Shirley didn't know what to think about becoming a grandma before she reached forty.

Don't forget, it was 1996.

Putting a ring on her finger and providing her son with the two parents that she didn't have herself growing up, was just how Tina wanted it done. Even if she didn't love Alfie. Even if she'd only had sex with him once before getting pregnant. Tina had already dumped her boyfriend, the one she'd cheated on with Alfie. It was the right thing to do for her child and she was going to do it.

Alfie didn't love Tina either. How could he? He still hardly knew her. But he had and still did lust after her. From her flowing red hair all the way down to the *'while you're down here'* inscription tattooed on the inside of her right ankle, he lusted after her. Just like all the young women before her and those that would fall for his charms in future one-night stands. Just like Tina had been a one-night stand, only the consequences of this one were going to determine the outcome of both their lives, for better or for worse.

Alfie didn't want to get married. He certainly didn't see it as a 'better,' and wasn't sure if it was a 'worse,' although right now it felt like it might be. Yes, he said that he wanted to support Tina, play his part, and be there to raise his child, but he was only twenty-four and not ready to make, as he saw it, the ultimate sacrifice. Not yet. He felt unknowingly trapped by impending fatherhood and Tina's demands for a gold ring to legitimise it.

He didn't share his doubts with Tina or Shirley. Not yet. Tina seemed so genuinely happy now she'd had her second scan, discovered everything was 'normal' and that it was a boy. Any thoughts about how they might support an infant hadn't even registered yet; if the truth be told, neither of them were very capable of supporting themselves! No thoughts either for how it might impact her employment at the DIY superstore crossed her mind.

Tina still lived at home with her single mum Shirley, in the small three-bedroom detached house that she had no idea belonged to her. For her first ten years, Tina had grown up in Ireland amongst the innocence of a rural farming community that provided a haven for her and her mother. But here, in the small Worcestershire town of Droitwich where the school, the town centre and the park were all five-minute walks in different directions from their home, Tina enjoyed friendships, discovered boys, and enjoyed teenage freedoms that would not have been possible in Ireland. Alfie was not her first sexual encounter, but significantly older, he had been her best. She was on the pill and it had been a spontaneous, drunken, one-night stand that both of them had willingly undertaken. In Alfie's flat. After an evening of drinking and flirting in the Hop Pole Pub.

Alfie and Tina never got married, but Tina changed her name by Deed Poll before Jake was born so she could take Alfie's surname - Rogers – and give their impending son some outward notion of conformity in the community. Almost five years later [in 2002] Jake's life was turned on its head with the arrival of Sophie, his baby sister, and the family was complete. Alfie and Tina moved from privately rented accommodation into a small housing association home to continue living their dysfunctional existence. The children were well looked after and loved, and Shirley was always there to pick up the emotional and especially the financial pieces on the many occasions when the things fell apart. They were both unfaithful, both had walked out on each other at times, but ultimately always gravitated back to each other and the responsibilities of their children.

# FIFTEEN
## Summer 2017

There's not a great deal to tell you about the proceeding twenty-one years.

Alfie and Tina, despite their best destructive efforts, managed to keep their family together. During this period, they lived in a small number of housing association and privately rented homes and, when things were really bad financially, spent six months with all four of them living under Shirley's roof. Between them they had a large number of full and part-time unskilled jobs.

Shirley's health has deteriorated badly in the last few years.

Back in 2010, at the age of 74 Edward's own health was starting to slow him down considerably, and his daughter Michelle left her insurance job in The City and moved back to Lance Dune House to start running *Heat at Home*. She took over completely in 2014 when 51% of the shares were transferred into her ownership. Although she was christened 'Helen,' in memory to her mother who died during her birth, shortly afterwards the 'Helen' was dropped and she has been known to everyone all her life by her middle name, Michelle, including us now. When her mother discovered that a little girl was on the way, she and Edward originally chose Michelle, and it was only after the Christening when Edward decided that Michelle would be more appropriate than the constant reminder of her mother. He would have to move on, and calling her Helen wasn't helping.

As a consequence of his failing health Edward, now aged 80, is a resident in the Avalon nursing home which specialises in providing healthcare to those with the condition he is afflicted by. Dementia. There is no polite way to put it. He is a permanent resident in cuckoo land, and sadly no longer recognised Michelle on the rare occasions she visited. She didn't really feel much of a connection with her father. If the truth were told, she'd had more of a relationship with his wallet than his fatherhood. He'd never been tactile or taken time to play with her. Nanny Julie had efficiently brought her up. Edward had been too consumed by work, golf, and womanising – but never beyond the boundaries outside *consent* again, and not with someone so young, even if she had been eighteen and technically legal. From that day back in 1977 when Shirley had stood on his doorstep clearly showing the early signs of pregnancy, he had bitterly regretted that day, even if he wouldn't allow himself to acknowledge or admit it; even to himself. When he'd been admitted to the nursing home, Edward's Dementia was thought to have been just Alzheimer's, but the experts there soon determined that there was more to his condition, and a diagnosis of 'mixed dementia,' a more debilitating combination of Alzheimer's disease and vascular dementia, was made.

Michelle's private education concluded with a place at Rochester College Oxford to read Economics and Management, with the Economics bit taking place within the college itself, and the *Management* bit being taken at the *School of Management Studies*, a school that transitioned to become the new Saïd Business School for the start of her second year. She went down from Oxford with a 2:1 and was truly gutted with her degree award, no, seething would be more accurate. Founded in 1246, and the very first of all the Oxford Colleges, for the first seven hundred and forty-four years of student enlightenment, Rochester only admitted male students. At the time of Michelle's graduation in 1989, female undergraduates had graced its cloisters, towers and banqueting hall for less than ten years, which when converting higher education years to real life equates to less than a weekend, and there were still Masters and Dons aplenty who despised such frankly unnecessary modernisation. She remained convinced that her lack of a penis had prevented her getting a 1st. There were male contemporaries, many the latest incarnation from generations of Rochesterians, and far less capable academically than herself, who were duly decorated with their comparatively undeserving top honour. With the benefit of 'new' family money enabling her to join in and become accepted financially, she had massively enjoyed her time at Oxford but had clearly joined the wrong college. Rochester would not benefit from any philanthropic support coming from Michelle that alumni were encouraged to bestow upon their Alma Mater, declining to join the *Old Members*. Fuck them for the sexual inequality of her 2:1.

Oxford is the strangest of Universities, despised by many, along with Cambridge, for its elitism which, for those that concern themselves too much with the social and economic mobility of higher education, too often confuse that elitism with academic prowess. Academically, these people believe that students with less favourable economic and social backgrounds should be afforded the same academic opportunities as those that who arrive at Oxford with the privilege, like Michelle did, of a private education behind them.  Academically, those young people might thrive, but socially, there is the potential that they will be damaged for life.  Academically, beyond their one-hour tutorial, a one-and-a-half-hour class and two hours of lectures, there are a lot of hours to fill, and if you want to be a part of 'Oxford' socially, then that takes money, social standing and networking to join in.  There are plenty of boys and girls from quite ordinary backgrounds who were captivated by the false equality promise at 'Oxford' [and Cambridge] and found out the hard way that it isn't so.

Michelle had been groomed to take over the family business, she never married despite a string of serious relationships and two engagements, and even before her father moved to the nursing home, from which he would not return, she had moved into the family home of her difficult childhood.  Lance Dune House had been too remote for friends, and from the age of eight she had been away at all-girls boarding schools followed by university, where her friends similarly went home in all geographically different directions for the holidays.

Michelle was planning her 40th Birthday party.  A marquee on the lawn with mainly friends and work colleagues.  With Edward in a nursing home, her only family were her mother's parents, and their own health was also deteriorating. The monthly payments to Shirley's company for marketing consultancy ended long before she joined the firm full time, and a long time before she took over the responsibility and applied the benefits of her Oxford education.  The legal I's were dotted and the T's crossed long ago; 51% of equity in *Heat at Home* – still a private company – had long since been transferred into Michelle's name; Edward still owned 49% of Preference Shares so that the dividend would go some way towards his healthcare costs.  Those shares, the house and other substantial investments that she didn't even yet know about would all pass to Michelle on his death.

Over the years Edward had walked near the small, detached house that he felt coerced into buying for his unacknowledged daughter, and had seen the young girl with red hair playing in the street with her friends. He didn't want to be involved.  He knew that he hadn't been involved enough with Michelle's upbringing, apart from funding it, and he took a conscious decision not to bequest anything to Tina in his will. He knew her name from the passport required to set up a trust fund that had been arranged by his solicitor, with no documentation linked back to him. He'd not seen Shirley since *'their business'* had been concluded in his office twenty-nine years ago.

Michelle also held two Statutory Powers of Attorney over her fathers' financial and healthcare needs, both of which had been signed before the onset of dementia took away his mental capability to determine almost anything for himself.

Before his mind was ravaged by Alzheimer's, Edward assumed that his dirty little rape secret would go with him to his grave. Would Michelle be ready for the truth that would soon be revealed to her?

# Part Four

## SIXTEEN
## I Love You, Goodbye

Shirley Phillips was one of those people who had never smoked but somehow managed to contract lung cancer. Tragically, around six thousand non-smokers die from lung cancer in the UK each year. Perhaps it had been during the years she lived with Uncle Fergal in County Wexford? He never smoked indoors or in the lorry, but outside he regularly had one on the go. Or maybe it was the log burner and the sods of dried peat that often fuelled it? Or just maybe plain bad luck? Like Roy Castle, a brilliant entertainer and musician throughout the 1960s, 70s, and 80s, who, having never smoked, died of Lung Cancer in 1994.

Three years ago, Shirley had undergone lobectomy surgery having been diagnosed with a non-small-cell cancer in her right lung. A dose of chemotherapy followed, but six months later the cancer was not only still present, but it had now spread to her left lung. Seven weeks of radiotherapy complemented another four cycles of chemotherapy, which made her extremely sick throughout the duration.

Over the last two years as her lung capacity gradually diminished, Shirley had increasingly lost her mobility. Severe breathlessness now followed even the lightest of energetic tasks and slowly but consistently her ability to cope with living ebbed from her. The small lounge on the front of the house became her bedroom some months ago, and social care provision was provided to help get her up in the mornings and back to bed in the evenings. It was undignified, but Shirley knew, and accepted, that despite being only fifty-eight, her death would not be far away. Not having any faith, Shirley wasn't reconciled to it. It was just now inevitable, even if it was much earlier than nature normally takes its course.

She needed to get all her affairs in order. It was time to let Tina know who her father was and that she was about to inherit a house now worth around £250,000, although technically and unbeknown to Tina, it was already in her name. There should have been some additional assets too. Joan and Patrick had left most of their estate, apart from a few small cash bequests, to Shirley, but ironically some of those small bequests ended up almost as much as she had been left with. Joan and Patrick had been persuaded to release the "Equity" from their home. It funded a couple of latter years memory-making cruises; up the Norwegian Fjords one January and then further north around the top of the world to catch the Northern Lights, which unfortunately they didn't. And then 18 months later a September cruise in Alaska and some whale watching. They'd signed-away fifty percent of the value of what had been a fully mortgage-free property, received around fifty percent of its value in cash thinking that was the end of the matter. They assumed that after their deaths the house would get sold, the company would take its fifty percent of the then increased market value, and fifty percent would still remain as their asset. Well, in fact that wasn't it. It never is. There was a six percent annually compounded interest that would be added, and by the time that Joan and Patrick were both dead, the 'debt' to the finance company pretty much wiped out the entire value leaving only a modest residual positive balance.

Shirley hadn't got around to making a will. The house wasn't strictly hers of course, although everyone assumed it was rented, but she had £20,000 in Premium Bonds that she'd invested all the money from her parent's home in, together with a Santander savings account containing £8,000. Shirley lost her job at the Alliance and Leicester in 2011 when it was fully taken over by Santander following troubles during the 2008 financial Crisis.

But it was time to get her most important affairs in order.

There was the Trust document from Edward's Solicitor with the house deeds in Tina's name, the 'Phillips' one she had before she changed it to Rogers.

An envelope from National Savings and Investments with her Premium Bonds.
The envelope with strands of Edward Claudius Claines hair. [She had burnt the skirt and knickers, as originally intended, almost as soon as she and Tina had moved into their new home.]

Her Santander savings passbook.

And finally, the letter she had written on Tina's 21st Birthday, the 7th March 1999, having sent *"Heat at Home"* her final invoice for Marketing Consultancy at the end of the previous month.

*7th March 1999*

*My Darling Tina*

*I am writing you this letter on the assumption that you will find it once I am dead, although I hope we will have had an opportunity for me to explain personally about the things you have long asked about and which I now want to clarify.*

*Your father is a man called Edward Claines. You will read why I couldn't tell you that before now. He owns a window company in Droitwich called 'Heat at Home,' and was just over 20 years older than me, so I expect that he too is now also dead. I have never once regretted having you. A life without you would have been no life at all. But the harsh, still uncomfortable reality, is that when I was just 18, your father took advantage of my young age and slight figure and raped me.*

*When you were born, Edward already had a young six-month-old daughter and had no interest in you or me. His own wife died in childbirth. He denied the rape, denied his responsibility, and it would have been his word against mine. As I was unmarried and just 18, my Catholic parents sent me to live with Aunty Nuala and Uncle Fergal until you had been born. I was supposed to give you away and come back to Droitwich alone, but I couldn't bear that, and Nuala and Fergal kindly offered to share their home with us for as long as was necessary.*

*I am writing this today on your 21st Birthday, because today the Droitwich house that you grew up in becomes legally* yours, although I have permission to continue living out my days here as it is also my home.

When you were 10 years old, DNA was discovered that could scientifically prove who your father is. The small, sealed envelope with this letter contains strands of your father's hair so that this DNA proof can be used if such confirmation is still required. I don't know how you do that.

When you and I came back from Ireland, I confronted Edward with the new scientific possibility for DNA to prove his paternity and requested that he now did the right thing by us. He was already wealthy when he took advantage of me and today he is a very wealthy man.

This house was purchased by his solicitor and put in Trust for you to own on your 21$^{st}$ birthday. Since we moved into the house, I have been paid a monthly allowance towards our upkeep. That arrangement also ends today with your 21$^{st}$ Birthday.

I hope you are reading this because my life has ended and not because you accidentally found it. You and Alfie now have Jake to provide for, along with any other children that come your way. Cherish this house in that same way that you and I did, and enjoy the benefit of being rent and mortgage-free. Please don't squander it!

Much Love

Mum

xx

## St. Richard's Hospice, Worcester

When Shirley knew that the plans in place to move her to St. Richard's Hospice for end-of-life care were imminent, she climbed her stairs for the final time to take the letter, Trust Document and Deeds, and the envelope with the hair strands from their hiding place in her wardrobe and propped them alongside the wine glasses in the kitchen cupboard that were hardly ever used.

On the outskirts of Worcester, opposite the Worcester Woods Country Park, St. Richard's Hospice is the most wonderful place to be when a last breath is taken. All the rooms are spacious and have direct views and access onto the landscaped gardens and pond. Someone is always available with time just to hold your hand, or with words of comfort, or to provide you with some welcome medication to reduce the physical pain. There is no gloom or doom, everything is explained clearly, honestly, openly. For Shirley, that was a comfort. There was nothing wrong with her mind.

Not knowing it would be Shirley's penultimate day of life, on Saturday 12th August, just over a week after Shirley was admitted into the hospice, Tina, Alfie, Jake and Sophie came to visit her again. Weather wise, it was a gloriously sunny British summer's afternoon. In their hearts and souls, it was the depths of winter. They were all visibly and audibly upset and found it impossible to hold back their tears. When they were about to leave, Shirley told Tina that she wished to speak to her alone, and would the others mind waiting outside, just for a few moments?

"There's no will, but a letter by the wine glasses in my kitchen cupboard will tell you who your father was, and with it are documents confirming that the house is yours. I'm sorry I couldn't tell you before. I was sworn to secrecy.

You've been a beautiful daughter to me. I am going to desperately miss every part of you."

Tina couldn't reply. She couldn't hold back her tears long enough to get any words out. She hugged and sobbed on her mother for what seemed like eternity, holding her hand not wanting to pull it away until Shirley, exhausted and in desperate need of rest, bid her to re-join her family.

Tina, knowing it wouldn't be long before her mother would be gone forever, planned to go and see her again tomorrow, but before the sun rose early the following day the last painful breath left Shirley's lungs.

# SEVENTEEN
## Nature or Nurture?

Once they were back in the car, Tina checked her handbag to make sure she had her key for mum's house and then asked Alfie to stop there on their way home so she could pick something up. She hadn't been in the house since Shirley left for the Hospice. She checked the fridge. It would need a clean out soon, but for now she just tipped the sour lumpy milk from its plastic container down the sink. Just as her mother had said, there were the documents in the cupboard that she took and put into her Tote bag to read when she got home.

Once home, Sophie and Jake went out separately to meet their friends; Sophie's at the Lido park, Jake was taking the train into Worcester.

"Mum wanted to tell me about these documents," she told Alfie as she took them from her bag and held them aloft.

"What they about?"

"I believe that I'm about to find out – at the fecking age of thirty-nine – who my father is. I'm just about to lose my mum so I'm not sure I want to know just yet, if at all."

"It's your call bab."

She hated it when he called her 'bab.'

"Have we got any JD?"

"There's a drop left."

"Pour me one and we'll get this over with."

Before Alfie came back from the kitchen with an Aldi beer for him and a JD and Coke for Tina, Tina had taken the letter from its envelope and started to read.

"Oh my god.

Fecking hell.

Mum was raped.

NO WAY!"

"What way?" he asked.

"Alfie, Alfie, it's too much to take in."

"What is?"

"The house, my father, mum."

She passed him the letter.

If Tina hadn't been expecting that, then Alfie was completely oblivious to the fact that learning who her father was for the very first time was totally bewildering. Tina had enjoyed a better relationship with her Mum than Alfie had with two parents. Probably a girl thing. And how could Alfie have realised that not knowing who your father is, or why it seemed to be such a secret, can play so much on your mind if you've never experienced it for yourself? It was therefore surprisingly easy for him to be unintentionally insensitive towards Tina.

"Wow - we might be rich," was his first comment, because that single 'fact,' that her father was *a very wealthy man*,' had the biggest potential impact on him as far as he could tell. Still no thought or consideration for how Tina might be feeling to have suddenly learnt who her father was after all these years.

"We. Really. WE are not even married. Remember that one?"

There was now a long silent tension between them.

"He might still be alive. Shirl wasn't expecting you to have this until, well, much later on. If he's twenty years older, then yes, he probably is still alive.."

Tina hadn't even considered that possibility. Firstly, she'd always assumed that her father would be Irish. She hadn't known that her mother was sent there because she was pregnant with her. And now come to think of it, it was almost thirty years since they moved into the house he provided, he lived locally, and not once had he come and found her.

Tina wasn't to ever know that he had seen her occasionally, but only from afar. He couldn't risk the 'rape' accusation being levelled at him again. It didn't matter that it was true, he just couldn't face the public backlash, potential prison; it would have ruined his business and he'd have been asked to leave the golf club, Club Captain or not.

"Feck, Feck, Feck. I don't know what I should do. I wish I didn't know, having the house is brilliant anyway."

And Tina resolved that she'd ask her mum tomorrow after she'd slept on it, and before it was too late to ask her these questions.

Alfie used his smartphone to Google *"Heat at Home"* and couldn't help inadvertently poking the Hornets' nest again. Not on purpose, it just came out.

"Just looking at their website. Say's here that the business started in 1973 and that in 2014 the daughter took over when Edward retired. He was seventy-eight at the time."

"What you on about?"

"*Heat at Home*, d-a- a-a-d-d-y's company silly. The one you might now be worth half of?"

"Don't be stupid Alfie. I don't even exist. No, that's not true OBVIOUSLY, what I mean is that he's not even on my birth certificate, there is no family link or proof for what mums written. I'll ask her tomorrow."

She hoped he'd just shut up now. But a few moments later.

"I've just Googled what he's worth. Reckon the company's worth over £12 million and that he's refused to sell it a few times."

"ALFIE, not now. Don't get ahead of yourself again."

He didn't know which of his 'get rich quick' ideas she was referring to, but he kept thinking about it even if he didn't speak about it. Wouldn't that be a great T-Shirt slogan everyone would want to pay for? *'Just because I haven't said it, doesn't mean that I'm not thinking it.'*

"And his daughter Michelle owns 51%. Doesn't that mean you've got a sort-of sister?"
ALFIE, FECKING LEAVE IT WILL YOU. LAST BLOODY WARNING."

The following morning, Tina's mobile rang whilst she was still half in slumber in bed. It was almost 9am.

Alfie was still asleep next to her, but the soft buzzing and vibration on the bedside cabinet was enough to disturb him from his sleep too.

It was Janice, the senior nurse at St. Richard's Hospice, with the news you learnt earlier about Shirley's passing during the night.

"There is no rush," said Janice, and Tina agreed to go and see Janice around 2.30pm that afternoon to start 'sorting a few things out.'

Before they'd gone to bed last night, it had been agreed that they would tell the kids about moving into Grandma's house when the time comes, but nothing else. Not who her father supposedly is. Nothing about the business. By the time they sorted themselves out, they'd most likely be nothing to sort out anyway, so best not raise any false expectations. Alfie reluctantly agreed to hold his tongue.

Tina went and woke Jake and Sophie to give them the sad but expected-any-day-now news about their Grandma. Afterall, in the normal course of events, there's only one reason for leaving a hospice when you've been a much-loved resident on an end-of-life care pathway. Death – that comes to all of us without exception – is something that's still got too much taboo about it, and Shirley had been a monthly direct-debit supporter of *'Dignity in Dying'* to support their much-needed opinion-changing work. Like many others, she wanted the UK to offer us a chance to die here when the time was right instead of going to Switzerland and forced into taking that final action before it was strictly necessary, but crucially before you were too ill to travel there.

"Grandma's left me her house, so we can move there when we're ready." It was way bigger than their Housing Association home, plus it had the garden too and in a much better location. That was something positive to look forward to amongst the current sadness permeating throughout the household.

Shirley had done a great job of bringing Tina up single-handedly and had always been there for the grandkids too. She may have been unhappy with her daughter's actions on occasions, like the first tattoo she'd had on her eighteenth, like her teenage pregnancy that would take away other choices about college, work, and would ultimately come to define her. But then that was to all intents and purposes no different to Shirley's own circumstance of being a teenage mum and having her life defined by it. What would she have done differently with her own life if she'd finished her college course and had a family as part of a normal relationship? At times she asked herself the question; by the school gate in Ireland, assisting a sheep to safely deliver its lamb, circumstances when she'd had no control. But since returning to Droitwich, she'd enjoyed her work, her parents had accepted the situation, it just was what it was. If Shirley had ever judged Tina, unlike her own mother she had kept those judgements internalised.

# EIGHTEEN
## Unremembered Contents

Shirley had never been truly sure what she made of Alfie, but in truth Tina had been every bit as rebellious, no that wasn't the right word, more like as strong headed, as Alfie. They were equally as good and as bad as each other and for each other. As volatile as Den and Angie Watts in EastEnders one moment, as harmonious as Tom and Barbara in the Good Life the next. Simultaneously perfect and then positively flawed for each other, and twenty years on, they were still somehow miraculously together. Perhaps it was simply because they didn't have the money or the intelligence to 'consciously uncouple?' Perhaps any dreams had been smothered by their Groundhog Day circumstances and there was no compelling sense of any alternative possibility?

And then there were the grandchildren Jake and Sophie. Shirley was the reason why Jake had been the first in the family to go to university. When he was just a few years old, Shirley taught him to play cards. For hours and hours, it was Uno, Snap, and Rummy. Jake developed the ability to add-up, use logic and apply strategy, all of which fuelled his ability and curiosity for maths. And then as luck would have it, there were a couple of great maths teachers at the High School and Sixth Form who challenged and developed him into an 'A' Star pupil. Something Tina could have applied herself to be, but she hadn't.

Tina went to St. Richard's Hospice on her own this time. Thankfully, they didn't have to walk past the room where her mother had died to get to Janice's office. Janice came to meet her in reception when she got the call to say Tina had arrived. It's not just with patient care in the most difficult of clinical and emotional circumstances where St. Richard's excel, but with the time and support close family, relatives and even friends receive. Today was no exception and there seemed to be as much time as Tina wanted. Did she want to see her mother? She wouldn't be moved to the undertakers until tomorrow. Could they help her with choosing an undertaker? No, it had to be Crumps. A *Certificate of Cause of Death* had already been prepared. Shirley's illness and interventions were well documented so there was no requirement to report her death to the coroner or for a post-mortem. Tina would now have five days in which to take the Certificate and register her mother's death at any of the Council offices listed on the form.

Tina told Janice that it was a great comfort that her Mum had been able to spend her last days in such a beautiful place. Not just the garden and pond she could see from her bed, but the staff and volunteers who looked after her. It must be hard, Tina thought, to cope with a conveyor belt of patients where no one rings the bell before walking out, cured of their illness. She didn't know how to ask the question tactfully. It wasn't something she thought she would be able to cope with herself. Tina left with a small bag containing the few possessions Shirley had arrived at the Hospice with. When she got back into the car she looked in the bag. It would have been too rude to have done that in Janice's office. Some toiletries, her necklace, and a small brown purse with £65 in it.

As she drove home Tina now wished, yet again, that she hadn't yet seen the letter, but it couldn't be unseen or the contents unremembered. The information, exposing for the first time who her father was and how she had been conceived, was intended to comfort Tina, give her some closure but, in fact, it did the opposite. There had not been any hint throughout her childhood or adulthood that her father would one day be revealed, or even that he was 'known.' She'd never thought once about trying to track him down; she hadn't been adopted, she'd seen her birth certificate, never thought once about contacting *Long Lost Family*. Yet now, annoyingly, Tina was thinking more about Edward Claines and his daughter, his other daughter, than her own mother right now. That just wasn't right. Was he still alive? Would he want to see her? Should she try or even want to see him now that she knew her mum had been raped by him? Would she like her new half-sister? Was she aware of Tina's existence? These questions, without any answers, were hurting her head.

It was heading towards 5pm when she got home, and nobody had given any thought to what they might eat that evening. Alfie had been to the pub for a lunchtime drink, so with the £65 already burning a hole in Tina's pocket, she suggested that they walk through the alley to The Castle and have a Sunday pub roast. They were all happy with that.

## Sister Act

Tina had a few part-time jobs on the go. The following morning, Tina rang Peter at the *Spinning Wheel Café* where she chatted to customers as well as serving them their coffee and home-cooked lunch, and told him that Shirley, who he knew well and had persuaded him to give Tina the job, had died and that she wouldn't be in for a few days. He'd have to do some work himself now while Tina was off on compassionate leave and sorting Shirley's affairs out.

The Spinning Wheel was a brightly shining jewel amongst the small selection of independently owned cafes and restaurants in Droitwich that is now much missed by many people in Droitwich. By day, when Tina worked there, it was a bustling little café contained within a few ground floor timber-framed rooms that offered a selection of home-made sandwiches, jacket potatoes or ham, egg and chips. Peter could be a little abrupt, but that was part of Peter's charm for those who became regulars, and almost friends. On Thursday, Friday, and Saturday evenings, without changing anything apart from dimming the lights, adding a few tablecloths and a meal-only menu, the Spinning Wheel transformed into an intimate Bistro offering its small selection of home-cooked delights. Marie, Peter's wife, did all the cooking, and her signature dish was an eight-ounce Sirloin with hand-cut chunky chips, mushrooms, tomatoes, onion rings and a smattering of French mustard. Just perfect when washed down with a moderately priced bottle of Malbec or Rioja.

When operating in Bistro-mode, Peter roamed as front-of-house and offering bonhomie to guests throughout the evening, leaving the order taking and waitressing to Lexie and Francesca.

By day, the café attracted a wide range of customers from infants with their parents, to the wrinklies from the Bowling Club in the Lido park who came in for a good value pensioners' lunch after a morning roll-up. By night, individuals and couples came in for a drink at the bar; there wasn't the space or ambiance to attract larger groups, and the price of a pint was a good notch up from the Hop Pole, The Castle, and others. For meals, it was mostly couples, and small groups of friends who were mostly past their prime in life. It is sadly missed following Peter's retirement.

The more she thought about it, the more going to see Michelle Claines and finding out what she knew made perfect sense. Tina hadn't told Alfie her intentions, she wanted it to be her own decision and not for him to talk her out of it. Otherwise, that doubt of not knowing would eat away for who knows how long. After she'd rung Peter, it was first on her short to-do list:

To Do:

1. Visit Michelle Claines.

2. Register the death at the office in Worcester.

3. Visit Crumps the undertakers and find out about a funeral.

4. Go to Mum's house and sort out any things that need sorting. The fridge for one.

The "Reserved – MD" space now had a BMW Z4 parked in it. In black. Whatever happened to Bavarian Blue? Was that a good omen?

# NINETEEN
## Long Lost Family

"I'd like to talk to Michelle Claines," Tina told the receptionist.

"Do you have an appointment?"

"No"

"Can I ask what it's about?"

"It's personal, not business."

She asked Tina her name and instructed her to wait. A few minutes later she came back.

"Come this way please. Miss Claines hasn't got long, she has another meeting starting in 10 minutes."

"Tina is it; how can I help?"

Without any apology for arriving without any notice, Tina came straight out with it, and somewhat aggressively she asked,

"Have you any idea who I am or why I might be here?"

"I'm afraid I don't. Is there a problem with some work we've done for you?"

"I don't know any other way to do this," she said, "but I believe that you are my half-sister. Did you know that you have a half-sister?"

Michelle had also seen "*Long Lost Family*" where unknown family members unexpectedly appear from the past, some welcomed, some not, but always after an intermediary had been in touch and ITV had arranged for the cameras to be there with Davina McCall and Nicky Campbell both gently preparing and smoothing the way for the big reunion. There was no Nicky Campbell with a cameraman present.

Michelle was in complete denial. Why would she not have been?

"My father has never mentioned anything to me about another child," which was the absolute truth, he hadn't. "What makes you think after all this time - you must be at least forty – that you're suddenly his child too?"

"I'm thirty-nine actually. I've never known who my father is, but my mum has just died, and she's left me details to say that Edward Claines is my father and some DNA so I can prove it. He raped her you know." She didn't know.

"Well, I never knew my mother, so we've got at least one thing in common." It was all a bit crass and unseemly, and not true either because Tina had known her mother very well, but Michelle was playing for time to give her some thinking space.   If it had been one of her suppliers she'd have said, 'That's a great question, one I need to investigate fully before I can give you an answer.'

"Are you after money?  I've seen his will, there's no mention of you or anyone I don't already know, and it can't be changed now?"

"Is he still alive?"

"Ah, did you think he was dead then?  Is that why you've come?"

"I told you, my mum just died.  I knew he was considerably older than my mum, so just assumed he was already dead."

"He's alive, sort of.  He has advanced dementia.  Doesn't even know who I am anymore. I hardly go to the home now.  Can't see the point.  But the point is, his will is very clear and there's no mention of you in it."

"He bought mum a house, paid her a monthly allowance until I was twenty-one. That must prove something?"

"I don't know what it proves.  You can have your DNA test but what will that achieve? He might be your father. That wouldn't surprise me given all the women he's had. You're probably not the only one. But even if it's true, there isn't a single penny you can get from him. Not now. Not ever."

"I wasn't after any money you cow.  I thought you might want to get to know me if we're half-sisters?"

"I don't care if we're half-sisters, full-sisters or even twins. I've got to forty without you in my life and I can't see any point in changing that.   You're thirty-nine you say.  When are YOU forty then?"

"Next March."

In an instant Michelle, with her Oxford 2:1 in Economics and Management, worked out that if what she was hearing was true, then her mother would have been seven months pregnant at the time this stranger now before her was conceived. Would he really have raped someone whilst his wife was heavily pregnant? Not out of the question, she thought.

"I'm sorry I can't help you anymore. If you want to do your DNA thing then go ahead. Here, have some of mine" as she pulled a few strands from her own hair and thrust them at Tina, which she automatically took without thinking. "There's no point going to see Edward, they won't let you in to the home unless you are an immediate family member that they know. Can't change his will now to put you in it."

"I wasn't after any FUCKING money."

No goodbye. Tina turned and left with her dignity just about intact, she thought.

Michelle was tall like her father whilst Tina was a little shorter, more like her mum. It was only after Tina had left that she admitted that they both had red hair and similar facial features; his. Only Tina had never met her father and she didn't recognise any of Michelle's physical features resembling her own.

Alfie would.

Michelle was now late for her meeting, the party organiser for her upcoming 40$^{th}$ birthday bash was waiting in reception as Tina hurried silently past.

Apart from the name Tina, Michelle didn't know who she was or if she'd be back again any time soon.

Did Tina want a sister? She wasn't sure and on reflection it would be difficult to find any common ground when Michelle knew everything about their father, and she knew nothing. Well not quite nothing. Her mother had told her that Edward had raped her. It must be true. She had no reason to make it up. Why else would he buy them a house and pay her an allowance for all those years? Why else? Apart from sharing a father, their lives were clearly miles apart. It would only end up causing, well trouble. She remembered as a teenager watching *Pat and Margaret* on the TV with her Mum, a Victoria Wood drama where two sisters raised apart in different social worlds were reunited after decades with neither knowing anything about the others' life, nor having any connection or reference points to it.

It didn't end well, and that was how she thought any moves to force Michelle to be a part of her life would end too.

Michelle certainly hadn't projected any interest in finding out more about Tina, not even if there was the slightest chance of it being true. Money. Michelle thought it was all about money. Maybe it was. Here was the one daughter with all life's opportunities in her bank account, whilst the other one, born just a few months apart and from the same father— the man who could provide those opportunities to both of them — was struggling to exist in so many ways, and not just the hand-to-mouth existence her and Alfie scraped by on for most of the time.

Tina might not have been certain about her thoughts towards Michelle Claines or if there was any real injustice in her newfound situation, but Alfie was certain where his own thoughts were focused. Money, lots of money, and the prospect of him getting his hands on some of it as soon as possible.

# Part Five

TWENTY
## Up On The Ride

Before Tina told Alfie about her day; he'd known that she was going to register the death, visit the undertakers, and see if anything needed sorting out at mum's house, he had some information of his own that he was champing at the bit to share.

"The house is worth over a million too."

"What are you on about?"

"The Window man, he's still alive and his house is worth at least a million."

"How do you know this eh?"

"Jimmy told me. He's worked for him for years fitting windows. Used to do some jobs up at the house from time to time."

"What the FUCK are you doing talking to someone else about this? Didn't we say that we'd keep everything to ourselves? DIDN'T WE? Didn't we agree that just YESTER-FUCKING-DAY?"

"I didn't tell him anything I shouldn't. Just asked him if he knew anything about him or his family. He doesn't know anything about you. Trust me."

"He better not. You and I need to think carefully about this."

She was going to tell Alfie about her meeting with Michelle, but not now. Perhaps tomorrow when she'd calmed down and thought more carefully about it, and when Alfie wasn't so fixated on just the money.

After they'd heated and eaten their Aldi frozen pizza, Alfie wanted them both to go up The Castle Pub for a drink so he could talk to her away from the children.

She told him she didn't feel like it. She wanted to be on her own and think about it all.

"Do you want me to stay?"

"Not really. Need to get me head straight before we decide what to do. Got to let Crumps know if we want a burial or a crem. What do you think?"

"Dunno, did she never say what she wanted?"

"Na. My grandparents were Church people and both of them were buried. Mum and me never went to Church. I bet she'd probably want to be cremated just to annoy her Mum."

"Sorted then," he said as he unhooked his keys from the rack and headed out into the early evening sunshine, leaving a "Don't wait up" hanging in the air. He'd have to blag a few drinks if he wanted to stay out all evening, but Alfie was in a good mood and was already dreaming about the equivalent of a six-number lottery win coming their way.

How many times had she told him that they couldn't afford drinking in the week unless he got himself some full-time work? Her head shook in disappointment with the thought.

Tina had no idea where the children were. Jake would be going back to Nottingham Trent University for his final year in a few weeks and Sophie would be starting her GCSE year at the High School.

She switched the TV off – bloody repeats on *Dave* all the time – to give her mind some peace and quiet to think through her options. She found a pen and paper to make a list which she headed and underlined; Do Nothing and Do Something:

| Do Nothing | Do Something |
| --- | --- |
| Rent-free house | Visit Edward |
| Little bit of money | Challenge the will |
|  | Ask Michelle again |

## Do Something

Tina looked at her 'Do Something' options and realised that there wasn't really anything she could do that had a realistic chance of changing anything.

The nursing home surely wouldn't let her in, not that she yet knew where it was, and even if somehow they did, what would she say to an old man with

Dementia who no longer recognises the daughter whom she assumed he'd been devoted to for almost forty years?

She couldn't contest the will; he wasn't even dead yet. Besides, she'd got a house in her name, so he'd known about her but, according to Michelle, not mentioned her in his Will at all. So that was a deliberate omission and not because he was unaware of her existence. Plus, if he had dementia, which Tina had no reason to doubt, then he probably now wouldn't be able to change his will.

The only potential action left was to appeal to Michelle's better senses again. Maybe she'd caught Michelle on a bad day? What she didn't know was that she'd actually caught Michelle on a good day. She was really excited to be sorting out the final arrangements for her 40$^{th}$ birthday bash in a few weeks, which was a welcome distraction from the mundane business, as she considered it, of making and fitting bloody windows.

Tina was in bed and fast asleep before anyone else arrived home. Alfie, pissed as the proverbial Newt on his return after midnight, fell asleep on the sofa watching repeats on Dave, which is where Tina found him when she went down to make a cup of tea shortly after 7am the following morning.

He hadn't received a text the night before, so the garden and leisure distributor didn't have any hours of his zero-hours contract working in the warehouse to offer him. He could be a liability; he'd been that far too many times in the last twenty-one years, but more recently he'd developed a much better work ethic and wouldn't have stayed out if he'd had a 7am start.

Tina fetched him a coffee and made him shift his feet up so she could sit at the end of the sofa.

"Listen, before the kids are around later, I've been having a good think. Look, we've got Mum's home so there's no more rent to pay. That's a massive help, but that's it. There's nothing to come from my father; that's just the reality."

Alfie perked up quickly. The idea of having enough money to work even less than a zero-hours contract appealed to him, and in his mind, he'd already been spending the money on his Villa season ticket, maybe even a corporate box for a few years, a holiday in Malaga, and a new car.

"Well let's at least have a go. There must be summut we can get? He might have left you something when he dies?"

"Honestly, there's really no point. I went to see my supposed half-sister yesterday. I was going to tell you but when you went on about how much his house was worth and that you'd already been talking to Jimmy, well you really pissed me off. She's not a bit interested in me and anyway, he's already made his will and with the Dementia or whatever, he couldn't legally change it. He knew about me. He gave me the house – not mum, so it's not that he didn't know or anything like that. It would cost a shit load of money to challenge it legally, but on what basis? There just isn't one and we should be glad just to have the house. I always assumed she rented it anyway."

"There must be summut. She's got all that money and a fucking massive house and you're exactly the same amount of daughter that she is. It don't seem right, does it?"

It didn't seem right, but was there really anything that could be done? Was such an injustice in Alfie's mind, if that's what it was, just down to which daughter had been born to which mother?

Alfie clearly thought so.

# TWENTY-ONE
## What's It All About?

Alfie Rogers is everyone's friend. His good looks attracted Tina to him in the first place, and plenty of other women before and since. With a bit of application, he could have made so much more of his life. If someone like Edward Claines had taken him under his wing, given him direction, motivation and a purpose, then he would have excelled in sales. Who wouldn't want to buy from him? But a liking for the ladies, his weakness for whacky-baccy, and a penchant for pubs, got in his way. He was far from stupid, but the harsh reality is that success requires parental support, great schooling that identifies everyone's specific talent, and the willingness of students to own their own learning. A minimum of two are usually required, and great things can happen when there is a full house. But for Alfie, none out of three consigned him to be one of life's chancers in order to get by. Yes, the odd thing might go missing from whatever warehouse, building site, or place of work he found himself, but nothing truly criminal and never violent. He'd never had to raise his hands to attack someone or defend himself. His charm did that alone. He could mix with anyone. He was a Chameleon that could take on other people's accents and behaviours just to fit in, and he also instinctively understood that was also achieved by spending more time listening to other people than talking to them. A couple of times he'd been on the pub outing to Cheltenham where hospitality required a jacket, shirt and tie and he'd scrubbed up with the rest of them and had no problem holding his own with those for whom such occasions were not a once-in-a-lifetime or even once-a-year treat. He'd charmed his way to free Guinness and glasses of Champagne all day long from those with too much money of their own or with access to corporate expense accounts.

But Alfie wouldn't let this one go. It was the once-in-his-lifetime opportunity and he had to think of something. The potential get-rich-quick prize was too alluring, and it seemed morally right to Alfie too. After all, Tina was every much the rich bastard's daughter too.

"I should marry her, then divorce her, so we can have half the money ever after." He wasn't in it just for himself, he really did want to find a way that would benefit him, Tina and the kids.

"What did you just say?"

"I should marry her, divorce her, and we can have half the money."

"And why do you think she'd give you a second look then?"

"Well you did, and she's got the same DNA as you."

"Fifty percent the same I think you'll find. I can't believe I'm having this conversation with you. Let's just stop this now."

"But what if we could. Just think what half of that money would let us do."

"Let us do? What would you do if you had ALL THAT MONEY?"

"That is exactly my point, I wouldn't have to do *'feck all'*, he said mimicking. "There's always stuff in the papers about young women marrying rich old geezers who then inherit everything when he pops his clogs, leaving the family with nothing. Look at that Jerry Hall marrying the old newspaper guy. He owns Sky Sports and loads of stuff and she'll cop a fortune when he dies. Why not the other way round?"

"I bet SHE had to sign a pre-nup, and she wasn't short of a bob or two in the first place so that doesn't count."

"Got to be worth a go. Millions, gazillions maybe? And just for a couple of years' work maybe."

"Get out of here Alfie Rogers. I've never heard anyfing so fecking stupid in all my life. Work indeed. Don't sound much like work to me. Anyway, she might be married already.

I'm going for a shower you crazy fool."

## Something Had Started..

Some people do their singing in the shower, but for Tina her shower this morning was longer than usual simply because the stupid *honey-trap-thought* that Alfie had started just a few minutes ago was now revolving louder and louder around her brain like an earworm does after the last truly awful and annoying song you hear on the radio. You don't want it there, but it's got a hold of you, even if you listen to something else. Except that Tina was not only replaying what he had said, SHE was now playing out the possibilities and potential consequences in her head of them actually doing it. In her mind, Tina was already making a mental list.

1. How could it be done?
2. How long would it take?
3. What if he fell in love with her and didn't come back? Wouldn't that be just typical!
4. They'd be having sex together. How would she feel about that? She didn't know.

Tina knew that there was a difference between sex and love, but what if he fell in love with her and it ended up being more than just sex to entrap her? If it was just sex, would that make the situation alright?

The truth is that even though everyone assumed they were married, they had both been unfaithful to each other several times. Twice Alfie had left her for someone else, but ultimately came back, whilst for her she'd only 'done it' with someone else to get back at him. To show him that she didn't need him. She probably didn't, but she did want him, and he was after all the father of her two children and she bitterly regretted the occasions when she had been unfaithful. She'd devalued her own self-worth, that was the point.

But potentially several million pounds coming their way. When would they ever get an opportunity like that again? Or even to just dream about it actually being possible.

'Oh my god, I can't believe that I'm starting to think this might be a good idea,' she thought, 'and it would help the kids with whatever they want in life too.'

Tina not only remembered the way that Michelle had treated her with utter contempt, but also thought about how being raped by Michelle's dad, her own dad, had probably ruined her Mum's life. Maybe that's why she never had anything intimate to do with another man?

The noise of the shower pump and her hairdryer had not raised either of the kids from their slumbers. When she went back downstairs Alfie was still on the sofa watching Piers Morgan spouting off again on Good Morning Britain. *'Why isn't that man locked up for phone hacking?'* She thought.

"Put that bloody thing on silent," she instructed.

"What you said about marrying her, divorcing her and getting half of her money, is that a thing? I mean is it really something that YOU could do?"

The biggest grin awoke on Alfie's face. Tina was starting to listen to him.

"Unless she's a *muff diver* how could she resist me?" he laughed. "Never thought of that possibility did we. I've looked on Facebook and her status is single."

'*God no,*' Tina thought, and then thinking that's she's almost forty and that presumably 'Miss Claines' is unmarried too. Whatever that might have to do with it.

"I don't know," she continued, "let's just pretend it's somehow genius and it looks like a crimeless crime, if that's a thing, how could you get to even meet her for long enough to get things started? What if you fell in love with her and didn't come back? I was just thinking about that in the shower. How do I know you won't just *feck off* and leave the three of us behind? You'll be spellbound by her money long before you get to a wedding, let alone creating a divorce, and then you pair could keep the bloody lot."

He didn't know what to say. It was just a waking dream that was now turning quickly into a 'what if.'

"Then I'd be the victim twice, wouldn't I?" she asked.

"What do you mean twice?" replied Alfie, not understanding her point.

"Well, everything's already been left to her, and now if you *copped off* with her and didn't come back that would be another slap in my face, wouldn't it?"

"I think you're getting ahead of yourself. You didn't even want to talk about it an hour ago. Told me that you'd never heard anything so *fecking stupid* if I remember right?"

"It's your bloody fault for putting the stupid idea in my head in the first place. I was also thinking what if it don't work, then we've not really lost nothing have we?" It was a statement more than a question. She continued.

"Don't say a word to anyone, specially not Jimmy and not even the kids. Let's go up the Castle tonight, find a table outside on our own and talk about it some more."

Alfie continued to dream his dream smiling from ear-to-ear.

Maybe, just maybe Tina was going to let him have a go at changing their lives.

# TWENTY-TWO
## Funding The Deceit

Either Shirley had thought that her end of life wasn't so imminent, or that things would just take care of themselves after she had 'gone,' but although she had left all the important documents for Tina to find, she hadn't sorted all her affairs out.

Tina visited the Citizens Advice Centre in the Library to ask about how she should deal with her mother's affairs. Apart from Shirley's possessions, and there was nothing more valuable than her old car and the flatscreen TV, she showed them the passbook and Bond Certificate. No, she didn't have a property, she told them, and confirmed that Shirley wasn't married and that she was an only child too.

"As there isn't a will specifying an Executor, you need to apply for what's called *"Letters of Administration"* in order to deal with your mum's estate," she was told.

"How do I do that?"

"That's a good question; I don't know. Bear with." The Citizen's Advice volunteer, it said so on her badge, went off to tap her keyboard and shake her head a few times before coming back.

"You have to complete a form PA1A on the Gov UK website. You can either do it online or print a copy off and fill it in. Have you got a printer at home?" She didn't. "We can print you a copy off here but there is small cost per page."

So, they printed her out a form which she was going to take home to fill out.

From the Library in Victoria Square, Tina walked the short distance to the traffic lights and up the Hanbury Road to Crumps the Undertaker to see if they had got a date for the Funeral yet? Yes, it was going to be Thursday week. They asked if Tina wanted to put a *Notice of Death* in the local paper with the Crematorium details? Yes she did, and it was going to cost £55.

With just one additional car to the hearse, the funeral cost still seemed expensive to Tina. The Celebrant would charge separately for the service. Aunty Nuala and Uncle Fergal, now just into their 80s, were going to come over from Ireland, and apart from Tina, Alfie, Jake and Sophie, there were no other family members.

She told Crumps that her mothers' assets were tied up until she could get Probate. She had just got the forms and would be sending them off tomorrow [the Probate Office wanted an upfront fee of £215] and that she'd pay him in full as soon as she had the funds. She showed him Shirley's Building Society Passbook with over £8000 in savings and said that she had some premium bonds too.

They were happy with that. Tina was in a permanent state of limbo until her mother's assets could be released to her, which would take almost three months.

Later that August day, Tina and Alfie walked up to The Castle Pub whilst the late afternoon sun was still warm enough to sit out. It was burger and a pint special night, so they did, and started a grown-up conversation about duping Michelle Claines out of half of her wealth. Tina told him that if they were going to have a go, then she had three golden rules that couldn't be broken under any circumstances:

1. The children must never know that they deliberately attempted this.

2. It must stay just between the two of them. If anyone else knew then they were open to blackmail or possibly being done for fraud or something; she didn't know exactly what.

3. Tina needed some assurance from Alfie that if their plan was successful, that he would carry the plan through and come back to her.

Maybe he had to sign something; again, she didn't quite know, but she sort of didn't trust him one hundred percent. She'd think about it more, but he willingly agreed in principle.

With his simple, spontaneous throw-away comment, Alfie had set the wheels of an unlikely, but substantial, attempted fraud in motion. But more than just the trappings of consumerism that the money could buy, it was a way out of their hand-to-mouth existence that excited Tina most. That and to give the kids a proper start in life; exactly like Michelle had been given.

Alfie had planted the notion of an injustice between what Tina had, compared to Michelle, and that perceived injustice was now beginning to eat away at her. Especially as there was now a possibility, however small, to right that wrong.

Nuala and Fergal were going to stay at Shirley's house whilst they were over, but once the cremation had taken place and they returned to Ireland, Tina was going to move into her house with the kids. Alfie was going to stay put and as far as everyone else was concerned, they were splitting up. It was part of the deceit. He'd ask the housing association to provide a smaller place for just himself. Neither of them had considered that one of the kids might want to stay with their father or that they might want to take sides in the seemingly amicable separation they were fronting. As the windfall inheritance coming from Shirley would be well over £20,000, after funeral and other costs were taken into account, they would lose the income support that went towards their housing association rent. She didn't want to squander the cash, there was no new car or holiday being planned, Alfie would need money to have better clothes and whatever else needed investing in him to give their stupid plan the best opportunity to work.

They agreed that they would give it twelve months.

# TWENTY-THREE
## Life Begins

Forty people had been invited to celebrate Michelle's fortieth birthday. A marquee on the lawn that thankfully wasn't required to escape adverse weather, was organised to host a five-course sit down meal. The party very closely resembled a wedding, with exquisite flowers on each table, but without a Groom. Two almost-Groom's would be there. Monty and Giles, the two Oxford undergraduates that Michelle had been engaged to; Monty whilst she was at Oxford and Giles a few years later. From her days at Rochester College there was a group of ten of them, four couples and two singles, that met up religiously every February for a week's skiing in Avoriaz, and sometimes in the summer, usually at someone's villa on Portugal's Silver Coast, near Nazaré where enormous Atlantic waves crash down on to the golden beaches and international surfing contests are held. Or occasionally in the Caribbean! They were great people to be with sporadically, but she soon realised at Oxford that whilst her *'new money'* gave her the currency to join in with anything socially, it didn't provide her with the language and connections of *'old school tie and money'* that all these friends were all a part of. Twenty years later and she was still the outsider in many ways. Both her ex-fiancées, arrangements that Michelle had purposely ended on both occasions through fear of 'the forever' commitment, had married other members of their social circle, and thankfully it hadn't made it difficult for any of them. *'Old money and Old School Tie'* talking. Some of her father's friends who had been like aunties and uncles to her growing up, the grandparents on her mother's side were both still alive; her mother had been ten year's younger than Edward and they'd had Helen at a much younger age, so they were almost the same age as her father. Bob Munday the builder was there. His wife had died the previous year and he was glad to be there having retreated into himself since her death.

"I remember your dad having a great party here when your mum was expecting you. Queens Silver Jubilee if I remember correctly. Not as posh as this, but great fun. Don't know why he never did another one."

Half of the people were from *"Heat at Home,"* not just the managers, but some of those that had been there over thirty years with her father and now her. Cars were banned. Michelle arranged taxis both ways for anyone local, and for her Oxford friends and others who had travelled to be there, they were being put up at the Chateau Impney Hotel with executive minibus transport each way.

The transport back would also mean that the party would end on time with no hangers-on! That also tells you something about Michelle, for whom spontaneity and commitment had always been difficult propositions. Skiing in Avoriaz, and especially the *red run* down to Morzine with the dramatic cable car return across the 1800m cliff face, was just about the only high-octane part of her life. Outwardly her BMW Z4 looked fun, but it had chosen her, not the other way round, when her father gave up driving and no longer had a need for the X6 that was only a few months old. It was way better value to swap it for an almost new Z4 than take a massive cash hit selling the X6 back to them. Michelle was also a victim of her boarding school childhood and relationship with a distant father who provided the money for whatever she wanted, but not his time nor expressions of love. Edward worked for money, amassed it, provided employment for hundreds of people over the years, but the money never really worked for him. He'll go to his grave a very wealthy man and what use will that money be to him now? Oh, there'll be some nice bequests to friends, family, even the bloody Golf Club will establish a competition in his memory with money entrusted to them, but he missed out on time he could have spent with Michelle. What pleasure he could have witnessed on the faces of those he was making his bequests to, if he had done it whilst he was younger and in good health. It wasn't as if he needed to be dead for his wealth to fund those gifts. His holidays were on golf courses, or thigh deep in fly fishing waters, and later in life, once he developed an appreciation for expensive red wine and put the cellar at Lance Dune House to good use, on vineyard tours. But never time in the sunshine or a European city break with his own daughter. For Edward, *'Rich Dad, Poor Dad'* was a juxtaposition, he was both. There are many like him.

Back in the birthday marquee, there was purposely one place-setting too many set on each of the eight tables. Rather than having a top table, Michelle decided, or rather her party planner suggested when Michelle didn't know who she should have on her table, that during the evening she could flit from table to table and have a proper seat and conversation at each. Starter with one table, main at another, and so on.

For the final hour there was a live Rhythm and Blues band to warm up the dance floor.

Her birthday party only had one aim. To impress her Oxford friends.

It did. Especially the party bag that everyone got as they left, containing Chocolate, Paracetamol, Cheese and Onion Crisps, and bottles of Lucozade Energy and still water. The perfect hangover accompaniment or cure she hoped that everyone, everyone but herself, would require. They did. She didn't. She even had one waitress specially coached to bring her *Seedlip Spice 94*, a non-alcoholic spirit with tonic water that looked as if she was joining in with gusto. Her glass would be slightly different to the others and she would be offered the tray first.

Or if, just like Michelle, you're just a bit too anally retentive to truly have a great time for fear of letting your guard down. Especially when you only got a 2:1, or because like the former leader of the free world, your election victory was stolen from you! Yes it was.

Yes, Michelle's 40th birthday party had been a great success, but wandering around the lawns and patio made her realise that the garden needed more attention than she was currently giving it. The flower beds were weeded, the lawn beautifully striped, cosmetically everything was fine, but wasn't this a garden only fit for someone of the 'Saga generation' and not for someone who had barely turned forty? There was no personality to it. No fun in it. Bland. And now come to look at it, perhaps the rendering could do with a fresh coat of paint too?

As Michelle looked around her garden wondering what it would take to make Lance Dune House better epitomise her own character, she could have no sense about how personally disastrous her next actions would prove.

# Part Six

## TWENTY-FOUR
### Sowing The Seeds Of Love

Shirley's funeral service passed off without anything remarkable happening. Tina didn't appreciate it as she sat in the Crematorium hearing the comforting words of Kate the Celebrant, but not really listening, that Shirley had been a far better mother and father to her, than Edward had been a father and mother to his other daughter Michelle. She didn't know what courage it had taken for Shirley to confront Edward so that they both had a far more comfortable existence than would otherwise have been the case. Shirley had invested her time and love in nurturing Tina, whereas Edward had opened his wallet to allow others to do the same for Michelle.

The newspaper announcement attracted a few ex-work colleagues to the crematorium, but no real friends. It was a sad reflection on her life. She'd missed all the opportunities that people have to make friends when children are first at nursery or being dropped off at the school gate. That all happened in Ireland where she hadn't been welcomed, and when they moved back to Droitwich, Tina had been old enough to walk the short distance to school with new friends after her first day at Witton Middle School.

Nuala and Fergal stayed on for a few days. They invited Tina, Alfie and kids – they were not really children anymore – to come and visit them in Ireland. The small sheep farm in County Wexford was but a distant memory for Tina, unbelievable that it was almost thirty years ago since she had lived there.

Long before the funeral took place, Tina was back at the *Spinning Wheel* waitressing for Peter, and once Nuala and Fergal had gone, Project MC, or just MC [*Michelle Claines*] as Alfie and Tina had agreed was the only way to refer to it between them, started. For the next week after work, which finished mid-afternoon when the café quietened down, Tina visited her new house to sort out her mother's belongings and clean the house from top to bottom before they moved there. Any clothes in reasonable condition would go to the St. Richard's Hospice Shop in the town, any real keepsakes she would keep, but there was no sentimentality for keeping anything just for the sake of it. Shirley wasn't a hoarder, something Tina had inherited, probably from their time in Ireland where, for ten years, they were living in someone else's home and didn't have the luxury of space for superfluous belongings. Nor did they have the luxury of cash to buy them in the first place.

In the drawer of the bedside table was a sealed envelope with substantial contents.

"Tina. For my Funeral." Was handwritten outside, inside was over £2,500 in mainly £20 notes. There was no other note or explanation. Had her mother just forgotten to tell her, or had Nuala and Fergal left it for her? She had told them that her mother had left £8,000 in a savings account when they asked how she was paying for the funeral and that it would be several weeks before she could get access to it. She didn't tell them about the Premium Bonds, or that the house was already hers. Or maybe it had been her Mum after all. Either way, the following day she went and paid the undertakers half of what she owed them. She didn't want to be completely broke until the money came through, and now she'd be able to give Jake a few quid for when he returned to university.

This was going to be her new home, a fresh start for herself and Sophie. Jake would be heading back to university in Nottingham soon, and Alfie was starting his new life. Despite the long-term project MC, she was looking forward to having time on her own, without the constant penny-pinching and hand-to-mouth existence that the money from her Mother would shortly alleviate, and without having to continually pick up the pieces around Alfie. She thought she would miss him not being there, but life would soon be easier without him and she would enjoy her own company. Again, probably something instilled in her back in Ireland when the adults were working on the farm, and she had to make her own entertainment and cope with what seemed like boredom at the time. She so wanted to have some boredom time again.

## Jake and Sophie's Choice

There hadn't been a big bust up, no fingers pointed, no voices raised that had been full of post-watershed words, and neither of them had been absent from the family home. In fact, they'd been out for a Sunday roast as a family and Alfie and Tina had been to the pub together, so it was quite surprising for Jake and Sophie to learn, when their parents sat them down for a never-before family discussion, that they were 'consciously uncoupling'!

It wasn't put quite so bluntly, but Mum was moving into Grandma's house, dad was staying here, and where did they want to live? The choice was theirs to make, and Tina and Alfie would accept whatever decisions Jake and Sophie came to. They didn't need to know this minute, but dad would need to know pretty soon so he could sort something out with the Housing Association. It was all very amicable, they were still friends and would still be a family, but they didn't love each other anymore. It was probably the most honest assessment of their relationship, and yet their habitual lifestyle would have probably continued indefinitely were it not for Project *MC* creating the opportunity for change.

"I don't need to make a decision," said Jake, "I'll be back to Uni in a couple of weeks, and I doubt I'll come back here to live and work." He wasn't being ungrateful. He had been the first in his family to make it to university and hoped that after he graduated next summer [he'd be well happy with a 2:1] he would find a job that would allow him to work in Nottingham. He bloody loved the city, the City Ground football, the live music, the nightclubs, and he took after his Dad because he loved the women there too. His favourite bar in the whole wide world was there, not that he'd travelled very much, a Tequila den called *400 Rabbits* just off the Market Square.

"So, it's just Sophie's choice really," said Jake.

"*Sophie's Choice*; I've seen the film," said Alfie thinking he was being funny, but it went right over all their heads.

"What film?" asked Jake.

"*Sophie's Choice*. Haven't you seen it then? We were made to watch it at school. A bit more serious when the choice determines who lives or dies though."

"A choice about what?" asked Sophie.

"Oh, just bloody Google it; *Sophie's Choice*. Meryl Streep. Won an Oscar," added Alfie when they continued to ask him what the hell it had to do with them.

"Why do I have to make a choice?" asked Sophie, "I mean, can't I just stay with both of you at different times if you're really doing this?"

"Well it's not like we are going to be miles apart," Alfie replied. "But if you want to go with your mum, I can get a smaller place, and you can still come round any time of course."

"Well, that sounds like you've made a decision for me. Why did you bother even asking us if that's how it's gonna be? Uh"

"When you movin' out Mum?" That sounded brutal, but Sophie wanted to know when she'd need to pack her stuff up.

"Probably next week love."

That had definitely gone better than Alfie and Tina anticipated, and the right decisions had come about without either Sophie or Jake actually having to voice a preferred choice between their parents.

Once her and Sophie had moved all their belongings to their new home, Tina went to the Housing Association with Alfie to find out his options. They had been jointly named on the tenancy. Larger properties were desperately needed, and they would be able to arrange a one-bedroom home quite quickly as they had several unoccupied. Alfie would need to go and look at those available and sign a new agreement. Given Tina's inheritance, which now counted as savings over the £16,000 threshold, Alfie probably wouldn't have qualified for a new Housing Association property but would have been entitled to stay at the current home, but the Association were happy to get their hands on a much needed three-bed 'in exchange' for a one-bed.

Tina still had her doubts about where this was all going to lead but was happy with her new living arrangements.

Alfie's friend Jimmy had got him a job in the factory at *Heat from Home*. As soon as that happened, Tina closed down both their Facebook accounts. She didn't want any opportunity for Michelle to have a window into their real lives. Those that actually run a factory with machinery that flatten and bend sheet metal, laser cut holes, and weld bits together before they head off pegged to a line through a powder-coating oven to have different colour finishes applied, would probably laugh at the term 'factory.' The works sheets containing customer orders spat out of a printer, and Alfie's new job was to feed lengths of uPVC into a machine, press a few buttons, and take out the finished cut. He then put some neoprene seal into the groove on the inside of the frame and trimmed both edges with a Stanley knife. Any imperfections to the machine cut uPVC would have to be filed off, and then he'd move on to the next one. When all four cuts with their seals inserted for one complete window frame were done, he wrapped some industrial cling-film around them and attached the 'job sheet' with some tape before placing the bundle into a rack so the next person in the process would put them on a bench and fix the four sides together using steel pins and screws to complete the frame.

Nobody knew that shortly after Michelle sold *Heat at Home* to a German company, that a new German machine would be installed that would automatically take in the next super long length of uPVC extrusion, cut the four required lengths and join them together with a mix of uPVC welding and fixings that also improved the security of the windows. Within a few minutes it would spit out the finished, fully assembled frame, ready to have the sealed glazed unit installed. So long as someone made sure that the hopper was kept supplied with long lengths of uPVC, the machine would run unaided to create finished frames all by itself. German engineering.

For Alfie, *Heat from Home* was much better than working in the Garden Supplies warehouse. It was warmer, the radio was on in the background all day, except at 10.30am when a 15-minute coffee-break purposely coincided with Pop-Master and everyone tried to pit their knowledge against the Radio 2 contestants. With a guaranteed thirty-seven hour working week, plus potential overtime when demand required it, he was better off too.

Michelle didn't venture into the factory very often. All the non-managerial employees wore the company work trousers with matching polo shirts emblazoned with the stunningly boring *Heat at Home* logo. Tina suggested that he start wearing a brightly coloured bandana to hold his long hair back. It would make him standout. But on the few occasions that Michelle did come through to see the works manager, he always found a reason to move and get something that would bring him close enough; initially just to have the opportunity to say something like "morning boss," but eventually, after many weeks, to be able to make other comments; the colour of her nails, compliment a nice hair do, admire her blouse. The sort of thing that only a charmer could get away with without it sounding too familiar or creepy or causing any unease. A comment without the expectation of a reply. Enough to be noticed. Alfie had been clearly told by Tina to play the long game. He mustn't do anything that jeopardised their cunning plan and might halt it in its tracks.

Throughout the autumn Alfie worked more diligently than he had in his entire life. The opportunity for someone pretty much unqualified [not uneducated] to have their eye on a multi-million-pound lottery jackpot was almost unbelievable. He stopped drinking in the week, but still got hammered on Friday and Saturday nights, and took advantage of his newfound bachelor status to test the mattress springs in his new home whenever the opportunity presented itself. He was also fully enjoying his own 'uncoupled freedom.'

# TWENTY-FIVE
## It's Christmas

Every year *Heat at Home* held a Christmas party for the staff, their partners and spouses and young children. Usually the Sunday before Christmas, they took over the Dining Room at St. Augustine's Golf Club once the Members' Lunch was finished. Santa had presents for all the little ones, staff had already been able to choose between having a fresh local Turkey or some bottles of wine. Most choose the Turkey as wine was not the drink of choice for the majority.

This year, after the triumph of her fortieth birthday party, Michelle wanted to do things differently, and she consulted the staff well in advance to see if they wanted to carry on the Christmas party tradition or have a complete change. They all wanted a change. No partners, no kids, no Santa!

When work finished at 5pm on Thursday 21st December, everyone gathered in the factory for their Turkey or wine gift to take home, and for the first time instead of those in managerial positions keeping all the Christmas gifts that had been received from suppliers and would-be suppliers, every member of staff was given a raffle ticket and could choose from the various bottles and gifts arrayed before them if they held a winning ticket. The following day, work finished at midday, and then everyone was off to The Spinning Wheel Bistro opposite the increasingly derelict Raven Hotel, which had been reserved for their private party until 5pm.

Tina, not wanting to encounter Michelle, had told Peter, on the pretext of Alfie being at *Heat at Home*'s private party and it being too upsetting for her following their break-up, that she couldn't work, and he'd have to get Lexie and Francesca in early instead. Alfie, when he wanted a quieter evening than a noisy pub, would sit at the bar for hours and chat to Lexie especially when she was fixing drinks for diners. He liked Lexie, he liked Lexie's trim figure, the allure of her mixed parentage skin colour and long black hair, and he liked the fact that she wasn't averse to topping his pint up for free when Peter wasn't in the bar. Peter wasn't unhappy that Tina and Alfie had split up. Their kids were almost adults, and he didn't much care for the fact that with Tina at home he'd sit and chat to Lexie or the customers for hours at a time. It never stopped Lexie from doing her job, Peter just felt sorry for Tina being home alone with the kids.

At the *Spinning Wheel*, Michelle had paid for a hot buffet lunch and stuck £1,500 'behind the bar,' roughly £25 per person, for booze. Once it was gone they were on their own, although the managers, who were all on a three-line whip to be there, could continue to buy drinks for their own staff and expense the cost if the money ran out. The money ran out well before 5pm.

Some of them were in their work clothes, but Alfie popped into his flat on the way there to get changed, putting on his favourite cowboy boots, black jeans, colourful shirt, and still had a bandana to hold his hair, but not the bright orange one he wore in the factory; a black one to match his jeans and boots.

Tina and Alfie had determined that this was the opportunity to have his first meaningful conversation with her. What should he say?

"Tell her that you appreciate it and that the last place you worked didn't do anything at Christmas for the workers." This was true, the Garden Distribution company hadn't. They did a big staff summer BBQ instead which their suppliers provided all the equipment for, as much for a real-life demonstration of what they might want to stock for next summer, as for a staff reward that didn't cost the company a penny.

"This is really great," he told Michelle, "my last company didn't do anything like this for their staff at Christmas. It's really appreciated."

"Where did you work before?" And that was it, the conversation was off. He told her where he had worked, and that his name was Alfie as they hadn't met properly before.

"I know," she said, "I make it my business to know about everyone who works for me."

She meant from a business point of view; their name, how long they had worked there, what their role was and who their line manager was. But it sounded more sinister than that to him. Sure, anyone being employed in a more senior position would have their background checked, but not factory workers or installation engineers, except for those working on Council contracts where an official DBS Check for criminal records was required.

"What plans have you got for Christmas?" he asked.

"Nothing much, but I'm really looking forward to 'going off grid' for a week. No phone or emails, read some books, watch some Christmas films, some walking if it's not raining, and just forget about the business 'til the New Year. What about you."

"Ah, not sure," he lied, "I'll be in the pub with friends most of the weekend, but this is the first Christmas since me and my partner split up, so we might be together on Christmas Day just for the sake of the kids. There wasn't anyone else involved, just fell out of love I guess, so it won't be too complicated or awkward."

She was about to ask if he had any children, but Tina had coached him to end it on his terms and not to show too much interest in her.

"Anyway, thanks once again for doing this. I'll try not to get too pissed. Enjoy your peaceful Christmas." Alfie ended the brief conversation and moved away to talk to Jimmy about meeting up over the weekend.

Michelle didn't mix with anyone particularly well and stood there on her own for a few minutes before one of her managers came over to speak. She'd enjoyed speaking to Alfie, he held a conversation better than most of the managers and had actually bothered to ask about her. Very few people did that.

If the truth was known, Michelle detested Christmas. She was looking forward to the break from the factory, but not to being on her own. She felt compelled to visit her father; she hadn't been since the summer, there really wasn't any point. That would mean taking some wine and chocolates for the nurses whose employers were already robbing her blind. She could stay on the beach in Cornwall at the exclusive Watergate Bay Hotel for less than they were charging. She had thought about going away to a hotel for Christmas but being the middle-aged singleton when it was all loved-up couples, or families, was a far worse prospect than isolation.

None of her Oxford friends thought to invite her for Christmas or New Year as they all wrongly assumed she'd have loads of options and invites for the festivities, and they all had great social circles in the places where they lived. They would all be seeing each other on the French slopes for their annual skiing trip in five or six weeks anyway.

By 5pm there were not many people left inside the *Spinning Wheel* before it opened to the public and Peter's regulars. Most of those with young families to get home to had left, Michelle and her managers were still there; they'd had their own Christmas dinner at the *Chequers at Crowle* last Saturday evening and were effectively still working. The £1,500 was long gone. A few had taken advantage with shots and shorts, and everyone that Michelle asked preferred the *Spinning Wheel* to trapesing out of town to the golf club on a Sunday afternoon, where everyone had been out of their comfort zones and social circles. The rest of Christmas was all about kids, so it was great to have a kids-free afternoon in such a great little boozer.

Alfie was indeed going to the family home on Christmas Day where he met "*Teddy*" the cute new Cocker Spaniel puppy that Tina had spent £850 on for Sophie and had managed to keep it a secret until Jill the breeder had arrived mid-morning. Jill bred *Working Cockers*, so the gorgeous little thing's tail had been mostly removed, even though *Teddy* was unlikely to do a day's work in his life. Let's be honest, when have you seen a nine-week-old puppy of any breed that didn't look adorable.

Alfie being there, even though she knew he was coming, confused Sophie. She'd taken their break-up particularly badly which had affected her schoolwork and seen her retreat into herself considerably. The kids had always wanted a dog, but it had been against the regulations in their Housing Association home, and Tina thought it might bring Sophie back to some normality. She'd given Jake the equivalent in cash for university, this just equalled it up.

In the kitchen, as Alfie was helping Tina with the food preparation, he filled her in on the progress he was making. The conversation had gone just like Tina told him. Alfie opened some tins of cider that he'd brought, and he and Tina were getting on better than they ever had. Come to think of it, he'd never helped her with any Sunday lunch or Christmas dinner preparation before. Internally, they both asked themselves why they hadn't done this before. But they also had a common purpose which, apart from the children, was also a first.

The "*Letters of Administration*" had come through from the Probate Office in early December. Tina had been into the building society, opened an account in her name, and put five of the eight thousand from her mother's account straight into it. She went to Crumps and paid them the outstanding amount for the funeral. She'd rung National Savings and they were sending her a form that she'd need to complete and send back with her Probate letter. In the week before Christmas a cheque for £20,000 arrived, which she immediately paid into the building society.

With a new puppy and Alfie not going to the pub, everyone was in a positive mood in their obligatory Christmas jumpers. It had the makings of their best Christmas day ever, which they normally spent exactly where they were now, at Shirley's house. Well, they were here altogether in the same house of course, but it was very different without Grandma. For the first time in all their years together Alfie hadn't disappeared off to the pub for that 'quick drink' that always ended with him being there until they shut at 2pm, and then coming back to eat dinner and sleep in front of the TV.

After the turkey crown dinner and Christmas pud had been gorged on, Sophie and Jake were going to take Teddy out for his first walk. He really wasn't supposed to go out yet and mix with other dogs until he'd had all his inoculations, but they desperately wanted to show him off and promised to keep him away from other dogs. Tina really didn't want them to take the dog out, but it would give her and Alfie some time on their own, and so she stressed how important it was not to let Teddy off the lead or socialise with any other dogs. No exceptions.

Alfie helped Tina clear the pots from the table into the kitchen where he spontaneously kissed her. She held him tight and kissed him back. She had missed him desperately. "Shall we?" he suggested, nodding over towards the stairs. Unable to resist, and with a craving to satisfy her own neglected sexual needs, she didn't need asking twice.

"God yes please," and they left the clearing up for later and headed upstairs to Tina's bedroom on a mission to be back downstairs as if nothing had happened before the kids returned from the Lido park.

They could have spent longer entwined in her bed. It was almost dark when *Teddy* returned with the kids by which time the dining room table was clear, the dishwasher full, and a few pots that wouldn't fit in were soaking in the sink. Alfie and Tina were in the lounge. They were sat apart.

# TWENTY-SIX
## Michelle's Christmas

Michelle had done a great deal of soul searching whilst she'd been *'off grid.'* She made a list. It was noticeably short.

| Things I love | Things I Want to Change |
|---|---|
| Money | Work – hate it |
| The House | Being single |
| Skiing | No Social Life |

Michelle was good at her job. Unlike her father, who had not benefitted from the insights provided by the Saïd Business School, she delegated responsibility to people who were employed by the company to be fully responsible in their areas of expertise. But *windows* for fuck's sake. How dull was that?

It may have been intellectually dulling to Michelle, but she was shrewd enough to realise that her relatively privileged upbringing, education and all the things she loved doing, were only possible because of the profit generated from the *windows* that her father had been so successful at selling. The company was now so well established with a great local and regional reputation that business just kept coming in. Edward had also been astute enough, throughout all forty-five years since he started the company, to continually scan the horizon searching for the next trend that he needed to be on-board with ahead of the curve and give himself a head-start over potential competition.

But Edward was gone; gone from the business, his cognitive senses taken by dementia, and Michelle didn't think she should sell the business until after he passed. She was sensitive to what others might think.

She loved Lance Dune House. Edward had always loved what the house said about him. She didn't know why she loved it so much. Most of her life was now confined to just three rooms within it: kitchen, bedroom, lounge. Four, in the summer months, with the conservatory. Friends rarely came to stay, she wasn't on any dinner party circuit, her grandparents were too old to visit now.

Her lack of a social life and being single were potentially one and the same. Solve one and maybe both would be fixed.

When 'daddy' was working, as a young child she had been discouraged from interrupting him in his home study – he'd had one of those before anyone knew a *home office* was a thing! Once there had been a *Brother* computer on the desk, an amber mono display and floppy disks, but that had eventually been replaced with a laptop. She spied some photo albums on the shelf and took a look. Mainly pictures of her that he'd taken when she was a young girl, summers in the garden, down by the stream, picking up autumn leaves. Then she realised why the house seemed so important to her. It hadn't changed. Not a thing. It was here when she was born, when she came back from boarding school, back from university, and it was here now; exactly the same as in those thirty-five-year-old photos. The same lawn, same garden layout, same rose bushes, same gravelled drive, same white render. To the trained eye, only the windows had changed when the original wooden frames with their secondary glazing were upgraded with uPVC look-a-likes that didn't need any painting or any maintenance. Edward had put the cost of the new windows against his own marketing budget and their home had been used as the visuals for a *Before and After* marketing brochure and campaign. Edward was always proud to point out, especially to the right people at the Golf Club and elsewhere, that it was his own home so lovingly transformed in the glossy brochure they were now holding, and not to overlook the difference that new facias and guttering would make to their own homes too. Another little uPVC goldmine in the colour of your choice. Come to think of it, the lawn got mown once a week when she was at work. She didn't even know who did it, or how they got paid.

Lance Dune House needs a transformation she determined, and in the New Year that would start with the garden. She added '*The House*' to her '*Things I Want to Change*' list so it now featured in both columns.

# New Year – New Beginning

> *Gardener Required*
> *for Lance Dune House*
>
> *Recommendations to*
> *Michelle Claines*

On the first day back in the New Year, the small card appeared on the staff notice board in the factory kitchen.

"What's Lance Dune House?" Alfie asked Jimmy pointing at the board.

"It's where the boss lives. Beautiful location in the middle of nowhere on the way to Feckenham."

Common-sense would have been to Google 'Landscape Designers' and take it from there, but common-sense wasn't always a strong point in a world where everything had been taken care of by people being paid to do it.

At break time, Alfie took the note down and made his way to her office, knocked, and waited.

"Come in. It's Alfie, isn't it?" She knew but didn't want to seem presumptuous. She'd forgotten that she'd told him it was her business to know who all her staff were.

"Yes, that's right. It's about your note Mrs Claines. The gardener for the house. I might be interested myself, you know, if its weekends."

"It's Miss Claines," she corrected him, "or Michelle when we're not in the factory. Have you got any gardening experience?"

"It's been a while, but I used to work for the Council Parks Department. The Lido Park was one of ours, as were the hanging baskets on all the lampposts across town. I really miss it and working outdoors."

It was true, Alfie had once worked for the parks department, but he omitted to say that it was a temporary summer job when he was sixteen and had just left school. They let him mow the lawns that needed a hand mower, he wasn't allowed anywhere near the sit-on machines. Watering flower beds and litter picking were the other main duties that summer. Twenty-seven years ago, the hanging baskets were also watered by hand.

"Well, I'm looking for some ideas to change the way the garden looks. Why don't you come and take a look on Saturday morning and we'll see if it's something suitable for you?"

He agreed and asked for the address and what time would be convenient for her. 10am was settled on. Alfie kept hold of the card from the notice board so that no more conversations about potential gardeners would jeopardise his own chances.

Roses, daffodils and tulips were about all Alfie could identify if pushed. He phoned Tina that evening and told her the news; it wasn't just mowing and weeding she wanted, she was looking to change things. Tina hadn't seen that opportunity coming, nor had he. But it would be a great fortune to be at the house with her – he just had to convince her he could do the job. Tina was going to call him back.

She consulted Amazon for books on Country House Gardens, finding two that looked sensible: Monty Don's *The Complete Gardener: A Practical, Imaginative Guide to Every Aspect of Gardening* and *The Royal Horticultural Society's Gardening Through the Year: Month-by-month Planning Instructions and Inspiration*.

She also searched to see if there was an App on her smartphone for identifying plants. WOW, there were loads of them with *iNaturalist* rated as the best of the free Apps.

Tina phoned him back, told him about the App and to download it. She ordered the RHS book as it was 50% off and would be delivered tomorrow, and after work she'd go to the library to see if they had anything. She'd come round about 7pm.

Alfie downloaded the *iNaturalist* App on his phone, but you had to capture a photo of a plant for it to identify, after which it would tell you all about it. Right now, it seemed pretty useless.

There hadn't been any books that looked suitable in the library, but the Amazon packet was propped against the door when she got back. The house was in darkness in the mid-afternoon January dusk, and *Teddy* wasn't in his cage when she got to the kitchen. She hoped Sophie had taken him to a friend's house and not the park again. She messaged her and was pleased that she was at Megan's house – her idea of a puppy to bring Sophie out of herself was working. When the novelty wore off a bit and she found herself doing the morning walk before work every morning come rain or shine, Tina would find out how a puppy attracts everyone to come and talk to you and brightens up any morning.

"I'm just popping to see dad," she told Sophie after they'd had their dinner. "Is there anything you want from the shop on the way back?"

It was the first time Tina had been inside Alfie's new Housing Association flat near the Freemason's Pub. He greeted her with a kiss and embrace once she was through the door. She couldn't refuse; didn't want to refuse. Last time they had been together was Christmas Day and they'd both more than willingly had sex. She'd had a shower and changed her underwear before going out on the anticipation that it might happen again. She hoped so. It was like dating all over again.

They looked through the book together. There were so many plants and shrubs, where to start?

Alfie opened the App and took a photo of a rose in one of the coloured photos. Bingo, it identified it as a *Hybrid Tea* and presented a plethora of information on history, planting, pruning, moving. Didn't every formal garden have roses? He was going to read up on when was the best time to do anything with them and from there he would have to wing it. He could photo her plants and look them up afterwards before going back with his recommendations.

Tina told him to take a notebook and make some sketches too.

With Tina living at the house and Alfie in his flat, this was such a strange, contrived situation they had knowingly put themselves in. "Shall we?" he suggested. Tina nodded her agreement and he led her through to test the bed springs again. She didn't want to think if she had been the only women he'd had in the three months since he'd moved there. She hoped so and enjoyed the moment until it was time to go home.

# TWENTY-SEVEN
## Lance Dune House

It was bloody freezing when Alfie ventured outside early on Saturday morning. The temperature had dipped to minus three overnight and although it was just creeping above freezing now, Alfie still needed to scrape the ice from every window of his car before he could set off to find the house somewhere just outside Feckenham. Google maps had locked it in.

To the side of a small lodge, at the end of the drive where it met the road, was a sign with the house name and an arrow pointing up the drive. "Impressive," he thought as he couldn't see the house from the road. Completely '*out of my league*,' he thought.

"Did you find it ok?" asked Michelle.

"Google Maps brought me straight here."

"Only the postcode covers a few farms as well so sometimes, you know."

"Come in, Come in. We can look at most of it from the Orangery instead of getting cold."

'What the feck's an Orangery?' he thought.

He stopped on the giant front door mat and bent over to unlace his work boots.

"If they're not muddy you can leave them on. It's all tiles where we're going."

He'd cleaned his boots the previous evening, put his only other pair of jeans on that Tina had freshly laundered for him, and had the cowboy-style hat that he'd worn in the pub for the company Christmas drinks, as much to keep the cold morning off his head as to keep his hair under control.

"I was just about to make a coffee. How do you take it?"

"Do you live here on your own?" As soon as he uttered the words, Alfie realised how creepy that might have sounded, quickly adding, "I mean, it seems a big old place for just one person to look after."

The entrance hall, with its sweeping staircase was bigger than his whole flat, so was the kitchen. There was a central island with a sink unit it in and four bar stools gathered around one end. The oven didn't have a window in the door and most of the units had glass doors. Michelle pressed a few buttons on the machine in the corner which started to grind, steam and froth, and out came his milky coffee. Hers was a double espresso in a much smaller mug.

"It was always just Dad and me, and the nanny when I was young, so I've never known the house full of people. It's a bit strange at times being just me. I should really get somewhere more sensible, but I can't sell it whilst dad's alive; he's in a home with Dementia if you didn't know?"

"I never met him, but one of the guys told me he was in a home now. Said he was a really down to earth great guy."

"Oh, he could mix with anyone. I think he would have liked you." What did she mean by that? he thought, 'would Edward have liked me or does Michelle think that I'm like him?' That was interesting. Don't too many women leave home only to marry men that have the same damaging attributes of their fathers? Controlling perhaps. Had Edward been controlling? Alfie certainly wasn't that driven.

"Right let's take these through," gestured Michelle. She handed him his mug of coffee and he followed her out of the kitchen and down a different short hallway into a conservatory. The Orangery.

The terracotta floor-tiled room was more than double the size of the kitchen, had a dinner table at one end, three casual rattan 2 seat sofas at the other, and ten or so big stone pots around the room with trees in them. There was a pair of double doors with a couple of steps down to the patio with a fabulous lawn beyond the flower beds.

"It's really more of a 'Lemonery' than an 'Orangery' seeing how there's only one Orange tree still going," explained Michelle pointing to one of the trees nearest to the dinner table.

The room was also warmer than his flat as the underfloor heating created the constant temperature required for citrus trees to survive and thrive in non-Mediterranean climates.

"Do you live in Droitwich?"

"Yes, just over the canal near the Freemason's Pub." She didn't know the pub by name and looked unsure. "As you turn at the lights and go over the canal heading towards the A38 and the Chateau Impney, just where the train goes over the road."

Now she knew where he meant, but it didn't look to Michelle like the sort of pub that she would venture in to. In fact, there were very few pubs in Droitwich that Michelle had ever ventured into.

Which was a shame, because as well as being world famous for the natural Brine streams and the medicinal healing qualities of bathing in salt-infused water, far more salty that even the Dead Sea, Droitwich was once accorded the title of Britain's Booziest Town – bar none! Our friends at the entertaining website *Ooh Aah Droitwich Spa* report that records from 1906 show that the borough had a greater number of public houses per head of population than anywhere else in the country – one for every 100 inhabitants. It seems that Salt making, and the intense heat used to extract salt crystals from the Brine, was thirsty work. However, townsfolk could clearly handle their beer as convictions for drunkenness were only one per 300 people, lower than elsewhere in the country. Today within Droitwich, which has grown substantially in the last thirty years thanks to the many developments of modern plasterboard commuter homes that serve Birmingham, there is one pub for approximately every 1,600 residents.

Back outside Feckenham, at Lance Dune House, about nine miles from Droitwich, Alfie was with Michelle looking out of the Orangery.

"Well, I can see straightaway that all those roses need cutting back before the spring's out," he offered having read the previous night in the RHS book that this was the perfect time to cut Roses back to the base."

"NO!" Alfie thought she meant 'no' to the Rose pruning.

"No, I want more than that. Those Roses have presumably been cut back every year for the forty plus years since Dad moved here, then every summer they grow up again only to look the bloody same. I've had a really good think about it this week. If I'm going to stay here I want to put my mark on the place, change it about. Radically, not just some cosmetic pruning. Completely modernise those bloody boring flower beds. I don't know; it's just got to be different. Better. More like me. Whatever me is?"

*'Oh shit.'* Alfie now considered that such a task would be beyond his capabilities. It would require much more than just the weekend gardening work he'd come to talk about with Michelle.

"What do you think?"

"That's a very good question," Tina had coached him to say something like that to give himself some thinking time.

"Well, that sounds like a bit more involved that just some gardening I thought you were after. But change is good, I like change. If it were me, I'd be asking two questions. How much do I want to spend? What do I want for me? If this place were mine, I'd have a big screen TV in here, that crazy paving would go – probably have some high-quality Astroturf instead along with outdoor heaters and a bar area so I could really enjoy it."

"Enjoy it. That's it. That's what's missing. We've been too concerned with making it look perfect and not thought about enjoying it. I should have a swimming pool. I'd enjoy that."

"Do you swim then?"

"No – but if I had a swimming pool here I would."

"That's an expensive swim."

"It doesn't matter about the money. I've not got anything else I want to spend it on. Oh, this is exciting."

"Well what else would you want do if you had the facility here at the house?" Alfie urged her to share more of her thoughts with him.

"I wanted to have a pony when I was a child, but Dad said it was too dangerous. I imagine horses take a lot of looking after. Dad said Mum wanted to have a tennis court built. That would be fun, but I've not got anyone to play with. Do you play?"

"When I was a kid," Alfie laughed.

"Let's go in the kitchen and make a list."

*'What is it with women and bloody lists?'* Alfie thought to himself.

For the next hour she made a list as they discussed all the potential nice-to-have additions to her home. The swimming pool, the stables, the tennis court, a new patio with a hot tub and what about an inside gym? Alfie suggested. She'd love a water fountain somewhere, maybe as a turning point in the drive?

Michelle was excited by the adventure on the list in front of her. What use was the money to her just sat in a bloody bank account, she should enjoy it, hell she was forty. Now she asked herself why she was working so many hours? She should be working to live and not living to work, or was that just a stupid cliché? In fact, come to think of it, why was she working at all? Because it was just what had been expected of her as her father got past retirement age. She looked at her list again; swimming, horse riding, tennis, and even the hot tub were all things she would enjoy and indulge in if she actually spent any time at the house. What did she do at the house apart from sleep, eat, and watch a bit of TV, mostly whilst sat in the kitchen?

"Alfie, that's been brilliant this morning, thank you so much. You've opened my eyes more than you can imagine. I'd like you to help me with this; I'm not sure how. I'm going to work on my ideas, but I'll talk to you on Monday at work if that's OK?"

"Sure. Do you mind if I go and wander around the garden before I head off?"

"Not at all, help yourself."

"Does the field beyond the lawn belong to you as well?"

"Yes. That field goes all the way down to a small stream. Dad bought it off the farmer after we'd been here a few years. I think he was going to create a couple of golf holes so he could practice his golf there, but he never got around to it."

"I shouldn't be too long. Have a nice weekend."

"You too."

Alfie remained there for over an hour. He paced out the size of the patio, made a few sketches of the current layout noting where the winter sun was coming from, and took a few photos to jog his memory later. The drop down beyond the lawn into the field puzzled him; he didn't know it was a *ha-ha* or what the dry moat thing was for, and hadn't seen the frost covered stones that acted as a way down until he was coming back, making him jump down onto the far bank before walking the length of the field to the stream.

Alfie didn't know that for much of the time he walked around the garden and then headed into the field, Michelle was watching him from her bedroom window. She was intrigued that someone who didn't have paper qualifications and who had worked in warehouses and now in her factory, had such creativity and could hold such a good conversation, again. Nor had he just rushed off after their meeting, but he was taking time to find out more. Michelle opened Facebook on her iPhone and searched to see what it would tell her about 'Alfie Rogers,' but she couldn't find him there. 'Oh well, he's not bad looking anyway,' she thought.

Most Saturday lunchtimes he would have found a pub, probably The Castle as their food was good, with Premier League football on the big screen. If it were two top teams playing each other he'd probably watch some of it, but it was the busyness of the pub and the likelihood that he'd know people there more than the football itself that attracted him to it.

Alfie wasn't aware that the football over the weekend was all about the 3rd Round of the FA Cup. No giant clashes, Spurs beat Tranmere away 0-7, and Manchester City stuck another seven past Rotherham later in the day. Instead of the pub, Alfie was off to WH Smith in Victoria Square to get himself a drawing pad and some fine coloured pens. He sensed she really wanted to bring about some big changes, and he had some ideas to build on what they'd spoken about that he now wanted to sketch out and keep the momentum building.

He messaged Tina to tell her the morning had gone really well. Did she want to come over sometime tomorrow to discuss MC?

# TWENTY-EIGHT
## Capability Brown

The global coverage and capacity of Google Maps is really quite frightening. Like many technology solutions that make life more convenient, it also has the potential for evil. Consult a satellite view down Corbett Avenue and Lyttelton Road in Droitwich, the latter being the most desirable residential address in town, and you can clearly see which properties have swimming pools, tennis courts, and which garden in one street backs on to which in the other. You can do the same pretty much anywhere and everywhere. Alfie used Google Maps to give him a more accurate layout of the garden at Lance Dune House so he could provide more detail in the sketches he wanted to create and show Michelle on Monday.

The patio could be slightly lengthened and flower beds removed so the Orangery opens up straight onto the lawn. There was plenty of space round to the left to create a home for a Hot Tub and beyond that a BBQ area with an outdoor Pizza Oven. Did she like pizza? The flower beds could be rotated 90 degrees and moved over to the right to create an avenue either side of a new track that would lead down to the field where the new stables would be located. Alfie had googled about stables and planning permission, discovering that as long as they weren't being used commercially, none would be needed. But they would need to get electricity and water down there. Maybe some security lights? The field could have some jumps put in it. He'd seen those in a couple of farms as he'd headed home. And then to the far side of the new track could be the tennis court. Would she really use a swimming pool? Beyond where he thought the tennis court might go there was room for a swimming pool and a home gym if she wanted it separate to the house. He hadn't seen enough of the inside of the house to know if one of the rooms lent itself to a gym transformation. There just had to be space for one in that big house.

Happy with his work, and really energised by the prospect of having a purpose to help create something that would be appreciated, he went to the pub.

When Tina came around the following morning he couldn't wait to show her his designs.

"They look great," she encouraged, "But if I lived there, and remember it's our plan to try and live somewhere as posh together, I'd want a vegetable patch, possibly in a walled garden if its affordable. Having somewhere to grow all your own vegetables is all the rage on the TV cooking shows."

He needed to keep Tina onside, make her feel fully involved even if she couldn't be there.

"That's a great idea. Really in keeping with the house too. I'll do some more sketches this afternoon and add it in somewhere."

Tina didn't stay long. She was on her way to Aldi to get something for lunch. Jake was travelling back to university in the morning, and she wanted to cook the kids a proper meal. Alfie hadn't been invited and felt a little deflated. Still, he'd got some new sketches to do and they were all consuming. This was the opportunity and his chance to really move the potential for a sexual relationship with Michelle Claines forwards.

Michelle didn't really know what she was worth financially; the house was already in her name, and she was the majority shareholder of a cash-rich company that hadn't needed to borrow any money for years. Even when the financial meltdown happened in 2008, Edward had kept everyone on and maintained pay levels even though the company made a loss for eighteen months. This careful advance planning would reduce the eventual inheritance tax bill that would inevitably be coming her way when Edward died.

If she sold the company, would she keep the profit from previous years that the company still has in the bank, should she pay herself a dividend and withdraw some cash, or would a prospective buyer take that cash sum into allowance when making their offer? She'd make some discrete enquiries with her accountant as she wanted to release the funds necessary to make her former family home feel like her own 21$^{st}$ century version of the same house.

## Brilliant Meetings

It was shortly after his thirty-minute lunch break that Michelle sent for him. Alfie collected the sketches from his locker, walked to her office and knocked.

"They're brilliant," and she was genuinely surprised when she saw his best three sketches laid out on her desk and the attention to detail. "I can see you've put a lot of time and thought into those."

"Well yes, but I really enjoyed doing it."

"I really like what you've done with the flower beds to separate the tennis court and bring the lawn closer to the house, and the vegetable garden, how did you think of that? Not that I know the first thing about growing vegetables or anything, but I love the idea of it."

"Well," she continued "I spent most of yesterday thinking about what could be done and what I'd actually use rather than what would just look good. I couldn't remember the last time before Saturday when I'd been in the *Orangery*, how mad is that. So, I asked myself why, and it's because it's just so boring. I don't need anywhere to escape for some peace and quiet and there isn't a TV or anything and all dad's furniture is so old fashioned. My thinking is to turn the Orangery into an indoor swimming pool with a sauna and a small changing area with a loo and a shower. I don't know if it will all go in or if it'll need a small extension? I was trying to get a feel for how big it is without the furniture, and you can get those pools, I had a very quick look, with jets so you can fully swim without needing a massive pool.

My office is next to the Orangery, you didn't see that, but we could put a doorway through and convert that into a small gym, and I'll move my office into one of the upstairs bedrooms and have a great view to look out onto when I'm working in there.

I'm going to re-do the kitchen. Turn the aspect 180 degrees and build an open conservatory with a dining area off it that then leads onto the new patio with bi-fold doors that fully open along the whole width.

Just like your sketch, I'm going to move the flower beds, so the lawn comes right up to the patio. I do want a hot tub; that'll be so much fun. Just don't know if that should be on the patio or somehow with the swimming pool; I think we need a bit more thought around that one, and I will have the tennis court.

I'm not going to bother just yet with horses and stables, but your idea of a track down to the field could be added. I think horses and stables would be too much of a commitment and expense unless I dedicate loads of time to it. So, I think I'd want to have some lessons somewhere to see if I'd enjoy it first. We can always add horses at a later point."

She was now talking about major construction projects, swimming pools, tennis courts, a new kitchen conservatory, and not the bit of gardening that Alfie had hoped to get involved with and which would take him to the house on a regular basis. But she did say 'we.' '*I think we need a bit more thought around that one*' and '*we can always add horses at a later point.*'

"At this morning's production meeting I asked Nick [the factory manager] if he could spare you for a couple of months to work on a project for me. I thought it might be possible as January is typically not so busy, although we are waiting on a council contract that will need fulfilling by the end March if we get it. Anyway, he said that would be alright with him. So, if you want to, I'd like you to help me work out what all this is going to cost and how long it would take. It's going to take a couple of months to get an architect and plans, quotes for building, patios, hot tubs, saunas, swimming pools, etc., find out what we need planning permission for. Once we have all that, we can determine what's affordable and the timescales to get it built, and then what project management is needed. Now I've made my mind up to do this, ideally I'd like to have it all completed by the beginning of the summer if that's possible.

Does that sound interesting to you? Whilst you're working on this project there'll be a good pay rise, but when you go back to the factory it will be the same pay as everyone else, unless we can find you a better permanent job by then."

What did Alfie think? That it was less than two weeks since Christmas and now all his Christmases had come at once; more interesting work, more money, more opportunities to be with Michelle and make her get to like him more and more each time. More chances of their stupid throw-away idea, his stupid throw-away ides, to '*get rich [almost] quick*' to actually happen.

"Honestly, that would be brilliant, thank you so much for this opportunity. It would be a real privilege to help you. When do we start?"

"Next Monday. I've decided that I'm going to work from home every Monday. All the traditional Monday morning meetings are going to take place on a Wednesday from now on, which makes far better business sense too. If you finish this week in the factory and come out for 10.30am next Monday, that will give me time to get any emails or calls out of the way and then we can spend a couple of hours working on a *To Do List* for you to tackle. Is that OK with you?"

It was more than OK with Alfie, and he couldn't wait for next Monday to come, even though it was all going to start with yet another bloody list!

# TWENTY-NINE
## Alfie.Rogers@heatathome.com

Not wanting to be late, Alfie arrived far too early and pulled up outside the Lodge at the end of the drive and had a wander around the outside to kill a bit of time. Clearly it had once been lived in; looking through the window there was a kitchen that the outside door opened into, with an outside tap and drain too, so it was obviously on mains water. The windows had been updated with uPVC, but it was quite some years since they had been fitted. It was small, but there were two further rooms too. Quite a little apartment. Alfie wasn't to know that although it had been modernised, it hadn't been lived in for over forty years, since before Edward purchased the main house, and it was included in the sale as part of the grounds. Who knows what he had planned for it? He must have had a purpose in mind when he arranged for the new windows to be fitted.

He was still a few minutes early arriving at Lance Dune House, where Michelle had organised for IT to provide a laptop with Microsoft Office and an email account already configured for him. "Project Manager" it stated below his name in the email signature. He was well made up. The To-Do List they were going to work on together had already been done; Michelle couldn't stop thinking about the project either. She also had a list of the local architects who had designed for customers that needed planning permission for one of their *Heat at Home* conservatories, together with builders who used their windows and conservatories too. "Wherever possible we should use these companies," Michelle said, "but when it comes to more specialist stuff like the swimming pool and the tennis court, then it doesn't matter."

Michelle's list was:

1. Orangery / Swimming Pool / Sauna / Gym / Hot Tub
2. Kitchen / Conservatory / Furniture
3. Patio / BBQ / Pizza Oven / Furniture
4. Tennis Court
5. Vegetable Garden
6. Gym Equipment
7. Home Office / Wi-Fi

They sat at the kitchen island and discussed which bits were the *chicken* and which bits were the *egg*. For example, should they determine the space a swimming pool had to fit in, or find the right pool and create the space to accommodate it if the current size wasn't sufficient. Money isn't unlimited, she told him, but she'd prefer to do it right rather than make false savings and regret it.

'Buy cheap, buy twice' her father had often used to put the fear of cheaper competition into the minds of his customers. 'Buy wrong, buy twice' was also true if you had the financial means to correct your first error, and Michelle's list had been constructed in a process-driven order where the first decision might impact on the next. When it came to moving forwards, Alfie said that the first thing to be done should be her new home office. If she was going to work there more frequently, then she would need to have that ready before her current space was turned into the gym.

She liked his clear thinking.

Alfie determined that the underused *Orangery* would make a great space for his temporary office. It was light, warm, and he pulled the table across to the wall so he could use the power socket for his new laptop; he'd never owned one before. Michelle suggested that he create a list of companies, their contact details, etc. in Excel. He'd never used Word or Excel before and only ever sent WhatsApp and Texts from his smartphone, so she told him to spend some time looking at YouTube tutorial videos and the Microsoft help files.

For the next three weeks he only saw her on Mondays. She gave him a key to the house so that many different tradesmen could come to the house, hear what they were planning, and ask them for their suggestions and ball-park costings. He would get formal quotations once Michelle's architect had drawn up the final designs.

A suitable swimming pool with swimming jets would fit in the Orangery, but there wouldn't be enough room for a sauna or any changing rooms. By the time that Michelle headed to Avoriaz for the annual skiing trip with her Oxford friends, who would all hear about Alfie, her project manager, and the simply marvellous redesign of her house, the architect they had chosen was instructed to design both a new pool room to replace the Orangery, plus the new kitchen with its conservatory dining area that opens fully to the patio. The pool room, with its toilet, shower and changing room, was to have a door to an outside hot tub area that would have a wooden pagoda-style structure to keep bathers dry when there was rain or, god forbid, snow. Apart from spa days and hotels with hot tubs, the *Hot Tub Experience* uppermost in Michelle's mind was at the holiday home in Portugal, on the Silver Coast, belonging to the parents of one of her Oxford friends. Located on the patio, there hadn't been an outside loo and she didn't know if it was an unspoken acceptance or just herself acting somewhat feral, but unlike in a swimming pool or the sea, secretly having a pee in the hot tub did not create a small oasis of warmth around the top of your legs. Within the heated water, that almost nobody put their head into, constantly circulating with the force of the jets, any additional liquid had 'circulated everywhere' almost as soon as it was passed. The things are stuffed full of chemicals to keep it clean, and it's better, safer, than dripping all the way through the house to the downstairs loo by the front door surely? Well at least she had consoled herself with those thoughts even though trails of drips were created by others most evenings. Her friends were too polite to even think that Michelle's purposeful leakage would even be an option, and that she must have great bladder control instead.

Once Michelle's own hot tub location along with the rest of the transformation had been determined, at that point Alfie was able to confirm to all the potential suppliers exactly what was required and to get at least two or three formal quotations for each. Everything was put into a spreadsheet with costs and notes about how long it would take them. For example, a 'simple' tennis court would require two hundred tonnes of material [equivalent to fourteen lorry loads] and would take around a month to build. The cost would depend on whether a hard tarmac or *Sporturf* surface was used. The latter might allow more use from the court. For example, they could remove the net posts and use it for 5-a-side, netball, etc. The next owners might be interested in those options, but Michelle wasn't.

# THIRTY
## The Reimagination Begins

March was getting close by the time the architect had drawn up the plans. The only part of the build that would require planning permission from the District Council was the kitchen as the original outside wall would be removed. The *Orangery* had originally been given planning permission but such a room, that used the original house wall and had its own heating controls, no longer needed planning. Alfie was surprised to learn that a swimming pool didn't require permission either.

Currently the council were advising planning would take around 8 weeks minimum.

"Could we start whilst Planning is going through?" She asked the architect when Hannah came to present her designs.

"I can't see any reason why this would not be approved. There's no impact on any neighbour, the additional square footage that it adds is in single digit percentages, and it's not protruding any further than the *Orangery*. But, if it's still refused after any appeal process, then you'd have the expense of restoring it back to how it was. I can't advise you to go ahead, but I think it's an extremely low risk."

After she'd left, Michelle asked Alfie *"What should we do?"*

"If it were my money I'd get the Planning Application submitted first and then instruct a builder so that you can clearly document that the application was made first, before any actual work started."

Previously, Michelle would have been very cautious, played everything by the book. But she had started to change, loosened up even, and decided *"What's the worst that can happen? Let's do it."*

With that confirmation, the reimagination of Lance Dune House was set in action and the builders, landscape gardeners, and tennis court builders were all contracted to make it happen.

Alfie's one month away from the factory had turned into two, and now Michelle confirmed that she wanted him on-site as her project manager until the constructions were complete. That meant being around her until at least the summer.

In truth, she'd enjoyed working from home on Mondays, it was better than any other day of the week in the office, and she looked forward to Mondays more than the weekends.  Having Alfie around, making him coffee and a sandwich for lunch, people coming to measure up, offer advice, trying to sell their goods and services.

"Can I ask you about that Lodge at the end of the drive?  I mean what's it used for?"

"It's never been used as far as I'm aware. I've never even been in it.  Why do you ask?"

"Well, I just thought it might make a great little…. well, not a flat exactly, and if I'm going to be here every day for the next four or five months I wondered if I could rent it?"

"I've no idea what condition it's in.  We could take a walk down, but I haven't got a key to get in."

It was a good third of a mile walk to the Lodge, along the way Michelle discovered that Alfie had two children, one was at university the other doing CGSE's at the High School, that he hadn't been married and it was a vague *'some years'* since the on-off relationship with their mother ended.  No, he hadn't got a current girlfriend.  Curious that she should ask that.  They had both forgotten that at the *Heat at Home* Christmas drinks in the *Spinning Wheel*, Alfie had told Michelle that this was the first Christmas after splitting from his partner.

Alfie, who had never met Michelle's father, asked her about her mother and if she had any brothers or sisters.  She told him what had happened to her mother during her birth. It had been a blood clot, a thromboembolism, not because she was pregnant, it was just the pressure of childbirth that made it happen at that moment.  Her mother had gone into labour at home about ten days before she was due. She'd tried to hold on for several hours until Edward got back from golf but called for an ambulance once her contractions became too painful and frequent to cope with alone.  When the ambulance arrived from Worcester, Helen was in such acute pain that she could hardly open the door.  On examination, the baby's head could already be seen and there was no alternative but for the ambulance crew to deliver the baby in the entrance hall at Lance Dune House. The baby had been successfully delivered, umbilical cord cut, and the infant placed on Helen's chest whilst the crew fetched the mobile bed from the ambulance to transport mother and child to the maternity ward at Worcester's Ronkswood Hospital. When they returned to the house Helen was unresponsive and despite their medical interventions, Helen couldn't be revived. With no one else at the house, they were just wheeling mother and carrying baby towards the ambulance when Edward arrived home and was confronted with the emergency vehicle outside his front door. He ran from his Jaguar to discover the elation of a baby daughter in the medic's arms and encounter the utter devastation of Helen's body covered by a red blanket. There were no visible clues to why Helen's death had occurred, and almost 48 hours elapsed before the post-mortem allowed the pathologist to discover the blood clot. That was everything Michelle's father had told her.

Edward had never remarried, and she was *'an only and, all too often, lonely child, especially during my school years.'* She seemed calm, nothing defensive in her voice about being an only child, and as her red hair escaped from under her bobble hat and down the outside of her ski jacket on a cold winter's day, the similarities between hers and Tina's looks were obvious to him.

They couldn't get into the Lodge, but Michelle recognised that the replacement uPVC windows and doors must be 'theirs,' so either her Dad might have a key somewhere in his study, or they might be able to order one from the supplier. Underneath where the key went in the lock was a four-digit number that was the code for the key. 'Doors haven't had those codes for years," she told him, "as it was then too easy for anyone to order a spare key and break in without actually breaking in." She did know the company inside out. From outside she could see exactly what Alfie had seen a couple of months earlier and that it appeared to be a property that had been lived in and could be again, assuming the water, electricity etc. were connected. "There's no letter box," she observed, "any services must come from the house otherwise there would be letters," she deduced.

As they walked back she said that if it were suitable, he could live there for free whilst the project was ongoing. She would look in the study drawers – which had been her dad's study – to see if she could find any keys. Michelle had never felt uncomfortable living in the house on her own; there were some CCTV cameras that recorded onto a DVD-player thing in the study, but it was more of a deterrent and she'd never once looked at any footage. They might not even be working now, and the house didn't have an alarm. But nevertheless, she felt better for knowing that someone she knew would be sort-of living 'on-site.' Unconsciously, there was a new feeling of a vulnerability about such isolated living that hadn't ever been considered by her before. She would like to have Alfie around for some reassurance. She might even see more of him with him being so close by. She'd like that.

Some keys were found later in the day when Michelle remembered to look for them, and Alfie waited until his workday was through before stopping at the Lodge on his way home. He already knew the key would fit as it had the same four-digit code stamped on it. As he got out of the car and walked to the door, Alfie was a little apprehensive as to what he might discover on the other side. There were trees and shrubs surrounding three quarters of the property and he thought of someone stumbling across a hidden cottage in the woods and being drawn to what wasn't really theirs to find.

There was no heating on, and it was bloody cold. The lights worked, the water was connected, which Alfie already knew that from the outside tap working a couple of months back, the windows had curtains and a small double bed was made in the room that couldn't be visible from outside. And there was a layer of dust on everything. If someone had lived here once, it was a very long time ago. The lightbulbs were old fashioned, the TV wasn't a flat screen, and the kitchen had a small electric stove and fridge, neither of which looked as if they had ever been used. There wasn't a microwave, nor any food in the cupboards. The bedroom and living room both had an electric night storage heater. He turned them on, but of course they wouldn't activate until the night. The Lodge needed a good clean, some fresh linen, his flat screen TV and PlayStation, toaster and kettle from his current flat. There wasn't any storage, but he could soon organise a small wardrobe and chest of drawers. There were no electric or water meters, so either the feed came from the house – a third of a mile away – or someone had just unofficially connected the lodge to the supplies; he wasn't bothered either way. Free rent, no utilities to pay, no council tax. Just one question in his mind. Who was the intended occupant when the windows had been updated and kitchen equipped?

# THIRTY-ONE
## Getting Closer

Alife arranged to see Tina the following evening to tell her the great news about managing the project to completion and moving into the Lodge; he told her that it wasn't going to cost any more than his Housing Association flat which he would now give notice on. He hadn't lied to her, just not told her the truth. It wasn't going to cost any extra to live at the Lodge, but nor had he wanted to tell her that it was cost-free living for the next four to five months.

He was earning more money than ever before, had more responsibility than ever before, and fewer overheads since the time he was himself a child. For the first time in his adult life there was the opportunity not to be living hand-to-mouth and to make the money in his bank account last until the end of the month.

"Have you thought about what you're going to do to spend more time there after the building work's been done?" Tina asked.

"Not really."

"If there's gonna be a tennis court, she'll need someone to play with. Why don't you join the club by the Lido and get some lessons at the weekends? We've got the money to pay for it."

"I'm alright for money, I got a pay rise whilst I'm doing this job and I'm not spending as much in the boozer as before."

And that's what Alfie did. He gave notice on his Housing Association flat, moved into the Lodge, and for the next four months from Monday to Friday he was at Lance Dune House supervising all the building works and on Saturday mornings he had a private tennis lesson with the coach and some Sunday mornings he joined in with the social tennis session. There was loads of *eye candy* of all ages, why hadn't he done something like this before? He'd been good at football and cricket as a kid but lacked any parental support to take it further and keep it going. In never dawned on Alfie that if he'd foregone just a couple of pints every Friday and Saturday, that not only would tennis have been affordable, but he could also have gone and watched The Villa too.

Although Alfie was really enjoying the tennis, enjoyed feeling fitter and improving his game, he was doing it with an eye on the bigger prize ahead that would give him and Tina a lifetime of better choices. That was his motivation. Throughout their lived experiences of what had been for them normal circumstances, that of a family living hand-to-mouth for over twenty years, there hadn't been the time or money or any inclination for any such indulgence; *'normal'* people like Alfie didn't usually do that sort of thing. As their kids were growing up he'd have been more interested in going to watch the Villa but couldn't even make his money run to that. Not in addition to or instead of the pub.

At Lance Dune House, the wall between the kitchen and the new conservatory had been knocked through well before the necessary Planning Permission was routinely granted unopposed, and Michelle decided on the Savanna surface for her tennis court; according to the marketing blurb it was the kindest to aging limbs, only needed an annual clean, and could be used for other sports.

As a new building was being constructed in place of T*he Orangery* for the swimming pool, Michelle opted for a slightly bigger pool that had both a propulsion system for fitness swimming and an underwater treadmill. Who knew such things existed?

Whilst all this construction work was going on, Alfie didn't just stand around keeping an eye on things, he was happy to help out when necessary and put his own sweat into it. On the day when the small fleet of lorries delivered the sub-base for the tennis court, one of the labourers from the tennis court company was ill, and without asking Alfie stepped in to ensure the process went smoothly. It was a Monday, and Michelle was there to witness how much of himself he was investing in her new home. It didn't go unnoticed or forgotten.

Heavy storms towards the end of April delayed the building of the patio which couldn't start until the two new structures for the kitchen and the pool were fully erected. Then there had been a delay getting the moulded pool liner which needed to be in place before the internal flooring could be started. Michelle had originally hoped that everything would have been completed at the house by the start of June, but it was in the final week of June when she held a small party to celebrate the project's completion.

Seemingly no friends, just Alfie, Hannah the Architect and all the owners of the companies they had used. Although by now Alfie had become much more than just a friend.

Michelle Claines had a strange relationship with sex and commitment that even confused her.

She had been a virgin when she went up to Oxford in 1996, and that had been preceded by a winter season working in a ski resort as part of a Gap Year across Europe. Funny that, seeing how most years when she was single and returned with her Oxford friends to Avoriaz she always 'got off' with one of her fellow skiers or an instructor, or just one of the Après Ski tribe as a consequence of too much jollification outside La Folie Douce after a hard day on the slopes, that invariably led to holiday sex. Without strings, without commitment, without any intention of future contact. Michelle had been engaged to two of her Rochester contemporaries, one whilst at Oxford, the other following graduation, and one of her ski trips had been made as a couple with Monty. Monty's wife Lucinda had been part of the *Rochester set* throughout, so it was both a surprise and perhaps even a triumph that they were all still able to socialise, although it really wasn't that often these days; one-week skiing and perhaps once in the summer for an occasion, like Michelle's fortieth birthday party. Then, in their younger days, there had been the ski chalet sauna challenge when all the couples took it in turns to have sex in the 90-degree heat; the year that Michelle and Monty were engaged, and Lucinda was there with her boyfriend at the time; yet another of the Oxford ski pals to this day. All very aristocratic; apparently, and events that never get mentioned *'when the ladies are around.'* Nobody could remember whose drunken idea it had been, or why they all went along with it?

It had been Michelle that had called both her engagements off. She was consciously afraid of the longevity expected with just that single other person, not in a sexual way, just a fear of seemingly eternal commitment. Given the death of her mother during her own birth, Michelle convinced herself was that this was the reason why her father had never found anyone else, and therefore internalised the blame on herself. There had been an absence of any real tactile love during her childhood, and she had never been exposed to mature relationships featuring *happy loving couples*. She had no benchmark to guide her, no mother to explain the benefits and warn her of the consequences and put it all in perspective. Saying 'no' before it was too late was the way that she dealt with it. She should have said 'no' and turned down the offers of engagements, but Monty and Giles were both persuasive and had chased her relentlessly. She was, after all, a very good-looking woman, with an inferior but nevertheless 'acceptable' degree to them [but not to her] and had always been fun to be around. But it was also clear that in the families Monty and Giles had themselves grown up in, the woman's role, however academically bright she was, however entitled herself, was always one that expected her to remain in the shadow of her husband. That wasn't a situation Michelle could either knowingly accept or be able to adhere herself to.

Alfie was different to any other man she had spent time with. Very different. She wanted him to be attracted to her, she enjoyed teaching him new things, watching him develop, and Michelle admired the fact that he accomplished for her everything asked of him, and especially the tasks that he had no prior experience of and set about educating himself in. Like Excel. He hadn't had her birth advantages of education and money, but Alfie was far from stupid, and in recognising that, she also recognised two things about herself and her own personality.

1. Without question she had all the academic and business skills, but it was Alfie who possessed the common-sense that she lacked as well as displaying an *I-can-do-that* attitude to everything.

2. Based on their upbringing and lived experiences, there was no doubt that both Monty and Giles had expected her to be subservient to them in a marriage situation. Alfie was, well almost deferential to her intellect and her money. More than just liking that, she considered that perfectly acceptable to her for a long-term relationship. On her terms. Was she any different to Monty or Giles in this respect?

Plus, thankfully there wasn't any of the *baggage* that parenting someone else's children seems to always entail. Michelle had read in novels and magazines about many experiences where the new stepmom had experienced the brutal *'you're not my fucking MUM'* and had to put up with the rejection from other peoples' children in much worse other ways.

Michelle came to these conclusions in order to allow herself to contemplate the possibility of having a sexual involvement with Alfie as a positive choice that she could make, and not as a mistake. There was nothing she disliked from being around him, and with him working at the house, where she worked on Mondays, they had got to see a lot of each other. She was sexually attracted to him; and the very fact that he had shown no signs of any interest towards her other than a working relationship, made her even more determined to get what she now wanted. If it happened and it went wrong, she had the financial resources to 'make it go away.' What was the worst that could happen? She reassured herself with.

# THIRTY-TWO
## Lady Chatterley Requires A Lover

Once Michelle had made the decision to allow herself the indulgence of a sexual encounter with Alfie Rogers, she felt it was her duty to make it happen. There was no escaping the reality of the unspoken class distinction between them, not one based on entitlement and history, just money and to a lesser extent education that put them into different classes. Don't like the idea of class? Then what would you call it if it wasn't a class divide?

| Michelle | Alfie |
|---|---|
| Big country house | Housing association |
| Millions invested | Hand-to-mouth existence |
| Five-star foreign holidays | No holidays |
| BMW Z4 | Dilapidated Ford Focus |

Would Alfie feel intimidated by those social differences? She hoped not and didn't think so.

In May 2018, at Lance Dune House the two new buildings for the kitchen extension and pool house were up, the patio was now under construction, and the tennis court was already finished and waiting for its first use.

"I just need to find someone who can play tennis now," Michelle half-laughed out as they were inspecting the finished court.

"I used to play at school," he told her. "Probably nowhere near your standard though," which came out sounding like a veiled threat.

"My standard. Ohhh yes," sounding like Churchill the dog, "I have very, very high standards," she teased him, "including a Blue at Oxford."

"What's a Blue at Oxford got to do with tennis then?"

"That's the colour of the jacket you're allowed to wear if you're good enough to play in the first team for an elite sport against Cambridge. You know, like the Boat Race and the varsity rugby too. I played in the ladies tennis team for Oxford."

"Have you still got it?"

"What? The jacket or the tennis skills?"

"The jacket I meant."

"Probably in a wardrobe somewhere. Don't expect it will fit. Why, do you fancy a game then?"

"I can't remember the last time I held a racquet," he lied, "But I'm quite willing to make a fool of myself."

"Let's finish early on Friday and have a game around 4pm. I'll get a couple of new racquets and some balls. Winner chooses supper and the loser pays. So, bring your wallet loser."

It was eighteen years since Michelle graduated from Oxford, and she hadn't been a member of a tennis club since. There was the occasional game at David Lloyd and she tried to play when she was on her summer holiday, but the Caribbean sunshine was generally too hot, so it was only on those occasions in the Iberian sunshine north of Lisbon when she unleashed her competitive spirit, which was not always her most attractive side. But Michelle was driven to be as good as she could be at whatever she took on and losing at anything did not sit well. She was her father's daughter.

When Friday came Alfie was ready for when Michelle got back from the factory shortly before 4pm.

"I didn't bother bringing my wallet," he greeted her. If his serving had been better – too many double faults – some purposely to ensure that she narrowly won – his recent lessons and regular playing would have been too much for Michelle.

"What would I be paying for if you had won?" enquired Michelle.

"Domino's Pizza. It is Friday night."

"It's going to cost you way way more than a pizza," she teased. With that she phoned the *Chequers at Crowle* to see if they could squeeze the two of them in at 7.30pm. She was a regular – the best gastro pub for miles – and told Alfie that not only was he paying, but he was driving.

By the time he showered, put on the smart casual clothes to impress that Tina had chosen for him, and driven back from the Lodge pleased with himself that he'd taken the tennis lessons Tina suggested, she was waiting by her car.

"Lock your car, you can drive mine."

"Am I insured?"

Being insured didn't usually bother Alfie, but this was a Z4 after all.

"As long as you've got a licence with not too many points on it. It's covered on the company insurance for anyone with my permission to drive it." She threw him the keys and got in the passenger seat to navigate the most direct route she knew, along narrow county lanes, as the best way to get there – and back, if you were worried that the country-set's 'five-and-drive' drink-driving policy needed to keep you off the larger roads for fear of encountering a marked Police car.

Alfie would have enjoyed the drive more if he'd been on his own instead of worrying about how he imagined she thought he was driving her expensive Z4. He'd never driven anything so powerful, and she had no idea how powerful the engine was when he enquired.

The *Chequers at Crowle* is a gastronomical delight that appeals to people far beyond its village setting. Only a few miles from the Worcester Warriors Rugby ground at Sixways, Saturday nights can be really noisy following a home game when the bar is buzzing as gin and tonics and foreign lagers are quaffed. Alfie's world wasn't paying £8 for a starter and £17 for a main but it was a world that he would have to get used to. They shared a baked Camembert with some tearing breads to start and, avoiding the items for mains that Alfie had no idea if he would like them, he opted for the Roasted Pork T-Bone with loin meat on one side of the T and tenderloin fillet the other. Alfie had never heard of a Pork T-Bone before, but it turned out to be an inspired choice. Michelle had her regular go-to, the wallet-numbing Fillet Steak, medium rare, for which she chose a bottle of Argentinian Malbec to accompany, having the first glass with her starter once the Chase G&T had disappeared.

Michelle was alive to the fact that the cost of their meal would be more than Alfie would have been expecting or used to, but he'd had three months' rent-free accommodation, and she was testing his reaction. She didn't know that he didn't own a credit card, he didn't know that she had an account there. But he thankfully had a couple of hundred pounds in his wallet in preparation. He was forty-four years old, had never experienced such a fine meal in his life, nor one so expensive; not even at the Cheltenham Races. In fact, he had never spent so much in a pub and walked out almost sober having had just the one pint of lager and a small glass of Michelle's Malbec. Michelle's intention had been to take the bottle of Malbec home and finish its contents on the sofa, but it slipped down all too easily, not just as accompaniment to her Fillet Steak, but in gleeful anticipation of the sexual encounter ahead that she was orchestrating in her own mind.

When the car came to a standstill on the gravel drive, she was ready to seize the moment.

"You've hardly had a drink tonight. Come on, let's go and find one of daddy's special bottles of red wine in the cellar to celebrate my sporting prowess together."

Alfie wondered where this might be leading, he hadn't heard her talk so, well he didn't know quite how to describe it. It wasn't quite intimate, but it was less than informal, almost as if her guard were down, assuming she had a guard to put up in the first place. Playful even.

The cellar wasn't just a cobwebbed wine cellar, but a large cellar with a small snooker table, things being stored in boxes on one wall, and a work bench across the shortest wall. Just one of the long walls was racked along its entire length and pretty much full of wine bottles. Each of the bottles had a small manilla tag hanging from its neck with a rubber band, on to which Edward had recorded when and where it had been purchased from, how much it had cost, how long to leave it before the optimal time for drinking, together with another value if that was substantially different to the cost price. All these wines that Edward had spent a small fortune collecting, he would never taste their magnificence. Maybe just owning them was enough? Like a painting.

"Now then, don't look at the price or the age, let's choose one we both like just based on a label or the bottle," Michelle suggested.

They both spent some time picking out bottles, asking each other 'what do you think of this one?' and putting it back as they hadn't both been enthusiastic with it.

In her choreography of the afternoon and evening, after coming back from The Chequers, Michelle had been contemplating a shared bottle of wine on the sofa, possibly with a little cheese and Nigella Beetroot biscuits she'd got from Waitrose, and then asking Alfie if he would like to stay for the night, or maybe telling him that she would like him to stay for the night. No spontaneity, carefully planned, with the option for him to make an excuse if we wanted to decline her advances. That would make the remainder of the house transformation awkward, but she'd figured out that they would hardly have to work together if that came about.

"OH" Michelle said forcibly; almost startling herself having picked out a bottle that sent goosebumps through her and wondering if she dared ask the question that instantly came into her head.

"What?" he asked, as she was reading the label more closely. 2006. 50% Nebbiolo grapes from the Barossa Valley and 50% Shiraz from the Clare Valley, blended into a wine that she rightly assumed her father had purchased only for the comedic value of its name and not its Australian wine heritage. The pop-art label featured a young blond woman with Marilyn Munroe curls and curvy physique in a black boddice slip and red-topped suspenders and the wine was simply called '*Quickie.*'

She held the bottle with the label clearly visible in his direction just a few feet away, so that the 'QUICKIE' in big white block lettering on a red background was instantly readable.

"Well," she couldn't believe she was asking him with no hint of irony in her voice, "Are you up for 'A Quickie' with me then?"

"Do you mean that wine, or the other type of quickie?" Alfie gestured with an incline of his head across the room, adding, "On the snooker table perhaps?"

# THIRTY-THREE
## A Disappointing Quickie?

Michelle calmly put the bottle on the floor, kicked off her shoes and removed her knickers from under her skirt signalling her consent for what she now hoped was to follow. Alfie took her hand the short distance to the table, lifted her up onto the green baize, calmly lowered his jeans and pants, and 'the quickie' commenced. Her bedside drawer had been calculatingly prepared with some condoms for him and some *'personal lubrication'* for her; it had been a long time since the last time. Neither were needed as silently on the snooker table he dominated her 'pink' with his 'cue' and a white ball unintentionally fouled the brown [now that really should be worthy of at least a short-listing in The Literary Review's Bad Sex Category of Awards] until they were both satisfied, both glad she had asked the question, and both mindful, if not quite apprehensive, of how this would change their relationship? It had been a very British 'him on top' but it hadn't been over in a whirlwind, neither was she blown away like a hurricane, if we're continuing the crass snooker analogies! Having entered her forties last summer, Michelle was all too aware of 'being left on the shelf,' and during her thirties it had been ok so long as she was getting 'dusted down' occasionally, but she knew that she had to willingly let her guard down if she didn't want to end up a lonely, depressed, and regretful spinster.

When it was over, they had still yet to kiss.

"Let's go back upstairs" she gestured towards the stairs in the corner, "and we'd better take that bottle of Red with us." Michelle grabbed her knickers, shoes and the bottle, and headed back upstairs to the kitchen where she used some kitchen roll to clean herself, put her underwear back on, and was unscrewing the bottle top when Alfie re-appeared.

"Well, I wasn't expecting that tonight," he stated, "Where does that leave us or put us?" he asked, "I don't want it to be awkward between us."

"Let's have a glass of wine and talk about it," her voice assured him that it wasn't going to be a problem.

Michelle, in an attempt to reassure Alfie, explained that what just happened in the cellar was unusually impulsive for her, and that her being impulsive was not something that came easily, adding that she really liked him and had intended to ask him to stay the night with her and that she wanted to know him better in every way. It all came out in a rush. She didn't tell him, but she had been slowly falling in love with him for some time.

He was flattered, especially given their clear differences in personal circumstances and backgrounds, and she reassured him that it was only really her family money and the choices it provided that differentiated them. Now they had taken this step – which they had both willingly embarked upon – Alfie was worried about what might happen if things didn't work out for them. There was no undoing what had been done. "I don't know," she honestly offered, "I hadn't given that any thought, but if the worst thing happens, I've got the financial resources to help you. I know that sounds really crass and shallow, and I really don't want that to happen. Listen Alfie, it wasn't my intention for this to be just a one-night stand and I won't have you come to any harm because of it, because of me, is what I'm trying to say."

The wine was truly disappointing. It was never intended to be laid down for any years let alone so many, but it was still just about drinkable, it was of the moment, and it would have been kind of awkward to go and fetch something better. To reject the wine might have been a metaphor that signalled what had just happened between them also wasn't good enough.

They moved from the kitchen to the lounge and talked further. Michelle asked Alfie to stay the night and he did.

After all, getting closer to Michelle and winning her affections was exactly what Tina and Alfie had set out to achieve over nine months ago. When they went to bed they kissed for the first time and made love again. It was a sexual union that instantly felt comfortable to Alfie. As soon has he had been inside her on the snooker table earlier, the carnal feel of Michelle instantly reminded him of Tina, and there was more. Not just her obvious long red hair, but her facial features so much clearer with her hair fallen to the table surface, that feeling of being inside her was eerily almost identical, and he'd never experienced that same physical sense of being with Tina in any of the other sexual encounters he'd encountered. Now they were both completely naked in Michelle's bed, her breasts that he explored whilst spooned into her back, were uncannily like Tina's; The way she shaved her pubic hair was identical too. He was worried that Michelle and Tina were so alike he might accidentally use Tina's name.

The next morning, her mobile ringing on the bedside table a little after 7.30am woke Michelle. When she saw on the screen the name of who was calling so early, she correctly predicted the news. Alfie, already awake, had been looking through the news and sport on his phone, not wanting to wake Michelle, nor wanting to leave without her knowing. Wouldn't that make it look like he was uncomfortable about what had happened the previous evening?

"Hello, Michelle Claines" she announced, grabbing a pillow off the floor and sitting up in anticipation as she told the caller what they already knew.

"Hello Michelle, I'm sorry it's so early on a Saturday, but it's Sister Margaret from the Avalon Nursing Home." Michelle stayed silent; she knew what was coming.

"There's no easy way to tell you this, but your father Edward passed away peacefully during the night. I'm so deeply sorry for your loss."

"Thank you Margaret. I lost him a long time ago really. Do I need to come and see you?"

"I'm afraid you do, there's the legal stuff that only you as next of kin can do, so the sooner you can attend to those matters the better it is for everyone."

"Very well. I'll be over mid-morning if that's ok?"

"I'm here until 2pm today so that would be just fine. Thank you."

"I'm very sorry to hear about your father," said Alfie who had heard all of the conversation and was now thinking only one thought. Jackpot. She was sure to inherit the lot now, and soon.

"He's had Dementia for a good few years, and he hasn't known who I am for a long time now. When I realised that he didn't know who I was or even if I'd visited him or not, I figured out that I was only visiting him for myself, just to avoid the guilt of not going. The staff were very honest about the reality of his situation, and that sometimes my visiting actually made it worst by confusing his routine. I stopped going, apart from Christmas and his birthday, and that was really more about taking some gifts for the nurses. I'm not a bit sad. Frankly, it's a bit of a relief and it was bound to happen sooner rather than later. He was always disappointed that I hadn't given him the grandchildren he….." Michelle stopped her sentence abruptly. Grandchildren. Something made her think now, for the first time, about the woman, Tina she recalled instantly, who came to her office last August claiming to be Edward's daughter from another mother. 'Did Tina have children?' she asked herself. 'Had Edward got grandchildren that he or she didn't even know existed?'

"What is it?" asked Alfie after she failed to continue her sentence.

"Oh, just thinking about grandchildren."

'Grandchildren' thought Alfie, and it dawned on him for the first time that his own children, Jake and Sophie, were actually Edward's grandchildren and Michelle was their sort of Aunty too. Why hadn't that been obvious to Alfie before? Probably because as much as he loved his children, he hadn't been the most reliable father, he couldn't always remember their birthdays, he'd never even been to visit Jake in Nottingham, and it wasn't about him being narcissistic, he just never thought of others first. Had Tina made the connection? Alfie wondered.

"Dad so desperately wanted grandchildren, which he'd have spoilt to bits, but apart from that I think he had a great life. He pretty much did everything he wanted and built up a brilliant business from scratch that enabled those things to happen. The private nursing home costs over six grand a month you know, it provides brilliant care for Dad and those like him with Dementia that can afford it, so I think they'll be more upset at losing him than me. He had no cognitive quality of life."

There was a silence for a few minutes. Alfie wasn't sure what she meant by 'cognitive,' but didn't want to show his lack of education.

"I'm not sad now Alfie. I cried so many times when I drove away from the nursing home, but I came to terms with that a long time ago. And talking of grandchildren, we got a bit carried away without any protection last night."

Before she could add anything to her statement, he put her mind at rest.

"It's ok, you won't be having any children with me," he gestured a pair of scissors 'snipping away' with his fingers, adding "I've been done!"

"Why don't you stay here," she suggested, "I'll go and fetch us some coffee now I'm awake," and with that she sprang from the duvet allowing him to marvel at her naked form from behind as she walked to the bedroom door, took her white dressing gown off the hook and put it on before disappearing out the door.

Alfie used her en-suite bathroom, freshened his breath with some toothpaste on his finger to brush his teeth, and put his boxer shorts back on before getting back under the duvet. At home he would have put a t-shirt on but felt putting the collared shirt he had on last night would have made him look and feel somewhat awkward.

"What do you have planned for today?" she enquired after getting back into bed and sensing that 'the-morning-after-the-night-before' situation wasn't as difficult as she had anticipated. Her father had just given her the necessity to go and sort out his affairs, so that was a positive distraction that couldn't be put off. But then Alfie already had his own key for working at the house during the week.

"It's the Cup Final this afternoon. Always watched it as a kid, regardless of whoever was playing, so I was planning to watch that. Chelsea v Man U, so it could be a good game."

"What time will that be over by?"

"Starts at five fifteen, so should be done by about seven unless it goes to extra time. Why?"

"Well, if you're still interested in me, I could get some pizzas and we could have a chat about how we work things out together. What do you think?"

"Yeh, that'd be great. I'll be here by 8pm then."

"I'll get a couple of different pizzas and we can share. Anything you don't like?"

"Anything but seafood for me please."

She leant across to kiss him, the coffee now masked the fresh breath Alfie had a little earlier, and with a "Right, you can get out of here now and I'll see you this evening," she went to her en-suite to shower and allowed Alfie to get dressed into the clothes he wore last night with a bit of privacy and dignity. It was not even 8.15am when he left the house for the short drive down to the lodge and a hot shower himself.

There was still time for him to make his tennis lesson, but he texted the coach to tell him he couldn't make it. His need for tennis lessons was over too. After some toast and marmite at the Lodge, Alfie called Tina and arranged to meet her in The Castle Pub at 5pm. They hadn't seen each other for a couple of months, and he had some positive news to update her with.

# THIRTY-FOUR
## No Going Back

The Castle Pub was heaving with all sizes and shapes of people in their ill-fitting replica football shirts designed for professional athletes; and that was just the women! It was warm enough for them to sit outside and talk.

"It seems really strange and almost wrong to be telling you this," he started, "but I stayed at the house with her last night. Which is what we both wanted. I mean it's what you and I both wanted to happen if we are going to succeed with you know, Project MC."

"Ahh that's good then," but in that precise moment of recognition that 'I stayed at the house with her last night' meant that Alfie and Michelle had last night experienced sex, Tina was both upset and jealous. She tried not to show it.

"What's she like?"

"What do you mean?"

"Well, everything. As a person, and you know, the sex stuff," she said, getting Alfie to confirm her suspicions.

"Ah cum'on, I can't tell you that – that's not fair on me. You wanted me to do this after all. Not that I didn't too.

But she's alright. Quite down to earth really, and what scares me is that beneath her expensive hair and make-up, [by which in his own mind he meant naked] apart from a little difference in height, you could be almost identical twin sisters. You are so alike in many ways."

"Such as?"

"You just are. That's it. Oh my god. Her father died last night and talking about how alike you are, it's only just dawned on me that he was your father too. When I heard I just thought that it would only mean everything would fully belong to her now. I'm sorry Tina."

"Well it's not like I knew him, is it? Good riddance if it helps us. He clearly wasn't bothered about me."

"Listen, forget that, I just wanted to let you know that I've got an 'in' and it's heading in the right direction. That's far more important. She really seems to like me, so fingers crossed I don't fuck it up. She don't seem the impetuous type, [even though their snooker table moment had been spontaneous, he now knew that she was planning to ask him to stay the night, so it wasn't quite as impromptu as it initially seemed to him in the heat of the 'Quickie' moment], so if it happens at all, it's going to take a long time to move it along without causing any suspicion. Like you suggested, she has to believe that everything is on her terms. She has to think that she's the one making the play and calling the shots. She likes being in control I think. I know we haven't been in contact much, but if I'm going to be with her more, then you can't call or message me unless it's life or death about the kids or something."

Alfie wasn't in the mood for another pint. He'd got to drive back to the lodge and the Cup Final was on the BBC anyway. So he drove back and, having unknowingly missed Hazard's only goal of the game for Chelsea in the first half, saw most of the second half in the Lodge before walking up to the house as arranged earlier.

Michelle had been to Waitrose and according to the empty boxes on the island, Spinach and Ricotta and a Salami Sourdough pizza were in the oven as planned. There was a bottle of red wine open. If he'd prefer a beer – she'd remembered that he'd had a lager at the pub the previous night – then there was one in the fridge.

He asked her how her day had been at the nursing home and she told him about the papers she'd had to sign, that she would have to register the death on Monday, and that she'd already been to Crumps in Droitwich to arrange for them to collect his body and organise a funeral.

"It'll be quite a big funeral. There are the people from work, the golf club, and he was Mayor of Droitwich on two occasions. He wanted a 'send-off' at the golf club; I haven't been there in years.

This afternoon I took a walk down by the stream to think about us. Have you given us any thought?"

"Hell yes, I couldn't think about anything else today. Didn't really watch the football properly."

"Well, what have you thought then?" She wanted to know how he felt about things before telling him her own thoughts.

Alfie explained to Michelle that he felt a bit confused by the situation because he works for her, and that although he really likes her, he wouldn't have done what they did if he thought it was just a one-night stand. He'd like to go out with her, even if that did sound a bit silly for people in their forties, but he was very aware of their different life circumstances and that she might view that situation differently to him.

"Alfie, I really enjoyed myself last night. The tennis, the meal, not just the other stuff, which was great too." When she'd been walking across the field and down by the stream she recognised that yesterday had been the first time in many years that she'd just been herself. She wasn't worried for one minute what Alfie thought of her, not because she didn't care, but because it just didn't matter. It was liberating. When she was with her Oxford friends she was always consumed with being the best version of herself, keeping up appearances if you like, having a great dress, jewellery, eating at the best places, spending a bloody fortune, like her 40$^{th}$ birthday party, just to impress. What had that achieved? Nothing. And that was only twice or so a year.

"I'd like to give you and me a go too. See if we can make it work," Michelle confidently told Alfie.

The oven alarm buzzed to let them know the pizza was ready, and they sat at the kitchen island to eat the pizza and continue the conversation in fits and starts. Michelle suggested that until the house renovations were all completed, they should take it gently and confine their relationship to the Friday and Saturday evenings and Sundays, but not Sunday nights as workmen would be arriving early Monday mornings. She was conscious that she was putting up a barrier during the working week but explained that she had a big responsibility to the business and for the next few weeks her dad's funeral was going to be all consuming of her time.

Alfie stayed the night at her further invitation.

Unknowingly, Michelle had been successfully hunted. Like a fish on a line, could Tina and Alfie keep her going until they were ready to reel her in?

When they were ready to go in for the kill.

# Part Seven

## THIRTY-FIVE
## Another World

Edward Claudius Claines had lined his grave with gold. Not literally. But throughout forty years he'd built up a business that had provided him with the money to do pretty much anything he wanted. He had enjoyed his golf, travelled modestly, and indulged in a collection of red wines only let down by the humour in a bottle of 'Quickie,' but Edward had never thrown caution to the wind and acted excessively. He'd been more concerned about his public reputation, keeping the business going and amassing as much wealth as possible to pass on to Michelle. Both of which were virtuous aims.

There was no more £6,000 a month required to pay the nursing home. Since she'd taken over the day-to-day running at *Heat at Home,* profits had increased each year. Not by much, but it underpinned Michelle's capabilities in a male-dominated and highly competitive industry. But Michelle was all too aware that many people viewed her value as *just keeping daddy's business running.* Only now that Edward was dead, honoured by employees, friends and business contacts alike at a standing-room-only service in St. Augustine's Church, Michelle sensed that time for the changes she'd wanted for some time had now arrived. A monumental change was in order. Time to set herself free from a dull business environment and live her life to the full.

Alfie didn't attend Edward's funeral; it was too soon in their relationship for that. But Tina went. The details of the forthcoming ceremony had been all over the local papers. "Former Mayor and Successful Business Owner Dies" was big news in a small provincial town, and as the hearse and the accompanying limousine containing Michelle and her grandparents arrived outside the church following the twenty-minute drive from Lance Dune House, Tina was stood amongst those paying their respects. Michelle saw and recognised her from that single time she had been in her office but didn't acknowledge her. Tina's presence confused her. She hadn't been back for money and maybe, just maybe, she was here today at Edward's funeral because her father really was Tina's father too. Did she have a half-sister after all? Did Tina have children and had Edward unknowingly been a grandfather? And, come to think of it, were there any others that Michelle didn't yet know about that would come out of the woodwork now he was dead?

A few weeks later, after the small but enjoyable Friday afternoon party on the penultimate day of June to celebrate completing their modernisation of Lance Dune House and the guests had gone, Michelle challenged Alfie to another game of tennis.

"I've got to use the place now it's finished," she laughed. It didn't matter who won, neither of them would be able to drive and they shouldn't really be playing tennis after the drinks party. It had been six weeks since Alfie had first stayed the night and their relationship was very much in the honeymoon stage with both of them being equally attentive to ensuring the needs of the other were being fully met.

As Michelle was raiding the fridge and freezer hopeful of finding something suitable to eat, Alfie asked her the question that had been playing on his own mind since their relationship became sexual.

"So Michelle, what happens to me from Monday? Am I back in the factory then?"

"I hope not. I've been giving everything a lot of thought and I certainly don't want your talents being wasted in the factory." But for Michelle it really went much deeper than that; something she couldn't be open and honest with him about. She didn't want to be 'going out' and developing a relationship with anyone who 'worked in a factory.' Not even Alfie. That wouldn't be acceptable as an answer when in polite conversation the question of 'and what do you do?' comes up.

Michelle wanted to say that she had given him a chance to prove himself with the project at Lance Dune House and that he had surpassed all her expectations, only she thought it might sound a bit contrived. Condescending perhaps. Or maybe that 'nobody puts Alfie in a factory,' but it wouldn't quite have the same Patrick Swayze flow to it. So, she didn't. Instead, she unburdened her own thoughts.

"There's a...," she hesitated, "Look, I don't want this to come out the wrong way and I want it to be more of a conversation than a 'this is how it's going to be.' I'm not sure I'm making much sense but so much seems to have happened in the last six months: meeting you, making this house feel like my own at last, dad dying. The company is super successful, but it's deadly dull and I just don't enjoy it." She thought he might say something. But Alfie just stayed silent, like Tina had coached him.

"Dad has left me everything and I'm quite a wealthy woman. That's not meant to sound like a brag, it's just the fact of it. But what's the point of just making more money if I don't enjoy the job and I can't make time to appreciate and enjoy the money that I've already got? That money should be about more than just removing the worries of life. That money should give me – maybe give us – the luxury of some choices that can be fun instead of business. So, I initially thought we might just leave everything behind and have a mid-life-crisis gap year and travel together. Have you ever wanted to just set off only knowing where your first destination is? I've not wanted to do that before, but that's what I now feel I want to do with you. But then it makes no sense to go away for a year when I've just invested so much in transforming this house. I guess I thought about a year away because that would be an ok period of time for someone to step up and look after the business. But knowing me I'd just worry about what state it might be in the whole time.

I've already made one decision. Something that I had to make by myself, but what happens after that is down to both of us. I'm selling the business. The German company that makes most of the uPVC we use tried to buy it from Dad before so it can extend its base in the UK. We've agreed a price. Unless I'm bloody stupid, I won't have to work ever again, which is also a scary thought at my age.

Now the transformations here are all finished, I'd like you to move in permanently so we can both enjoy the house and these new fun facilities we've designed and built together. I'll pay you an allowance every month, which is no different to how things used to be for most households except with a modern twist of sex equality about it, and you can be responsible for arranging all the maintenance to keep the pool and hot tub going. As a condition of selling the business, I'm going to have to spend some time working with the new owners, maybe six to nine months, but I can still have time off to go away. Once the transition is complete, we can travel as much as we want to for as long as we want to. I'm really excited at the thought of doing that. Doing that with YOU Alfie.

Please, just don't let the money thing worry you."

For Alfie, it was late June 2018 and all his Christmases had just come at once; again. On the one hand, he was getting much closer to exactly what he and Tina had been planning as revenge for Edward Claines' actions towards Tina's mother. On the other hand, there was the prospect of care-free travelling to places he had only dreamed about, with a beautiful woman and without having to worry about a single penny. It was a win win win situation, and yet he didn't want to let her think that everything she had decided was perfect, otherwise he'd feel like he had no control over the situation. In different circumstances, Alfie, with that mindset, would have been the perfect protégé for Edward to teach. Maybe that's why Michelle was attracted to him? Her father had come from nothing, and the only real difference was that Edward had the support and advice of his parents.

"Wow, what's not to like about any of that? I agree with what you said about the last six months being a whirlwind, but they've also been the best six months of my life. Honestly Michelle, I've really enjoyed the responsibility of working for you and what we've found personally together is just a fantastic bonus. If I'm honest, I'm struggling a bit with the thought of a monthly allowance for very little in return, but I'm sure you can help me come to terms with it. I feel so lucky to be in this position, but I do love you and just want to make this work between us.

But I can see a problem," he sounded serious and she was a little concerned with what was coming next, "which one of us decides where we go?"

## THIRTY-SIX
## Venice

Despite an ever-looming Brexit, the German company proceeded with its purchase and Michelle was contracted to remain until 31$^{st}$ December 2018. She was paid £6 in million cash immediately, with the remaining 50% due on 1$^{st}$ January 2019. By the time Capital Gains Tax was paid, assuming she earned no interest, that would leave her with over £16,000 per month, every month for the next 40 years. Just from the sale of *Heat at Home*. Nice work if you can get it. But she already had other investment shares and the substantial wealth she inherited from her father. She felt blessed. Thanks to her father, she'd been used to a very privileged life by Alfie's and most people standards: private education, foreign holidays, 5-star hotels, business class flights, top restaurants, skiing holidays. And now her second-generation money provided the choice for pretty much anything she wanted to do. Perhaps even a London apartment. That was her reality.

During her transition period with the German owners, they had a late summer week on a Greek Island, and long weekends in London and Edinburgh. Once her time with the company had finally ended, for Alfie's birthday in mid-January, Michelle organised a long weekend in Venice. Her choice, and like most of the places they explored together, he had never been there, but she had. There are still enough tourists in Venice in January, but not the volume you get for the Carnivale festival in February nor the masses that Venice attracts throughout the rest of the year after March, and especially for the Venice Film Festival week each September. Michelle had been to Venice one February when she was still at Oxford. They'd been on a skiing trip high in the Dolomites about an hour north of Venice and decided to have a day in Venice when too much snow was falling and the strong winds blowing closed the ski lifts for safety reasons. It had unexpectedly coincided with both Carnival and a partial flood and she had memories of people running through the narrow lanes in capes and costume masks when they had none, and along raised walkways above the encroaching waters. As students they had got the bus from the ski resort and transferred onto a big public water taxi to take them across the lagoon and into the Grand Canal and the heart of Venice.

After their early morning easyJet flight from Luton, Michelle had arranged a private water taxi directly from the airport to their hotel by the steps of the Rialto bridge. Once clear of the airport quay, the elegant taxi sped across the lagoon, like a decadent scene from a 1960's Dean Martin film, before slowing as it headed into a narrow canal with high buildings on both sides that instantly reduced the daylight. From the amount of light that was flooding down ahead of them, Alfie could sense that this narrow channel was opening into something bigger and took out his mobile phone to video it. As the source of the light was reached, the small water taxi swung left into the Grand Canal and, illuminated by the winter sun now behind them, the wide canal was an unexpected bustle of activity; everything happens on the water in Venice. Every type of boat was there; large water taxis, gondolas with people, boats for international courier companies, boats delivering building materials and food and beer, and everything else. Hundreds of gondolas were parked up along the way, all covered by tarpaulins – goodness knows what it would have been like at the height of summer? At their hotel, right by one of the most iconic attractions, a small suite with windows overlooking the Grand Canal in January was 'just' a few hundred Euros a night; still far more than the Marriott Hotel near Luton Airport, but the same room in high season or during Venice Film Week would easily add another zero to the end of the cost and probably double the first number too. It was bitterly cold, but they were prepared for it. Outdoor restaurants that hugged the banks of canals everywhere, all adding to global warming with their arrays of gas and halogen heaters, were prepared not to turn any customer away. Gondoliers were doing deals towards the end of the daylight, and even the best restaurants could accommodate diners without an advance booking.

Alfie was enchanted by the alley-ways and small, short, sharp flights of steps up and down to get over canals around every corner. For their first evening Michelle had booked a walking tour with six different stops for food and drink. Over the years Michelle had learnt that a walking tour at the start of any city break was the best way to get your bearings and learn where the great authentically local places off the beaten track could be found, and this guided tour with drink and food was even better. It was how they found La Cantina and its selection of local Amarone Reds, their most expensive €30 bottle being the best. The following morning, the hotel organised a private water taxi for them and another couple to visit the glass factory on the neighbouring Island of Murano, where they were pleasantly surprised not to be even expected to buy anything. After the demonstration of artisan glassmaking, they were creating some hand-made red roses for a forthcoming Viennese exposition, there was an explanation, a short history, of why Venice, and Murano in particular, now has a globally acclaimed reputation for glass. On leaving the factory they strolled together along either side of the main canal, before leaving Murano on a public water taxi to the picturesque Island of Burano, famed for its narrow canals lined with brightly painted multicolour houses; Tobermory by an Italian canal for younger readers and their CBBC parents! But now, following their visit, Burano is today famed for the Pizza Calzone that to this day remains the gold standard of pizzas for Alfie that no one else has come close to before or since. MAGNIFICO. It would be a destination in itself worthy of another visit to Venice just to eat their calzone once more, accompanied by a sumptuous €18 bottle of a gorgeous *house red*. But if they were going to visit Venice again, they would also spend an inordinate amount of time in La Cantina, the amazing scruffy and inexpensive bar frequented mainly by locals with excellent wines and perfect for doing nothing but people watching. Michelle took Alfie to a five-star restaurant on the evening of his birthday, located just off Piazza San Marco. It was the recommendation of a friend, with antique wood panelled rooms and expensive tourist prices. Compared to the pizza restaurant on Burano and the La Cantina bar in Venice, it came a poor third despite being many times the price. It was a life lesson they discussed back in La Cantina the following afternoon. An experience that pointed them towards finding a middle way in many areas of their relationship moving forwards, and not just to seek out the four- and five-star experiences that had cossetted Michelle throughout her life.

'*Where to next?*' was a constant conversation, but now getting more real for Alfie than the previous fictional question of '*How would you spend your winnings if you got the lottery jackpot?*' in conversations he used to have with Tina.

Michelle wanted Alfie to come on her annual ski trip next month, but he'd never skied in his life and didn't want to be the only non-skier, especially amongst a group of people he didn't know. He would take some lessons at the Tamworth SnowDome and go next year, he promised. Next year. Michelle liked the sound of that. A commitment beyond twelve months.

When they were at Lance Dune House they swam every day, zoned out in the hot tub, occasionally having sex in it which meant Alfie had to drain it, clean and refill so it would be up to temperature for the next morning, and played tennis a few times every week. Michelle started riding lessons with a local riding school and enjoyed it so much that she persuaded Alfie to join her. Maybe they would build the stables after all, "or maybe we could go on a ranch holiday in the USA or Canada?" suggested Alfie. Places he searched on the internet looked great fun and had amazing wildlife and scenic panoramas around them.

"Would she like to do that?" Michelle thought the accommodation looked a little bit too 'horsey' for her, but if he could find one with much better accommodation and a five-star spa, she'd definitely go. There was that five-star mental trap holding her back again. The 'middle way' wasn't Michelle's way of choice!

Michelle was not afraid to spend her money. Every month they went somewhere: Vienna, Copenhagen, Kortrijk, Bilbao. All places she had been before, but Alfie hadn't. She loved showing him the places she knew, educating Alfie about wine, food, history and architecture, and discovering new experiences together.

For their summer holiday they flew to Cyprus and Tui's Sensatori resort in Aphrodite Hills, a five-star all-inclusive hotel around fifteen miles from Paphos. Isolated within a golf course, her father had been there for one of his last holidays before going into the nursing home. The location was stunning, food and drink a notch or three above most five-star resorts, and Michelle had opted for a swim-up room that provided another layer of privacy and satisfied Michelle's need to take every opportunity to indulge herself with the absolute best her money could easily afford. Everything was there to join in with or not, and without any entertainment team running around with whistles or cajoling people against their will. On a couple of evenings, they took a taxi into Paphos for cocktails with live music. Cyprus was somewhere that they both thought they could live for a year – which had been an idea of Michelle's for a future adventure.

# THIRTY-SEVEN
## Las Vegas

In Venice's La Cantina bar, Alfie and Michelle played the 'Where to next?' game. Before meeting Michelle, Alfie's only taste of anywhere foreign had been a couple of TUI package holidays with Tina and the children. One to Malta, the other a last-minute cheapie to Maspalomas on the Spanish island of Gran Canaria. They'd hired a little Suzuki Jimny for a couple of days and headed up into the mountains as a break from the incessant heat of the hotel pool and beach, and somewhere on that road they passed through a tiny little village called Las Vegas. Alfie had to turn the car around so he could have his photo taken next to the Spanish road sign with dull black lettering on a white background with red edging that proclaimed where he was. He'd always wanted to go to Las Vegas – the real one in Nevada – and had missed out on a couple of Stag Do's because he couldn't afford it. Michelle's only trip to North America was for a Canadian skiing holiday in Whistler and when Alfie suggested Las Vegas, well she really wasn't too keen; the thought of casinos 24/7, Stag and Hen parties, the 'Bunny Ranch' and other infamous locations of debauchery; all those horrid little cliches of Vegas just didn't do it for her. But then there were the Vegas shows: Celine Dion, Elton John, Barry Manilow, Cirque du Soleil, and tourist gems like the Hoover Dam and the Grand Canyon not too far away and, ultimately, a not-before-time realisation that it wasn't all about her. Maybe they could do a few days shopping in New York and a few days in Vegas. No, she was going to leave this one to Alfie she decided. Let's see what he could organise by himself.

"Vegas doesn't really appeal to me," she started, "so when you plan it, it had better be everything we will want to remember and nothing that we want to forget." She couldn't remember where she'd heard that before.

"Let's go in the autumn."

Whilst Michelle was away on her skiing holiday in February, Alfie spent the whole week researching when to go, where to go, where to stay, and had prepared a full itinerary for a seven-day visit based on his research for when she returned. It was just as well that she approved of his plans, as he'd decided that he was going to pay for it and had already booked the flights and hotel as a package. She'd been paying him a generous allowance every month that he hardly touched, so thought it would send a good signal about not taking her, and especially her money, for granted.

She was impressed.

On Wednesday 13th November 2019 they travelled standard class with British Airways on a 3pm flight from Heathrow with far more leg room than Michelle imagined would be the case in anything other than Business or First. It was surprisingly acceptable, with big seatback TV's, drinks included, and unusually someone to talk to, Alfie!  With an eight-hour time difference, their ten-hour flight landed around 5pm local time, bang in the middle of rush hour, but by the time they eventually got through immigration – twenty-four *'Welcome to the USA'* booths but only four humourless operatives working! – and were reunited with their bags and then stood in line for a taxi, it was now almost 7pm. Come on America, why is it always thus? You can do so much better. On the plus side, rush hour was over and the taxi ride now barely 20 minutes to their hotel at the north end of *'The Strip.'* The SLS – Sahara Las Vegas Resort and Casino. And yes, if your cab drops you outside the front of the hotel like theirs did, then you have to walk through the casino pulling your case behind you before you reach reception and have to stand in line again.

Alfie had never been in a Casino before. The mirrored glass panels in the hotel doors hid the inside from the outside until you were safely through the second set of doors after a small flight of three marbled steps. For as far as he could see in front of them there now stood machine after machine after machine. Slot machines, card machines, horse racing machines. There was a just a single aisle of machine-free carpet that suggested where to walk. Not in a straight line, but first over the left to where people were sat at a bar, then over to right where the card tables and roulette wheels that were tended by croupiers at the far end of the room could only now be seen. Only it wasn't the far end of the room, there were yet more machines and tables before the walkway though the casino ended, and the start of the hotel lobby began.

As they waited in a small queue to check in, the Casbar Lounge opposite reception caught Michelle's eye.

"Why don't you go and get us a couple of drinks whilst I check us in? They'll arrange for someone to take our bags to the room," said Michelle. "I'll have a G and T please."

The hotel looked fine on her first impression, but Michelle, who had let Alfie organise their trip to Las Vegas and had booked a British Airways combined flight and hotel deal, wanted to make sure the room would be to her liking; her five-star expectations, or as close as possible. And that meant more than just 'fine.' They were travelling out of season, there were thousands of rooms in just this one hotel. Alfie's starting point was the fact that they wouldn't actually be spending any time in the room except for sleeping. Michelle's starting point was the massively more expensive and exclusive Bellagio Hotel and Resort in the middle of *The Strip*. Or at least one of the other hotels that Las Vegas is famous for; The MGM Grand, New York, New York, Caesars Palace.

And whilst Alfie was organising a Gin and Tonic for Michelle and a beer for himself, Michelle upgraded their standard room to a top floor, top-of-the-range Marra Legendary Suite, with three times the floor space, a separate living area, the biggest flat screen TV either of them had ever seen, and spectacular views across the mountains. Their bags were taken up, and reception called the Casbar lounge from across the lobby to inform the barman that their drinks would be complimentary. It wasn't just a bigger space that money bought. Somehow bar staff, restaurant staff, and casino staff all knew the potential spending power of their new Marra Legendary Suite guests and made sure that they were treated accordingly.

The casino was bright and noisy. The bar was heaving. It was busy, machines whirring and their lights flashing. No, chink, chink, chink of machines paying out. He'd discover that this was Vegas, and you could put all the money you wanted into a machine, but when, if, you won, you got a voucher with a barcode instead. You could take that to a cashier and get dollars in exchange, or more likely you'd put it into the same or a different machine as a credit to carry on playing. Every machine in the casino would willingly accept your barcode voucher and let you play on.

They were knackered. Both of them had slept a little on the flight, but their bodies were telling them that it was 3.30am the following morning UK time. Most flights to Las Vegas from Europe arrive at the same time each day [and still immigration have only less than 20% of their booths open – Welcome to America] and Alfie had read that you must go and eat, drink a little, and try to stay up until 10pm. With their bags unpacked into the suite's walk-in wardrobe, passports and valuables stowed in the safe, they walked down *The Strip* in the balmy evening dusk where unknowingly to Michelle, Alfie was heading to The Venetian Hotel complete with a replica Venice Canal that would bring back memories of their Venice trip ten months earlier when Alfie's idea of heading to Las Vegas had been given the green light. The pizza was ok, but nothing close to eroding Alfie's memory from Burano Island. They were determined to walk the thirty minutes back to their hotel, glad that they had their jackets with them, taking in the bright lights and people watching the whole time. Las Vegas, as they would shortly experience themselves, never sleeps. Ever.

# THIRTY-EIGHT
## Road Trip

The next morning, after brunch in the hotel, the keys to their hire car - a bright red Ford Mustang Convertible, and yes, Michelle was very impressed with his choice – were waiting for them at the Enterprise rental desk, and with an overnight bag they were off to the Grand Canyon, top down, via a stop to look at the Dam retaining wall and an army of steel pylons and network of cables that distributed electricity from the Hoover Dam. When they left the Hoover Dam they were instantly across the state border into Arizona from Nevada, and the clocks went forward an hour – which meant that after the four-hour drive they would be arriving at their hotel an hour later than Alfie had expected, making their reservation for dinner in the town a little rushed. They were spending the night in the town of Williams, Arizona, where the gradual but seemingly endless increase in altitude throughout the four-hour drive from Las Vegas completely changed the climate. It was cold, cold enough for both a jumper and a jacket even before the sun went down, a situation which Alfie hadn't factored into his planning or their overnight bags. He'd never checked the expected temperature at the Canyon. Thankfully, it was only a short walk from The Grand Canyon Railway Hotel to Rod's Steak House, which Alfie had found highly recommended on TripAdvisor, especially for their 16oz T-Bone steaks.

Their standard hotel room was, even by Alfie's expectations for *experiencing the luxury of a bygone era,* that their website clearly implied, more than a little disappointing. And without Alfie knowing, Michelle discovered that the few suites along with the *Rail Baron Suite*, were already taken. It was the kind of place that people only stopped over for a night or maybe two. But something was going on as the suites were all booked, the vast car park was almost full, and they couldn't find a space to park near the hotel's entrance. The reception had two big couches in front of a log fire and the Christmas tree, fully decorated, was already in place. When they got back from Rod's Steak House, the couches in reception were full of spritely pyjama-clad women of surprisingly mature years, all very excited about something.

As Michelle was to find out the following morning, every day the train leaves Williams on a mostly single-track line heading to the Grand Canyon's South

Rim. The two-hour journey is entirely open country, alongside rivers, through woods and cuttings, but it's just as much about the on-board experience of riding in 1950s railcars, entertainment from wild-west singers, and stories from your conductor – each carriage has their own. On the return journey your train is brought to a halt by actors on horseback pretending to be gun-brandishing bandits who have blocked the line and boarded the train looking for goodness knows who and fleecing the tourists for tips. What fun! Most passengers stay at the Railway Hotel before their early morning departure to the Canyon. The Christmas tree was up, signalling the start of another service the railway runs from early November until beyond Christmas. The Polar Express. On which passengers all travel bedecked in their PJs, as the *Casey-Jones* locomotive heads forty-five minutes up the track towards the Canyon where a "North Pole" town has been constructed and is illuminated for all the passengers to view, and it's where Father Christmas enters the train to give all the kids a present that their mums and dads have paid for in the ticket price! Based on the Polar Express book and film, two trains a day for nine weeks sell out months and years in advance. The middle-aged women in front of the fire in their PJ's had all been on the first train of the season that evening, and hence why the hotel car park is so big and was almost full.

The following morning, in the train station café where the hotel's buffet breakfast was self-served, Alfie and Michelle were able to buy commemorative sweatshirts, a distress-purchase necessary to keep them warm. They were taking their overnight luggage with them, as unbeknown to Michelle, Alfie had booked an overnight stay in one of the lodges overlooking the Canyon. When he told her, she thought it was a lovely touch and definitely 'an everything we will want to remember' moment.

The car park was now almost empty, and Alfie moved the car closer to reception for some added security. Security from what? They were almost in the middle of nowhere, but it seemed the right thing to do with a convertible hire car. The bottles of water they had left in the car overnight were frozen solid, and the weather App on his smartphone now reported expectations for a daytime high of twelve degrees with a night-time low of minus twelve degrees. From Las Vegas their route to Williams had climbed over five thousand feet - that's more than the height of Ben Nevis - and they were now at almost seven thousand feet of altitude, no wonder it was so cold in November and the air noticeably thinner. It was only a few hundred feet higher at the South Rim of the Canyon where their train was heading, but boy would they need those hideous Grand Canyon tourist sweatshirts.

## The Extremely Grand, Grand Canyon

Venice was superb and looked just like on the TV travels show with Joanna Lumley, only noisier and colder.

The 'Little Mermaid' in Copenhagen's Harbour is a fraction of the size you imagine it to be and massively disappointing.

When the solitary bugler plays *The Last Post* at the Ceremony of Remembrance that takes place every night of the year under the Menin Gate in Ypres, the hairs involuntarily stand up on the back of your neck.

But neither Alfie nor Michelle had seen a photo or video of the Grand Canyon that created an accurate representation of the sight seen with their own eyes the first time and every time they got to the edge of the South Rim and looked in awe at the vastness before and below them. The images on their sweatshirts certainly didn't capture the moment. Little wonder that the Grand Canyon is on every list for the seven natural wonders of the world.

It was just a short walk along the rim of solid ground to their hotel; they had actually walked past the lodge entrance with their bags, so keen were they to see the Canyon with their own eyes. The concrete path and small wall really gave an impression of being at the very edge of civilisation. Nothing else could be seen in front of you except the vast wilderness of the Canyon stretching out far beyond the horizon ahead and deep below where they stood, with the occasional human hikers looking like ants on the trail that came into view as it zig-zagged in the few places where the track could be seen.

It was not yet midday; as they were unable to check-in to their room, they left their bags and went to explore the tourist opportunities in the Grand Canyon Village. They jumped on the bus that would take them along the Canyon edge to the tourist centre, from where the hotel's reception had advised them to start their exploration.  In truth, the twenty-seven hours they now had until their return train was really too much time for anyone not hiking one of the trails into the Canyon. The El Tovar Lodge was comfortable enough, the reception and public areas decorated to make you think you were in a wild west setting – which you were, but it was functional more than luxurious, and not the place to linger. Again, most tourists only stopped here for a night or two, and they found out at the tourist centre about the overnight hikes down to the Colorado River, the river rafting, 2-hour mule rides so long as you weren't a person in excess of 90kg, or 198 pounds in local money, which would have been ok for Alfie and Michelle, just not most of the Americans they encountered! There were any number of activities they could do next time. Would there be a 'next time?' Alfie knew Tina would love it here too, and she'd want to do the overnight mule trek down to the Canyon floor and see the Colorado River from standing on its banks. And the white-water rafting, if possible.

# THIRTY-NINE
## The Stag Party

The following afternoon, as they waited on the platform outside their carriage for the train boarding to start, the young man, dressed from head to toes in a bright gold Tequila bottle fancy-dress outfit with a big red top, was waiting with his friends near the same platform markings as themselves, which meant they were going to be sharing their return train ride to Williams in the same carriage with a Stag Party. They were Brits too, and Steve the groom was there with his father, prospective father-in-law, brother-in-law to be, and four friends. None of them were drunk and they were also driving back to Vegas once the train ride was over. A couple of the younger ones had been to Las Vegas on Stag-Dos before, but none of them had been to the Canyon. They'd already had a couple of days on their five-night trip in Las Vegas and they willingly shared some experiences and their recommendations; the zip wire at night from the rooftop bar of the Rio Hotel to an adjacent building, brunch at the Luxor was a must and Old Vegas, away from *The Strip* at Freemont Street, was a completely different experience. It turned out that they were staying at the Sahara too [same deal as Alfie had booked with flights and accommodation from British Airways holidays] but the eight of them had to return their hire van to the airport before getting a couple of Ubers back to the hotel. They all got on well and had been really helpful with advice, so Michelle said that she'd like to buy them all a drink, and 8pm in the Casino bar on Sunday evening was arranged. Alfie thought that he'd have enough time to make it.

On that slow train back to Williams, held up by bandits, Alfie and Michelle did discuss coming back and making the Canyon a destination rather than a fleeting visit. Even now, out of peak season, there had been loads of enormous American RV motorhomes parked up, perhaps they could rent one and do their own big American adventure? The high street in Williams is on Route 66, there are music bars and diners, but it had been too cold just to wander along it and seek any out. Maybe early summer?

For their current adventure, it was just getting dark as the train pulled back into Williams at the end of the tourist-only line, and they now had the return four-hour night-time drive back to Las Vegas ahead of them. Most of it theoretically capped at 65mph, but not in a Mustang with the roof closed. On the plus side, they would re-enter the Pacific Time Zone as they crossed back into Nevada by the Hoover Dam and regain another hour to their day.  Once past the Dam, the road dropped down and towards Las Vegas which, according to the Sat Nav, was still over twenty miles away, and they could clearly see *The Strip* illuminated by skyscraper hotels and office blocks with their millions or billions of adorning lights in the centre of the surrounding darkness. Their hotel was almost the furthest north before *The Strip* ended at the Stratosphere, and Alfie intended to drive the whole length of *The Strip* – three traffic lanes in each direction, but once on *The Strip*, and just before the New York New York Hotel with its roof-top rollercoaster, the road was shut to traffic, and they had to take a diversion and up a side road to the hotel. Alfie knew why.

They were back in Las Vegas, it was just after 8pm and being five thousand feet closer to sea level, warm enough again to be out on a Saturday night in only a long-sleeved shirt with a light jacket or jumper for when the temperature dropped a couple of degrees.

On the advice of the Stag-Do lads they'd befriended on the train, after a gourmet burger in the hotel's sports bar, Alfie and Michelle took the Monorail directly from the stop at their hotel, down to The Bellagio Hotel, waited ten minutes to see the famous Bellagio fountains dance to the classical music and then started walking back to the Sahara through the maze of interconnected Casinos that every hotel had.  They played a little *blackjack,* sat at fruit machines designed for couples to sit together at, were told by the Stag group that if they played the machines slowly, the casino hostess girls would bring them free drinks just for the cost of a dollar tip per drink.  They did and it was all vastly different to Alfie's own experience of fruit machines in The Castle Pub and elsewhere back in Droitwich. Even the Departure Lounge at Las Vegas International Airport had a mini-Casino in it; just in case people hadn't had enough or were still desperately chasing their losses.

Casinos have no windows or clocks and, according to urban myth, have pure oxygen pumped into them so you don't get more tired as the evening wears on, but rather you feel like you can go on forever, cashflow and financial willpower permitting.  The casino hostesses hand out free drinks to customers they identify as properly spending their money, as yet another way to keep them there for longer. It was 4am when Michelle and Alfie arrived back at the Sahara. Their Uber dropped them at the front door and both the Casino, and its bars, were still buzzing as they walked through to get the lift by reception up to their room at the top of the Marra Tower. Alfie had more to drink than was sensible given what tomorrow would bring, but he wanted it to be a surprise for Michelle and so hadn't yet told her about it.

They were now spending their fourth night in America but were still struggling to acclimatise to the eight hours' time difference to the UK. By 9am they were both wide awake, if not exactly bright-eyed, and decided to go and have a swim in the outside pool, grabbing a coffee from the Starbucks in reception on the way there. Refreshed by the coffee and the outside pool, they now chose to walk off last night's booze by heading up to Old Vegas, as had been recommended, and get some breakfast there. Michelle hadn't noticed it last night, but outside their hotel a stage had been built in the still closed-off *Strip*. Today was the Las Vegas *Rock 'n' Roll Marathon* and Alfie had entered in the 10k run that started from just outside their hotel at 5pm. At every mile along the route for all three events [10k, half and full marathons] there was a live band playing to encourage the runners along. All the events finished outside the Bellagio Hotel after dark, so the final couple of miles were lit up by those millions and billions of Las Vegas lights as the finish line was reached, along with an ear-busting accompaniment of American heavy rock. Their walk to Old Vegas was mostly traffic-free in preparation for the afternoon and evening runners. The intersecting roads all had busses and lorries parked perpendicular across them so no [terrorist] vehicles could access the route – it must have cost thousands for the security alone.

As they walked along Las Vegas Boulevard towards Old Vegas, Alife recognised the Gold and Silver Pawn Shop, also known as Ricks, from the *Pawn Stars* TV programme he'd occasionally watched. It was too early to be open on a Sunday, so maybe he'd get to have a look in on the way back; get a fridge magnet?

Along the road were bars, gun shooting ranges, conveniences stores, motels, and wedding venues, 24-hour and drive-thru ones where you didn't even need to get out of the car to get hitched. Even an Elvis, in the building of course, could marry you. Uh huh. Outside the Little White Wedding Chapel, before 11am on Sunday morning, a young couple who had just stepped out of the chapel asked if Alfie or Michelle could kindly take a couple of photos for them using the groom's mobile phone.  The groom, strikingly as tall as Richard Osman [but a bit thinner] had an eastern European accent and looked to be restricted in movement by what gave the impression of being an ill-fitting borrowed suit. The Bride, as diminutive as he was tall, didn't speak but was clearly of Asian origin, maybe Japanese, in her full white lace-edged bridal gown.  Alife took a couple of photos with the white decorative iron fencing and whitewashed chapel walls behind them, and over brunch they theorised about who the couple might be, why there were getting married all alone in Las Vegas and why he didn't appear to have the money for a suit of his own or a few professional photographs. Their conversation made Michelle contemplate her own situation. Here she was, forty-two years old, two broken-off engagements behind her, the last one fifteen years ago.  No family: her mum's parents were both now in a nursing home and Edward's parents both long dead. But she was now falling more and more in love with someone completely different to her, and who she now realised that she'd been 'going out with' for longer than both her engagements put together.

# FORTY
## It's A Nice Day To Start Again

The breakfast hitting Alfie's alcohol-laden stomach from the excesses of last night, made him feel worse than before he'd eaten, and he now had less than five hours until the start of his 10k run. Las Vegas was crazy. He was crazy to have contemplated a 10k run. Here they were eating brunch at a pavement table outside a deli but still under a roof that covered the entire road and pavements for hundreds of metres in each direction. The roof was also a giant LED screen with visual entertainment and advertising for anyone who looked up, and along the entire length four zipwires allowed wannabe superheroes to fly past at great speed. All for $49. There just wasn't time to do everything that Las Vegas offered, and neither of them were feeling like making their maiden flights right now.

When Alfie came across details of the running event by accident, it was that uniqueness of the Rock 'n Roll run and the close proximity to their hotel that attracted his entry. A closed Las Vegas *Strip*, out of the relative dark to finish in the neon, a different rock band every eight or nine minutes or so. But any thoughts or hope of a decent time in the ideal running temperature had been taken away by the excesses of Las Vegas and Alfie's lack of will power and then, when he was around 6k into the run, and crucially before getting to the crowds on *The Strip* cheering all the runners, Alfie had to make an impromptu detour into the Oyo Oasis Hotel for a call of nature that couldn't be done stood next to a pine tree in the central reservation as other male runners had! Not something to remember.

There were rock bands, gospel choirs, Caribbean steel drums, the obligatory Elvis impersonator, Country and Western duos, and more spread out along the way. Despite how he was feeling, running down *The Strip* to the finish line under the lights from all the hotels with cheers from thousands of strangers had been a brilliant experience. Thrilling even.

While Alfie was running, Michelle, now acting instinctively on the self-reflection of her own situation over brunch, made her way back to the Little White Wedding Chapel just to enquire about, well, how quickly a wedding could be arranged. Her wedding. Their wedding. She had both their passports, collected from their hotel room safe with her. It was the thought of a spur-of-the-moment Las Vegas wedding that seemed a little *seedy* to

Michelle, but when she learnt that Frank Sinatra, Paul Newman, Sinead O'Connor, Britney Spears, Joan Collins, Bruce Willis and Demi Moore, had all got married at The Little White Chapel, well it wasn't all just about spontaneity. Following in the footsteps of all those five-star celebrities, well that didn't seem such a bad thing to be considering after all. Michelle discovered that they would both need to visit the Clark County Marriage Bureau, situated a couple of blocks before Old Vegas, prove their identity, swear an Oath that they were free to get married, and sign a pre-nuptial if they wanted to use their Licence within thirty days, and pay the $77 fee for the Marriage Licence. Las Vegas licences three hundred weddings a day, three hundred and sixty-five days of the year, and to cope with such demand, the bureau was open seven days a week from 8am to midnight. Once they had their licence, they could get married immediately. They just had to turn up and wait in line at the bureau, usually no more than twenty to thirty minutes. How could something that should be so carefully considered be so blinking easy and carried out on impulse? Exactly like Michelle herself was now acting.

"When was she thinking of?"

Tuesday, before they flew home on Wednesday. And with availability confirmed, Michelle paid the Little White Wedding Chapel a 50% deposit for the $75 ceremony, plus there would be a $50 cost for the minister and further $95 for 18 professionally taken digital images they could take away instantly on a USB stick.

All Michelle had to do now was ask Alfie if he would like to marry her.

Was 2019 a leap year?

Would Alfie say 'yes?'

## Let's Get Married?

Michelle was waiting in the Casbar Lounge at the hotel where they had agreed to meet after his race. She'd arrived there early and had been contemplating again the potential consequences of her rare display of spontaneity. She'd never even met his children, but then again, at no point did she ever want to experience his previous world of warehouse work and window frame cutting and everything that came with it. This just confirmed that Michelle had brought Alfie into her world. Not the other way around; it would be alright.

"Well?" She asked as he pulled a chair back from the table and sat next to her.

"Fifty-six minutes – ok under the circumstances."

"Circumstances?"

"Still massively pissed from last night. And I had to stop for a sit-down comfort break as well!" With it being ideal weather, he'd been hoping for something more like forty-five minutes. But he'd got his 10k finishers' medal around his neck on its gold ribbon - although in truth it was more like a mini trophy than a medal as it had a flat base and could sit on a flat surface.

They were meeting the Stag-Do guys from the train in under an hour, and then she didn't know where they were going that evening. She'd been spontaneous [almost] going to the wedding chapel, so she might as well just take the plunge. How would Alfie react. 'Here goes,' she thought.

"Before you go and get showered, before we meet the guys later, I want to ask you something Alfie."

She seemed a bit serious or at least preoccupied and not herself. Had he forgotten to book something, had she regretted coming to Las Vegas with him? Had he been selfish booking the run and leaving her alone for a few hours?

There were a few people sat by the bar and at tables throughout the small lounge.

Michelle was about to proclaim her own 'everything we will want to remember' experience for Alfie.

"Alife" she started as she rose and moved her chair completely from the table and got down on one knee in its space, "Alfie Rogers, will you marry me?"

A few people near them noticed what was going on and tapped glasses and 'shushed' everyone to be quiet.

All Alfie, completely and utterly dumbstruck and genuinely taken aback by what was being asked of him, and remembering what they had seen at the Little White Chapel this morning, could say was, "WHEN?"

"This Tuesday at noon."

And as he said "YES" and helped Michelle to her feet to embrace and kiss her, the whooping and cheering started across the lounge.

"Get these two folks a glass of champagne each," shouted a complete stranger across to the barman.

Everyone wanted to talk to them and offer their congratulations when the Stag-Do guys arrived. They had coincidentally made the Casbar Lounge their own meeting point before going to the casino bar to meet Michelle and Alfie as arranged. Steve, the groom, was now dressed in a suit covered in casino-related images; cards, dice, dollar bills, roulette chips, cherries and other slot machine fruit. Now everyone in the lounge wanted to have their photo taken with Steve at their side.

"We have to go to the roof-top bar at the Rio and you two have to go on the zip-wire to celebrate," suggested Duncan, Steve's father-in-law to be. So, with the first plan of the night made, Alfie was given an unrealistic ten minutes to grab a quick shower and change. It could take that long just to get back to the room if the lifts were busy! They would all be in the Casino bar waiting for him.

The hotel had a 12-seater van used for airport drop-offs and pick-ups that would get all ten of them in to take them to the Rio.

Neither Michelle nor Alfie really wanted to go on the zip wire. It seemed so flimsy; two bucket seats with just a car-like seat belt across your lap to restrain you. Admittedly you couldn't get to the buckle that once in place was out of reach behind your seat, but nevertheless, it wasn't reassuring. But you just have to tell yourself that it's been in operation for years, you've seen it go across the void a dozen times in the last thirty minutes, and they would surely have to be fully insured and licenced to operate. Not that much comfort would be taken if it did plunge the forty-two stories to the ground below. In fairness, the fast-as-a-bullet zip ride down and across to the destination building was so quick that it was over in seconds, but now the motor had to slowly wind you backwards to your starting position at a much slower speed, with your back now facing the uphill direction of travel. That was an altogether different sensation. But from their suspended vantage point, hands clasped tightly together, the view out across a highly illuminated Las Vegas and into the pitch black of the desert beyond was a wonder to behold and did take their minds off the one hundred and thirty metre drop that their legs in the flimsy bucket seats were dangling over.

Apart from Groom Steve in his suit, the Stag-Do boys were all in garish shirts. Some sort of 'shit shirt' competition which Duncan won hands-down with purple and mauve flowers on a light blue background; totally hideous. Despite the heaters, the roof-top bar at the Rio was already getting too cold for just the short-sleeved shirts that most of them had. Alfie and Michelle needed to eat too, so the boys headed down to the Casino and to see if they could get any tickets for the Comedy Club in the hotel's basement, whilst our husband and wife-to-be grabbed an Uber for the 10-minute ride back to *The Strip* and a late dinner in New York, New York's steak restaurant before taking a ride on their roof-top rollercoaster.

Over dinner Michelle had the time to explain in full and told Alfie that they were getting married at the Little White Chapel where he'd taken the photos of the Asian bride this morning, that they would both have to go together and get a marriage licence tomorrow morning, after which they could go and find some rings and clothes; not a white dress and tux, nor Hawaiian shirts, but something new, elegant.

# FORTY-ONE
## A Legal Requirement

The next morning, all evidence of the *Rock 'n' Roll Marathon* had disappeared from *The Strip* and Alfie ordered an Uber to take them to the Marriage Bureau, a most undistinguished building from the outside that contained 10 desks solely for the processing of wedding licences, with a Disney-style queuing system to get you to the next available counter. Eight of the desks were open; there were twenty something couples in the queue, but with more council operatives processing wedding licences than there had been Immigration Officers welcoming tourist dollars at the airport, it was around half an hour before they were showing their passports, signing to say that they were free to marry and not being coerced, and signing the required pre-nuptial form as they were getting married tomorrow. If Michelle had spoken to her Accountant, she would have advised that Michell should get Alfie to sign a bespoke pre-nuptial to protect the huge difference in their financial circumstances should something go wrong between them. The Las Vegas mandatory pre-nuptial would also not allow Alfie to get a substantial divorce settlement if the marriage did not last a minimum of three years, which was exactly what he and Tina did not want. But he couldn't object; that would only make it look as if it was her money that he was after, and after all it wasn't Michelle asking for a pre-nuptial, but a legal requirement of getting married so quickly in Clark County, the capital of which is Las Vegas.

Fuck. He'd come so far with their plans and everything had looked like it was Michelle that was making all the moves and driving their relationship forwards. She'd seduced him initially, she'd asked him to move in with her, and it really was HER idea to get married in Las Vegas. But now they were both having to sign a pre-nuptial that would protect her wealth for three years in the event of their marriage souring into divorce. Alfie and Michelle signed the papers, paid their $77, and walked to the Little White Wedding Chapel to provide them with their wedding licence and pay the balance owing. From there they got a cab back onto *The Strip* to take them shopping. First to the jewellery store to buy wedding rings together, and then they were each on their own to buy their outfits. Alfie wanted something to wear – he didn't know quite what – that would remind him that his wedding had been in Las Vegas and not a UK church or functional registry office. New jeans, new cowboy boots, a collared white shirt and a bright jacket, a bit like the memorable style of shirts the Stag-Do boys had been wearing, only far more tasteful. At Macy's he found everything that he wanted, apart from the cowboy boots, and they advised him to go to a specialist shop – Wild Boots – back up near Old Vegas, where he also spontaneously purchased a white cowboy hat that he hadn't even been looking for. In Macy's he fell in love with an oriental-looking silk-effect jacket, beautifully tailored in bright red with embroidered gold dragonflies fluttering all over it. It cost less than the jeans and considerably less than both the cowboy hat and boots, but it was for him simply perfect. Whilst he was on his own, Alfie thought about phoning Tina to tell her the news. Did she even know he was in America? He couldn't now remember. He desperately wanted to share his news with someone, but the kids had never met Michelle and they didn't explicitly know that he had a full-time girlfriend. It might all seem a bit strange and rushed to them. A sham marriage situation was exactly what he and Tina set out to achieve, so she would be pleased, wouldn't she? Alfie wasn't sure. She hadn't reacted that well when he first told that he'd stayed overnight at the house. Alfie decided to wait until he next saw Tina in person; he wasn't now so sure that it was a phoney marriage after all.

Secretly, Michelle hated the jacket as soon as she clapped her eyes on it, she knew she should have gone with him, but she was thrilled with her own trip to the Forum in Caesar's Palace and her purchases of Jimmy Choo shoes, a dress and jacket from Louis Vuitton, styled with a clutch bag from Kate Spade. Michelle was overjoyed with her outfit and she'd never known shopping to be anything other than a solitary experience with the ability to buy anything and everything she wanted. Most brides-to-be would have their mother or bridesmaid with them for such an adventure, but Michelle never thought for one moment that it should be any other way. By the time she first saw Alfie's jacket, as they were getting dressed in the hotel the following morning, the day of their wedding, it was too late to do anything about it, except just go with it. And that white cowboy hat, just what was he thinking of?

The Little White Wedding Chapel is far from little. Within its whitewashed walls are four different wedding chapels plus a facility for those that like their weddings, like their favourite dining arrangement, drive thru. With just themselves, the Pastor and a photographer, Michelle had chosen the Crystal Chapel. It wasn't the prettiest room, but just the two of them would have looked lost in the other much bigger spaces, and ironically the red drapes with gold edging perfectly matched Alfie's jacket.

Within ten minutes vows had been made, rings exchanged, photographs snapped, and the next couple were waiting for their 12.15pm slot, by which time Michelle and Alfie were in a cab, with their wedding photos on a USB stick, taking them back to *The Strip* and the Cipriani restaurant at the Wynn Resort Hotel for a celebration lunch.

Barely forty-eight hours ago, whilst they were having brunch in Old Vegas because they hadn't been able to sleep, the idea of getting married popped into Michelle's head after a chance encounter with the newlyweds who Alfie took a couple of wedding photos for. Here they were now, Mr and Mrs Rogers, married. All legal and above board. Only in America. Only in Las Vegas. But with a pre-nup. How would Alfie explain that to Tina?

And it wasn't just in Alfie's mind where thoughts of Tina came into play. As they sat in the sumptuous splendour of Cipriani's restaurant for the rich and famous, Michelle wondered if Alfie would have wanted his children to have been at his wedding – yes it was his wedding too. And what if that Tina really was her half-sister, wouldn't that have been special too? Only, what did she really know about the woman that had come to her office a little more than two years ago, and who she had only seen once more at Edward's funeral eighteen months ago? Didn't she say that Edward had bought her mother a house? She hadn't come asking for money, so maybe she was genuine after all? So many unanswered questions in her head that Michelle thought that it might now be alright, after all, to allow herself to find out more. The house Tina had been given. How might she find out about that?

After lunch they walked the short distance back to their hotel. They made love for the first time as a married couple; Alfie kept his cowboy hat on. Then after Michelle had showered and changed into clothes more suitable for 'doing Vegas' and Alfie has showered and re-dressed in his wedding clothes, perfect for 'doing Vegas,' late afternoon they left the hotel to spend the next 12 hours before their flight home the following evening, 'doing Vegas.'

Las Vegas, which Michelle had reluctantly agreed to visit as it was Alfie's choice, had been her best holiday ever.

With the excursion to Williams and the Canyon they had not spent seven days there and Michelle hadn't been at all bored like she expected; hell, they hadn't even found time to go to one of the big shows. The Grand Canyon had been both spectacular and fun. The train ride, all the ladies in their PJs round the Christmas Tree, the Stag-Do lads had been fun too; even tight-wad Tony in his bright gold lamé shirt!

Without exception, it had exceeded everything she wanted to remember, and maybe the zip wire was the only thing she wanted to forget. But at least she had done it and it was actually memorable too.

Everything they had done, the expensive restaurants, expensive clothes, first class train to the Canyon, had all been normal for Michelle and her money.  Alfie would love to have taken Tina to Las Vegas, she would have loved it, loved it, loved it. But it would have been a vastly different trip on their budget.  But now Alfie was a giant step closer to an ever-growing possibility that he could take Tina there in same style one day. Maybe not real soon, but soon enough. A thousand and ninety-five days didn't sound too long when you said it like that. A thousand and ninety-five days was the harsh reality of a three-year pre-nuptial before he could think about getting his hands on Michelle's money.  Just to bring a little perspective to the situation, it was now only seven hundred days since they had first met properly at the *Heat at Home* Christmas party. Didn't that make the three years ahead of them sound like an eternity? Uh huh!

As brilliant as it was, their fabulous holiday by Alfie's standards was expensive, but what he didn't know is that Michelle's wedding clothes, from Louis Vuitton, Kate Spade, and Jimmy Choo, had together cost even more than the holiday. But then her extravagance, as Michelle had justified it to herself, could also be seen as a massive saving compared to even a small wedding reception in the UK with all her Oxford friends.  Cipriani's restaurant had been fantastic, the food was a bit 'fussy,' watching extremely wealthy people eat lunch had been fascinating, and Michelle had loved being the centre of attention after she let the staff know why they were there. Alfie had preferred the raw authenticity of Rod's scruffy Steak Restaurant in Williams; the constant chatter of people enjoying their food not quite enough to deter the country music from the speakers, and just a brilliant steak.

Michelle and Alfie's relationship was a kind of *Pretty Woman* in reverse. She was the one showing him how to enjoy and appreciate the finer things in life. The experiences that he wouldn't be able to afford without her money, and yet she also recognised her own newfound liberty from only being 98% fixated on exclusive designer brands and doing things and going to places just because it would look good to others. Alfie was happier, more comfortable, more relaxed in his Macy's Jeans and Jacket than Michelle, physically and mentally constrained by her must-have designer-dressed look. But boy did he like those cowboy boots. Having that money readily available on a payment card, meant the following day they were able to take advantage of a $250 each upgrade to World Traveller Plus seating for the ten-hour direct flight back to Heathrow. More leg room, more people like Michelle around them.

The new Mrs Rodgers and her husband Alfie were both blissfully happy.

For hugely different reasons.

Alfie's sham marriage was now far ahead of the schedule in their minds, but the three-year pre-nup had now placed a massive obstacle for Tina and Alfie to deal with. Would they both be resigned to the new requirement to play a much longer game, or could another way to get their hands on Michelle's wealth more quickly be found?

# Part Eight

## FORTY-TWO
### All Is Full Of Love

*'Just got back from the most amazing and surreal holiday in Las Vegas. I'll be introducing you all to my new husband, Alfie, when we get to Avoriaz.'*

Then with a little press on the white arrow in the blue circle, off went the message to the 'Oxford' WhatsApp group that immediately sparked a deluge of *'congratulations,' 'send us a photo,' 'God you kept that quiet,'* wedding emojis, and a deluge of questions and comments in return. In response, all Michelle sent was a picture of her and Alfie looking beautiful together - despite his red and gold jacket - at the Little White Wedding Chapel, with a "WE will tell you all about it in February." She just knew that the *'girls'* would all *pinch and zoom* the photo to discover she was wearing Louis Vuitton.

Arriving back mid-afternoon on Thursday from their overnight flight, it took a couple of days for the body clocks and sleep patterns to start adjusting to their old normal. On Sunday morning, Michelle took Alfie to the Tamworth SnowDome, kitted him out in the Ellis Brigham Mountain Sports Shop with all the gear including his own ski boots, and sat with a cappuccino from Starbucks as she watched him, like a mother would her small child, survive his first two-hour group ski lesson. He was booked in with the 'beginners' group for the following three Sundays too, and then for Christmas she was going to buy him as many one-to-one lessons with an instructor as was necessary to be Avoriaz-proficient by $4^{th}$ February when their easyJet Birmingham to Geneva flight would be on its way to meet all her old university pals and their partners.

Everything that Michelle wanted Alfie to do just seemed to work. It had to be his positive mental attitude to everything she thought, and then there was the psychology for Alfie of knowing that if he got it right, there was the growing prospect of a million pound pay day and then he could do what he wanted. Like most people in the UK, maybe with the exception of those living in the Scottish Highlands, skiing wasn't something they did, but everyone grew up watching David Vine in their living rooms on Sunday afternoons as Ski Sunday brought the likes of Alberto Tomba and Peter Mueller from the Austrian, German and Italian slopes with a sense of foreboding as they sped through the downhill and slalom courses at potentially break-neck speed. Alfie didn't need to be that proficient, but he just wanted to be.

Tina was now working at *Coffee No. 1* in Droitwich town centre. Peter and his wife had retired, and the Spinning Wheel café had been taken over and, after a lengthy refurbishment, transformed into the Panda Chinese Restaurant. It wasn't the change that most of Peter's Spinning Wheel regulars embraced. Alfie ordered a latte and Tina went on a ten-minute break so they could catch up. He held his left hand up so she could see the gold band on his ring finger.

"O. M. G." she half-mimed, half-shrieked almost in slow motion, "Is that for real?" and Alfie told her precisely what happened in Las Vegas a week earlier, with just one exception; he purposely omitted the small detail of having to sign a three-year pre-nuptial to comply with Nevada State Law.

"I almost rang you from Las Vegas," he finished, "but I decided to let you know face-to-face. It caught me by surprise too, I can bloody tell you."

"That's fecking brilliant, how long you gonna leave it before, you know?"

Alfie explained that he'd allowed Michelle to make all the advances, so it looked and felt like every advance in their relationship had been her decision. He hadn't pushed or rushed her into anything, and the 'falling apart' would need to be the same. It had to be, otherwise if he were blamed for a divorce, then his settlement – their settlement he now reminded her - would be reduced. It was going to take time, maybe another eighteen months to two years, but wasn't it worth doing right? For the jackpot they were in clear sight of. It wasn't a stupid, crazy idea any longer. Michelle's money was now tangibly within touching distance.

"Should I tell the kids about you getting married?" she asked.

"I don't see what telling the kids will do. It'll only upset Sophie even more, and she hardly messages me anymore as it is."

"And what about Christmas? Are you going to see us this year?"

"Best not until we've got through this. Anyway, we're going to some upmarket Center Parcs on the south coast for a few days. Back for New Year I believe."

Not for the first time, Tina was filled with conflicting emotions when she returned to serve customers waiting at the counter. He'd married her, it's what they both wanted, and she absolutely knew that a wedding had to happen for their plans against Edward and Michelle Claines to work. But Alfie had never wanted to commit himself in that way to Tina, and that still irked her, massively. 'Maybe I should have asked him too?' Tina now thought. Perhaps 2020 would end up being a great year if the next twelve months of their fraud proved to be as productive as the last twelve.

## FORTY-THREE
## Ready For 1800 Avoriaz

The 170m long slope at the Tamworth SnowDome was supposed to be the equivalent of a *'Blue Run'* in ski resorts. Not the easiest level, but no opportunity to add any complexity either. Apparently, the Avoriaz gang all did *Red Runs*, and some of them, but not Michelle, did *Black Runs* too.

The minibus transfer from Geneva airport took about 90 minutes; it was dark and late afternoon when they arrived in the resort. Once they'd left the motorway, the climb along narrow winding alpine roads was constant until they reached Les Gets, at which point the inclines up to the small alpine town of Morzine got steeper, the roadside snow got deeper, and from Morzine to 1800 Avoriaz, even steeper still. The 1800 was added to the official name to let everyone know that at an altitude of 1800m, good snow conditions were more likely, and therefore a higher price and more exclusivity could be assured. Great marketing. It seemed incredible now that when Michelle and Alfie had been in Williams on their way to the Grand Canyon, they were at a considerably higher altitude than this stunning mountain setting with its frozen lakes and sheer drops over the cliff walls towards Morzine in the valley far below.

Michelle was still uncomfortable with the possibility of her friends finding out the truth that Alfie, her husband, had worked in her factory, and before that as a warehouse hand. She just knew that they would make a judgement based on that alone if they got the opportunity. Alfie was the sort of person that people like them employed, and not went on holiday as equals with. But he could hold a conversation with any of them, and unlike most of them, he could talk a bit about almost anything. He would discover himself during their skiing week that not everyone could join in with a discussion when something outside of their immediate experience was the conversation's subject. And we all know people like that! She didn't want to 'give them the satisfaction' she explained to Alfie, adding that it sounded stupid her being worried about what they thought, but nevertheless she did. And she was proud of him. Maybe he could vaguely say that he'd been in Supply Chain Logistics and not working in a Warehouse!

"Well, you just tell them that you've sold the business and that we're free spirits on a gap year and that neither of us have a job. If they push me for information, I'll just tell them that *'it's too painful to discuss right now!'"* But they needn't have worried. They were desperate to know all about the whirlwind marriage in Las Vegas, and beyond that they were all more interested in talking about themselves and bragging about the simply marvellous places they had themselves been, how successful their careers were, and for some of them how 'so advanced for their age' their precious sounding, stupidly named children are.

Alfie started the week with some one-on-one skiing lessons at the official French Ski School in the resort and progressed from the gentle wide *Green Runs* to the narrower and steeper *Blue Runs* in no time, managing to control his descent with a combination of snowplough and parallel turns that he learnt as Michelle watched over him at the Tamworth SnowDome. It was exhilarating to ski for miles without having to stop and a world away from the thirty seconds it took to descend the SnowDome before heading back up on the travelator lift again, which at the time he'd thoroughly enjoyed from knowing no different.

Avoriaz is a fully car-free resort where the eco-friendly buildings, designed in the 1960s before eco-friendly was even a thing, hug the mountains to provide spectacular views and maximise as many hours as possible of the sunlight that each day provides. According to its own website, Avoriaz [you don't pronounce the z], is the best French ski resort in the French Alps. That's the French for you.

From the transport reception, the end of the road for cars, minibuses and coaches, visitors and their luggage are whisked across the snow to their hotels, apartments, and chalets in large snow-friendly vehicles with huge tank-like caterpillar tracks. The village remains vehicle free and is fully accessible on foot, on skis, or in a horse-drawn sleigh.

If you don't ski, snowcats and snowshoes allow you to explore the area, otherwise over 200 lifts provide access to a staggering 650km of fully linked ski runs. It's also a top resort for snow boarders.

It was nothing like Alfie had experienced before. He didn't know that such places even existed. Every aspect of the week was new and exciting, and he felt at times like a child at a funfair with its mum. Michelle had brought Alfie into her world, and this alpine wonderland was better than Venice,

Copenhagen and Las Vegas combined. There were no people like the true Alfie Rogers in Avoriaz, apart from Alfie Rogers himself.

By the third day, Alfie was getting on so well that he joined Michelle and a couple of her friends on what they thought and sold to him as an easier *Red Run*. Turned out that for them it was manageable, but for Alfie is was a descent too far and he ended up abruptly on his bum too many times when the icy slopes were too different, too challenging for such an inexperienced skier, however willing, to handle. He was really happy exploring the green and blue runs that interlinked and allowed him to ski for miles, and each time he repeated the route, he got more confident in his abilities. 'Tina would bloody love this too,' he thought, but like him, before he met Michelle, she never had the means, let alone the opportunity, to afford such a fabulous experience.

From their catered Chalet on the edge of the village, they could put their skis on, literally by the front door, and go almost anywhere from there. Ski into the village for drinks or lunch, ski straight onto the slopes and ski literally all day without coming back thanks to a vast network of ski lifts that would get them anywhere and everywhere. "Not all ski resorts are like this," Michelle told him. In fact, most are not like that and you pay a considerable premium not to have to catch a bus from your accommodation to the slopes. Alfie had no idea what the week in Avoriaz was costing Michelle. He knew that at the La Folie Douce, during Après Ski, bottles of Prosecco were a €40 touch and that small bottles of Carlsberg beer in distinctive black bottles were €9 each. The resort was full of beautiful young people, and some older ones who'd visibly spent their money on cosmetic procedures in a failed desperation to keep up.

Alife hadn't experienced anything like the Après ski where Michelle and her friends all religiously congregated every afternoon at 4pm. For the next two hours before sunset, the La Folie Deuce restaurant and bar operate an outside club area where skiers head to directly from the slopes, before they put their skis back on to slowly meander homewards for a shower and the evening ahead. Pulsating music that can be heard far and wide across the whole resort, as enticing as the call to prayer from an Islamic minaret, attracts party worshippers by the hundreds. So popular is it that security guards are employed to get as many people in and to the tills as possible.

For two hours your personal space is constantly invaded not just by the friends you are with, but the people heading to and from the bar, people losing their footing as they dance in their ski boots close-by. There is no dancefloor. Everyone just raves exactly where they are. There are balcony dancers, Ibiza DJs, Eurotrash pop groups playing in their fur coats to keep away the cold. Alfie had never been to a rave and he bloody loved it. He recognised the wafts of cannabis that permeated so much that there was almost no need to spend any money yourself in order to get a little high. Looking back, with everyone breathing in close proximity over each other's faces, even though nobody yet knew that Covid was a thing, it must have been a spectacular outside environment, the best, for the Covid-19 contagion to multiply its number of victims. The only social distancing going on in Avoriaz was with the people who couldn't afford to be there. La Folie Deuce really lived up to the *sheer madness* of its literal translation.

## But that was all about to change....

.. Because on Saturday 8th February 2020, sometime a little after nine whilst they were having breakfast together around the communal table in the Chalet that Lois, their chalet maid, had prepared a selection of hot and cold options for, everyone's phones pinged in unison as they were presented with the same BBC News Alert: Five Britons had tested positive for Covid-19 in the French Ski Resort of Contamines-Montjoie. It wasn't in the same Portes du Soleil area where Avoriaz was located, but it was only ninety minutes away, and the suspected virus carrier had travelled there from Singapore for a skiing weekend on his way back to the UK. But, somewhat alarmingly for the occupants of this chalet, that infected traveller was now back in England having flown from Geneva with easyJet to Gatwick. Until that very moment, the Coronavirus was being called the *China Virus*, where almost 35,000 Chinese people, mainly near the city of Wuhan, had been infected and 723 had so far died. Nobody was expecting it to get any worse, and certainly not to have a global impact. Ninety minutes away. Hadn't Saddam's weapons of mass destruction been capable of deployment within forty-five minutes? Was this the potential mass destruction we should really all be worried about?

But today, by the time they returned in the afternoon from the slopes, there were eleven confirmed cases in France, and in the UK our compatriot who had enjoyed four days skiing on his travels from Singapore to the UK, had not only tested positive, but was now successfully infecting others. The contagion was proving contagious. And quickly.

The resulting conversation was one that they could all join in with.

Absolutely nothing changed in Avoriaz. Everyone continued to Après Ski at La Folie Douce, still in the closest proximity to each other, the bars and restaurants continued to heave during their main winter season, and today was the first day that the slopes were crammed full and there were considerable queues waiting for ski-lifts, all resulting from an influx of the French arriving at the start of their half-term break. The perfect storm. The Oxford lot were all flying out from Geneva the following Tuesday with easyJet to Birmingham, Luton or Gatwick. The plane cabins were being sprayed with disinfectant as a precaution, delaying take off by thirty minutes, which they all then thought would be as inconvenient as life would get.

Little did they know.

Little did we all know.

Except the Chinese. In Wuhan.

But many places in the Far East were reporting infections: Japan, Thailand, South Korea, Hong Kong, Singapore and more, and from all those places scheduled flights full of passengers continued to criss-cross the globe, and in the UK, no testing or temperature checking was put in place to identify infected travellers arriving. No self-isolation was required in the UK. The infection could carry on being infectious with greater and greater success.

# FORTY-FOUR
## Lockdown One

Four weeks after returning from Avoriaz, Covid-19 had replaced Brexit in everyone's conversations and had become the lead story on every TV and radio news and current affairs programme. The UK had hundreds of people testing positive, the first death attributable to Covid-19 had been officially registered on 2$^{nd}$ March, although it was later found that some pensioners had died from Covid in late January. But because Covid was not 'a thing' that anyone was looking out for in January, and very few people outside of the medical research community even knew that a SARS-CoV-2 respiratory illness originating in China was so deadly to people already in ill health, those people with the *underlying health conditions* that quickly became an everyday phrase, that the connections to the *China Virus* were not initially made.

Northern Italy was already in Lockdown with regions banning all travel and non-essential work, closing schools, etc. The virus, spread both as an airborne disease carried in coughs and sneezes and from physical contact with infected surfaces, was highly efficient at being passed from person to person, especially in western communities that hadn't previously been faced with SARS and Bird-Flu influenza. Very effectively where close-knit families live with or in close proximity to each other; with Covid-19 you are most likely to be killed by acquiring the virus from a family member.

Only essential travel from the UK to Italy and then France and then Portugal and then Germany was permitted. But everyone, from Wuhan to South Africa. could still happily come to the UK; without requiring a negative Covid test, without having to quarantine, without a temperature check. Eventually, on Monday 23$^{rd}$ March 2020 the UK was put into lockdown. Offices were closed, schools closed, pubs restaurants and cafes closed, and the doors of non-essential shops closed too, causing queues for supermarkets and the hoarding of toilet rolls and some food stuffs; but mostly toilet rolls.

Stay Home. Protect the National Health Service. Save Lives. We were told, but anyone infected could still come to the UK and bring more death with them.

Those emergency food stores that many households had in garages and cupboards ready for the inevitable supply chain chaos of Brexit, would now have another potential purpose. There were reports of food shortages in Italy, so hey those people weren't so stupid after all. Factories would continue to operate where 'Covid-secure' measures and 'social distancing' could be observed, but everyone who could work from home was told to do so.

In April, Ryanair cancelled Michelle and Alfie's flights to Limoges, an anonymous French City with a historic medieval centre that was picked for the convenience of the flights, but which now looked on closer inspection like a hidden gem waiting to be unearthed. Having enjoyed their 2019 Sensatori holiday in Cyprus so much, they were really disappointed that their holiday in June to TUI's Sensatori resort on Ibiza was now postponed, initially to September 'when this would all be over' by, and then by twelve months to June 2021. Michelle had really wanted to go long haul to the Sensatori Resort on Mexico's Riviera Maya coast, but when she found so many poor comments on TripAdvisor, and then read that a really poor experience by devoted Sensatori junkies was featured in *Carry on Complaining*, a customer service book that also featured poor experiences with BMWs, VWs, and Microsoft. Ibiza was chosen instead.

But hey, they had a beautiful house with not just spacious gardens and their own field with a stream at the end, but they had a home gym, a tennis court, a swimming pool with in-water treadmills and a hot tub. They were hardly cooped up like those families in small gardenless inner-city flats with small children that were supposed to be home-schooled by ill-equipped parents and insufficient broadband, and remote teaching that had no chance of being effective. The notion of *Death by PowerPoint* in physical meetings was being replaced with *Death by Teams* over the internet. For the 44,198 people in the UK who lost their lives to Covid by the end of Lockdown One, it was just 'Death.'

For everything the government got right, like the Furlough job-retention scheme, like the Nightingale Hospitals, it got more things wrong. Not enough Personal Protective Equipment [PPE], too slow to lock the country down, to slow to insist on isolation periods for people entering the country, too slow to introduce mass testing and a wholly ineffective, world-defeated, still-frozen, track and trace system. Then, potentially the biggest mistake of all, and certainly the one that resulted in the general public considering the whole situation and their own willingness to comply with government advice through their own lens and no longer feeling any compulsion to be acting for the greater good. Not sacking Boris's chief advisor, Dominic Cummings, for breaking lockdown rules to suit his own selfish family purposes, however well-intentioned they might have been to such an intelligent individual. The *Green Light* was effectively given for everyone throughout the UK to now act as they saw fit personally, and not to obey any personally inconvenient local and national lockdown restrictions put in place for the common good.   And people started to care only for themselves, mentally freeing themselves from the restrictions of lockdown. Raves took place. Pub lock-ins took place. Everyone went to climb Mount Snowdon. Some in flip-flops.

Lockdown One ended at midnight on Friday 4$^{th}$ July. Pubs and restaurants reopened with Covid-secure measures in place, but still no mass events for music or sport, and rightly so. Some idiots decided that holding their own raves would be OK, or that pubs could be visited without the need to consider the consequences to their own family and friends from getting up too close and personal with others.  It wasn't just at La Folie Douce on the French slopes where examples of *sheer madness* were reported on a daily basis. Still no culture or insistence of mask-wearing prevailed for now.

For Michelle and Alfie, lockdown together was far better than lockdown alone. Someone to share hot tubs, play tennis, go for walks with. They definitely got closer to each other, the space and facilities afforded to them at Lance Dune House meant that they weren't on top of each other, except for the times when they wanted to be on top of each other. Alfie's son Jake might have been the first in the family to attend university, but Alife, thanks to Michelle's influence, was the first in his family to purposely listen to Radio 4. Ok, so Saturday Live, The News Quiz, Dead Ringers, and Money Box are not the political and current affairs heavyweights that some might interact with Radio 4 for, but nonetheless a big step up from Kiss, Magic FM and Heart, and a good improvement on Radio 2 that was played all day in the factory as windows were cut and assembled.

At Lance Dune House, Alfie and Michelle drank every evening. One bottle of wine between them became one each, became wine once when Michelle had finished her G&T and Alfie a continental lager. Mealtimes became something to pass the time, so there were always three a day when in previous times there would often only be two.

Despite this, Alfie got fitter.

Michelle got a *little wider* and her dress size increased.

Ironically for a country where we head off to Mediterranean beaches because we can't rely on the weather here, during Lockdown One the long spell of warm and dry weather enjoyed in the UK was for the most part the very thing that allowed so many people to maintain socially distanced contact in outdoor settings.

At the start of lockdown, Michelle and Alfie each made a pledge, like so many well-intentioned people, to learn something new, an additional skill that would forever be their 'it was only because of Covid lockdown that I can now do this' triumph. Alfie, who had played around with the guitar as a teenager but long since given up, now wanted to build on his new cowboy boots and cowboy hat persona, ordered an inexpensive banjo from Argos. By the end of lockdown one, it was still in its box, unopened, at the side of the filing cabinet in Michelle's new study upstairs. He knew there couldn't be a half-hearted attempt; he had to absolutely nail it if he was going to play it, and a fear of failure has prevented him from opening the box; even to look at it and strum its five strings.

"When are you going to start playing that banjo?" not so much of a question as a challenge she prompted him with time and time again.

"I need to write a song first," was his stock answer to deflect what was really a fun jibe.

But he hadn't known who to write a song for or what it should celebrate. Michelle, her money and appetite to take him new places and provide him with an education that the school system failed to? Or Tina, who had desperately wanted to be his wife and was never really convinced that he really loved her. Wasn't it just the fact that they created two children that had kept them together?

So Alfie decided to write a song for Tina, *'You Are Already Loved,'* but it was Michelle who when she read the lyrics assumed it was herself that Alfie was writing about. Maybe he'd confused lonely with self-esteem, something she had never lacked, but she didn't put him right.

## You Are Already Loved

*I know you're scared of getting hurt*
*Especially those times when you thought [that] you and I don't work*
*I hated myself when you were down and low on self-esteem*
*'Cause you're the one that transforms us into our can't-be-broken team*
*So, don't look too hard to find your 'for evermore'*
*Because my love [that] you think you're searching for, is already yours*

*Not everything in life makes sense*
*I should declare that 'I love you' more, there is no defence*
*But we won't be broken, even when those words aren't spoken*
*I'm just as scared of getting hurt, and don't want to be heart-broken*
*I don't want to make loving me a chore*
*Because my love [that] you think you're searching for, is already yours*

*The clothes you wear, how you fashion your hair*
*What we share, and everything about you goes beyond compare*
*DJ play us our special when-we-first-met slow song*
*And we'll show all those gathered here just how much we belong*
*Take my hand, let me lead you to the dance floor*
*Because my love [that] you think you're searching for is already yours.*

*Real love ain't like in the movies or on the TV Screen*
*But that won't stop me treating you like my beauty queen*
*From now to the end of time, we'll make each day brand-new*
*And you don't need to make me love you, because I already do.*

Who doesn't want to know that they are already loved?

# FORTY-FIVE
## At Least That's What She Told Herself

Alfie was so pleased with his lyrics – even though he couldn't play it – or anything – on his banjo yet. He didn't even have a tune in his head for the words, but he could envisage James Blunt taking it to Number 1 in more countries than *'You're Beautiful'* had topped the charts with back in the day. How many requests for his song would Steve Wright get every Sunday morning?

He needed to write about Tina. It was cathartic. An apology for living in his new world, where he could pretty much have anything he wanted, where there was always food in the fridge and drink in the cellar, where his hand-to-mouth existence was all but a memory. His song for Tina and the sentiment around it reminded him of the only reason why he was really with Michelle. It wasn't lost on Alfie that their two children had been more than let down by his own and Tina's actions with their crazy notion that they could do this. There was no doubt that at times Alfie had been himself swept up by everything happening to him and he'd sometimes lost sight of the real reason why Michelle and he were so happy together. They genuinely were.

Only Tina didn't know that there were still two years and four months of his pre-nup left. Or one hundred and twenty-one weeks, or eight hundred and forty-seven days. It didn't sound any easier however Alfie calculated it in his mind. Then how long would it actually take after that to sour the relationship to the point of Michelle actually being the one to want a divorce? Would either of his children still be speaking to him by then? He couldn't follow them on Facebook anymore, and it was pretty much only the occasional text message from Sophie now as things were. Jake had a new life working in Nottingham where he remained after graduating. He too would have loved Avoriaz. Alfie hoped they would all get to experience it together.

His song made him sad and almost regretful for his actions. He'd been the one that had goaded Tina to get even with Edward Claines, but he wouldn't have been able to execute it without her help. Tina was the one that suggested he got tennis lessons, to leave Facebook, to add a vegetable garden to the plans, not to make any advances before Michelle made a move. They were all small details, but there was no doubt in Alfie's mind that they had made all the difference.

Michelle decided that if Alfie was going to learn to play the banjo during Lockdown, then she was going to learn something new too; a foreign language. She'd learnt French for 'A' level, and initially that had been a great help on many skiing trips to the French Alps, but nowadays everybody spoke English in Avoriaz and Morzine and Les Chats. And if you tried to speak some French to the waiter, they just answered you in English; probably because most of them weren't French. Only which language should she learn? She didn't fancy German, Chinese might once have been good for business, but Spanish was the language in many of the places she was now interested in visiting. She'd taken Alfie to so many places that she already knew, and especially after Vegas had opened her eyes, she had an as yet unfulfilled lust for discovering new places. Costa Rica for the jungle, Peru for the Machu Picchu Inca Trail, Cuba for its dilapidated magnificence of a bygone era. They all spoke Spanish. That is what she would do.

But just like Alfie needing the words before he could think about playing his banjo, Michelle was spending her time researching Costa Rica, Cuba and Peru for authentic experiences and not package holiday trips, and had only managed a few personal lessons using the *italki* website. In truth, she hadn't got on with the tutor, so was looking for another one; there were hundreds to choose from. She just needed the right person on the other end of the Zoom connection to motivate her, and she'd start to fly.

O al menos eso es lo que se dijo a sí misma.

In September the schools reopened, and Michelle decided she needed to get away, something to do with there being less kids about if they're supposed to be back in school.

"I've booked us a long weekend in Cornwall," was her throwaway line at supper. "You'll looovve it," she purred, "It's right on the beach, got a bit of a spa and you can learn to surf if you fancy it."

Alfie didn't really know Cornwall except you couldn't get to it until the M5 had ended by Exeter.

"Whereabouts?"

Michelle told him all about the Watergate Bay Hotel that her dad had taken her to, the long beach at low tide, the stunning walk across the skyscraper-high cliffs to Mawgan Porth and Bedruthan Steps heading north or Porth and Newquay heading south.

"When are we going?"

"Next Monday. We're booked on a "Taste the Bay" experience for three nights, and then we've got another two nights tagged on."

"Taste the Bay! That sounds like lots of seafood."

"It just means we have one evening meal in each of their three restaurants, one of which is on the beach."

Alife assumed that "Taste the Bay" had put the price up, but in fact it was a non-weekend offer that saved a bit on the normal 'don't-stay-here-if-you-need-to-ask-the-cost' prices. It was great having the financial means and time to do things spontaneously, stay in nice hotels and eat great food, but just occasionally Alfie missed sitting for hours on a stool at the bar of a scruffy little pub and putting the world to rights with the barmaid in between her actually doing her job. There was no such bar or timeframe at the Watergate Bay Hotel.

Alfie overheard the hotel receptionist advising a dog-owner to be careful on the cliffs. At least one dog a week dies from not correctly sensing the imminent danger after their culpable owner has unclipped their lead, she warned. *'Perhaps I could push Michelle off a cliff?'* came a spontaneous thought from nowhere. Then another equally chilling thought came quickly, building on the first. *'If she died, we wouldn't have to wait for the pre-nup to expire.'*

Physically it would have been quite easy to push someone from the footpath high above the rugged, perilous beauty of almost vertical and terrifying rocks from which it would be virtually impossible to survive. If the impact from the fall itself didn't take away life, then being tossed around within the full fury of the Atlantic waves crashing onto the rocks and the resultant injuries before the RNLI arrived should do it. A quick shove in the back to get them over the edge to a certain death. A split second was all it would take, but your OWN HANDS would have to do it and there was always the chance that someone, someone maybe you couldn't see, might see you.

The early September weather was kind to them, and the morning following their arrival and after breakfast they walked in shorts north along the *South West Coast Path* through Mawgan Porth and to the National Trust property at Carnewas, where manmade steel steps lead down to a fantastic beach with giant stone stacks that dominate at low tide.

The now Covid-secure café at the top of the cliffs was operating again, albeit with a very strange queuing protocol, and they were able to have a Cornish Pasty and coffee before retracing their steps to Mawgan Porth and an outside drink at the Merrymoor Inn that overlooks the beach, before the steep climb to the cliff top and back to the Spa in their hotel.

Within those few miles, maybe three in each direction at most, there had been so many places where a loose foothold could easily have been attributed as the reason why the deceased had fallen from the cliff. Alfie knew that he would not be capable of pushing Michelle to her death. Not with his own hands, but the growing thought of her death as the 'answer' to his pre-nuptial predicament had been a seed now firmly sown in his mind. Playing the scenario forwards in his mind, apart from himself, who would actually miss her? All that money and she didn't have anyone in her life close enough to raise a concern that something might not be all it seemed. He hadn't pursued her, he hadn't demonstrated any cause for concern by his behaviour. The Chequers, where they regularly ate, would vouch for the harmony they displayed. Yes, of course lots of people would be sad; her Oxford friends, the original *Heat at Home* family, and yes, of course Michelle was far too young to 'pass,' but who would actually have any concerns, who might suspect any foul play? Was there anyone?

## FORTY-SIX
## **Wind Of Change**

Alfie had held back from telling Tina about the pre-nuptial that was in place for three years from their wedding, not even ten months had yet passed. But the prospect of a death? No, he couldn't do it and he certainly couldn't tell Tina and implicate himself if he subsequently determined he was capable.

While Michelle was in the bathroom drying her hair before getting dressed and going down to dinner; they were eating in the Beach Hut tonight, Alfie lay on the bed with the hotel's blue and white bath towel wrapped around himself, watching *Spotlight*, the local Cornish BBC News.

It wasn't even the lead story, but a young twenty-one-year-old woman had been found dead on the beach at Newquay by a woman walking her dog at daybreak. The large woman who had found the body, being interviewed with her Border Collie, was holding one of those plastic ball throwers for dogs; the long thin plastic contraption with an ice-cream scoop on the end that holds a tennis ball so the dog can over-exercise its joints whilst the owner checks her iPhone. 'Shouldn't it be the dog throwing the ball to give that lard arse the exercise she needs?' thought Alfie half listening.

"Just one of them druggies I 'spect," speculated the woman, "judging by the stuff around her. There must have been more of 'em here."

'*That could be it*,' thought Alfie. Yes, a drug overdose, but we'd have to be at a festival, Glastonbury or somewhere and they're all bloody cancelled because of Covid until at least next summer. Another ten months, but that would still save at least eighteen months of waiting; maybe three years or more if he really needed to wait to make it look convincing and then the time for the inevitable protracted legal hostilities of a divorce to take their course before any cash settlement was made. It could easily be five or six years now.

Returning to their lead story, after almost two months without a single Covid death in Cornwall, there had been a Covid death in Truro's Royal Cornwall Hospital, across the South West Region another eight people had been diagnosed with Covid-19, making Devon and Cornwall one of the lowest affected [and infected] areas across the UK where in the last twenty-four hours four thousand three hundred and twenty-two new positive infections cases had been recorded. Anyone who had tested positive for Coronavirus and died within twenty-eight days was officially recorded as a Covid death and further investigations into their death, unless there was anything highly irregular, were not being conducted.

'So, if Michelle caught Covid, that would be the time to strike,' continued Alfie's thought process.

Only here they were, in a highly Covid-secure hotel, in statistically the safest place in the UK, and back home they had the perfect isolation at Lance Dune House. How the hell would Michelle ever contract Coronavirus?

The food at the Beach Hut was great, but the restaurant had removed tables to reduce capacity for Covid-compliance, thereby inadvertently creating a sparseness of atmosphere from the Beach Hut buzz that Michelle remembered. Across from the restaurant, the new Watchful Mary bar that looked great in the sunset photos on the website and should have been open until October half-term, had closed early. They didn't know why.

They were planning to have a drink in the bar and watch the sunset themselves, so had to go straight into the Beach Hut instead. Once their drinks had arrived, Michelle had a Tarquin's, a local gin with tonic, and Alfie a pint of Peroni, Michelle's announcement out of nowhere was gut-wrenching to Alfie.

"There's something I want to tell you Alfie. I might have a sister; well, a half-sister. It's been playing on my mind for a while you know, knowing but really not-knowing. But, I've decided that I'm going to try and find out if it's true."

"What do you mean? I thought you told me you were an only child. When did you find this out?" Alfie replied trying to find out if she meant Tina or if another 'sister' from Edward's errant ways had now unknowingly turned up.

"I wouldn't be surprised if my dad had several children I don't know about. I think it suited him with the ladies not to get married again after mum died, if you know what I mean, and he had the money to make things go away if needed."

"What's this about a sister then? Sounds like a *Long-Lost Family* secret. Who's looking for who then?"

"Before dad died, before I'd even met you, a woman came to the factory and claimed that she was my half-sister. Supposedly her mum had just died, and she'd found out my dad was also her dad." Michelle purposely omitted the claim that Edward had raped her – he wasn't able to defend himself now. "I thought she was just after money, but then I saw her again at Dad's funeral. She was outside the church beforehand, but not there after the ceremony. And then when we got married in Vegas it occurred to me when I was shopping for my outfit that having a mother or a sister or a Bridesmaid might have been a nice experience to share."

Alfie was now furious on the inside. He didn't know Tina had been to Edward's funeral.

"Has she been in touch again then?" he asked.

"No, and I don't really know anything except that her name is Tina, and that I might be able to track down details about the house that she claimed dad had bought for her mother. It's just being here again. Well, it's brought back a few memories of being here with dad, me failing to learn how to surf whilst he read his paper on the beach. And if it's true, then it's not really her fault, any more than I'm his daughter too. I didn't get any choice in that either! Do you think I should try and look for her?"

"Wow, that's a difficult question. I don't know how I'd feel if it were me. Guess I'd probably be too curious to leave it alone. But then what if you don't like each other at all? It would be too late to go back and undo it. I think I'd want to know, but I don't know how you go about it or what can be done whilst we're still in this pandemic mess. You know, with all the offices closed everywhere. Do you know her surname?"

"No. Only Tina, and I've no idea where she lives. But I think I'll give it a go. I'll find out if the solicitors have got any records for dad buying a house. Probably wait until Boris has sorted everything out with the virus and the vaccines first."

Outwardly Alfie showed all the signs of being supportive, offering to help Michelle once she started looking. Inwardly, he was so cross that Tina had been to the funeral, planted an extra seed of interest in Michelle's mind, and if Michelle Rogers now discovered that Tina was Tina Rogers, the mother of Alfie's children, then their game would be over, and with the pre-nuptial signed in Vegas it would all have been for nothing. He'd be broke again in no time.

On the Saturday morning after breakfast, they headed back to Droitwich. Expecting it to be a four-hour drive, Alfie looked at Google Maps on his smartphone to find somewhere convenient for a half-way coffee stop.

"Have you ever been to Glastonbury?" he asked her.

"The festival or the place?"

"I meant the place, it's a bit more than half-way back, but it's the same place as the festival, right?"

"I guess so, but I've never been to either."

On the drive home, north of Taunton they exited the M5 near Bridgwater and followed Google Maps across the Somerset Levels to Glastonbury where the strangest of experiences was waiting for them.

# FORTY-SEVEN
## Strange Phenomena

It was September, but Glastonbury, which they discovered is six miles from the Worthy Farm where the original Pilton Pop, Blues and Folk Festival, now renamed Glastonbury Festival, takes place, emanated an air of Halloween, witchcraft, and everything mystical. People, mostly exposing just a single tooth each when they smiled, were dressed in the strangest of clothes, almost pirate-esque, but more impish than sinister, no eyepatches or cutlasses. There was a quaintness about Glastonbury too. The High Street had relatively few shops that were not independent – some weird and wonderful choices of quirky clothes, pagan sculptures, and even self-love and pleasures from a shop that promoted itself as not just open, but 'very open.' The potions and lotions and artifacts designed to take you to another place where not just in the shops, they were being openly traded along the pavement too. Quite Bohemian.

They followed the walking signs from the top of the High Street for Glastonbury Tor, only a mile. When they had walked for fifteen minutes another sign told them it was still only a mile away, and when they made their way upwards through the fields beyond the last houses and the vegetarian Yoga retreat centre on Dod Lane [at least it wasn't Vegan] they finally caught their first glimpse of the tower protruding from the top of Glastonbury Tor, it seemed like it was still at least a mile away. The steepest of climbs was ahead of them, but from the top the views were stunning, the wind rasping. Bristol, Wells Cathedral, the new Hinkley Point Nuclear Power Station, and the Glastonbury Festival site could all be seen after the twenty-minute climb.

Back in the town centre, Glastonbury Abbey and King Arthur's Tomb would have to wait for exploration on another day, and also the George Hotel, dating back to the 1400s, looked like the perfect place for Michelle and Alfie to stay when they did come back. As they made their way back to the car park, Alife noticed several pubs where – in normal times – sitting at the bar and chatting to the barmaid for hours would make him a local. Alfie loved Glastonbury's vibe. He almost wished he had his cowboy hat and banjo with him.

# Time for Action

The following week, Michelle and Alfie went into Droitwich. Whilst Michelle was having some part of her body waxed, shaved, or exfoliated at *The Pamper Pot* Beauty Salon, Alfie had thirty minutes before meeting Michelle in Waitrose to visit Coffee No. 1, hoping that Tina would be working. The café wasn't busy, and she was able to take her ten-minute morning break early.  It was almost ten months since Alfie and Michelle had got married and Tina had hoped that spending almost twenty-four hours together, each day, every day during the strangest of years, would have made Michelle regret her spontaneity in Las Vegas. It hadn't, and to make matters worse, Alfie now told her for the first time about the pre-nuptial agreement they had both had to sign in America.  Tina, with huge disappointment, immediately recognised that his pretence with Michelle had more than two years to go before they would be in a position to 'cash in.' Much more, unless, as Alfie now quietly whispered into her ear, "unless she were to have a fatal drug overdose. Could we do that?"  He explained what he'd seen on the BBC news in Cornwall, and how they would go back to Glastonbury where experimenting with substances seemed to be a pre-requisite for visiting. They could both smoke some dope, drink too much spirits, and he could administer something tragic. A *Speedball* would do it.

"A *Speedball*! Fucking hell Alfie, you're playing with fire there."

Alfie was a little surprised that Tina knew how explosive the mixture of Heroin and Cocaine could be. Where had she got that information? Even if you knew what you were doing with a *Speedball*, that particular mix is well known to paramedics for the finality to human life that statistically results, along with it being the wrong combination of illegal substances to play with even if you did supposedly know what you were doing with drugs and chasing another high.

"Well, unfortunately it's not that simple anymore.  When we were in Cornwall, Michelle told me that she is now thinking of looking for you. Told me that she'd seen YOU at Edward's funeral.  Please tell me that's not true?"

Tina had truly forgotten until that point that she'd been to St. Augustine's the morning of Edward's funeral.

"Yes, but I didn't think she'd seen me. I didn't go into the church. I just wanted to see him arrive at the church. Pay my respects. After all, he was MY father too."

"Michelle now thinks that because you didn't make further contact after you first confronted her, and then because you were at the funeral, that you might now be a genuine sister after all. She's going to wait until this Covid thing is over, and then she's going to start making some enquiries. If the old man's solicitors have still got any records of the house being purchased for Shirley, then she'll soon find the probate stuff and we are done for. Alfie Rogers, Michelle Rogers, and now Tina Rogers. How do you think that will look to her? You and me, parents to my children and now me married to her. Us, the parents of Edward's grandchildren too. It won't be something that I can just say that I didn't think was important to mention. That's not going to look great is it?"

It turned out to be a rhetorical question as they both knew the answer, and Tina remained silent waiting for Alfie to calm down and continue.

"So now do you understand why there has to be no chance of her recovering or we're done for. It's either that or we're going to get found out when she starts to look for you. Is that what you want?"

"Oh, I don't know Alfie, I never thought anyone would get hurt like that. We only wanted to hurt her financially. Are we fecking mad even contemplating killing someone? How did we get here? Maybe we should just end it now?"

"End it now? I can't just walk away.

I'm married to her.

Michelle looking for you changes everything.

If the truth came out now I'd probably still get done for some sort of fraud or entrapment or whatever the heck it is. Have you forgotten that I'm doing this for US? For you, for me, for the kids. Isn't that what we set out to do? I'm quite happy with the life I've got now you know. But if she finds you, then like I said before, we are both well and truly done for and she won't want anything to do with either of us."

That, 'I'm quite happy with the life I've got now' hurt Tina. HER being Mrs Rogers still hurt Tina too.

"Listen, have you still got some money left?" he asked.

Tina nodded.

"Well, you need to start getting some stuff for a *Speedball* together. The sooner you start the better so that there's as much time as possible between when it happens, and any people being subsequently questioned about potentially supplying the stuff. Get a small amount several times from different people, in that way it shouldn't seem significant or suspicious to anyone."

"I'm not happy with this Alfie. You're talking about it like, like it's already decided. Like you're really going to kill someone. Could you live with that?"

Tina had almost doubled her ten-minute break and there was a queue forming at the counter and she needed to get back and help her colleagues.

"Just text me with something about a problem about Sophie's schooling when you've got all the gear for me."

# FORTY-EIGHT
## Could You Live With That?

Their talking had been so intense that when Tina went back to work, Alfie had barely touched his now lukewarm coffee. Could he live with that? He sat and contemplated the question for a while. Michelle was his wife, but then Tina had been his wife in everything but name and paperwork for twenty years. He almost wished he'd got a pen and paper to resorted to making a list himself, but however implausible the situation seemed, the alternative of not now killing Michelle seemed far worse for Alfie and Tina. They would be found out. It was going to happen unless they stopped her.

If Tina hadn't gone to the funeral. If Tina hadn't gone and confronted Michelle in her office. But the latter was a red herring really, because it was Michelle's complete ambivalence towards Tina at that meeting which started the whole chain reaction. If Michelle had been more empathetic instead of brushing her aside so she could plan her birthday party, they wouldn't be here is this situation now. They could have met up, got to know each other, which ironically is exactly what Michelle now wants to do with Tina, and which Alfie and Tina cannot let happen. Yes, ironic because it was probably only the experiences of her new life with Alfie, allowing her to view the world slightly differently, and becoming more confident in her own world – the changes to Lance Dune House, allowing herself to be taken to Las Vegas, her impromptu decision to get married there – that made Michelle feel that she'd been wrong, perhaps been too hasty to deny her half-sister's existence. Probably also because at that time Edward was still alive, even if no longer capable of his own cognitive thoughts.

It was with a heavy heart that Alfie admitted to himself, without the need for making a list, that the last three years had been the best of his life. Yes, it was all down to Michelle and her money and the choices it gave them, but if Michelle were now removed and they got away with it, that good life could continue with Tina instead. There was no other way it could continue. Michelle would start to find Tina sooner or later and then all their deceit and lies would come tumbling down around them all. There was a pre-nup still in place. Alfie would get nothing. It would be hard to prove that they had purposely engineered a plot, but Michelle wouldn't believe him or trust him after that. Far too much coincidence, even though all their decisions had been made by Michelle; for Alfie to move in, for them to get married in Vegas. She'd shown Tina the door. This was too much coincidence.

Before Alfie left Coffee No. 1 he'd decided that a return to his old life, even in Tina's house instead of the small housing association flat, would be too difficult to contemplate when there was a luxurious alternative, however unpalatable it might be to acquire, within arms' reach.

For the rest of the day, Tina was distracted in her work by the conversation she'd had with Alfie, and after work spent the whole evening fretting and reflecting on the situation and whether or not she could be complicit in Michelle's murder. There were so many questions in her head she now formed a mental list.

1. If she told Alfie to stop, would he just remain with Michelle forever?
2. Maybe he could explain everything away to Michelle?
3. How hard would it be for Alfie to walk away from his new life of privilege?
4. Would she do it if the tables were turned?
5. Could Alfie really make it look like an accident?
6. Was Alfie the benefactor of Michelle's will?

She'd have to ask him if he knew that or not.

Tina assumed by 'Glastonbury,' that Alfie meant the music festival where drug overdoses were sadly no longer the news sensations they once were. In fact, wasn't there a case recently of someone dying from an overdose at a different festival, and the person with her being sent to jail because he'd bought the drugs and hadn't shown any duty of care towards her?

*'Hang on,' she thought, 'whether Michelle dies, or they wait it out and Alfie gets divorced, there's nothing to guarantee me anything. We're not married and never were. If he wanted to just continue his high life on his own, I couldn't do anything about it. Where's my evidence? There bloody isn't any. What a fecking mess. I so wish we'd never started this stupid vendetta; my mother would never have wanted this. Why why why did she have to tell me?'*

Tina didn't know what damage Alife and her actions had already done to their children, but she was also alive to the likelihood that if Covid-19 hadn't exposed frailties in Alfie's new marriage, that in another two years the potential from a vaccine to live normal lives and travel again would only bring Michelle and Alfie closer together. Would Alfie still want to go through with a mock divorce?

Then Tina remembered the time that she had confronted Michelle in her office shortly after her mother had died with the news that they were half-sisters, and Michelle being cold and distant and assuming it was only about money.

Maybe she would have gone back and tried again if Alfie hadn't been so fixated on the money and talked her out of it.

Well, it wasn't anything to do with money then. It was about family, the truth, some sort of, well not compensation but acknowledgement of a need to put things right. Yes, that might take some money, but it hadn't been about the money itself. Tina had wanted a sister and now instead Alfie had a wife. A very wealthy wife.

What were Tina's choices.

1. Call it off. In which case she'd probably lose Alfie forever.
2. Wait over two years for the pre-nuptial to expire. She'd almost certainly lose Alfie.
3. Help Alfie 'get rid' of Michelle. If he could do that then even if she lost Alfie, he'd do alright by her financially, and she'd be able to look after the Jake and Sophie better. After all, she'd have something on him even if it implicated herself too.

Did she now have any meaningful choice?

And if Alfie screwed up the overdose attempt, how could any of it come back to her?

# FORTY-NINE
## Sophie's Schooling Is A Problem

It was six days before Christmas 2020 when Alfie received the coded text from Tina letting him know she finally had the drugs.

It had taken almost three months for Tina to accumulate enough heroin and cocaine to neutralise a small horse. She purposely hadn't gone looking and asking for any, it was only when some was being 'offered' around the pub she was in that she took advantage, and not too much at a time, which is why it had taken so long. To make sure that her illegal stash wasn't accidentally found by Sophie or anyone else, she placed the drugs in a small resealable plastic bag, folded it and folded it twice more until it was about the size of a matchbox and using a spoon to hollow out space, Tina hid the small hoard below the surface of her mother's ashes, still in the ugly plastic container they came in from the crematorium, that she collected from Crumps over three years ago.

The text from Tina reminded Alfie that he needed to get the children some Christmas gifts; perhaps one for Tina too. He was a different person. A better person. He didn't know if Jake was coming back from Nottingham and Sophie's 18th had completely passed him by. Tina didn't feel it had been her place to remind him. It was all part of the 'estrangement' game they were playing. Tina hadn't even told them that Alfie was married, and the topic of Jake and Sophie never came up in conversations between Alfie and Michelle. His children had never been a part of their relationship and, given the game that Tina and Alfie were playing, there seemed no point it trying to create relationships that only had the potential to confuse and then cause future upset as lives untangled and re-tangled themselves.

Michelle was quite surprised when Alfie told her after breakfast on the Monday morning that he was going into Worcester to buy some Christmas gifts for the kids and would drop them off with their mother.

"So you know where she lives then?"

"Unless she's moved since I last had any contact. Which I doubt."

Michelle wanted to ask, '*And when was that then?*' but just knew that there wasn't a way she could ask without it sounding plain wrong, or even a touch jealous. Or without it sounding like an accusation of something more than it was. Whatever his previous family life had been, Alfie had shown nothing but devotion to Michelle, she reminded herself in time.

"Ok. I'll see you later then," was all that came out.

In Worcester, the Boots perfume assistant recommended *Miss Dior* for Sophie and *Joy, Eau de Parfum Intense* for Tina. Alfie saw some Jimmy Choo perfume locked behind the glass in the same cabinet and got that for Michelle too; he'd pop it as a surprise inside the Louis Vuitton clutch bag that she'd asked for. Gift wrapping for Christmas was included! For Jake, he got a *Tommy Hilfiger* dressing gown from *House of Fraser* that was the most expensive of the lot, yet still attracted a small additional fee for their gift-wrapping service.

"I come bearing gifts, and to talk about Sophie's schooling," was how he greeted Tina when she took his order for a Gingerbread Latte after he'd waited in line for what seemed like ages at Coffee No. 1.

"I can't get a break now, we're rammed; can you take them to the house? Sophie's at home."

London and the South East had just gone into a new Tier 4, the government's relaxation of social distancing rules over Christmas had been reduced from the promised five days to just Christmas day itself, and everyone was being told that just because you can mix with other people, doesn't mean that you should. Here was Coffee No. 1, and the Muffin Break across the way, rammed with shoppers enjoying a drink together. The drive-thru queues at KFC and McDonalds in Worcester had backed up onto the main road, there was no shortage of shopping going on, just in case the rules changed yet again, and it now proved to be last-minute shopping. Now the French had just stopped all ferries, Eurotunnel freight and Eurostar passengers from leaving the UK over concerns about a new variant of Covid-19 that had been detected here. The Belgians and Dutch were now joining in. Alfie was sure that he'd heard on Radio 4 some time ago, probably during all the talks on Brexit, that the UK's just-in-time food deliveries from mainland Europe mean that supermarkets only have on their shelves and in their warehouses enough food for another six meals each if supplies stopped abruptly. Like supplies were now being abruptly stopped coming in from Calais. Like people had expected for Brexit. Was that just another urban myth? Was this just a great excuse for the French to highlight the error of our June 2016 referendum?  Or was it really just the French trade unions flexing their Mussels [and Scallops] over the imminent loss of their Common Fisheries Policy rights to fish anywhere in UK waters?

"Are you OK to keep Sophie's report until I need to see it in more detail?" he asked.

And Tina nodded her willingness to hold onto the drugs that she'd acquired until they were needed.

Alfie's relationship with Sophie had deteriorated under the circumstances, and he'd gone to Coffee No. 1 precisely because he didn't want to have any confrontation with her.  Sixth form had finished the previous Friday so he rightly guessed she might be home.  It was almost midday now; would she still be in bed like most teenagers were supposed to be?

He rang the bell.  An upstairs window opened.

"You can't come in.  I'm self-isolating, my friend Dominic tested positive."

Alife raised the bag indicating that he had something for her.

"Just leave it on the step and I'll come down in a minute."

"Are you ok love?"

"I'm fine.  Happy Christmas."

"You too love.   I hope you like what I've got you."

Alfie got a 'thank you,' before Sophie closed the window, but no mention of the Dad-word, no *'hang on a moment, I've got something for you,'* not that he was really expecting that.

Apart from the crackers and themed place mats and cloth napkins, Christmas Day at Lance Dune House was pretty much like any other one since the second lockdown started in early November.  There was no opportunity to pop to *The Chequers* for a pre-dinner drink, there was no one else to form a 24-hour bubble with.  For Christmas Day lunch, Michelle had gone off-piste with two small guinea fowl from the farm shop butcher supplying meat from the Ragley Hall Estate near Alcester, accompanied by a selection of roasted root vegetables, roast potatoes, and cranberry gravy.

The days dragged until New Year, when 2021 was welcomed in with the best, or at the least the most expensive bottle of red wine they had searched together for in Edward's cellar, instead of champagne. A 2004 Italian Sassicaia from Tuscany that, according to the attached Tag, Edward had bought for €800 during a wine society trip in 2006. Michelle did a Google search and discovered that the same ungenerous 600cl bottle was now selling for almost £4,000 at a UK merchant thanks to its heritage and not, according to the online tasting notes, necessarily its quality. Michelle decanted the bottle in the afternoon and placed it on the coffee table in front of the fire to breath until the evening. It was good, very good in fact, but not, in both their amateur opinions, as good as the bottles of €30 Amarone they had enjoyed in Venice. In La Cantina. Maybe they had been intoxicated as much by their fledgling love and Venice's ambiance as well as the fine wine from the foothills of the Dolomites?

Two small glasses each, effectively costing £1,000 per glass at today's prices, was way beyond decadent, but what good would another two or ten years residing in the cellar achieve? Once the small bottle of self-indulgence was consumed, Michelle opened a bottle of Pol Roger Champagne anyway for herself, and Alfie resorted to a continental lager.

Happy New Year. What would 2021 bring?

Before Christmas, following comments from Sir Paul McCartney that Glastonbury was no longer in his diary for 2021, and he was supposedly booked to be a headline act, there were rumours that June's Glastonbury festival had already been cancelled. The organisers reassured the public that no decision had yet been taken, but Alfie and Tina both separately suspected that any notion of inflicting yet another narcotics overdose on the UK's premium music festival was now dead in the water.

## 2021 Starts Badly

On Wednesday 6th January 2021, an official looking letter arrived for Michelle Claines, sent by Royal Mail Special Delivery Service. It was from the solicitor acting as The Executor for her grandparents on her mother's side. Michelle hadn't seen them since they came to her fortieth party. She hadn't even let them know that she'd got married.

But that was all now too late as they'd both died before Christmas as a result of Covid rampaging through their nursing home. The solicitor wanted to setup a video call as Michelle was the main benefactor of their will. Michelle's mother Helen had been their only child.

Yet more wealth was about to come Michelle's way; wealth that just increased further the unfairness in Alfie's mind between what Michelle and Tina each had. How long was it now going to take Alfie for him and Tina to have the wealth he thought should have been Tina's by right? Would he still be able to create a death for Michelle that looked only like a tragic accident? Or would Michelle find Tina before his plans could be executed?

# Part Nine

FIFTY
## The Lowering

Jake had been planning on coming home for Christmas with his girlfriend for three of the five days that were originally declared by Prime Minister Johnson to be a Covid-free-for-all-spread-fest. Train tickets had been purchased, a sufficiently expensive fresh turkey to feed four was in the fridge waiting, and then everyone's plans got scuppered by the U-turn supposedly in reaction to the new and very virulent virus variant, but more likely because of the impending January 2021 pressures that such social mixing, with everyone overheating in Christmas jumpers and making best use of the mistletoe dangling invitingly from light fittings to make people who would never normally kiss each other, kiss each other, would create for already-near-maximum-capacity hospitals.

Frontline NHS staff and the super-old, who had thus far survived the almost life-ending certainty of what a Covid infection would have entailed, were the first to be inoculated with the Pfizer-BioNTech Vaccine, and by mid-January would have the presumed immunity. But there would be another government U-Turn on that one, with an unpopular decision to increase the distance between the two vaccinations from four to twelve weeks. That would allow more people to have their first jab, but the distance of twelve weeks between the two inoculations wasn't scientifically robust.

We don't know the true death rate…..

Since the start of the pandemic, governments around the world published infection and mortality rates. In the UK, and elsewhere, a Covid death is officially recognised as a *'Death for any reason, within twenty-eight days of a positive Covid test.'* Trying to explain that as straightforwardly as possible, it means that *dying with Covid* as opposed to *dying from Covid* are lumped together, because the sheer volume of post-mortem examinations required to tell the difference would just take too long and be too costly. In any case, and this may be too difficult for those recently bereaved to concur with, if the person is dead, what difference does it make if Covid-19 was the only cause or just the trigger that pushed the pre-existing medical condition over the edge?

And there isn't the time, money, or desire for anything more precise.

Sophie self-isolated until the New Year and thankfully hadn't been unwell, so unless she had been asymptomatic, she didn't appear to have Covid herself. But when a teenage girl believes she is perfectly healthy and understands self-isolating to mean that she just has to stay at home, then if she is infected and asymptomatic, chances are that it will be passed on to anyone in the same household. Ten days into January, Tina caught Covid. Her new cough and loss of taste and smell suggested she had two of the three symptoms that made her require a coronavirus test for confirmation.

The Gov.co.uk website asked a series of questions before the process efficiently gave Tina a 4.15pm appointment on Tuesday 12th January to have a drive-thru test at County Hall in Worcester. The process, a large cotton bud probing the soft tissue around the back area of the throat and then gently swirled just inside each nostril, was not as uncomfortable as she'd been expecting, nor did it make her gag. The kit had been placed onto her rear car seat by the testing official, which is where Tina placed it once she had re-sealed it, and the official retrieved it through the same open rear window. The whole process had taken just five minutes after her booking details had been digitally verified from her smartphone on arrival.

It was Thursday morning when Tina received her text message to confirm the positive diagnosis; but she'd already had her lightbulb moment. When she arrived at the testing centre she was wearing her facemask as instructed, and the only *identification* they required was the QR code from her smartphone that had been provided when she completed the online booking with her personal details. As instructed, Tina held her phone against the window so they could scan the code. Armed with the booking time and the QR Code, it could have been almost any woman sat in the car taking that Covid test in Tina's name.

Coffee No. 1 now had to close their Takeaway-only service as the small team had all worked with Tina either on the proceeding Friday or Saturday and needed to self-isolate. Tina was going to be at home for the next 7 days at least. She would have to proceed quickly, whilst she was herself still infected with Covid, if her plan was to work.

On Thursday afternoon she sent Alfie a text.

"Need to talk urgently about Sophie's University plans. Call me."

His phone was on silent, but he felt it vibrate the top of his thigh from inside his jean pocket. It was only usually Michelle who called or texted him, and she was sat on the sofa opposite. On the pretence of making a cup of tea he moved into the kitchen so he could read it.

"Do you know what," Alfie announced to Michelle, "I could do with some fresh air. Do you fancy walking up to the lodge? I thought I would just check everything's OK after the New Year snow and the cold weather."

Michelle, reading a great *whodunnit* novel, *Youthenasia*, on her iPad, told him that she really wanted to finish her book and definitely didn't want to go out in the cold air right now.

Walking along the drive to the Lodge, Alfie made the call.

"Tina. What's up?"

"I've got Covid Alfie. Just had a positive test result come through."

"You'll be OK. Are you feeling alright?"

"I'm fine, just a bit of a cough. I've had far worse. But It's given me a brilliant idea for our plans. If you get HER a positive Covid test, you can then do the other thing, and everyone will just assume that it was Covid that did for her."

"Only one problem there Tina. She hasn't got Covid, so unless you were thinking of giving it to me and me to her, I don't see how."

"We shouldn't talk about it on the phone, but I know how we can definitely do it. We need to move quickly; can you meet me early tomorrow in the Lido Park? I'll take Teddy for a walk and we can meet in front of the Cricket Pavilion. Say 9.30am? Great. Bring a mask and don't get too close."

The following morning Alfie made an excuse about going to the hot tub section at Webbs Garden Centre to get some chemicals. It was another frightfully cold morning and no, Michelle did not want to go.

Ever since Alfie tasked her with getting the drugs, Tina had determined for herself that both her and Alfie needed to be equally involved, so neither of them could innocently walk away nor could one of them pin the blame on the other if they were detected. At times Tina had been genuinely concerned that Alfie wouldn't include her in his post-Michelle life.

Alfie's unlikely 'I should marry her, divorce her, and we can have half the money' idea had set in motion their plans to defraud Michelle Claines of some of her wealth. Tina never for one moment expected their windfall to be half of what she had. She was bound to have a smart lawyer minimise her losses. But with the pre-nuptial and then Michelle's change of heart about wanting to find Tina, Alfie had taken them down a more sinister path, from which there didn't now appear to be any turning back from. Tina wished there was another course of action open to them.

How would Alfie get her to ingest the drugs? Wherever it happened, there would be an investigation with the prospect of some comeback, some unforeseen consequence. Tina was far from comfortable. She wished there was a way to stop it; couldn't they just go back to the fraud? But that just didn't seem possible now.

# FIFTY-ONE
## Not Covid Secure!

Alfie was at the Cricket Pavilion before Tina walked across the cricket outfield with Teddy to meet him. They were going to walk together around the perimeter of the pitch, but the ground was saturated after yesterday's rain had melted the deep snow that had hidden the grass for the last few days. Tina would have been ok in her wellies, but Alfie only had some Ecco leisure boots on that Michelle had bought him for their trip to Venice. They walked down the path instead, to Al's Kitchen, a café by the Lido pool where they got a couple of take-away coffees. Al had only taken over the café in the summer, and it was the first time ever that the café next to the Lido pool, itself only open from May bank holiday to October half-term, had been open all winter. Alfie asked Tina how she was feeling, and she told him that she was still feeling OK despite being Covid positive. More importantly, she had something brilliant to share with Alfie.

"Can you get her properly drunk tonight?" Tina asked.

"Probably, it's Friday. That's seems to be what we normally do on Friday's these days. But why?"

"You need to book HER and you a Covid test for as early as you can tomorrow morning. It's dead simple, you only have to confirm you've got a couple of the symptoms they list on the website, and you can book on behalf of you both, just using your own phone or email. For confirmation, they send you one of those black and white squares that are scanned when you check-in. If she's drunk and I take her place in her car with you, then my positive test will be officially recorded against her name, any CCTV will show that it looks like her too. You just need to bring one of her coats for me to wear, the more distinctive the better."

Tina was so pleased with herself for having worked out that this could be done. It just seemed so bloody simple and obvious, she wouldn't have been surprised if other people were doing it just to get furloughed or into self-isolation and a government cash handout.

Her next suggestion, she thought, was another one of genius too.

"There's some non-alcoholic spirit called "*Seedlip Spice 94*" that you can get at Waitrose. I checked their website yesterday. It smells and tastes just like gin, so you need to get a bottle of that and decant it into a proper gin bottle. One of my colleagues says that she drinks it if she's driving. You can give HER real Gin and you can drink the non-alcoholic stuff."  Neither of them knew that Michelle already knew about the non-alcoholic *Seedlip Spice 94*. She had drunk some at her 40$^{th}$ Birthday party to make it look like she was joining in when she wanted to keep her head.

"But I don't really drink gin."

"That's not the fecking point, is it?" replied Tina, "she needs to be hung over and sleep in, whilst you need to be capable of driving first thing in the morning. "Assuming that you get my positive test back in her name, four or five days later you can give her the other stuff I've been collecting and then everyone will assume that it was just a tragic unfortunate Covid death. There was someone on the news last night who was only in his thirties. Died at home, bit overweight, had some breathing difficulties but not enough to call an ambulance his family thought. But no suspicion, no requirement for a Post-Mortem because he was already Covid-positive.  There are thousands of deaths not being checked properly and just being certified as Covid if that person has had a positive official test in the previous twenty-eight days. You just call an ambulance the following morning, and so long as they can check she was Covid-positive, they'll not want to take her to the hospital morgue or do a Post-Mortem because of further risk of infection."

"But what if the paramedics swab her for Covid when the ambulance turns up?  Or they do it at the funeral home?  That'll just test negative, and they might do more checks then," stated Alfie.

"I hadn't thought of that."  But then quick as a flash, Tina had the answer for that too.

"Well, you're going to have to clear up any trace of the other stuff, and between now and then I'll have to start saving my saliva. It's Covid positive so that you can put that into her nose and mouth then. Hey, I'd forgotten that her and me have got 50% of the same DNA, and nobody but the three of us knows about that."

Yes, although the majority of people being killed by Covid were in their 70s and 80s, and most of them with pre-existing underlying health conditions that were sparked into death by the Covid, there were nevertheless so many younger people in their forties and fifties, including *frontline workers* who were probably getting infections whilst already infected, and the accumulated *'viral load'* did for them. The new Covid variants from South Africa, Brazil and elsewhere were spreading faster and affecting more younger people too. In similar circumstances, and especially now with the post-Christmas surge that was overloading hospitals whilst GPs were overloaded with vaccine rollouts, the timing for Alfie and Tina to hide their murderous intentions in direct view was perfect.

Tina, so pleased with what she was suggesting added, "God, if ever there was the perfect time to do something like this, it is now. Don't you think?" Her previous reservations about killing Michelle had ebbed away a little; partly because of Tina's own Covid infection now provided them with the perfect cover up. Covid also highlighted the fragility of life for all of us.

"It almost seems too good to be true," Alfie replied, "and I DO now think that we are going to get away with it. Clever you!"

"You better get to Waitrose then. Just text me the time you are going to pick me up from outside the barbers where the Post Office was at Witton. Don't forget her coat."

Alfie knew that he had no choice. He'd had a brilliant two and a half years with Michelle; hell, they'd been married for fourteen months and even the Covid situation hadn't spoilt their time together. Now he was about to cut that marriage short. Well of course he had a choice, but the potential damage to his real family would be far greater than the damage, in his opinion, to Michelle. It wasn't lost on Alfie that he'd been with Tina for twenty years and Michelle for a little over two and a half, but the experiences that he'd had in those two and a half years, with the sole exception of the children, were far greater. But now he could have some great experiences with Tina, Jake and Sophie. And it wasn't just Alfie who knew that if they didn't attempt this now, the opportunity for just a random drug overdose would be so difficult to carry out, and if Michelle found Tina beforehand, then their game would be up too.

For Alfie, it had all been because of money. The money that Michelle had wrongly assumed Tina was after. The same money that Alfie and Tina were anticipating that shortly they would have lots of and could then do exactly as they pleased with it. The same money they had been chasing after Alfie's stupid throw-away line started it all: 'I should marry her, divorce her, and we can have half the money.'

For Tina it wasn't about the money, as lovely as that prospect now seemed. When her mother had revealed the truth, Tina wanted her newfound sister to like her, but she also wanted revenge against Edward Claines, the father she had never met, for raping her mother. God it was complicated. If Edward hadn't raped Shirley, would Tina have ever existed? Once their little scheme was underway, there was never any prospect of Michelle and Tina ever being able to have a relationship. Alfie had made Tina believe in the injustice between Michelle and Tina's situations. He was the one that planted the seeds for revenge against Edward. Just for the money. It was what Alfie wanted. Not Tina.

Only now the reality facing them was not only that Alfie had already married her, but jointly they were now seriously contemplating killing her, and if they got away with it, they'd get all Michelle's money and not just the half they originally envisaged. Not so much a National Lottery Lotto-win pot, more of a Euro-millions sized jackpot. How might that ruin their lives?

Before he bought the *Seedlip Spice 94* from Waitrose, Alfie sat in the car park and used his smartphone to book the Covid tests for him and Michelle. On the application he confirmed that they both had a high temperature and a new continuous cough for more than three days, Alfie had a photo of her passport on his iPhone which he consulted to make sure her date of birth was correct. The earliest slot he could get was 8.40am, so he sent Tina a text. '08:15' That would give them plenty of time to get there. Two QR Codes confirming their tests came through to his mobile almost immediately.

By 10pm Michelle was completely and utterly bladdered. They usually watched *The Last Leg* at 10pm on Fridays, but tonight it had started an hour earlier and was on for thirty minutes longer than usual. Alfie had tipped the contents of half a perfectly good bottle of *Chase* Gin down the sink and replaced it with the *Seedlip Spice 94* he'd got from Waitrose. He'd had a couple of small continental lagers and the odd glass of Red, but then substituted a non-alcoholic deep and full-bodied Merlot Grape Juice, that he'd also found at Waitrose, for his own red, and had remained relatively sober.

Michelle's Gin and Tonic's had all been double-doubles, the strength disguised in part with a Clementine tonic, and she'd drunk – without realising it – two bottles of a 15% Grande Alberone Zinfandel from Puglia. The second Brandy she'd asked for, and a clear sign that her self-control was not in control, remained untouched as Alfie helped her up to bed. She would not have got up the stairs on two legs unaided.

# FIFTY-TWO
## Days Like These

Alfie set the alarm on his iPhone for 7am, watched the rest of *The Last Leg* before some stupid *Big Fat Quiz of the Year* thing was on. Sleeping in the spare room would have looked odd, whereas him sleeping on the sofa would have made it just seem that he was as pissed as her and unintentionally fallen asleep there. It had happened before. It was not uncommon for one or both of them to awake on the sofa in the middle of the night. Shortly after 7am he made some instant coffee so that the machine grinding the Colombian coffee beans wouldn't wake her. To be honest, he didn't think anything would. The non-alcoholic contents of the Chase bottle tipped down the sink and the empties from last night were consigned quietly into the recycle bin. Before Alfie left the house at 7.55am - still un-showered - he checked that she was still asleep and grabbed one of her coats for Tina to wear.

Using Michelle's Z4, they were at the drive-through Covid-19 testing centre by County Hall ten minutes before their appointments – not because it was a Z4, just because they were both early and the roads were empty – and they were checked in immediately for their tests as there wasn't a queue.

When Alfie dropped Tina back at the old post office, where an alley cut through by the Esso garage to Blackfriars, they agreed to meet by the cricket pavilion at 10.30am on Tuesday morning. Alfie was back home by 9.15am. Michelle was still asleep, so he decided to use the hot tub and sauna. She remained asleep. He made some toast and coffee from the machine. Still no sign of Michelle emerging from her hibernation.

It was after 11am, thirteen hours since Michelle went to bed, when the pump in the airing cupboard sprang into life announcing that the power shower was in use.

Michelle entered the kitchen in her white dressing gown looking like the proverbial *death warmed up*.

"Coffee?" he enquired?

"Extra shot I think."

"Oh, that sounds bad."

"Worse. It's much much worse."

"What do you mean?"

"I pissed the bed last night Alfie. Forty-Three years old and I've messed the fucking bed. How much did we drink last night for me not to wake up?"

"Even I've not done that," he lied, then adding, "not that much really. I think we both must have been really tired. I fell asleep on the sofa with the TV on and didn't wake up till gone seven. I don't know what made me drink gin. Quite enjoyed it though."

"We should go to the furniture shop and get a new mattress," she urged.

"I don't think either of us should drive until tomorrow. And anyway, those shops are shut. We'll have to order one for delivery next week. Can't we just turn it or take one off a spare bed for now?"

"Can't use the one from the spare bed, it's smaller."

"Just turn it then. How bad is it."

"I don't know. Looks like a full-on bladder empty," she squealed in disgust with herself. "And it stinks. Oh Alfie, I'm so sorry."

"Do you fancy the hot tub?" he asked her, "We can sort the bed out after."

They spent a couple of cycles in the hot tub naked together. Michelle felt so ashamed, she sensed that alcohol was still coming out of her pores, and so sex was the furthest thing on her mind. Alfie, contemplating what he had put in action this morning, getting Michelle a positive Covid test so she could then be killed, was very quiet and withdrawn. Michelle just put it all down to the stupid alcohol excesses of the previous evening, vowing not to get so out of control again.

On Sunday afternoon they were sat in front of the real fire watching a Netflix film, *Peanut Butter Falcon,* that Netflix itself had recommended for Alfie's viewing preferences - when he felt the mobile phone in his pocket vibrate silently against his thigh.

Before he'd made an opportunity to look at the incoming message, ten minutes later the silent thigh vibration was repeated.

"Pop it on pause," Michelle had the control, "Do you fancy a cup of tea?" Alfie asked.

In the kitchen whilst the kettle was boiling the water for their tea, Alfie checked his phone.

\*\*\*\*\*\*\*\*\*\*\*\*\*\*\*\*\*\*\*\*

NHS Covid-19 Notification:
Hello Alfie Rogers
Birth Date – 12 January 1974
Test date: 16 January 2021

Your coronavirus test was negative.

\*\*\*\*\*\*\*\*\*\*\*\*\*\*\*\*\*\*\*\*


\*\*\*\*\*\*\*\*\*\*\*\*\*\*\*\*\*\*\*\*

NHS Covid-19 Notification:
Hello Helen Michelle Rogers
Birth Date – 26 August 1977
Test date: 16 January 2021

Your coronavirus test was positive.

You and anyone you live with must self-isolate immediately and keep in self-isolation until you're no longer infectious.

The self-isolation period includes the day your symptoms started (or the day you had the test, if you do not have symptoms) and the next 10 full days.

\*\*\*\*\*\*\*\*\*\*\*\*\*\*\*\*\*\*\*\*

## Game On

Alfie met up with Tina on Tuesday by the cricket pavilion as planned. He parked near St. Peter's Church, she walked from her home with Teddy. He'd got a small list of things that Michelle wanted from Waitrose; she would have come with him but the new mattress being delivered this morning had not yet arrived.

It was now a week since Tina had tested positive for Covid, so they had to move quickly. She'd been spitting regularly into an empty jar since Friday and she had the drugs, far more than needed for a recreational high, concealed within her mother's ashes.

"We should have done it on Friday, she was so pissed that she'd never have recovered. I'm now worried I won't be able to get as much down her again. But at least I don't need to pretend about drinking myself this time."

"What are her favourite chocolates?" asked Tina.

"Oh, she adores white chocolate. Why?"

"Because I was thinking that might be the best way to get her to take the drugs. You're not going to be able to inject them or get her to snort anything, are you?"

It was planned, simply, without any emotion, perhaps like a paid professional assassin might feel towards their victim, that Tina would get some individual chocolates from one of the supermarkets in town, probably Waitrose, and mix the drugs into their centres. Just the white ones, leaving Alfie to eat the milk chocolate ones. She would have everything ready for Alfie by Friday morning so that Friday evening they could make it happen.

# FIFTY-THREE
## Grant My Last Request

"I'm going to cook fish for us tonight," announced Alfie nonchalantly on Friday morning as they sat in bed drinking the first coffee of the day. "Some monkfish I think."

The monkfish was both an excuse to go to Waitrose so that Alfie could visit Tina to collect the drugs and saliva, and an indication of how far Alfie had developed as a person during his time with Michelle. Three years ago, Alfie had never even heard of monkfish; cod and haddock, not cooked in the pan at home but covered in batter, generously seasoned with salt and vinegar, and wrapped in the paper fresh from the Queen Street chippy, was all he knew. He'd now eaten monkfish at the *Chequers at Crowle*, the Watergate Bay Hotel, and at another of Michelle's favourite places, the Venture In restaurant.

Now the Venture In, in a little chocolate-box village called Ombersley, located a few miles the other side of Droitwich from their own home near Feckenham, was a place that Michelle knew very well, and one that Alfie was starting to like. Amongst the wooden beams that supported a low ceiling and divided the room into small intimate dining groups, the cost of their quite exquisite food and attentive service, really did keep the riffraff away. They even had fish-only menus, well for starters and mains at least.

Before he met Michelle, happiness wasn't a beautiful meal, a first-class flight, or a hot tub in the garden. Just getting £20 out of the cash machine for a few beers at *The Old Cock* was a triumph on occasions.

But before their coffee in bed was finished, Michelle suggested,

"Let's go in the hot tub then!"

Hanging up their dressing gowns and hot tubbing naked had become the thing. There were no prying neighbours overlooking or public footpaths crossing their land. They would hear the gravel if anyone drove up to the house. It was liberating.

"It's a good job you fetched some chemicals," she said, "I reckon you're gonna have to drain and clean this a bit later on." Which was Michelle speak for "I want you to give me a good seeing to, here and now." How could he refuse what would be her last ever request of him?

The previous evening, and against the government's lockdown rules, Sophie had gone to see her friend Dominic. They'd both had Covid now so assumed that they couldn't get it again. If either of them had bothered to Google that, they would have found out how mistaken they were. But Tina wasn't going to stop her going, it provided her with the opportunity to set about lacing the white chocolates with a combination of the cocaine and heroin she had acquired for the imminent *speedball* moment.

As she was creating her *death by chocolate*, it dawned on Tina how trusting Alfie was going to have to be. She could now lace the milk chocolates instead of the white ones. Or all of them! But what would that achieve? Alfie had a negative Covid test, there would be a Post-Mortem, but no way that it would come back to her. If she killed them both, would everything now be inherited by their children? She didn't think so as Michelle would surely have made a Will.

The small bags of white powdered cocaine and heroin, the brightness of which indicated a higher purity, were carefully tipped into an egg cup and mixed together with the wrong end of a teaspoon. Tina cut the base off the two small white chocolates, specifically chosen because they were more likely to be put into the mouth whole, and used a teaspoon to scoop out the fillings. Half of the deadly mix was put into each white chocolate, some of the original filling replaced too, and then she placed the cut-off base of the chocolate in the microwave on a 'defrost' setting for 5 seconds, just enough to start the melting process so that the top section containing the deadly concoction would reattach to the part-melted base. She repeated the base in the microwave for the second chocolate, and after they had cooled, sealed the chocolates into a new freezer bag and put them into her mother's ashes so there was no danger of Sophie accidentally eating them before they were handed over to Alfie the following morning.

It was almost lunchtime before Alfie, who had been to Waitrose in Worcester so that he could also collect the wine bottles that he'd ordered online the previous day from Majestic Wine, headed back to Droitwich to collect the items from Tina's as arranged.

With the High School and Sixth Form closed to help get the virus under control, Sophie had got up late and was in the Lido park with Teddy and some friends.

"Are we absolutely sure we want to do this Alfie? This, this what we're planning to do next, well it was never our intention. Wasn't it just supposed to be a stupid get-rich-quick scam where the only damage might have been a broken heart and a financial loss? Not someone's life."

"I don't see what choice we have now," said Alfie despondently. "There won't be a better opportunity to hide what we're doing, and we won't be able to carry on as we are when she finds you. She won't give it up you know. Now her mum's parents are both dead I think she's realised that you're potentially the only family she's got left, and I'll probably end up in jail. She won't want anything to do with you either if she finds out, and we'll both be skint again. That'll be really difficult having experienced what a positive difference having a bit, or a lot of money, makes to your choices."

Alfie was right. Going back to a hand-to-mouth existence did not appeal to him in the slightest, and if the *Speedball* did it for Michelle, with her positive Covid test they would almost certainly get away with it now.

"I've been looking at some *YouTube* videos of what happens after death, so we don't get caught out," Tina told Alfie. "I was just worried that if the drugs caused some sort of fit, her body might be in a strange position which you couldn't change once she goes stiff."

And Tina was quite right to be concerned. Anywhere from two hours after death, a stiffness – *Rigor Mortis* – sets in and 'temporarily freezes' the body's position. It then takes another couple of days before the body's state changes so that it could be manipulated into a different position. Tina also learnt, again from *YouTube*, that if Alfie discovered her dead on her front or back, he would have to leave her that way as the blood quickly settles, acting under gravity when the heart stops pumping it around, and would alert someone, someone who knew that they were looking for, like a paramedic, a doctor, or an inquisitive undertaker, that something was not right if the body had been turned over after death.

"Wow, all that from *YouTube*!" Alfie was astounded and recognised that would help prevent a stupid mistake and possible detection.

"I've also had a look at *Speedballs*," Tina continued his education. "There's loads more stuff in those white chocolates than someone would normally take. It's not going to take more than a couple of hours, so you need to check her no later than three hours to confirm it's done. If you need to move her, the Rigor Mortis shouldn't have started." There was a finality about that information, and Alfie didn't reply.

# FIFTY-FOUR
## Death Comes To Lance Dune House

Watching *MasterChef* throughout lockdown, experiencing first-hand the great food served up at the Chequers, Watergate Bay, the Venture In, etc., had given Alfie culinary ideas far above his capabilities, but the not-enough-food-to-fill-you portions he was attempting were perfect for the occasion. The less stodgy and smaller the volume of food, the more the alcohol and drugs would have their desired impact. And the greater the volume of alcohol he could get into Michelle's body, the more effect the drugs would have.

Having started the evening with a quadruple gin, the strength of which was sublimely hidden behind a rhubarb and ginger tonic, Alfie had very cleverly consulted the Majestic Wines website in order to select high strength wines appropriate for each course. To accompany his starter of Sesame and Honey Halloumi Fries, there was a 14% Domaine Prunier Chardonnay that really provided the *creamy marriage of vanilla and stone fruit* that the tasting notes hinted at. To pair with the main course of Monkfish roasted in red wine [yes, really], Alfie had selected a 15.5% Amarone, also from Majestic at just over £60 for the bottle; he'd bought two in the hope that last week's *'I'll never drink like that again'* declaration would be forgotten once this decanted nectar had been tasted. The fish had been roasted in a £20 Amarone and was served on a bed of wilted spinach leaves, with three Scallops each, pan fried in a lemon garlic butter, and a mouthful of watercress and beetroot salad.

"Oh Alfie, wherever did you find OUR Amarone? That's a beautiful touch."

Alfie hadn't realised it at all, but the expensive Majestic Amarone they were now drinking was the same as the best one they had drunk in the La Cantina bar in Venice. Michelle thought she recognised the label immediately, but it took her a little time to place where it had been. Their favourite little bar, almost exactly two years ago, where all the wine had been great, but this one exceptional. That was fitting for her final ever glass of wine.

For pudding, the Gorgonzola with oat biscuits were perfectly balanced with another high alcohol content selection; a mildly peated 46% single Malt

Whisky, with smoky and lemon notes, from the Isle of Islay. The perfect accompaniment for cheese.

Throughout the evening Alfie had been drinking with her, but far less than she had. They'd eaten in the kitchen and stayed there drinking and chatting as the two courses had been created and cooked. They hardly ever ate in the dining room, and Alfie reflected on the fact that although 2020 had been the strangest of years, in the three years since he first came to work at Lance Dune House, Michelle had never invited anyone to dinner. If this big house had been Tina's home, she'd have wanted parties all the time.

After their cheese, Michelle declined a second whisky, and Alife took their wine glasses and the rest of the second bottle of Amarone through to the lounge. With the three courses and two heavyweight G&Ts before it, the equivalent of eight single measures, Michelle had drunk much more than she thought. Did she want a coffee? No. They were both tired, and she indicated that they should go and watch *The Last Leg* in bed; hopefully it had started at the usual time tonight.

"Hang on, hang on," he said, "I almost forgot the chocolates."

He returned with a small plate from the fridge that had two white and two milk chocolates on it. As he was putting the plate down on the coffee table, Alfie took one of the milk chocolates and popped it whole into his mouth, subconsciously indicating to her that this was the right thing to do, and leaving her with a choice of three that only had one dark chocolate left. As Alfie rightly anticipated, she selected a white chocolate and placed it in her mouth whole.

For an instant, Alfie had a *'let's hope Tina's only laced the white ones'* moment of panic.

"Wow, that's heavenly," said Michelle unknowingly acknowledging Tina's great choice.

Alfie took the second milk chocolate and ate it.

"Let's go up," he said, and as she got to her feet, Michelle took and ate the remaining drug-laced white chocolate. One might have been enough on its own, but two would definitely seal her fate.

Alfie helped her up the stairs and into their bedroom. She went to the toilet and put her PJs on and got into bed.

"I'll just go and make sure everything is locked up downstairs and the fire's safe." The TV and the bedside light on his side of the bed were on, so he turned out the main bedroom light as he left.

Alfie was physically shaking with the fear of what he had just done, and the unknown hours ahead of him as he went back downstairs. He found her mobile phone, turned it to silent and placed it on top of a kitchen cupboard so she wouldn't be able to find it if needed in a hurry to call for help. That prompted Alfie to unplug the master socket of the house phone in the hall so the phone in their bedroom couldn't be used to dial out. If she started feeling ill, she now wouldn't be able to summon help before it was too late.

It was still relatively early, not quite 10.30pm. Thinking what Tina had said about leaving her no more than three hours, Alfie set the alarm on his phone for 1.30am and tried to settle down on the sofa. He tuned the TV on and watched the last half an hour of the *Last Leg* – something that he'd actually introduced Michelle to. Alfie couldn't rest. Once the *Last Leg* was over, not having heard anything from upstairs, he cleared the remaining crockery and glasses into the dishwasher, washed and dried the pans and put them away. Alfie returned to the lounge, turned up the volume on the TV and settled down, still feeling sick in the bottom of his stomach, to watch a film, any film on Netflix.

When Alfie looked around the room, there was none of his personality or anything of his choice in any of the decorations, ornaments, pictures. Yes, there was a photo of the two of them at the Little White Chapel on their Las Vegas Wedding Day, placed above the fireplace in a Pearl-edged frame, but it was over two and a half years since he'd moved into Lance Dune House full time; not even his PlayStation - or the Banjo - had made it into their joint space.

Whatever we think of euthanasia or the death we might choose for ourselves, a drug overdose was not something that Michelle had ever contemplated as a possibility for herself. A car accident could happen to any of us, skiing was comparatively less dangerous than many people thought, and most of us think it will be heart disease or cancer that takes us before old age sets in. Throughout 2020, even fit and healthy people added

Coronavirus to that list of unfortunate possibilities that might bring about a premature, gasping-for-breath, horrible death.

At 1.30am, the *Cosmic alarm* sound effect on his iPhone awoke Alfie from a deep sleep. The lights were on, the TV was still on, the remains of the fire were but a few embers glowing. He caught the time on his phone and knew that he must find out what had happened upstairs. There was no putting it off.

The TV in the bedroom had turned itself off, but the bedside light was still on. He could see that she'd been sick on the floor, projectile vomiting from the bed. The smell, the stench, was even worse than just the vomit alone. From the way the duvet had been lifted and thrown aside, the pillows displaced on to the floor and across the bedside table, knocking her light onto the floor, Michelle had encountered some sort of fit. She was motionless, face down, and when he touched her she was already cold. She'd defecated, hence the stench. Face down, he was initially glad of that, but Alfie knew that he would have to look at her again, the clean-up needed to start now, before her muscles relaxed and lost their flexibility.

Their purposeful removal of a human life had been successfully completed. It had been horrifyingly easy, frighteningly quick, and almost dehumanising. Michelle's eyes were shut and that was that.

# FIFTY-FIVE
## Coward's Courage

Alfie rolled her onto her back, picked her up off the bed and half carried her and half dragged her into the bathroom, removed her two-piece pyjamas, placed a shower cap over her hair and washed her down in the shower. He aimed the shower head into her mouth to clear out her sick, and around her bum and the top of her thighs to clean that mess too. Taking her deadweight corpse back into the bedroom, Alfie struggled to get her on top of the duvet before drying her. Despite the shower cap her hair was wet in places, so he found her hairdryer to dry that too. Now he put new nightclothes on her and, with all the strength he could muster, picked her up and carried her into the spare room and laid her on the double bed. Knowing that he needed to get her back on her front as soon as possible, Alfie ran down to the kitchen and he found the jar containing Tina's Covid-positive saliva where he's stashed it in the back of the fridge. Using cotton buds, he generously applied it up her nostrils, in her mouth, the back of her throat. He was thankful that her eyelids were shut, that made her look peaceful and gave Alfie the impression, from which he took some comfort, that she wasn't watching his ultimate disloyalty to her.

Alfie wrestled with the duvet to pull it from under her, and flipped Michelle back onto her front, at which point her body involuntary moved, there was a noise, a groan, from her mouth and she pissed herself too. In that instant Alfie wasn't to know that after death the body can expel gases, accounting for the groan, and her bladder had emptied as the muscles relaxed and the state of Rigor Mortis was beginning. Instead, Alfie, contrary to what he had already seen with his own eyes and felt with his own fingers, now thought that she was still to die. Perhaps she was not quite dead after all? In that moment, Alfie felt that he was going to shit himself with fear. But she was fully dead, and Alfie threw the duvet over Michelle, ruffled it and both pillows to try and give the effect that she had been there for some hours.

She was in the spare room. Alfie had planned to leave her in their bedroom, but that needed cleaning. In that moment it dawned on Alfie that Michelle being in the spare room actually helped. Because she had Covid and he didn't, she should have been in self-isolation – isolation away from Alfie.

That would help explain things and remove the need for the paramedics to go into their bedroom.

Alfie ran to the kitchen. Why was he running? Nerves, fear, disbelief at what he'd just done?. It wasn't yet 2.30am and he wouldn't call for help until he 'discovered her' in the morning. Alfie took a plate and dirty cutlery from the dishwasher, put them on a tray, along with a clean wine glass that he first dirtied with some of the remaining cheaper Amarone and then threw down the sink, and a salt and pepper mill. He took them upstairs, along with one of the empty wine bottles, and placed the tray on the bedside cabinet beside her.

Back in their own bedroom Alfie closed the door behind him, opened the windows wide, and set about cleaning up the mess. He did the bed first. Their new mattress, with just the smallest of stains from the pooh, was cleaned with a wet hand towel and then sprayed with Febreze fabric freshener before Alfie used the hairdryer and then turned the mattress over. The Duvet cover had a few pieces of sick on it but had otherwise protected the duvet itself. The bed was stripped, remade with fresh Egyptian Cotton linen taken from the airing cupboard on the landing, and then Alfie cleaned the vomit from the carpet. Likewise, the carpet was sprayed with the fabric freshener and the hairdryer used to dry it, after which Alfie fetched a bin liner from the utility to bag up the bed linen and Michelle's nightclothes.

He hid the bag in the pump room for the swimming pool, locked the door and went back to the lounge. Not yet 4am. He needed a drink and fetched a cold lager from the Fridge. Straight out of the bottle, Michelle would have hated that, along with him watching repeats of *Come Dine with Me* on Channel 4.

A wide range of random thoughts went through Alfie's mind as he sat on the sofa alone knowing Michelle was dead in the room upstairs. Knowing that he was very close to being a very wealthy man in his own right. Not dependent on a monthly handout; for cleaning the hot tub and pool.

1. Phew! Tina hadn't laced all the chocolates after all. Realistically she had nothing to gain by it.

2.  In a peculiar way Lockdown was going to help him. He couldn't suddenly go and spend any money on a holiday or a car. Avoriaz would have to wait until 2022, but he really wanted one of those Seat Cupra Ateca cars. He could part-ex the Z4 towards one of those without it seeming too excessive.

3.  Had Michelle made a will? He didn't know, it had never been discussed. What if she'd made a legally binding arrangement for her money before they got married?

4.  What would be a reasonable wait to get back together with Tina? Would it matter?

Alfie couldn't face going back upstairs. Several repeats of Channel 4's *Come Dine with Me* were followed by three back-to-back episodes of *Everyone Loves Raymond*, something he had never watched before, and then by three episodes of *The Big Bang Theory*. It was now 8.35am, Alfie was TV'd out, and in his mind it was now a respectable time to take his wife her morning mug of tea.

Using his mobile, Alfie dialled 999.

He'd seen enough TV documentaries to know that every 999 call is recorded.

"Ambulance please. I've just found my wife dead in bed. I think she's died from Covid. She tested positive a few days ago."

With the call made and their address provided, Alfie returned to the spare room to sit with Michelle for a little while, maybe until they arrived. Where was her phone, she'd have that by the bed? He fetched Michelle's phone from the top of the kitchen cupboard, which made him remember to reconnect the house phone into the main socket too. Not that anybody ever used the house phone to call anymore.

What was he going to tell the paramedics? That would be it. He'd taken her up a mug of tea but there wasn't any answer when he knocked the door. Where was that mug of tea now? He dashed to the kitchen, got the milk from the fridge as he waited for the kettle to boil, then made Michelle half a mug of tea, topping up the mug with cold water to make it lukewarm. He shouldn't sit with her; she has Covid right.

The paramedics were expecting someone older when their Control Centre sent them to the call where someone had potentially died at home from Covid. Alfie got out his iPhone to show them the NHS confirmation texts that they'd both had a Covid test less than a week earlier, and that the one for Michelle was positive.

"I cooked us both some fish last night that I put for her on a tray and placed it outside her bedroom door about 8pm, together with some red wine." He told the paramedics, still downstairs in the kitchen, that he'd taken her a mug of tea sometime around 8.30am, knocked on the door, but there wasn't a response, which is when he went into her bedroom and found her dead.

"You stay here sir. Where can we find her?"

"She's in the spare room because she was isolating from me."

"Which is where?"

"Yes, sorry. Turn left at the top of the stairs and it's the first door on the left."

It was not long before they returned.

"I'm sorry for your loss sir, as you said, she is dead. Unfortunately, as Covid's suspected, we're not allowed to put her in an ambulance or take her to the hospital. We've taken some swabs and will get a test fast-tracked. In fact, we'd like to swab you for a test too."

At the test centre he and Tina had to swab themselves following the staff instructions. But the paramedics, in full PPE, asked Alfie to sit on a chair whilst they agitated his throat and then nostrils with the oversized cotton-bud.

When they'd taken her details, including her GP practice in Corbett Avenue, details of their previous tests and his phone number, they left saying that he'd get a call as soon as the tests had been completed. In the meantime, Alfie phoned Tina, he didn't want the digital record of a text message and told her exactly what she was expecting to hear.

"Michelle has died from Covid. You don't need to say anything," he added, "I'll come to the house in a few days."

Alfie hung up with no further words exchanged between them.

The paramedics hadn't mentioned any need to call the police. She'd had Covid, thousands of people were dying of Covid, more now than at the peak during Lockdown One last year, with the authorities really worried about the new variants that were spreading across the UK from South Africa, California, Brazil, Japan, and other places that they shouldn't have been able to migrate from. It would be a few hours before he knew what would happen next.

Alfie decided to relight the log fire in the lounge, and when it was burning fiercely, he fetched the bag from the pump room, a set of scissors from the kitchen, and started cutting up sheets, PJs, duvet covers and towels, and fed them into the fire. When everything had burnt, he used the poker to hold the plastic bag in the flames above the logs, but it disintegrated into a molten mess and didn't go up in flames. The smoke it gave off smelt acrid and dangerous, so Alfie took out what was left from the flames, then opened the windows on both sides of the room.

The fire was still alight when the call came from the hospital to say that Michelle's Covid test was positive, and Alfie's was negative. They would send the test results to her GP, but Alfie would need to contact them for a death certificate. Given that she'd had a positive Covid test a week ago and was still positive, that would count as an 'explained Covid death' and the coroner would not need to be involved, unless the GP thought otherwise. He should call the GP as soon as possible.

When Alfie called the medical practice as instructed, another Covid-unique situation helped his cause. All the on-call GPs at the practice were involved in the mass deployment of the so-called Oxford Vaccine to the next group of citizens prioritized by Matt Hancock. When his situation was explained, the receptionist went to consult with one of the GPs and returned to say that they would attend Michelle's body at the undertakers on Monday, assuming it was one in Droitwich, and issue a Death Certificate then.

One more phone call, to Crumps the Undertakers, and it would be done for now. Part of the undertaker's Covid process was now to ask if the deceased or anyone else in the household had recently tested positive for Covid. They didn't tell Alfie, but for Covid deaths a special body bag was used to collect the deceased which, because it didn't contain any PVC or highly chlorinated material, could be put straight into the coffin, and then be cremated. There is still a high probability of Covid transmission from a deceased person, and this body bag procedure greatly reduces the risk. They would be at the house in the next hour and would let Alfie know on Monday when the GP had given them the Death Certificate for him to collect.

## FIFTY-SIX
## Nothing Breaks Like A Heart

Alfie went back upstairs to sit with Michelle. She had genuinely died from a respiratory illness. Her Death Certificate would state that SARS-CoV2 [Coronavirus] was the cause, but it was really the *Speedball* of heroin and cocaine on top of the alcohol already acting as a nervous system depressant, that combined to create a respiratory depression and death. Same outcome, different cause.

In that moment Alfie was now genuinely more heartbroken than he thought he would be. Tears fell down his face at what he'd done. At what he and Tina had willingly done. He took some comfort in the fact that he and Tina were equally culpable, and that he had only got physically and emotionally close to Michelle because they'd set out to defraud her. When their scheme had been dreamt up, they had only meant for Michelle to be heartbroken herself and defrauded out of some of her considerable fortune, and no doubt as angry as hell from a divorce settlement that would be more financially lucrative than Tina and Alfie would really need. But Alfie had never anticipated the life-changing discoveries of travel, places, fine food and wine that Michelle's money had provided and which she'd enjoyed educating him about. Yes, a sort of *Educating Rita* life-changing experiences that would no doubt have continued at pace throughout the last ten months if coronavirus hadn't happened.

From before their first intimate moment in the cellar on the snooker table, after Michelle had found the *'Quickie'* bottle of wine that sparked her inhibition, being with Michelle hadn't been a chore. She had always been fun to be around. Alfie couldn't understand why she didn't have a big friendship group. Maybe her solitary upbringing here in this isolated house? Or maybe the social divide of *'Old School Tie and Old Money'* from Oxford that Monty and Giles had tried to bring her into with their marriage proposals?

Had Alfie loved Michelle? He didn't really know himself. Their meeting and getting to know each other had been contrived, but after that it felt more like love than anything he'd experienced previously, even with Tina. Each time he'd kissed Michelle it had been for real. But then life before had been about paying bills, making ends meet, bringing up children, and not having enough money to do or buy the things you want, like a Villa season ticket. There hadn't been the time and carefree lifestyle for love. But he and Tina could have that now.

'Did Michelle love me?' he thought. Probably he decided. If she hadn't seen something in him or about him that she must have loved, the wedding in Las Vegas would never have happened. But that didn't matter now. He probably loved her too on reflection, but in a different way to Tina. Tina had stuck with him for over twenty years. Shirley had also been responsible for keeping them together at times. That hadn't escaped him.

Whether he loved Michelle or Michelle loved him, it no longer mattered.

As far as the world was concerned, Michelle was now just another tragic Covid statistic. A forty-three-year-old woman without any underlying health conditions who had caught Covid from somewhere or someone. A tragic Covid statistic. But then without Covid-19, and Tina recognising the opportunity to mask her murder, he wouldn't be sitting here next to her cold, dead, corpse.

If they got away with it, he'd enjoy providing the same enlightenment for Tina and the children; Avoriaz, and La Folie Deuce especially, was at the top of his list. Maybe he and Tina could get married in Las Vegas; they were well and truly stuck with each other now, so he might as well. Once the necessary grieving husband period was behind him. Then there was Venice, Vienna, Bilbao, Kortrijk, Copenhagen. As Alfie thought about each of those places that Michelle had taken him to, in his mind's eye there was an image of them together in each one. All these places that Michelle had taken him to, he now wanted to share with Tina once a life without Covid returned. It would, wouldn't it?

The sound of gravel moving under tyres announced the arrival of the men in black in their black car. He took off his wedding ring, undid her necklace, and threaded his ring onto the chain before clasping the two ends back together. He sensed that Tina wouldn't want him to keep it. It was a small part of him for Michelle to take with her. Was there another life waiting now this one had ended so abruptly?

Alfie led the two gloved Undertakers, protected behind their visors and PPE, up to the spare room where, with as much dignity as possible, Michelle was concealed within the zipped black bag. There was minimal chit-chat, a final "We're sorry for your loss," and an expectation that they would be in touch on Monday.

His pre-nuptial had ended. But did Michelle have a Will and either way, what would the full implications of her death be for him and Tina now?

Alfie had not found any sign of a will when he went through her study filing cabinet, but discovered investments and bank accounts that made her, by most peoples' standards, fabulously wealthy. Even more fabulously wealthy than Alfie had known about before her death. That would now make Alfie and Tina fabulously wealthy by most peoples' standards and provide an opportunity for them to ruin the rest of their lives.

The following week, Michelle's solicitor confirmed that a Will hadn't been made with her; Alfie enquired because he wanted to know if she'd left any instructions for a funeral. The grubby subject of money was not mentioned.

Without a Will, and without any dependents or close relatives, as her husband he would legally inherit her entire estate. The Jackpot. The Treasury, spending money to minimise the economic threats from Covid like there will be no tomorrow, would be very happy too with the 40% Inheritance Tax coming their way in due course.

Alfie left it over a week before going to visit Tina at home. She noticed straightway that he wasn't wearing his wedding ring but didn't mention it.

"How are you?" He asked with a heaviness in his voice. "Do I need to put a mask on before coming in?"

"It's almost three weeks since my test, so I should be OK. It's up to you."

They went and sat together at the kitchen table and Tina made two mugs of tea.

"It's done then." Tina stated. If they had just managed to only have defrauded Michelle of her wealth as originally planned, they'd have been ecstatic, high fiving perhaps. But the circumstances that made them take her life were not ones to celebrate.

"What happens now?" she questioned Alfie.

"There's another three weeks until the funeral. And then we'll have to leave some time, out of respect, until you move in with me," Alfie told her.

"No, no, no. I'm not moving in there. It wouldn't be right. Anyway, it's too isolated for me and everyday would be a reminder of the only reason we were living there. Of what WE did there. I don't want to have to deal with any of that."

"What do you suggest then," he asked.

"Is there really as much money as we thought?"

"No," Alfie answered. "There's far more; millions even after the tax man has got his grubby paws on what they're owed."

'We are the ones with grubby paws,' thought Tina.

"Well. there's really no reason to live here either if we can afford something bigger." Tina was testing his resolve. Did he consider it a 'we' or did he want to live at Lance Dune House without her?

"We," he now claimed almost triumphantly, "can afford any house in Droitwich. Where would you want to live?"

"Somewhere near the Lido would be good. One of them big houses on Lyttleton or Tagwell that backs on to the park."

"It's probably going to take months to sort out you know. She hadn't made a Will, but I can get her solicitor on it as soon as the funeral's done."

"What are we going to tell the kids?" asked Tina.

"I don't know," he replied, "but they'll find out about it soon enough. A Worcester Evening News journalist has already called; want to run an article about her. Got knows how they found out."

"Let's wait until after the funeral. That'll be the end of it. We can do what we want, live where we want, when that's behind us."

Alfie was glad that Tina didn't want to live at Lance Dune House. He couldn't face it either, the thought of sleeping in their bedroom where she'd been murdered, or in the spare room where he'd put her until the undertakers arrived or using the hot tub again. None of these were circumstances he wanted to face right now and so he'd moved back into the lodge on the day Michelle died.

Yes, he thought, Lyttelton Road in Droitwich, that's where everyone he knew aspired to live. He was sure that they could find a lovely, detached house that backed onto the Lido park, perfect for taking Teddy into the Lido Park for his daily walk.

Alfie had already taken all his clothes, the un-played banjo and his PlayStation into the lodge. Apart from their wedding photo, here was nothing else of his presence left behind, except maybe his influence on the reimagining of Lance Dune House. He would only need to go into her office for documents, or he could let the solicitor do that.

# FIFTY-SEVEN
## Covid Death Of Wealthy Businesswoman

The week before her funeral, the death of Michelle Rogers, née Claines, and one-time heir to the county's *Heat at Home* empire, was reported in the paper. Yet another of the Covid fatalities from those in their twenties to those in their nineties, causing endless heartache for thousands of families and loved ones across the whole of the UK. Michelle was only forty-three years old, and their report made no hint or suggestion of anything other than this being a Covid tragedy. That reporting of her death, survived by grieving husband Alfie, was also news to most people to find out that she was even married.

Alfie had his own list,

1. Positive Covid Test
2. Signed Death Certificate
3. Newspaper Article

where conveniently everything pointed to only one thing.

## Astwood Chapel – Wednesday 24th February 2021

It was just short of five weeks since Michelle had died. Covid meant that fewer cremations could take place each day and so waiting times had increased.

Within the Astwood Chapel at Worcester Crematorium, Kate the Celebrant stood before six mourners ready to share some treasured moments from Michelle's short life, shielded behind the clear Perspex screen that protected them from her and vice versa. Under Covid rules, only immediate family and close friends were allowed to be present, up to a maximum of thirty. Alfie had telephoned Michelle's Oxford friends. In the ongoing National Lockdown travel to a funeral was permitted, but every last one of them opted instead to watch the live stream of their recently deceased friend. Surely that's an oxymoron?

And so it fell to Alfie, Jamie, the General Manager from the Chequers at Crowle, Nick, Michelle's Factory Manager, Georgina, Michelle's Solicitor, Angela, Michelle's Accountant, and Brian, the President of St. Augustine's

Golf Club where Edward's bequest had financed an annual 'Foursome' Competition, to mourn Michelle's passing.

Tina had travelled to the Crematorium but had remained in her car at the far end of the sparsely used car park. If Michelle hadn't rejected her as a half-sister, today's service would not be taking place. Tina wanted to see the smoke leaving the chimney, once the short ceremony was over, with her own eyes.

Once Michelle's body had been in the Crematorium furnace, there was no way for their enterprise to be detected.

It was not just the proof of Michelle's finality. The smoke signalled the fact that her and Alfie's crazy stupid insane plan had not been so crazy stupid and insane after all.

Ill judged? Yes.

Murderous even.

Together, Alfie and Tina had achieved their revenge on Edward Claudius Claines for raping Shirley Phillips and not properly acknowledging Tina as his daughter. Michelle had been unfortunate collateral damage, and Lance Dune House now legally belonged to Alfie Rogers.

They had got away with it.

But did Alfie and Tina possess the capabilities between them to stop their new wealth, and the means by which they had acquired it, from destroying themselves?

# Part Ten

FIFTY-EIGHT
## Water Under Bridges

Alfie hadn't waited until the funeral to get back in touch with Michelle's solicitor. As they hadn't got a joint bank account, he quickly found that he couldn't do anything about her money without the necessary '*Letters of Administration*' from the probate office, and the solicitor now told him that because of Covid the usual four-week lead time had doubled. The house and all of her investments were just in her name too, so the sooner Alfie instructed Georgina the sooner she said she could draw up a list of everything that needed attending to.

'Another bloody list,' thought Alfie, but at least this one was in his best interests.

Either Georgina or Alfie should go through all her private papers to find out as much information as possible; *Moore and Moore* had helped both Edward and then Michelle with some of her investments, but there might be others they weren't aware of. Georgina was pleased when Alfie asked her to come to the house and take on that task. When acting for the company's wealthy individual clients, the associated 'day rate' was particularly good, and she pointed out that their costs would be offset against the value of the estate before any Inheritance Tax was levied. Alfie wasn't sure if that helped him or not. In the grand scheme of things, it was not important, including the additional day that Georgina managed to spin the work out too. With Covid, Alfie left her alone in the house and she took her time diligently recording details of everything she found.

His credit card was an additional card on her account, so he'd have to stop using that too. Her bank account was frozen, stopping Alfie's monthly allowance being paid at the end of January.

He had plenty of money in his account to last a few months, and he'd found the cash in her study – her emergency fund that she'd told him about – long before Georgina came to the house. The Z4 was in her name too, so he couldn't yet trade it in for his Cupra Sports.

Alfie felt that he'd won the Lotto jackpot, at least a *triple rollover* sum, but he couldn't have his money to spend on anything meaningful. That might have been a blessing in disguise.

Georgina had pushed the Probate Office hard, and in just six weeks, by mid-March, Alfie had his *'Letters of Administration'* and took up Georgina's offer to let her realise his inheritance and deal with the HMRC; all at her usual day rate!

Alfie's first purchase was his Cupra sports car now he was able to trade in the Z4. He'd intended to buy an Ateca but ended up with the sleeker looking Formentor instead. In Desire Red paint with copper-coloured alloys.

Lance Dune House was back on the market for the first time in forty-four years and its value had considerably appreciated with time and the addition of the tennis court and adjoining eight-acre field. There was tremendous interest, and with many offers for the full asking price, the agent advised Alfie to allow all those interested to enter a *Sealed Bid*. There were higher offers, but Alfie accepted a bid from a buyer who could buy immediately for cash. Alfie wanted closure and to move on without the stress of a prolonged sale; the house was sold completely as seen; furniture, wine cellar, a forty-three-year-old woman's clothes. Didn't that make his grief appear more real and remove the need to empty the place.

With the house sale going through, Alfie suggested that Tina might like to start looking for their new home in Droitwich, and to let the kids know that they were getting back together again. Dad was coming home, but it would be a new home with a fresh start.

"What's our budget?" Tina asked.

"There isn't anything we can't afford. Doesn't that sound crazy? Us, you and me. Tina and Alfie Rogers, with enough money for anything we want. We are millionaires. I could even buy a pub."

"Make sure you sort the kids out before you squander it all Alfie."

"I've already thought about that. Sophie can have your house when she gets back from university. We can rent it out for now. And we'll buy Jake a place in Nottingham. That'll help set them both up in life too."

Tina liked the fact that he'd asked her to find somewhere for them to live, said 'we'll get Jake a place,' and that he'd thought about the kids, but legally it was his money. 'The last thing you should do is buy a pub,' she thought.

Sophie should have been doing her 'A' Levels at the Sixth Form and then hopefully going to university, but the exams were cancelled at Christmas and right now she didn't want to go anywhere in September with so much uncertainty still around. The government were aiming to have everyone over fifty, together with younger people with underlying health conditions, all vaccinated by the end of April, but giving everyone their Covid jab was going to take until Christmas.  But neither could Sophie go on a GAP year or find work as things stood.

In early July, Alfie, Tina, Sophie and Teddy moved into a new home in Lyttleton Road. Well, it was new to them, but in truth it needed some tlc and modernisation.  But it was structurally sound, occupied a big double plot which gave Alfie plenty of ideas for improvement, and had a big garden with the Lido Park immediately beyond the privet hedge. Alfie would have a gate put in so they could access straight into the park.

Tina's house off Blackfriars, that Edward had originally provided for Shirley, was now put into Sophies name, and Alfie and Tina had been up to Nottingham to buy Jake a property.

The old council building by Trent Bridge had been converted into over 120 luxury and appropriately named Waterside Apartments, and a few of the most expensive 2-storey penthouse units were still available.  The views across the city centre and down the river Trent were amazing, the location, near to the centre of West Bridgford, was sought after, and with three bedrooms, it came with the obligation of providing accommodation whenever Tina and Alfie wanted to visit.

Jake couldn't quite fathom where they had got the money from; had they robbed a bank, won the lottery, and the fact they had already bought a home on Lyttleton Road only doubled his curiosity.

"Something like that," was all that Alfie would say.  Tina shrugged her shoulders.  Having agreed to purchase and passed over the details of Georgina, Alfie's solicitor, to the sales agent, with Jake's girlfriend they all wandered into West Bridgford to find some lunch.

## We're Almost Done

The last time that Alfie and Tina made any reference to what they had *'done,'* was the first time that Alfie went to visit Tina after Michelle's death when Tina had calmly stated "It's done then." They each had the same secret of their own and the other's involvement in something they both knew was despicable, but which also couldn't effectively be proved. And neither of them could turn the other in if they fell out; they both had their hands dirty; a joint criminal enterprise that wouldn't differentiate between them if somehow any suspicions were made and substantiated.

And knowing that they had each been responsible for one murder, would either of them be capable of a second?

On the drive home from Nottingham, Alfie surprised Tina.

"Well, that's the kids sorted. We'd better get ourselves properly sorted next."

Tina shrugged her shoulders and pulled a face that said, 'what do you mean?'

"Is there anywhere in particular that you'd like to get married then?"

That was Alfie's best understated offer of a proposal, and Tina was completely taken aback with it.

"Oh, I didn't think this day would ever come. Let me have a think about it." He hadn't properly asked, and she wasn't expected to say yes. It was more of a 'we are doing this,' it was only the where? he was asking about.

But Tina's thoughts weren't on where to get married, but rather that wasn't it a shame for what it had taken in order to get to this point, and she was upset that her mother never got to see her married. She would have been proud to have Shirley walk her down the aisle, whether a Church or a Registry Office.

"Just you and me or with the kids?" she asked.

"Whatever you want, wherever you want," he told her.

"Fancy Las Vegas again?" she asked him.

"Why not, only it might be a while before we can fly there again," he said, 'and a three-year pre-nup might come in handy,' he thought.

"Well, it's not like we're in any rush."

---

THE END

# Some Personal Thoughts on Covid

## June 2021

Coronavirus continues to be a dreadful blight on the UK and across the world, and this novel does not attempt to trivialise the serious devastation families have been caused by the tragic, and sometimes unnecessary, deaths of their loved ones.

The vaccination rollout offers us hope of a more normalised future where Covid may have the same ongoing impact as Flu, but we don't know for sure yet.

We do know that many of the same politicians who rightly praise our frontline NHS workers for their heroism, are the Cabinet Ministers who voted NOT to give nurses and other NHS workers a pay rise before Covid struck. The same Ministers who relied on the dedication of NHS workers to work in the early stages of Covid without PPE, or PPE that didn't meet the minimum World Health Organisation standards of protection.

When this is over, when the medics get a moment to catch their breath and wipe away tears, there will be an epidemic of PTSD to deal with. There will be a torrent of anxiety from children who will carry a consciousness about the finality of life that should not trouble them until much later in their own lives and way beyond their childhoods.

The ongoing effects of Coronavirus will occur in many places away from the illness itself.

Some might therefore feel that it is a little insensitive to incorporate an aspect of the situation around Covid into this fiction. That is a personal judgement. But books were available long before this one, that have the stark reality and bare experiences of Covid running through their pages:

Breathtaking: Inside the NHS at a time of Pandemic, and

Life Support: Diary of an ICU Doctor on the Frontline of the Covid Crisis, are both written by medics.

Many, if not all, real life situations that people judge to be horrific, ultimately find their way into art and literature and sadly the criminal courts.

According to a Sky News Report, at least fifteen people have now been jailed for falsely claiming monies as victims of the Grenfell tragedy or embezzling funds from a position of trust. Literature played a part in raising funds for the Grenfell charity when Philip Pullman agreed to name a character in his second *Book of Dust* series – *The Secret Commonwealth*, after one of the Grenfell victims.

In June 2020, the HMRC announced their first arrest in connection with an attempt to defraud the Coronavirus Job Retention Scheme. By October 2020, the National Audit Office estimated that the level of fraud in connection with Coronavirus Job Retention Scheme and other government support for Covid, including loans and grants, had reached £3 billion.

The UK statistics for infections and deaths during the second wave, and our circumstances for recording and dealing with Covid-assumed deaths, provided a perfect basis for the outcome of this fiction.

Monday 18th January 2021 – 599

Tuesday 19th January 2021 - 1,610

Wednesday 20th January 2021 - 1,820

Thursday 21st January 2021 - 1,290

Friday 22nd January 2021 - 1,401

Saturday 23rd January 2021 –1,348

These death statistics included people who had known pre-existing health conditions, people who had none, and increasingly younger and younger people were at risk of death too. And tragically, within that week in January 2021, deaths included fifteen residents of a single care home in Worcester.

Over eight thousand [*8,000*], British citizens died from Covid-19 in this one January week during Lockdown 3, some as a result of up to three households mixing around Christmas Day – as the Government allowed them to do. On the day Michelle Rogers fictionally died, supposedly from Covid-19, the UK Borders were still open to many. The inability of the Government to close our borders in spring 2020 was a mistake, but the key error of judgement that allowed so many people not to follow the guidelines for the greater good, was to allow Dominic Cummings to keep his job and set the wrong example of selfish personal judgement for other selfish people to follow.

With so many deaths, and the real potential of further infections from those bodies that still continued after life had gone, there was no appetite or capacity for post-mortems if a recent positive Covid test existed and there was nothing of further suspicion.

By comparison.

When, in February 2003, Tony Blair was leading the UK towards supporting the USA invasion of Iraq, a million people filled London's streets and squares in protest at sending our troops to the Middle East to die. In the eight years of hostilities in Iraq, one hundred and seventy-nine [179], British service personnel lost their lives.

179 lives in 8 years versus 8,000 Covid deaths in one week.

And yet there haven't been street protests in the UK.

Where are those protests for regime change in our own country? The regime, albeit in unprecedented times, that has allowed the UK to lead the world in Coronavirus deaths, now in excess of one-hundred-and-twenty-eight thousand [128,000], dead.

# Acknowledgements:

This book has been a collaboration, sometimes just between my own personalities and ideas, fuelled by a desire for constant improvement to achieve the best possible final manuscript.   I am indebted to the following friends and family who read my drafts, sometimes several versions, and provided me with a clarity of forthright feedback that enriched my story, removed personal approaches to storytelling that did not work, helped me tighten the words, reduced the number of grammatical errors, and better ensured historical and other factual accuracies.

Alphabetically, these generous spirits that I give my thanks to are:

Adrian

Daphne

Elaine

Georgina

Janis

Mandy

Sophie

Susan

Tom

Verity

Regarding the use of Deed Polls for changing names in the 1970s and 1990s, Andre Hill at the Deed Poll Office generously provided the necessary guidance.

For the cover and website artwork, Neil Duffy.

Before the first words of this book were keyed onto the screen, I'd had an earlier idea for a collection of short stories, grouped around explaining a single action, as a fundraising idea for charities struggling to maintain their incomes once the pandemic closed their shops and cancelled mass-participation fund-raising events.   It was my intention, right from the start, to use this book to help raise such funds.

Given the Covid elements incorporated into this book, and however successful or otherwise it proves, I'd like to thank Tricia and her fundraising team at St. Richard's Hospice for having the courage to be associated with it. I am sure that many other charities would put their 'corporate persona' first and be differently minded about the people they are trying to help!

Music is a big part of my life and the titles for the different sections of the book take their inspiration directly from those artists who have provided me with great listening pleasure and live performances over many years:

Cock Robin – Just Around The Corner
Thomas Dolby – She Blinded Me With Science
Nathaniel Rateliffe – Time Stands*
Thomas Dolby – I Love You, Goodbye
The Guillemots – Up On The Ride
Tears for Fears – Sowing the Seeds of Love
Joe Jackson - Another World
Bjork – All Is Full Of Love
The Avett Brothers – The Lowering
Gregory Porter featuring Laura Mvula – Water Under Bridges

Sadly, I failed to use an Abba track, nor did I get to see them in concert. That will be my challenge for the next book.

*On the stage of an empty Red Rock Amphitheatre outside Denver, Colorado, Nathaniel Rateliffe opened the *Banding Together* benefit concert for the Colorado Music Relief Fund in May 2020 that you can find on YouTube. That one open-air performance - in front of 10,000 empty seats - encapsulates so many aspects of Covid's effect on the world, providing me with the inspiration for a future destination that is more likely to entice my return to international travel than anything else.

And finally, there really is a wine called "**Quickie**" produced by an Australian winery **Some Young Punks**. Today, Quickie is only available as a Sauvignon Blanc, but back in the day it was red, exactly like Edward Claines purchased!

Should this novel be successful, the second book in the Covid19 Murder Mysteries, **Pilgrim Corner**, will be available later in 2021 from

www.thecovid19Murders.com

If you'd like to contact Duncan Peberdy, please email him at:

Duncan@thecovid19murders.com

# Also by Duncan Peberdy and set in Droitwich Spa, Youthenasia is available from Amazon as a Kindle eBook

On a cold October night, Debbie Green is abducted as she leaves a Droitwich pub alone. The fifteen-year old's poisoned body is found early the following morning and her seemingly motiveless death mystifies the police. Two weeks later the body of seventeen-year-old Jonathan Braidwood is found beneath a railway bridge he was decorating with graffiti. He too has been poisoned with the same homemade concoction, but his wrists are bound, and the murderer had tried and failed to strangle him first.

Almost a month after the killings started, the motives behind them and the person responsible continue to baffle Detective Inspector Jim Jarvis and his team from West Mercia Police. It was now time to call on the services of Professor Martin Noakes, a psychological profiler working with Birmingham's Regional Forensic Psychology Service.

Would he be able to pinpoint the identity of the murderer?

Who is the killer and how many more teenagers must die before his personal revenge is completed?

Centred on Droitwich Spa, Youthenasia will take you on journey that includes Munich, Cornwall, and the Lake District amongst its landscapes, whilst asking you difficult questions of morality along the way.